HOME

HOME

Len Varley

ISBN: 978-1-7384582-3-3 (Paperback)
ISBN: 978-1-7384582-4-0 (Hardcover)
ISBN: 978-1-7384582-5-7 (eBook)

Cover design by Diana Buidoso – Design Crowd

First edition published 2018

Len Varley Publishing
PO Box 331E
East Devonport TAS 7310
Australia

'A human being is part of the whole called by us 'Universe'; a part limited in time and space. He experiences himself, his thoughts and feelings as something separated from the rest; a kind of optical delusion of his consciousness. This delusion is a kind of prison for us, restricting us to our personal desires and to affection from a few persons nearest to us. Our task must be to free ourselves from this prison by widening our circle of compassion to embrace all living creatures and the whole of nature in its beauty'

- ALBERT EINSTEIN

CHAPTERS

CHAPTER ONE

THEY'RE STILL BREATHING

The Sun has only memory of flame
And for centuries has watched the
Earth dance like a clown upon one foot.
Someday it will drop and die
Laughing, laughing madly.
– ANNA SUJARTHA MODAYIL - 'On the Beach at Baga'

THE FAMILY REMAINED at the bay long after the youngsters were taken by the hunters. After three seasons of cruel ambush, the elders knew full well that the chances of their return were slim at best. And yet despite that knowledge they remained huddled close together and waited hopefully for the familiar calls of their young.

They had tracked the sun as it traversed a familiar arc across the wide expanse of blue water. From its lofty zenith it had watched over the painful scene of their abduction; accusingly illuminating the greedy casting of nets, and bearing silent witness to the confused cries of the infants and the plaintive calls and wails of their distraught mothers.

The broad swath of shallow water had turned rapidly to foam, the thin zephyr of salt air punctuated by the businesslike yells and calls of the hunters. On and on through the long afternoon it had continued. By the time of the long shadow, three youngsters hung lifeless, trussed painfully in a web of ropes and gaudy yellow plastic floats. Their once sleek beauty now suspended, motionless and mute. Oberon, Ganymede and pretty little Constant, whose mother Opal had desperately hurled herself over the straining nets in a vain attempt to rescue her first-born. Barely out of her wild youth herself, Opal now lay entangled and broken, her pectoral straining to touch Constant's flank. Her daughter never felt that last reassuring embrace. Even as mother Opal struggled wide-eyed in her own death throes to reach her; young Constant, already weary from the chase, had slipped away to the greater embrace of All That Is.

The remaining family continued to track the sun until it departed over the hunting grounds, the gathering of the clan all but forgotten and lost after the hunters calculated ambush. For years the hunters had watched the clan and knew their customs and their sacred meeting grounds. Twenty-file miles out to sea, Belaire held her pod in a tight protective formation. She had sensed the impending ambush and had approached the meeting point warily. It was her measured judgement which had saved her family. Focussed on scanning the area with her bio-sonar, she sensed rather than saw the reassuring bulk of her partner Columbus, driving steady and constant to starboard of her and the harem of females. The surety of his passage belayed his taut unease.

At twenty-five miles, Belaire and her forty-strong tribe had registered the faint distress calls. The fevered electricity of the younger bulls' desire to head shoreward and join the fight had momentarily confused her pod. But the wise old matriarch had seen all this before, and saw to it that she quickly re-established order, backed by the sharp whistles of authority from mighty Columbus. She placed the retreat call firmly and authoritatively. Begrudgingly the pod turned away toward deeper water, a testament to the respect and trust which they each placed in Belaire.

The only sign of their reluctance was the looseness with which the ordinarily regimented formation wheeled onto the track which ultimately turned their backs on Shadow's ill-fated pod. The matriarch issued a sigh and knew that they could do no more. Fly and Spark, two of the younger bulls, lagged dejectedly behind. For once, the wise old matriarch overlooked the deliberately slow execution of her order. She understood the reasons why and she recognized the cause of the pain transmitted through the brine. Spark had sensed the fate of his older sister Opal; his grief carried away in the slipstream of the departing ocean giants. And it was with that they said their last goodbyes.

'Water is seldom still,' thought Persia.
In the pitch darkness she bobbed like a cork, her pectoral fins barely able to extend to full spread; making it all the more difficult for her to maintain balance. After what seemed like agonizing minutes of frantic flailing, Persia drew breath, summonsed all her remaining strength and assessed the situation just as her mother had patiently taught her all those suns ago. She had quickly realized that her sonar was useless; the unexpected slap-back echo had added to her initial confusion and had sent her into a paroxysm of fear. Now, with sonar shut down, she could easily sense the imposing bulk of the rough wall mere inches away. The backwash from the slaps of her massive tail fluke similarly told her that the obstacle extended around her completely, effectively sealing her in. Shallow water with the familiar taste of salt, but more lifeless than a slack tide. The energy of the sea was gone from it.

She was floating blind, exhausted but alive. But where was the ocean, and where was the sun? And what had become of the family? As the initial cloud of blind panic cleared, Persia was slowly regaining her ability to think and assess. She now noticed the shallow slants of muted light breaking the darkened murk from somewhere above. Restricted in her movements as she was, Persia was unable to see the source of the light. It was not enough to be able to read the passage of time. She sounded the identifying call and listened. The returning sounds were muffled and unfamiliar. Persia's hearing was superior through water, but these noises came from beyond the dark cramped confines of her shallow tank. She persisted, trying to steady herself against the persistent roll and pitch of slopping water.

Semi-submerged as she was, and bereft of natural balance, the sense of dizzying claustrophobia rose afresh. Fighting the rising tide, she exhaled and drew a steady focussing breath; ignoring the wet spray falling back onto her flanks and dorsal fin. Sounding the identifier once more, she hunched low into the water and listened. Through the foreign mechanical rumbling she perceived the faintest squeak; far more narrowed and fine than the brash low surrounding throb. Encouraged she sounded again, and strained to listen and filter the higher frequency. Yes! There it was! Faint and muffled, but it was definitely Tristesse. She must be close.

Tristesse was Aura's second-born and only a year younger than Persia herself. Persia felt her spirits lift as she recalled the pure joy of weaving through the slow moving pod with Tristesse, climbing like twin bullets to breach and take breath. Tasting salt foam as they leapt under the vibrant blue arc of sky, before flashing all black-and-white torpedo-like down through the pod; dodging the school bus sized elders as they studiously ignored the high spirited duo. Past the matronly Shadow, quietly intent on navigating the broad expanse of sun dappled aquamarine water ahead of her fold.

An orca pod in full formation on an open ocean is a truly imposing sight. Their shiny neoprene black bodies, broken by curved saddle-patches of creamy white strike awe in the hearts of those lucky few whose good fortune it is to witness them.

A towering triangular dorsal fin surmounts a blocky yet surprisingly sleek body, which tapers down to broad muscular tail flukes. A blunt purposeful snout surmounted by dark, deeply expressive eyes and a wide mouth full of flashing white serrated teeth complete this picture of dominance and masterful power. Like lions in the savannah, they are the pride of the ocean as they slide confident and supreme into a broad bomber formation, rising unhurriedly in a majestic choreography to draw breath together with deft whooshes of expelled air. They remain unchallenged; the masters of their domain. Their sole enemy is an unwelcome intruder into their world; an opportunistic predator who walks on two legs.

A sudden bounce and the resultant sideways slap of water shocked Persia out of her reminiscence. Slowly mastering the quick compensating movements required of her slick glossy body to counteract the sway in the restricted space, she called again to Tristesse. The reply came back immediately, confirming Tristesse's similar predicament. Whatever, or whoever had them was removing the pair from the family, and they were powerless to resist it. Buoyed up by their new found connection, the pair traded reassuring whistles and squeaks across the waterless void separating them until they tired; letting the heavy dark tombs carry them like a rough surrogate mother.

Persia's blood lineage traced back to the grand old pod matriarch Shadow and her partner, the imposing alpha male Mars. Persia's mother Grace was Shadow's first-born. This completed the matriline; a bloodline forming the core around which the pod was built. This heritage accorded Persia an elevated status within the pod, and she had always been consciously aware of this fact. It had never really sat comfortably with her, and she did her best to studiously ignore the singing of the bloodline that connected her to the mighty ancestral whales now passed Beyond. Tristesse called once more; tired but hopeful. Little Tristesse, looking to her for guidance and answers. Persia secretly despaired that she could offer neither.

Instead, gathering up all of her remaining strength she quietly sang the old songs of family. Of happier times. Of Home.

It was when the coarse background thrum ceased, to be replaced with unfamiliar rough vocalizations that Tristesse became distressed. Fighting back her own fear, Persia again rose to the fore in a desperate attempt to calm her bewildered companion. The hunters, it seemed, had returned. Warily Persia hunched down into the dark water and listened. Muffled low noises sounded from points in front and behind her. The *'slap, slap'* of the waters around her, lapping against the walls. A foreign language that she didn't understand.

There was still not enough light to synchronize her body clock. The noises seemed to draw closer, becoming more defined through the water until they echoed in the brine. Tristesse sounded the warning call almost in the same instant that the staccato crunch of sound reverberated overhead, bringing the sun back with it. Persia was rolled anew with the sudden surge of water, catching her off-guard. The unexpected blaze of sunlight after the near complete darkness assaulted her senses; causing a further giddying disorientation as her body clock struggled to re-harmonize with the sudden anomaly.

The sky had returned; a watercolor pastel blue, its presence instantly reassuring. Automatically Persia sounded the pod call, though more for Tristesse's benefit, as the magnetics had already told her they had travelled well beyond the meeting grounds. Wishing that she had paid more attention to the words of the elders, she recalled vague tales of the hunters at past clan gatherings. The sun at morning shadow revealed more of Persia's present predicament and surroundings. The walls around her were foreign and artificial, the water fast becoming stale and lifeless. Its vigor and vibration spent. Tristesse must be nearby, but still remained unseen. Moving shapes, dark and ominous appeared in the sky above, fussing around her container; disappearing beyond sight above the rim only to reappear, sounding their blunt vocalizations to each other. A stabbing punctuation of strange language sounding in the thin air. And then, the suddenly faint but distinct smell of nearby water carried on the lightest of breezes. An ocean, perhaps?

'Woomph-shhh,' she exhaled in quiet anticipation.

This time the watery blow caught the sunlight and descended slowly around her in a million points of refracted light. A bejewelled crown for a captive princess.

There was a definite keening of the salt breeze and the calls of nearby seabirds sounded, faint through atmosphere. Encouraged, she sounded the pod call once more with a renewed vigor:

'Shadow, Mars, I need your help'.

Tristesse heard her, and took up the call hopefully:

'Shadow, Mars, this is Tristesse'.

Gazing down on the holding tanks lashed to the back of the truck, the men set about preparing the slings. To the long-haired hunter the two young orcas presented a beautiful sight, their perfectly streamlined and slick bodies unmarked. He stood entranced, his body language distinctly different from his peers who preferred to lean in slouches against the rusty old flatbed. He seemed expectant, coiled tense somehow, like some wiry whippet. There was a sadness and a conflict about him, Persia decided. Lost in his own private thoughts, he carefully studied the pair. He marvelled at their imposing presence – their cool intellect and keen vitality. The fine ivory glint of teeth standing out in perfect contrast to the broad flat pink tongues as they vocalised together. A precise symmetry of broad tail, and squat spade-like pectorals. Those dark eyes, inquisitive and alive with a cool intellect.

They were the last of the season's catch and the money was as good as in the bank. They were perfect specimens. Awestruck by their symmetry up close, he reached out a tentative hand to them like a fascinated child; his posture betraying a vague uneasiness. Persia felt it; a seeking of answers to questions still forming. An awakening of something as old as Time, and as wise as the Earth Mother.

The brash string of invective shook him from his dreamy reverie and galvanized him into motion. Catching the eye of the impatient crane operator he paused; momentarily chastened. The guilt again rising in him like an accusing finger. He shrugged it off awkwardly and returned to the task at hand, his curt yell of acknowledgement setting the wheels into motion. With a sudden asthmatic wheeze and a billow of oily black diesel smoke, the rough canvas sling was nudged closer until it was aligned over the holding tank.

The body of an orca is perfectly designed to function in water. Fifty million years of evolution have shaped this ocean predator as surely as a thoroughbred is groomed and honed for a single purpose. The only legacy of her primitive land-dwelling ancestry is the clever waterproof blowhole vent through which she draws air into her vast lungs. And that remains her only connection with air and the realm of the earth dwellers.

To live underwater, she must connect with the world of air above; and therein lies the first point of Duality and Balance. Immersed in the natural buoyancy of water, the orca is a finely balanced torpedo, capable of powering its massive bulk with an unexpected muscular grace. But taken from her aquatic kingdom, that power and majesty is very quickly subverted by the more ancient force of Gravity; reducing her to little more than a dark impotent jelly, slowing crushing vital organs under its weighty heel.

Unaccustomed to the overwhelming feeling of her own body weight, Persia thrashed against the coarse damp fabric of the cradle sling which now snugged up taught against her belly and undersides. Her pectoral fins hung limp and useless through the purpose made cut-outs; chafing her rudely as she flailed and flexed in an instinctive attempt to compensate for the crazed yawing of the canvas stretcher. Despite her relatively small size, the sudden crush of gravity as she hove clear of the water unsettled and confused her. Though greatly limited in air, Persia's eyesight served her well enough to now see her pod-mate Tristesse suffering a similar fate, no more than a few feet away from her; subdued and trussed, staring wide-eyed over the coarse aged canvas.

The naked glare of the sun was already at work, super-heating the bodies of the ebony mammals, adding a further dimension to their discomfort. Foreign 'smells' tainted the water – oil and diesel, rust and stale tobacco. An orca has no true sense of smell, though she is able to discriminate fine changes in the water around her. From above, a lone seagull swooped in a messy dive over the dark wetly glistening shapes, trussed and suspended side by side. Emitting a single squawk, loud enough to register to Persia's straining senses, it headed off towards water in an un-coordinated flurry of feathers; satisfied that the new arrivals had nothing to offer by way of food opportunities.

Allowing the motion of the crane to lead, rather than offering any resistance seemed to reduce the dizzying sway. Persia again became aware of the alluring whisper of salt water; much closer to her now. She vocalized this fact encouragingly to her companion. Relaxing into the thought of impending reunion with Tristesse, she was vaguely aware of the emptiness in her belly insinuating itself for the first time since her capture. The pair desperately needed to eat soon.

No sooner had the thought entered her mind, the mechanical buzz that had filled the surrounding air fell away to a starkly pregnant silence. The sway of the sling slowed until it became no more than a limpid pendulum swing. Persia sensed the sharp tang of brine rising from below, and she sank slowly toward it. And that was when she *saw* him. Realised who he was. Long haired, pale and tall; she recoiled from the surprise communion.

She had expected him. But not like this. He looked into her, and she in turn involuntarily looked back into him. But this time she saw nothing but a dark sea, confused and turbulent. Breaching at its surface, she bobbed for a moment, disoriented. The horizon was a thin scribbled line, all but invisible beneath the dense bank of sea fog that had gathered up; a moist air blowing aimlessly across the swell.

Drawing back, she felt her sudden nakedness under his probing gaze, and instantly resented his betrayal. Sinking soundlessly back into the Deep in a neatly executed tail slide, her eyes never leaving his; she withdrew from his questioning stare. She had no answers for him. And even if she voiced them, he seemed little more than a rudderless ship far beyond the range of hearing or understanding.

Suddenly recognizing her intentions, he desperately lunged for her as she sank back, in the same way that a drowning man clutches at a straw. Letting the dark water swallow her she left him flailing, mouth wide open yet soundless; his urgent calls all but snatched away in the maelstrom that blew up ominously in her wake.

Once again the rough tenor and baritone calls of the gathered hunters filled the void. This time she caught sight of at least three of them – primitive upright shapes gathering around the perimeter; their mannerisms, language and aura entirely foreign to her. Low, ugly vibrations. Begrudgingly she endured their brief caress, inwardly recoiling from their oily touch.

Away to one side, Tristesse endured a similar ordeal. A black-clad hunter appeared to be trying to pacify her, repeating the same vocalization in a low monotone. Again the revulsion rose in her. These savage intruders who lived outside of the Harmony, in haughty ignorance of the natural order of things.

'Some things remain a constant as surely as the moon and the tides; flow with them and yield to them.' Persia recalled her mother's gentle yet insistent teachings.

How she wished that she had paid more attention. And how she painfully missed her mother's reassuring presence; of being tucked in close, riding alongside Grace's dorsal as it effortlessly cleaved the waters, like a knife through soft butter.

'Some things cannot be changed and a wise being simply flows with them,' she had said. 'Be like water and take the path of least resistance, for this is the way of the Harmony. Know what you can change and accept what you cannot. Be like the water, my child!'

Shaking her mind free, she wriggled momentarily and flared her pectorals in anticipation of the waiting surf; hopeful of regaining some sense of lateral control. And then she met the water abruptly, not in the graceful diving arc which she was so accustomed to describing, but in the ungainly belly flop of a hooked fish. A sudden invigorating swirl of salt water rose around her. Or put more correctly, Persia simply fell into it; submerging herself instinctively in the jade green water; swallowed up as suddenly and surely as a seal swallows the silver streaks of passing salmon.

Heavy droplets of flume leapt in a broad arc as Persia swiftly exercised her strong flukes for the first time since her capture. The sudden wash of spray caused the gathered knot of hunters to jump back in shocked surprise, much to her quiet satisfaction. Tail slapping once more for good measure; she torpedo dived, as much to test the water as to relieve the painful heat build-up over her dark upper surfaces.

The sudden embrace of water felt good and reassuringly familiar as it streamed and curved around her. The faint surging pulse of current was there, yet before she could transmit the pod call, she had reached a sudden and unexpected impasse.

Cautiously scanning with her bio-sonar, Persia mapped the rocky seabed close beneath her. Heading to what appeared as an open bay, she quickly came up against the heavy netting; bringing back painful recollections of the hunters' trap. Images wheeled in sharp relief – of her mother Grace, of the panicked Aura. Of poor little Constant, spinning in a torrent of confused water and tightening rope as she fought vainly to draw breath.

Persia recoiled, hearing the *whoomp* of water at the surface nearby. It was Tristesse, bubbling contrails pluming back from her fins as she too dived into the emerald green on the other side of the dividing net. Snugging up against the criss-cross of coarse rope separating them, the pair exchanged greetings, re-energised by the renewed contact after the ordeals of the past few hours.

It is at this point of joyful reunion that I would like to share with you one singular and important fact. It is one which I pray you will keep in the back of your mind throughout this telling of this story. Wired deep into an orca's DNA is a powerful drive of allegiance to family and extended clan, evidenced by the complex social network that these enigmatic blackfish immerse themselves in. This familial loyalty arguably surpasses even that of human beings. Indeed, it is quite possible that no more powerful unity and social bonding exists on this planet than that demonstrated by the noble orca. It is this recognised truth which makes the deliberate calculated acts of their greedy captors all the more callous and inhumane.

The gentle ebb and flow of water seemed to wash away some of the trauma of the day's events, and the pair settled into quiet basking in each other's company. 'Logging' at the surface they traded easy whistles and clicks as they re-synchronized with the Harmony. The hunger pangs grew more insistent as the pair relaxed. Food. But where? Shadow's pod members are popularly described in human terms as transients. Unlike their kindred stable-mates who choose to inhabit a particular coastal region, these pods of nomadic wayfarers will traverse vast distances in their relentless travels; an inbuilt sense of wanderlust driving them onwards through the wild blue. The open ocean to these orca in not unlike the wide open plains that once lured the mighty buffalo. For them there is a place to feed, a place to breed and a place to rejoice in the reunion and meeting of extended family. Neither are they limited by solitary dimension, for they will plumb unfathomable depths as they travel; at times diving deep to where the blue fades gradually to black. To the place where light can no longer penetrate and the world above the surface no longer holds sway. This is the unchallenged domain of the transient orca as they journey far and range deep.

The diet of the transient orca pod differs markedly from that of their regional cousins. Shadow's kin were nomadic hunters, preferring a rich diet of seals, and other aquatic mammals like porpoises. In point of fact, the porpoises they feed on are closely related to the mighty blackfish and it is for this reason that some humans have dubbed the orca the 'killer whale'. But in truth, does this fact qualify them as 'killers'; a human term generally reserved for murderers and those who would take life callously and opportunistically?

There exists a natural order of things referred to as the Harmony. One eats to live. One kills only to eat. One takes no pleasure in the act, except insofar as it provides the benefit of sustenance. So says the Harmony and All That Is. It is only those who fall short of this deeper understanding who seek to call the noble blackfish the 'killer whale'.

A transient pod, unlike their sloppier and far noisier fish eating cousins, will stalk their prey in silence with the same precision and deft agility as a pride of lions. The calls and click trains that normally bounce back and forth across the waters between the ranging orcas are just as easily detected and recognized by the seals and dolphins that they stalk. Thus, Shadow's clan approach their prey like a vast bomber formation in strict radio silence. Any necessary information is transmitted only in short, curt bursts. *Running silent now.* A subtle electricity passes between the dark shapes; as powerful as any language. With the range closing there is an almost imperceptible pulse as the squadron lunges forward as one; fine contrails streaming from their muscular tail flukes. The lumbering giants are deceptively nimble courtesy of their strength and sleek styling. Silent bolts of slick black lightning.

Make no mistake, there is no ragged chatter and free-for-all scrapping as is evidenced by their fish eating relations who call the close coastal waters their home; surging and wheeling around schools of panicked fish like rowdy street fighters. Today though, it was the mighty hunters who had become the hunted.

Shaking herself out of the tiredness that was steadily overtaking her, Persia sensed she was alone in the darkening water. Tristesse was treading water up above at the surface, 'spy hopping' with her head raised out of the water. Immersed as they were in the close silence away from their captors' scrutiny, thoughts of assessing the surface had been temporarily set aside. Now Persia followed her young companion's lead. Breaking the meniscus of becalmed water warily, she exhaled with a steady *'woomfh-shh'* before drawing breath, assuming the 'spy hop' position with a veiled caution. The surface world had now become the domain of the hunters. With snout protruding and tail down, Persia extended her flattened pectorals like water wings, and with the huge buoyancy tanks of her lungs newly filled with air, bobbed in the salt water as effortlessly as a cork. Rotating her powerful squat body with the grace of a ballerina, she cautiously surveyed her new surrounds for the first time.

Woomfh-shhh. Tristesse locked eyes with her and did the same, turning in a similar easy pirouette. They were separated from each other by a narrow walkway of crude wooden planking which extended out and around the two pens, neatly sealing them off on all four sides. Across one side they could see and sense the wide curve of the bay. On the lee side, a long wooden jetty supported by weather-beaten timber poles connected the sea pens with the nearby shoreline. From it the lazy wash of breaking surf registered dimly to Persia. A gentle zephyr of breeze rolling in across the broad expanse of open water sung to the pair; seductive and insistent. With the fading light slowly leaching the ocean of its bold color, freedom felt so near and yet so far.

Out on the rough cobbled shore, seabirds tucked in their wings and roosted, hunched against the faintest of sea breezes. A threaded line of sea foam signed off on the darkening waterline. The hum and clatter of the day was falling away, broken suddenly by the steady slap of the hunter's rubber-soled feet as he made his way slowly along the length of sun-bleached jetty toward the pens. He paused at the rough planking forming the narrow walkway around the periphery of the tiny enclosures and waited patiently, brushing windswept locks of unruly hair from his eyes as he scanned the smooth surface. Precious minutes passed under his expectant gaze until the slick triangular dorsal fins surfaced like angular submarine conning towers, all gloss black and powerfully slick. *Wooom-fshhh.* A fine spray of salt water caught in the gentle breeze playing along the jetty. *Woom-fshhh.* Tristesse sounded a complimentary exhalation with a hollow reverberant echo.

Pulling the camera from a pocket of his weathered grey coat, he paused; awaiting the moment the sturdy dorsals broke the surface once more. His photoflash strobed once, twice. The nearer of the two orcas broke the surface inquisitively; drawn by the unexpected wash of light. Persia raised her head out of the small pen and locked eyes with the hunter. The photoflash fired rapidly, scaring her into a messy duck dive which showered the hunter with brine. He crammed the camera back into a protective pocket and scanned the area. Suddenly self-conscious, the young man spun on his heel and re-traced his footsteps back along the narrow jetty, much swifter this time. The others would be waiting impatiently for him to join them for dinner back in the old shanty tavern, and he too felt the hunger pangs in his belly. It had been a long, physically exhausting day and despite his distress he realised he needed nourishment. He would eat a quick meal and then excuse himself for the long drive north. His partner had been ill lately and he needed to be there. Not that his story really needed any refinement or embellishment. They would be far too drunk to care by now. The decision made, he cursed softly to himself as he beat his way back at a slow jog, uncertain and loose limbed. At least they were still alive and breathing.

With the lulling ebb and flow of tide, and the retreat of daylight playing quietly and insistently upon the beleaguered youngsters, a silence fell over the pens, punctuated only by the hollow pipe *whoosh* of their exhalations. At sunset the water's surface took on the impression of dappled gold, neatly washing the tragedy of the day's events away with a subdued finality. The perfect ivory eye patches of the pair assumed a dazzling hue of burnished bronze in the evening light; shining like golden tears until their longest day finally gave way to the approaching night.

ೞ ☯ ೞ

My crime is of no concern here. Justice, guilt, right and wrong I think I will leave for other tellers and other tales. It is simply of the consequences of my wrongdoing that I wish to speak now; the hard unfamiliar surroundings and the feelings that remain, raw like a fresh-opened wound. I wonder if it is a wound that will ever truly heal.

I am led away from the court in shock. From somewhere outside of my body, now mute and numb, I look down at the clothes that I'm wearing. It occurs to me that they now remain the last reminder of who I truly am. In my mind they symbolise all that remains of my life up until this point. And soon, no doubt they will be taken from me too. I decide solemnly that it is going to be up to me to remember exactly who I am, no matter what. No matter how desperate the situation becomes.

Fluorescent lights, grimy walls and gray concrete. The basement holding cells in the bowels of the building beneath the stately polished oak and opulent pile carpet of the courtroom present a darkly cruel juxtaposition. The short span of steps from the civil gentility of the court to the almost medieval grime of the holding cells comes as an unexpected slap to one's face. The world that we know, and take for granted; our comfortable façade of humanity and peaceable civility is wallpaper thin, and there is a dark brooding ugliness festering behind it. A series of glass-doored cages look out onto a central control room, and from them a succession of caged animals peer out; angry and unkempt. Expectantly brooding. Sparked suddenly from their sullen torpor by the distraction of another new arrival. They look for all the world like a pack of motherless lab rats. Abandoned and uncared for. Of precious little worth except as specimens to be subjugated, probed and dissected. Corrected.

Barked words, unregistered. I am a sleepwalker. A sharp metallic slam and the double click of a heavy latch, like the driving of coffin nails. I find myself enclosed in a stale brushed steel cabin, all rivets and heavy plates, and barely wider than my shoulders. It forms part of the rear flank of a large slab-sided van; a 'meat wagon'. Facing me, a white haired bespectacled old man stares back, eyes glazed in bewilderment. A startled rabbit caught in the headlights. I realise in a later reflection that his expression is likely a mirror image of my own. We sit in silence, our knees almost touching in the cramped angularity of our metal cocoon. I examine the thickness of the welds. The blind domed bolt heads. The heavy double glass side window muffles the sounds of the real world outside, a grim reminder of our impending removal from it. A crunch of gears, a sudden lurch and the extraction begins. The swaying of my stainless tomb makes me queasy and I struggle against a sense of rising panic in the airless enclosure. I am hyperventilating. Outside, groups of office workers laugh and banter over post-work coffees in the fading afternoon light. They are oblivious to my passing.

Razor wire and bitumen. Towering bastion walls permit only the narrowest glimpse of a starless sky illuminated by the eerie yellow-orange glow of sodium lighting. This will be my new home for the time being; or rather the home that has been chosen for me. This observation returns to haunt me time and time again over the next few days as my thoughts turn naturally to home and all its familiar comforts. Of my beautiful Maree, now in a prison of her own by virtue of our separation.

The jaws of the beast yawn open and I am shepherded in by an impatient blue uniform. More fluorescent lights; more grimy walls. More shouted instructions. Yet another holding cell. Lock by lock, cell by cell I am being swallowed alive. My gut is a hardened knot which pulls my innards tighter with each uniform that sweeps past the glass walled holding room. This is a processing area, and I can make a fair assumption as to what is to come here. Beyond that, however, I do not know. I feel like nothing more than a speck of lint slowly drawn into an eddying flow that circles a waiting drain, and I can only adopt the path of least resistance and allow it to carry me in. Correction – I can choose to flail out and resist rather like the cornered animals in the glass holding tanks at the courthouse. The thought sends a dry shiver through me which ends its travel by pulling on the knot of my gut.

I want to cry, but no tears come.

Shock overtakes me and a numbness persists throughout the next two hours of induction. Strip search. Shower. An issue of threadbare green prison clothes. A medical check from a disinterested prison nurse who spends the entire medical assessment with her eyes glued to a computer screen. Directions given by humourless, disinterested uniforms continue throughout the entire ordeal.

'Sit down. Wait. Go to the first door. Take these. Go over there. Wait.'

Finally, exhausted I am led to what appears to be a hospital wing. Linoleum floors, heavy doors, and always the same stark fluorescent lighting. I am pointed to a small hallway lined with heavy cell doors. Each door has a glass paned viewing slot in it accessed by raising a sliding cover. We walk to the very end of the hallway passing a cell which the officer accompanying me eyes carefully. Whatever is in there is trying it's darndest to get out; the heavy door vibrates hard enough to cause sympathetic shock waves of dust to fall from the surrounding walls with each dull thud. The hammering goes on rhythmically as we walk the length of the corridor.

Thud. Thud. THU-UD.

'This is you' says the guard, indicating the cell door at the far end of the corridor. Assessing the room gingerly, I find a spot for the pile of prison greens that I have been issued with. I have a plastic mug, plastic plate and bowl. Plastic cutlery. A crude metal bunk bed fills almost the entire room, bare and unmade except for an old stained pillow. I wait for the guard to leave and then mustering all my strength, I leave the cell to tentatively explore my new surroundings.

The remainder of my day passes like an ill-remembered dream. I am existing in some grim parallel reality. Normal life as I know it is going on beyond the stern razor-wire capped brick wall; yet it has now become a world that I can neither see nor hear. Just like the dreams, I am in a world within a world. The recollection makes me nauseous.

Seven or eight others are domiciled here in the small holding area with me. No-one speaks. No-one seems to take any notice of me; rather they roam the hall and common room area aimlessly. Backwards and forwards wordlessly like so many walking dead. It is surreal and disturbing. Five jaded prison guards oversee the hellhole, each one latently fractious or angry. Job satisfaction seems non-existent here.

A middle-aged prisoner who I have heard referred to as Johnny sidles up to me in the small common room adjoining the hallway. A yellow T-shirt sets him apart from the others and marks him as a 'trustee' prisoner; entrusted to assist with the welfare of new inmates. He must have recognised the shell-shocked look in my eyes, and his creased face breaks into a dry sympathetic grimace. I weigh him up swiftly – bearded and balding, he has a quiet sense of purpose and confidence about him. A warmth in his eyes belies the almost offhand businesslike mannerisms.

'I'm Johnny,' he says, offering a cursory handshake, 'I saw you come in earlier. You OK?

'Adam. Hi. Yes I'm OK, just a little overwhelmed, is all.'

'First time inside?'

'Yeah, first ever.'

'Take my advice – make it your last. You're gonna feel that shitty overwhelmed feeling for a while. But hang in and it will be OK. Are you finding everything you need?'

'I'm getting there slowly. The guards are no help at all. I'm still waiting to get a phone call out.'

'Evil pricks. Yeah, they do that. OK if they haven't set up a call for you by late afternoon, let me know and I'll make some waves. You have a wife? Girlfriend?'

'Girlfriend. We live together and she'll probably be beside herself right now.'

'Kids?'

'No.'

'That's good. Makes it a whole lot easier.'

I weighed up Johnny's words and decided that they sounded a little foreboding. Never mind. Push that creeping doubt down and try to ride this out.

'So where is home?' he continued, eyes continually roaming the room as he spoke.

'Upstate. A couple hundred miles from here. You?'

'Well my house is six miles from here. This is my home, for at least the next five years.'

'Ouch.'

'Yeah. Ouch.'

A commotion rose from around the corner in the hallway. Trouble. Johnny's body language telegraphed that he had already picked up on it, several beats before I did.

'Listen Adam, I gotta go sort this out. It's like fighting wildfires in here. Word of advice for you though – you look like a level-headed guy. Don't draw attention to yourself. Blend in. You act different or weak here, it makes you a target.'

The thumping grew more urgent from the nearby hallway as two overweight guards strode purposefully towards the fracas. Johnny joined them, but not before yelling over his shoulder:

'They'll move you to a permanent cell sometime tomorrow. Won't be as crazy as this, I promise ya! Let me know if you don't get that phone call.'

As the yelling grows louder, I decide that the relative privacy of my cell might be a more sensible option and peer warily around the corner into the hallway. A screaming prisoner, face bloodied and handcuffed is being manhandled by the two portly guards before being slammed bodily against the wall and pushed into an open cell. He falls heavily, like a sack of potatoes and doesn't get up again. The younger of the two guards deftly slams the cell door closed, and I take the opportunity to slip by, giving the officers as wide a berth as possible.

Without so much as a passing glance, Johnny and the two guards are gone, leaving me to step past the bloodied smear marks against the opposite wall. I reach my room and make for the tiny stainless steel toilet in the corner of the room. The dry retching eases some of the knot that has grabbed coldly at my gut.

Though it is only early evening, I remain in my small featureless room. I doze fitfully, a part of me aware of every passing sound. Johnny's words play on my mind. About this being his home. Could he really be that disaffected with his life that he could embrace this place as his home, and his place outside in the real world a mere house? I find his observation to be paradoxical and jarring. Maybe he has lost his family. Perhaps his wife and kids. I never did ask. Maybe there is nothing for him out there in the real world any longer. Or is it perhaps simply his way of putting a perspective on his imprisonment? Perhaps it is his way of enduring the long years before he sees his true home again?

I lie on my back and gaze at the unfamiliar surrounds. Featureless white walls. Stainless steel wash basin and toilet. Everything is bolted down carefully with blind domed bolts. There are no sharp edges on any of the fittings. I have turned off the overhead light, but the antiseptic glare of sodium lighting outside the heavy barred window keeps the room bathed in an alien half-light.

This is not my home. Nor am I ever likely to see it as such. It is simply a trial to be studiously and quietly endured. This is *not* a home.

I don't recall just when I fell asleep. I'm only thankful the dreams seem to have receded and given me some respite. My private nightmare world seems to have left me alone, at least for the time being. Sometime in the early hours of morning, a flashlight playing on my closed eyelids draws me up through the cottonwool cloud of sleep. I flinch involuntarily in response to the sudden unwelcome intrusion of light. The sound of the inspection slot in the door slamming shut. From outside my room a disinterested woman's voice yells down the corridor: *'They're still breathing!'*

CHAPTER TWO

LOCKED DOWN

*'When illusion spins her net, I'm never where I wanna be
And Liberty she pirouettes, when I think that I am free'*
–PETER GABRIEL - 'Solsbury Hill'

IF YOU'RE EARLY enough to catch it, the autumn light has a way of stealthily encroaching on sleep as it climbs high enough to peep through the eastern windows of the house. The warm shaft of morning sunlight advances slowly and inexorably across the floor; picking out the burgundies and golds in the thick Persian carpet before pouring like warm treacle into the bedroom. Quiet fingers of light endow the distressed timber walls with a warm yellow patina which reflects firstly onto the headboard before tracing its way down across the bed.

Tin-Tin the cat, who has surreptitiously laid claim to a large swath of the king-size bed under the cover of darkness, is the first to react to the insistent tendrils of morning light. The jet black feline twitches imperceptibly before performing a contented waking stretch like some proud heathen conqueror of the Alps. The oddly toylike squeak which he then emits somewhat undermines the credibility of his coolly regal demeanour. In what I'm sure is a deliberate act, Tin-Tin sprawls across the gap between me and Maree, gently touching each of us with a paw. Satisfied with the re-connection, he lazily closes his eyes and returns to some mystical cat dimension which, judging from his smug countenance I'm quite certain no human being may access, or indeed understand.

Aided by the set of sharp claws insinuating themselves on my shoulder, I drowsily shake off the last thick shards of sleep and I gradually become aware of Maree's outline on the pillow next to me. The glow of morning sunlight rises in intensity and highlights the tawny browns and tans in her long tousled hair. Tin-Tin's outstretched paw gently rises and falls rhythmically with her breathing. I'm at once comforted and at peace. The morning sun is matched perfectly by this beautiful woman's quiet glow.

With the return of consciousness, last night's dream is slowly bubbling to the surface and leaching out of me, like so much dirty water from a sponge. The dark memories feel so real – small dank cells, yelling and confusion, and everywhere the faded green of prison uniforms. I recall the anxiety sitting in a hard knot against my gut, like so much thick undigested food. Exhaling in a deep sigh of relief I reach out to touch Maree.

Slap. The wet sound of plastic milk pouches being dropped outside my bedroom door. *Slap.* The cat's body snaps to attention, wired and taut. Emerald eyes suddenly widening. *SLAP!* Tin-Tin leaps from the bed in a black fluid blur before disappearing like an apparition through the scuffed gray lino floor next to the small bunk bed. I rise up instinctively onto my elbows, the rough brick wall rudely grazing my left shoulder and drawing blood. Maree too has vanished, and in her place the dirty cell door stares back at me blankly. From beyond it in the void the public address system grates and then blares in angry metallic distortion:

'B and C wings, stand by your doors for morning muster. NOW!'

Johnny tells me that this feeling will pass. That things will slowly settle down and get better. Right now it doesn't seem so. I am wading through a mire of thick mud and quicksand which threatens to suck me down, and each step forward is a supreme effort.

In the cramped confines of my cell with its little inspection slot in the door, I feel little more than a caged animal, observed by my captors every few hours through the night. I'm told they do this to ensure the risk of an inmate committing suicide is minimised. The humiliation chafes at me like so much wet rope. The wounds of my incarceration are still fresh and raw, and I lay broken on my small bunk.

When I was a kid, I would spend endless days of my summer vacation at the beach. Heady days given to swimming, basking and boisterous play in the sun and salt air. To a young boy, the lingering smell of salt, sea and sand that clung to our clothes at the end of the day was like some seminal promise of freedom. Freedom from school and the string of endless tests and exams. From parents, chores and responsibility. Even now, recalling that smell takes me back just like an old half-remembered song draws you back to a particular era of your life.

One summer's day my pal Buddy and I discovered a makeshift cave dug into the side of one of the low grassy dunes. Seeming like a welcome respite from the midday swelter we crawled into the dugout, surprised at how perfectly the shock of cool, moist air enveloped us. The pungent smell of wet sand and the rotting roots of parched dry coastal bushes assaulted our nostrils. I sat happily in the muffled confines of the dugout, content to just let the world roll by. The dim cavern was a welcome change from the stark noonday sun.

Not so with Buddy, however. High spirited and prone to distraction – these days doctors would quickly declare his condition as ADHD – he scurried out of the cave to explore. Moments passed and I could hear him scrambling awkwardly across the dune overhead, breathing heavily from the climb. Sand began to dislodge from the low ceiling and matted in my wet hair; gritty and coarse to the touch. In almost the same instant I can recall my heart skipping a beat as I drew breath to yell a terrified warning to Buddy, but no words escaped. All at once the roof collapsed, falling in on me like a heavy dark blanket that winded me and pinned me with astonishing speed.

The piercing blue of the sky disappeared and my world faded to black; a muffled silence save for the racing sobs of my breath. I realized that I was hyperventilating; my heart and lungs racing beyond my voluntary control. The weight of sand made every terrified breath a painful effort and I felt the rising tide of fear.

Precious moments passed before I regained the presence of mind to consciously calm my uncontrolled breathing. My body was pinned up to the shoulders; my limbs all but useless against the weight. Trapped as I was in a small dank air pocket, a pained thought came to me in a sudden moment of clarity – I was going to suffocate and die here. *So this is what death is like.* No sooner had that thought crystallised and settled than the smallest shaft of filtered light broke through the dark roof overhead. The smell of that first deep draught of in-rushing air was sublime.

That day in the dune cave – that suffocating feeling of being buried alive which melted my guts to hot liquid – no words can better describe to you what I am feeling right now. What the experience of being in a prison for the first time feels like. If like me you are a person who is used to life outdoors under a wide open sky, prison is incredibly claustrophobic and stale. It smothers you slowly and incessantly. Closes in on you and suffocates you.

Even experience below decks on the trawler, in the greasy-stale confines of a small rolling cabin couldn't prepare me for this. The difference is that on a boat you know that you are always able to scurry up a companionway and draw in deep draughts of fresh sea air up on deck, when that liquid queasiness of claustrophobia overtakes you.

I am suffocating. And yet there is a small hopeful part of me that keeps looking for that slim shaft of light, just like that day so long ago in the dunes.

When an orca sleeps, you might say that it is in a cradle rocked by two worlds. You see, a blackfish cannot sleep in a conventional sense. At least, not in the way that human beings sleep. Indeed, no whale or dolphin can. For an orca, every single draught of breath must be taken consciously. Unlike a human being, there is no involuntary impulse that makes it so, and because of this only a part of an orcas brain goes into sleep.

The wakeful half, which perhaps we might refer to as a *'Night Watchman'* remains conscious in the physical world; quietly going about the mundane business of regulating breathing, keeping an eye out for threats and impending danger whilst the other half of the brain quietly submerges into the sub-conscious world of sleep. It is here the orca is free to seek out other dimensions and other times in accordance with the Harmony:

'Our spirits straddle the divide between the two Spheres. This is the Primary Duality and Balance.'

Through the stillness of that first night, Persia was aware of the insistent hunger pangs as she slept. She was fighting the desperate urge to eat. The watcher continued to scan the area for approaching threats, wary but satisfied. A logging blackfish is always most vulnerable at the water's surface, but she was safe at least for the time being. Persia knew she would need sustenance very soon. A ravenous feeder, the orca will eat as much as two hundred pounds of food each day to fuel the exertions of its tireless journey.

Harbor seals are not the easiest of prey to catch once they are alerted to the looming presence of a hungry five thousand pound blackfish. Imagine if you will, being the size of a very large sausage dog and being relentlessly pursued by a wildly careening black and white dump truck, intent on grinding you into an edible mince. Flicking a quick rearward glance as you dodge and corkscrew wildly, you see the business end of the black leviathan opening in anticipation; a deceptively cute baby-pink mouth surmounted by a cruel flange of flashing white serrated teeth.

The pair of plump seals which flashed past the nets like quicksilver bullets in the pre-dawn gloom scarcely noticed the two logging orcas. Not expecting the presence of a lurking predator this close to the shoreline, they had passed within feet of the pens leaving a silvered trail of rising bubbles in their wake as they sped toward the beach to haul out. Their presence registered to the two young orcas but neither of the pair reacted. They were all but powerless to pursue the seals even if they wanted to.

And so that long first night passed and around her the rest of the world began to wake. The first hint of the return of sunlight in the upper firmament is the break of pre-dawn hush by the delicate tinker of small songbirds. Long before the curve of gold reveals itself, the birds feel the onset of its warming energy as a subtle vibration which sets into motion the insistent pulse of blood through tiny veins. And slowly, one by one, tree by tree, their chorus rises in harmony with this pulsation. It is through this vibration that all life forms are connected, and understanding this is a key to understanding the Harmony.

After the birds, the creatures of forest and glade then similarly take up the call. In a neat counterpoint, the dwellers of the night lower their vibrations as the heavier pitch of darkness recedes. Returning to nest and burrow, hollow and copse, they blend themselves in with bark and earth until the day's prescribed trek of

Sun is once again complete. Mother Nature breathes in and breathes out and life follows its pulse. A truly wise man or woman will do the same.

Every day Navajo people would rise just before the dawn and greet the Sun with prayers to ensure the continuing harmony with their world. In Navajo belief, human beings have an obligation to preserve and protect this harmony. That was before the artificial world of mechanization and high technology encroached. Men and women who live their lives close to nature; who depend upon the Earth mother for their food, warmth and shelter touch upon this deeper understanding which orcas naturally embrace and take for granted.

Down below in the world of Water, a similar choreography is taking place. Here, in the same way, it also begins with vibration. The teachings of the Harmony tell us that this is a fundamental precept which is at the very foundation of All That Is. Vibration explains a great many things and importantly it defines and separates the spheres and dimensions of Being. To master that spectrum of vibration is the secret to mastering Time and Space.

As the first questing rays of sunlight strike the waters they similarly infuse it with a vibration – a vitality which dances insistently at a molecular level. A calling to the life forms of ocean and stream, river and brook to take up its compelling rhythm. To the casual observer there is a sense of lush serenity conjured by the casual lap of water against timber and rock. But beneath the surface the song birds of the sea are drawing into life, all but unheard by the human ear. The incessant crackle of shrimp rises like the dry static sound of snapping twigs. The croaks of gropers and large reef fish. From all manner of watery corners comes the moans, squeaks, whines, barks, chirps and grunts of waking aquatic life. Beneath the surface, the ocean is a busy place!

From her pen, Persia sensed the expectant quavering which heralded the break of day. The *Night Watchman* dutifully raised her from the Other side and drew her back to wakefulness, before he himself melted away like the other nocturnal dwellers, leaving behind him the unanswered question of sustenance.

When the hunters came again with their slings and their cranes Persia, just like water, offered them no resistance.

CHAPTER THREE

OLD DOGS & NEW TRICKS

*A full-grown horse or dog is beyond comparison a more rational animal
than an infant of a day, or a week, or even a month old.
But suppose that the case were otherwise, what would it avail?
The question is not 'Can they reason?' nor 'Can they talk?'
but 'Can they suffer?'*
– JEREMY BENTHAM (1748-1832) - British social reformer

THE BRASS NAME plaque on the heavy walnut panelled door was impressive, yet not ostentatiously so. It spoke to the discernment of the unobtrusive fair haired businessman who toiled quietly at the ornate wooden desk in the neat corner office. The solid black lettering on it read: *'Casper Barrett CEO Waterworld'*.

Casper Barrett might be best described as a collector. As a youngster growing up in the Californian southwest, it was baseball cards. Then postage stamps and first day covers. As his collections grew he developed a penchant and skill for acquiring the unique and the unusual. It had never been an interest fuelled by any sort of desire for profit or gain – rather it seemed largely a case of 'the getting rather than the having.'

There is an early distinction to be made here. Casper was always a discriminating collector; he was never what would be popularly termed a hoarder. He was never given to the senseless compulsion to hoard up all and sundry, like the crazy old cat ladies found long dead in damp, dark houses-cum-rubbish dumps; stuffed room upon fetid room with the floor to ceiling spoils of books and newspapers, pots and pans, toys, trinkets and heirlooms. A rotting, shambolic time capsule neurotically and painstakingly built from all manner of discards of a throwaway society.

As the quietly-spoken lad entered his teens, it was plainly evident that the rapidly evolving hobby of collecting was becoming obsessive and all-consuming, and his parents' sense of consternation grew in concert with their son's increasingly solitary focus. Despite their concern, they couldn't help but be privately impressed with his fine eye for detail and his sense of quiet determination in researching every field of interest that he engrossed himself in. They consoled themselves with the fact that it could be far worse; citing the steadily growing suburban tales of drug addiction, alcohol abuse and sexual excess that followed in the wake of the current crop of local teenagers. Not surprisingly, their first-born was never the normal American teenager, spurning ice rinks and shopping malls for the quaintly old-fashioned thrill of scouring through old bric-a-brac shops and antiquarian bookstores.

His father privately speculated on the question of whether this behaviour was a compensation for a confused sexuality; and yet the boy seemed comfortably engrossed rather than conflicted. If his mother harboured similar concerns, she never once voiced them; rather she showered her son with an unconditional love, as only a mother can. So when the Barrett family doctor recommended a referral to a local specialist and young Casper returned home with a diagnosis of mild autism, new light was shed on the boy's curious pattern of obsessive behavior and social isolation.

Casper's passion for collectibles continued unabated as the years passed. A chance visit to the Ventura County Museum of History and Art in later life sparked an interest in US pioneer artifacts, and ultimately led to his enduring passion for antiques of the Civil War era.

Running an upmarket antique store in Santa Monica marked Casper's first foray into entrepreneurship, fuelled by his now substantive knowledge of historical curiosa. Barrett never looked back from there, and the budding businessman quietly went from strength to strength, running a lucrative chain of furniture shops across five states. Taking pride of place in his rambling Santa Monica mansion was a glass covered weapons display which sported a rare 1863 Enfield Rifle Musket of English manufacture, so fondly used by the Confederate forces of the day.

Apart from a handful of close friends, and an extended family courtesy of his two devoted younger sisters, Casper had no wife or significant other to share his treasured spoils with. He never married.

The death of a well-to-do relative gave the aging eccentric the capital injection needed to make his next business speculation a reality. There is little doubt that his childhood fascination with touring circuses was a key motivator behind the purchase of the ailing marine amusement park which once held a prime position on the Pacific coastal strip. These days it presented as little more than a crumbling shade of its former glory; hidden from prying eyes behind a makeshift wooden fence which had been progressively coated and then re-coated with gaudy airbrushed urban graffiti. The wooden bleachers still stood, forlorn and empty. Standing silently whilst blocking out the incessant background thrum of nearby traffic, one could almost hear a haunting snatch carried on the warm wind – the echoed squeals of childish joy from past ages of spectators who once filled the stands; the young faces shiny with rosy smiles and smeared hot buttered pop-corn.

The old rock seawall remained, hunkered down against the wind and holding doggedly firm. It would endure another hundred and fifty years of insistent assaults of wind and water before finally crumbling under their unrelenting onslaught. The Pacific is destined to take back her own, and all the best efforts of Man cannot hold back this greater truth.

Native American legend tells us of the 'Earth Diver' – a mystical giant turtle that descended to the greatest depths of the Ocean, and returned to the surface with elemental mud from which she fashioned the Earth; the great mountains, the valleys deserts and plains. The earth shares an ancient connection with the ocean, having originally been born and raised from it.

The City of Angels will return to the sea floor from which the Earth Diver faithfully carved it, all those eons ago. There it will remain like a cancer; its low energy persisting for further millennia, until the endless wash of tide and time eventually heals it over once and for all. Nature has a way of washing Mankind from her hair. That is the way of the Harmony. But the journey of Man is a tale in itself; to be told at another time and place.

The lagoon and the connecting circular performance pool with the broad concrete ramp where the wet-suited trainers would muster their charges all sat intact. It baked quietly in the noon-day sun awaiting the next performance, beneath a hot tired looking row of tall palm trees. Abandoned and uncared for, it had fallen into a sorry state of ramshackle disrepair. What others had simply written off as an occupational health and safety nightmare, Casper's practiced eye recognized as a veritable goldmine in the making. Casting only a cursory glance at the old man's first draft business plan, Barrett's long-time financial adviser Morrie Lambert – himself something of a canny investor from 'old moneyed' stock – forced a patronizing grin before delivering his take on the situation bluntly:

'Casper, buddy. Listen to your old friend. Do you know how to make a small fortune in the world of marine amusement parks? Start with a large one!'

Lambert's dry assessment of the situation had not been enough to dampen the old eccentric's quiet resolve, and the plans for acquisition of the old park forged ahead.

The inevitable hours of research that followed saw Casper casting a far-flung net to gather information from oceanographers, marine mammal experts and professional fishermen. He decided very early on in the piece that what was needed was an act which was 'larger than life'. After all, the key to the success of the travelling circuses which had so enthralled him as a child was the thrill of seeing exotic wild animals at close quarters. Television had fired the imagination of middle America in the sixties with the rise of 'Flipper' – the tale of a dolphin who befriended a young boy and his family. Was it possible that an animal could be possessed of unique personality and bold intellect, such that it could rival a human? Viewers were enchanted with the notion, and it sparked an endearing national love affair with the dolphin.

Casper's imagination, tempered with his canny knack for acquiring the unusual took that seminal spark to the next level. To his mind the marine park concept was a two-stage rocket, and the now decrepit first-stage marine park which once rode high on the crest of a wave inspired by a television dolphin was spent. Slowly but inevitably the surge of excited patrons had receded like a king tide, leaving the park a flat and lifeless backwater. The fickle public had mostly flitted off in search of the next cheap sensation, perhaps a singing frog or a talking bear. Sallie the seal and the trio of tired bottlenose dolphins performing their trade-mark choreographed jump through burning rings of fire was no longer enough to entice the paying public back. The concept was good in its heyday, but Stage Two was now required, and it needed to be larger than life to draw the crowds once again. And what could be larger than the foreboding might of the killer whale?

Casper had been captivated by a mighty creature he had seen off Washington state whilst enjoying a game fishing expedition on a friend's boat. Where its smaller cousin the bottlenose dolphin was mischievously clever and playfully cute; in carnival terms the killer whale was the veritable lion to Flipper's pony. A veritable Dark Lord of the seas, Machiavellian in both countenance and reputation. The more that he discovered and learned, the more the wiry eccentric was enchanted by this enigmatic creature's legend. Drawn by mythological tales of their demonic world, he began to perceive that chance encounter in the swell off the Olympic peninsula as a rogue challenge; daring him venture into the watery staterooms of Orcus, god of the Underworld. The Hellish Whale thus became both the challenge and the prize. Its capture and subjugation would stand testament to Casper's victory over this emissary from the lower world.

History, it seems had found its grim repetition in the form of Casper Barrett; a modern day Ahab setting out upon a gruesome hunt to capture the great whale. In this case the object of his quest was a creature he perceived to be possessed of unfathomable evil. The black whale. The 'Pequod' that he commissioned to seek and capture his prize was an equally ominous looking black ship called the *Pacific Dark*.

⁗❦⁘

The old prison laundry is a scene straight out of a Dickensian novel. And Bob the crusty old chief guard looks like he has overseen proceedings here since Oliver Twist was a young lad. White haired, with the stern leathery face of a bulldog he totters around on skinny knobbly-kneed legs whilst watching the thirty-odd lags going more or less about their daily toil. He appears studiously oblivious to the childish carry-on of many of the workers, who invariably do little more than flock together like jailbirds of a feather.

Behind a pair of huge silver rimmed glasses, the hawk eyes have a warm glint that suggests that Bob sees more than he actually lets on. Pushed sufficiently, I suspect that his bark is probably ably matched by his bite. Dave my roommate, ever the wily observer, has also noted these qualities in old Bob. He has reached the conclusion that the old codger's massive pair of spectacles are equipped with special lenses not unlike those of a fly's eye; endowing the wiry old bulldog with some sort of panoramic 'wrap-around' vision. Over the years I'm certain that Bob has witnessed endless repeats of the scene that plays itself out like an aggravating one-act theatrical. The lags who scurry into the corners like cockroaches to avoid hard work are the very same ones who hover continuously around the toilet block throughout the day to drag on yet another surreptitious smoke. The whole operation seems to be carried by a small knot of hard working prisoners who pick up the slack, grateful for the relief from the monotony of being cell-bound all day.

The focal point of the ancient linoleum clad room is a massive old linen press; a mechanical contraption of motor driven rollers strung with an array of long felt strips which guide sheets and bed linen through the antique monstrosity. A team of fifteen inmates are engaged in the process. Fed by a group of green-clad workers at one end, the super-heated newly pressed linen is expelled at the other end to be neatly folded by a six cotton gloved men working in pairs to fold the sheets in a neat choreography. More workers then stack the sheets into trolleys for dispersal through the prison complex.

Against one wall, a line of large industrial tumble dryers revolve in almost constant motion. Their contents of towels, shirts, pants and underwear are routinely disgorged newly warm and slung across huge sorting tables, to be folded and stacked by a waiting throng of workers. Hovering over a table of steaming bed linen, old Bob dryly observes:

'If these quilts are slightly damp and some folks die of pneumonia, don't worry boys. That just means there'll be less for us to wash next week.'

Satisfied with the efforts of the scruffy band of laborers he totters off, loudly whistling *By the Light of the Silvery Moon'*, which is precisely half of the two-song repertoire which he repeats endlessly.

'He must have the lungs of a bulldog as well,' I venture to Dave as *'Moon River'*, the other half of his repertoire, wafts tunelessly across the room; rising over the din of the military battery of stainless steel dryers. The toilet block behind him lies underneath a semi-permanent fog of tobacco smoke, which he seems to studiously ignore in spite of the large metal *'No Smoking'* sign hung prominently on the wall.

I have been fortunate enough to have been paired up with Dave. Largely preferring his own company, and more often than not engrossed in a good book; we hit it off instantly. Being at such close quarters, I felt a compulsion to tell him about the nightmares. Or at least warn him that I may suffer from some sort of sleep disturbance occasionally. I needn't have worried, as he took it all easily in his stride; simply conceding that many people here suffered similar problems and the cure was sleeping tablets from the medical center. I let it pass with a smile and a nod. I've already discovered the nightmares are impervious to sleeping tablets.

With the day slowly rolling on I slip comfortably into a dreamy reverie, lulled by the mind numbing repetition of folding score upon score of faded army green T-shirts in the midst of the industrial clamor. This is how it starts. Sometimes noise and vibration set it off. I hadn't told Dave, or anyone else for that matter, that the 'nightmares' could also strike during the day.

The boat rocks again like a drunken sailor, caught in the wake of the second catcher vessel. It catches me off-guard as I am folding clothes and packing them neatly into my waterproof bag. I'll be needing them when I head back home from the wharf after our catch is complete. The golden rule for steadying oneself on any size vessel is *'One hand for yourself and one hand for the boat'*. In other words you always work one handed and steady yourself against something solid with the other. With both hands engaged in the process of stuffing my folded civvies into the zip bag, I have broken the golden rule and the sudden lurch of the big hull catches me off balance. I dash my forehead sharply against the small wooden bunk ladder, as penance for my sins. The blow is hard enough for me to literally see stars, and I clutch instinctively for a hand hold.

Reeling back in a daze, a wave of giddying nausea hits me in the sweaty confines of the cabin. The blow seems to bring my sense of smell into sharp relief and the cloying smell of stale tobacco and body odor makes me retch. Perhaps this was the first time that I really became aware of this strange keening of the senses that was slowly and inexorably beginning to overtake me in recent times. I'm swimming in a sonic ocean of diesel engine noise and muffled deck sounds as the duty deckhands keep a keen eye out for passing trade.

There is an odd feeling in the air which is putting me on edge. A quiet expectation. Suspended like a pregnant pause or a sharply held intake of breath. Something inside told me they were nearby, and in that same moment of lucidity the monotonous background thrum of the diesels fell away to an ominous silence. The ship was becoming a dead bulk in the water; slowly giving way until it took on the rocking motion of the ocean instead of its own surging momentum. It was as though the ship itself had taken to lying in wait. It readied itself to pounce, all black and dangerous; almost like one of their own. I bounded up the stale dank companionway to take position. It was neither hot nor cold on deck and the low scuds of gray cloud only made the scene feel all the more cramped and close.

After a series of distant sightings and false alarms, when they finally did appear they showed no signs of fear or reticence. Even being submerged as they were, and all but hidden to the naked eye, you could sense an imposing presence. Fear was definitely not one of their emotions that day. At least not that I could see. They made you feel as if the oceans belonged to them. No, it seemed more than that somehow. As if *they* belonged to the ocean. Am I making sense at all? For all my eloquence I cannot find the words to describe it. There is something mysteriously ancient and timeless about their connection. The sense of power is palpable. Maybe this is the territory that comes with the hallowed position of top predator on the food chain.

When you watch a seagull fly, it does so simply to get from point 'A' to point 'B'. It cares nothing for the graceful art of flying as an act in itself. An eagle on the other hand, displays a deft control of its aerial craft. A pure joy to behold; the imperceptible flick of an eagle's outstretched flight feather sends the powerful bird into a wheeling turn. In a raptor's precise aerial symmetry there is a deft sense of command that borders on regal majesty. And so it is with these killer whales.

As they rose together in formation on the swell to draw breath, they seemed to infuse the waters with the purest sense of a predatory might tempered with cool connection. They surfaced all wetly black, and displayed their tall triangular fins. Flashes of ivory white down their flanks. Their course neatly bisected that of our boats; the *Pacific Dark* in the lead with the smaller *Jonathon Lee* tucked in to leeward off our starboard quarter. Despite the collision course, the orcas drove on unperturbed by the squat metal hulls bobbing lazily at the surface. All at once, from the deathly silence of the gray waters, life and commotion had burst forth.

'Wooomf-shhh; wooomp-whoomp-shhh'. Their distracted blows sounded loud enough to be plainly audible over the din of diesels as they kicked hastily into life. The duty hands all whooped and hollered with a newfound excitement borne out of the boredom of the past few days. I knew in that instant just what it must have been

like to man an old Yankee whaler. Becalmed by long sulphurous days of slack water, mind numbed by the monotony of endless hours of whittling. The grimy scrimshaw-handled knife scraping against knotted wood. Then suddenly, unexpectedly the strangled cry from the crow's nest above; suspended stalk-like and timber-railed above the ratlines and the rigging. *'Whale-ho!'*

The sudden invigorating kick, keenly sharp after the schlub torpor and boredom brought me back to the present. My heart quickened palpably. A massive bull rose in the center of the herd, its huge triangular dorsal fin surfacing like the conning tower of a nuclear submarine; dwarfing the harem that now surrounded him. A ragged cheer went up as the game began. Roils of oily gray-black smoke pumped from funnels as the two boats sprung to life in unison; the deck shuddered underfoot as the massive engine in the beast's belly transformed the deceptively impotent hulk into a thorobred fighting machine.

A female orca close alongside raised her head and peered curiously at our plate-steel flanks, her small eye lively and surprised by the unexpected metallic clamor. Alongside her dorsal fin, her nursing youngling took fright and fell away from the neat vacuum of slipstream which had neatly towed her along. She was a beautifully fashioned replica of her mother's graceful bulk; tiny yet perfectly formed. Her smooth flanks still unblemished and supple in their youth. Feverishly the little one struggled to regain the lost ground and tried to keep up with her mother, unaccustomed to negotiating the sharp bursts of speed needed to match her sudden pace. Her panicked breathing came in rapid half-gulps with the exertion. I felt the terror in that soft eye as the youngster passed alongside, raising her head in confusion.

Seeing this, the deck crew whooped raucously; a sense of bloodlust overtaking them as they took the cue to run excitedly to their positions in order to make ready the ropes and nets. Ours was the business of separation – to steal the young from the cloying grip of their mothers. I imagined a scene of brutish Romanic hordes, feverishly anticipating the fall of a bloodied weary gladiator in some grim arena. Caught up in that fever I rushed to join them; the torpor and queasiness of the past few days all but forgotten with the blood pounding in my temples as the adrenaline rush kicked in. So I willingly became one of the Romans. There and then, I too took up the barbarian cry, losing myself in the quickening baritone of diesels. Rising mechanically against the blue wash of ocean and the dimly wet breaches of our quarry, I bayed for blood just like an animal.

The shrill persistent ringing of the wall mounted bells suddenly pounds in my temples, and with that the din around me pulls into fine focus. Bringing me back to my current reality. Loud, unsavoury voices yelling and whooping punctuate the steady thrum of washing machines and dryers. The now familiar involuntary flinch through my backbone is strong enough to knock my part-completed pile of laundry off the folding table, drawing a couple of mildly bemused glances from the rough poker-faces nearby. I am momentarily confused and the now-familiar sense of remote disconnection smothers me like a densely persistent sea fog. I quickly shake myself free of its cloying non-corporeal grasp, but the experience leaves me somewhat disturbed and off-balance.

Coming-to, I realize I am standing in a loose pile of threadbare green T-shirts, looking as sheepish as a drunken bum who has just pissed his pants in public. The heavies go back to ignoring me; deciding I am either another junkie coming down from something, or a newbie doing it tough. What the fuck is happening to me? My spirits sink, and I am once again a stranger in a strange land. I occasionally have this strong sense that I am looking down at myself, as though I'm searching for something. Or someone. What the hell am I doing here? Thankfully the siren sounds, marking the end of the work shift, and I file back to the unit with the others, lost in my own thoughts.

'You know, I think some of us simply swap prisons when we come in here,' mused Dave, who had sat in quiet contemplation for the past few minutes. Taking his reading glasses off and setting them down in front of him on the table seems to give his statement something of an air of considered authority.

After the maddening din of the laundry, the unit common room seems almost hushed by comparison. I put down the coffee cup I had been cradling, sensing another of Dave's profound observations in the offing.

'OK, how do you figure that?'

Wincing I lean back, realizing just how badly my back is complaining after a day's toil in the laundry. I'm very quickly losing muscle tone from the long days in confinement. Part of me also realises that the out-of-body spinal jolt didn't help matters either.

'Well,' Dave continued, 'I know of guys who work as drillers and underground miners, and they live in conditions not much different from this. They'll spend weeks away from their family in a small remote mining camp. They live in cramped conditions; eat three square meals a day at the mess. Working days are long – out at dawn and back at dusk. There's no social life to speak of so it becomes the same endless routine day in, day out.'

I nod my acknowledgement, seeing the parallel he is describing.

'So, you're saying it's like a jail of their own making?'

'A jail doesn't always have a barbed wire fence and bars at the windows. Sometimes we choose a prison for ourselves, all of our own making. Sometimes it's an office. Sometimes it's a house in the suburbs with a white picket fence. Or a lifestyle. And sometimes, it's a life sentence.'

Just a decade older than me, Dave had come to remind me of my thoughtful old boat skipper, and I liked the way that he carefully chose his words. They had a weight to them which I appreciated.

'You see, a prison can be anything that stops us from living today, something that we endure for a variety of reasons. Some stay in failed marriages thinking that it's better the devil you know. Some stay in a job they hate simply because the money is good. Or because they feel they will be setting themselves up for the future by denying themselves a life today.'

He looked away toward the far corner of the room. A shouting match is developing at one of the card games, the course of events going against one of the gangstas who is about to turn on one of his own breed.

'You see Adam, the thing is that all we really have is today. Yesterday has been written and cannot be undone. We can beat ourselves up continually over it, but that just keeps us rooted in the past. It paralyses us. Yesterday is done. But the choice is ours with what we do today, if we decide that we want a better tomorrow.'

ରେ❀ରେ

When the construction crew started craning in the old twisted metal components, Morrie Lambert looked on dumbstruck. It rather resembled a de-construction, if truth be told. The big multi-wheeled crane made short work of unloading the assembly of scrap from the low-loader parked alongside the old wire mesh fence. Old corrugated metal water tanks, three of them, sat in a cluster on the periphery of the natural rock lagoon. They looked antiquated and clearly beyond economical repair; rendered useless as water tanks with the patina of ancient rust barely disguising the multitude of weatherworn holes where rivets once lay. A closer inspection revealed that the old tanks had been used for target practice; their agricultural appearance suggesting they had at some stage in their retirement become the sun bleached targets for some hick mid-western teenagers with an air rifle. The biggest of the three tanks still bore the remains of dusty flaking white letters scribed around its mid-section: *Reynolds Airfield*. Hefty four legged tank mounts like squatting giants were dropped alongside them. The heavy angular metal supports, each scarred and rusting; perfectly matching the wear and age of the big circular barrels. A helmeted construction worker in a yellow day-glo safety vest waved in a bulky rectangular observation booth resembling a small control tower. The peeling livery of its black and white checkerboard pattern dully reflected the sunlight as the crane operator carefully jockeyed it into position amongst the cluster of palms and verdant shrubby greenery at the coastal end of the natural pool.

By the time the first of the three grimy low loaders disgorged their rusting cargo of drums, barrels and battered Quonset barrack huts, the beachside marine park was taking on the appearance of an old abandoned wartime airfield. Casper sidled up alongside Morrie Lambert at the lagoon; the early gusts of sea breeze, heady with the smells of seaweed and salt baulking and lifting around the newly strewn obstacles.

'What do you think?'

'I think we'll be safe from Japanese fighters, buddy. It looks like they bombed the place to hell already.'

'That's all part of the look, Morrie. We're giving people something interesting. Something different.'

'Yeah, I was at all the meetings remember? It's just a shock when you see it all actually coming together. Stroke of genius buying all of this junk as surplus I must admit.'

'Well we're on a schedule now. We'll be ready to move the first killer whales in as of next week. The clearances have just come through from the NOAA. Then we'll really give 'em something different.'

'Different is definitely the word. Though my idea of different is Lebanese takeaway instead of Thursday night pizza.'

Casper grinned at the man's dry wit. Morrie had always been the grounded constant since they met at a conference in New York all those years ago. The savvy numbers man, his stern leathery face more often than not buried in ledgers and reports; a cigarette and a coffee never far from hand. As such, he was the perfect foil for Casper's pie-in-the-sky kinetics. Despite the gritty Manhattan demeanour, the wise-cracking financier could not help but admire the canny vision and sheer energy of his eccentric friend, built over the years spent wheeling and dealing together. Successes had far outshone failures, and when Casper cut him a deal on the old marine park, Lambert had taken a punt with a full quarter share.

Waterworld had been born.

CHAPTER FOUR

BRAKE PADS & DEAD FISH

*'Jails and prisons are designed to break human beings.
To convert the population into specimens in a zoo;
obedient to our keepers but dangerous to each other'*
—ANGELA DAVIS - US civil rights activist.

NEARING LAND, THERE comes a point at which the relentless tide is welcomed by the earth. It is as if the ocean, after its long lonely journey, waves a greeting to the land and the long jagged expanse of the coast waves its answering welcome. Sailing through this zone, one has a distinct sensation of being almost cradled as the motion created by this warm 'hand-shake' transmits through the shoaling waters; rocked by the might of the ocean on one side, and the solidity of dry land on the other.

Perhaps this is an echo back to the early days of the Birthing, when mother Ocean was a rich primordial soup which bore the creatures that were to become the dwellers of the newly risen land. Thus these coastal waters became a virtual spawning ground as embryonic life transitioned from the world of water into the world of air.

The first time that Persia had encountered others of her own kind from outside of the Clan of Three Pods was in these very waters.

The water here carries a different energy and the rolling main is at last stilled and becalmed in the shallows. The hardness that she invested herself with in order to complete so colossal a voyage seems all but soothed away by the aloof yet welcome solidity of dry land. These waters belong to the nation of the resident orca pods.

Shadow had very carefully mapped the seascape around her charges and Persia, from her flanking position alongside Grace, watched on with interest. The youngster had already become adept at scanning the waters around her, easily charting the increasing number of obstacles that marked the coastal approach; translating the echoes into a picture of jagged peaks and rocky outcrops lining their track. Despite her youth, she was a natural navigator, much to the quiet approval of her proud mother. It was a quality of their bloodline, and the others knew this implicitly. Out in front of the pod, Shadow was a study of focus and deft precision; making delicate course corrections which caused intermittent surges of bubbly contrails to suddenly stream back like glistening sparks behind her, first left and then right. Occasional larger corrections gave her the appearance of a lumbering punch-drunk boxer.

The reason, Persia knew, was the fact that the gently sloping seabed was extremely hard to navigate even for the sophisticated natural sonar that the ocean giants possessed. Shadow's years of practice made the art of close-in navigation look effortless. The lead line of orcas instinctively widened out slightly into a ragged 'V' formation, allowing Shadow the space to carefully guide her tribe. Out here the waters took on a lighter coloration, dappled with increasing shafts of sunlight as the waters ran in toward the rocky shoreline.

Tristesse and Constant called across the pod and Persia caught sight of the commotion in almost the same instant. Off the port quarter, out past the flanking bulk of Oberon and Arcturus a thousand shimmering points caught the light and reflected it back through the rippling water. Suddenly there was noise everywhere, the sounds of clicks and whistles crackling back and forth through the pod, like dry lightning. Beyond a churning school of salmon cruised the source of the noise; a half dozen slab-sided orcas, their dialect totally foreign to Persia.

Having made a dart for the open ocean ahead of their pursuers, the run of schooling salmon now wheeled in confused circles, confronted with the unexpected arrival of Shadow's pod. Capitalizing on their delay, the pursuers were quickly upon them, swinging like huge black and white pinwheels into the mêlée. Persia watched on with interest, immersed as she was in the noisy chatter of the group of marauding blackfish.

This was Tani'm's pod, and just like other orca groups they spoke in their own unique dialect. A language which was largely unrecognized by Persia and her nomadic kinfolk. Closing on an intersecting course the running salmon found themselves trapped between the two converging pods, and the waters churned and blurred with their frantic movements. The light sparkled and danced off them crazily as the streamlined silver bullets broke off and wheeled erratically in a confused frenzy.

The chaotic underwater ballet was punctuated by repeated swoops and dives through the schooling fish by the wheeling giants. Each spontaneous opportunistic lunge caused the racing salmon to break and re-group into smaller protective schools. The steadily increasing cloud of blood and debris in the water showed the balance of power was beginning to favor the seemingly randomly sparring orcas – Skalus and Kosum, Spukani, Lúkwał, Sumshasat and Luqał, who were each taking their fill of the plump fleshy fish. Re-grouping for mutual protection after the attack the surviving salmon fled in silvered darts close to the surface, their shadows painting dark flickers over Persia and Grace.

As the feeding frenzy began to abate, Shadow's pod had disengaged from their cautious transit to circle lazily; as much to allow Tani'm's group space as to take the opportunity to rest for a while and curiously assess the inshore dwellers. Several of her pod had playfully engaged the six locals, breaching and tail slapping at the surface before diving together in mock competition. A human might assume this activity to be flirting; Constant finding herself surrounded by three curious bulls, all vocalizing, corkscrewing and posing to attract her attention.

It is interesting to note that, in point of fact, whilst residents and transients may occasionally cross paths inadvertently they do not generally mix or socialize and nor have they inter-bred in hundreds, possibly thousands of years. They have become culturally and genetically distinct, to the point that they are close to becoming separate sub-species. The reason for this behaviour is known only to the orcas and the Harmony. I am inclined to let them keep this one little secret of intimacy to themselves for now, because the story of DNA and bloodlines is rather a subject within itself, and humans may be confronted to learn the fuller truth of it. For now, let us understand a little more about the ways of the Harmony.

What can be observed here is that, when members of two tribes meet, there is understood to be a meeting at two levels. At the first level of Being, a meeting of two physical forms takes place. It is in this meeting that the aspects of the flesh are negotiated. That is, the elements of physicality are satisfied – predator and prey, dominance and submission, territoriality and boundary. At the second level of Being there is an acknowledgement of All That Is, and the recognition and affirmation of each form's rightful place within the Harmony.

In the First Form there is Balance, and in the Second Form, Equality.
For Balance to prevail below there must be respect of Equality above and vice-versa. So says the Harmony.

०३❂८०

The dead salmon that Persia now eyed lay lifeless, like so many limp fallen leaves strewn across the surface of the pool. She sank disconsolately like a lift to the bottom of the enclosure, idly watching Tristesse break the surface nearby and disperse the dead offerings in her wake. With two easy flicks of his tail flukes Tondo easily coasted the length of the pool, swallowing half of the salmon offering before diving lazily to the bottom.

Orcas are behaviourally conservative to the extreme when it comes to food. They are naturally slow at taking up new food sources. A casual observer may suggest that they are fussy eaters, however it should be pointed out that there is far more to it than that. There is a design and an inherent logic to their discrimination and it is one of the keys to their success as a species. To hark back to our recent discussion of the Harmony, this is a fine example of the Balance in first form which we spoke of.

Ranging orca pods will occasionally encroach upon each other's territories. Rather than compete, they complement one another. The territorial resident pods may have a predominant diet of fish. The nomadic transients typically choose a diet of seals and other marine mammals. Thus a complementary balance and a natural order are maintained.

Tondo and Kyrie had once belonged to Tani'm's pod and were used to shallow water and a diet of fish which ran and schooled in the coastal waters. For the two young nomads however, the change in diet came as yet another shock to be overcome.

The dead fish which were thrown into the enclosure were not natural to them, but in the absence of live food they would have to do. Begrudgingly, Persia and Tristesse followed Tondo's cue and began devouring the regular offerings.

It had been almost three weeks since the two young orcas had been transferred from the floating pens, and they were slowly developing a familiarity with their new surroundings. The rocky pool which held the four orcas was close enough to the shoreline for

Persia to recognise the familiar crash and roll of breaking surf. She quickly realized that just like the claustrophobic box she had found herself enclosed in after being removed from the family, her bio-sonar was virtually useless here. Although the pool was comfortably deep, the confused ricochet reflection of her sonar clicks off the nearby rock walls was much like the firing of a bullet in a metal bucket. She very quickly decided to shut down her sonar, at least for the time being.

Following the natural curve of the lagoon, she could sense the ebb and flow of the ocean pouring regularly in and out of the enclosure through a wide gap in the wall. Sensing this Persia and Tristesse had remained around the gap, assessing it for some time before deciding that the barrier of metal bars which formed a gate across the breach was firm and unyielding. A cautious sonar inspection through the stout metal bars revealed deep water on the other side of the barricade. The ocean. *Home!*

The pair had spent the best part of their first few days at the barricade, desperately vocalizing and repeatedly issuing the pod call. Persia knew at once that the magnetics were all wrong, but the surge of incoming tide brought with it fresh hope. When no replies came back through the breach, they had dejectedly resigned themselves to settling into the unfamiliar new surroundings.

Another grated barricade, narrower than the sea wall barrier, lay at the opposite end of the elliptical sea pen. Spy hopping at the surface, the two orcas decided that a further pool lay beyond the smaller gate. This one appeared unnatural to them – a perfect smooth circle which appeared far smaller than their rocky surrounds. Here the water became still, and the two orcas far preferred logging along the broad sweeping curve of the lagoon near the sea inlet.

Then there were the other orcas. When Persia and Tristesse had arrived at their new home, they had been met by the two residents; the older male Tondo and his younger mate Kyrie. Tondo, though hardly an adult himself, was almost three times the size of the young pair. His dazzling saddle patches blazed an almost perfect white, matching his imposing white belly and the massive triangular 'conning tower' of a dorsal fin sailed high out of the water as he ran along just under the surface. The uppermost portion of fin was just beginning to sag and fall in a sorry curl to the left, in the same way that a flower wilts as it becomes stale after being cut. Tondo had been in captivity for some time. Without the healthy slap of waves and swell in the wild, the fibrous sinew of the mighty orcas topmost projecting fin starts to weaken, causing the once proudly erect dorsal to flop over like wet spaghetti.

Kyrie, his mate, rarely left his side. She was some years older than Persia and Tristesse and eyed them warily. She had a perfect symmetry, save for the ugly scarred chunk taken from her fin; a legacy of her vain struggle with the hunter's rough ropes. The couple spoke an entirely different dialect to the younger orcas, a dialect that was foreign and yet vaguely familiar. Thrown as they were into close quarters with one another, an aloof stand-off occurred and the opposing pairs kept a wary distance from one another.

Tondo and Kyrie, as you may perhaps have already surmised, are the names given by the humans to the two original residents of Waterworld. Some of you might be curious to know their true names, in which case I will tell you that they are known to their clan as Xai'ałax and Snx. For the purpose of our story however, we shall continue to refer to them by their 'human names', not as a callous gesture but rather to symbolically supress their true names from those who enslaved them, as a mark of our respect. For the same reason, in the presence of the humans we shall refer to the young newcomers, Persia and Tristesse, by their newly acquired human names Pandora and Leda.

Anyone who has ever learned to ride a bicycle will be able to appreciate how a wild animal can be taught to perform a specific behaviour on command. Whether it be riding a mountain bike or leaping through a hoop, behaviour can be shaped in a series of progressive steps.

Kathy Quick could recall the day that her father had taken the small training wheels off the back of her bicycle. How the concrete sidewalk leading down the gentle slope to their house had looked suddenly daunting, despite the fact she had ridden boisterously down it so many times before. She remembered her father's voice, quietly excited yet comforting, and she felt that old feeling of wanting to please her pop. To make him proud of her. He had looked like Elvis in those days, she thought. Boyishly handsome, and she knew that she carried the same good genes. Even after he had gone, people would remark at the similarity, and remind her of that fact.

At thirty-eight years old, the tom-boyish Kathy Quick was a ball of wiry energy; athletic and lithe from her years of fitness training and swimming. Short spiky blonde hair and the perfect posture of a gymnast. Despite her diminutive frame, she cut an imposing figure poolside and she naturally commanded attention. The chief trainer handled killer whales easily and with a natural grace which belied the fact that she started her days as an awkward rebellious teenager.

It was the awkward girl that she pictured in her mind's eye now. The tricycle had quickly been replaced with a metallic pink bicycle, and despite her trepidation she imagined it looked that little bit sleeker and faster with its clunky little trainer wheels removed. With an encouraging word from her doting father and one firm push she was on her way.

We crawl before we walk, and walk before we run, and our own behaviour is shaped by a number of progressive small steps. And so it is with the training of animals. The three trainers stood poolside under a perfect California sky. Emma and Jodie in matching polo shirts and shorts. Kathy wore a navy blue spring suit – a lightweight neoprene wetsuit with short sleeves and legs cut off just above the knee.

'Always remember that we never refer to our training as 'tricks' ladies. A hooker turns a trick. A dolphin performs a behavior.'
The two young trainers giggled at the explanation given by their boss.

'What we're doing here is connecting with the whales and communicating a desired behaviour, or sequence of behavoirs to them.'
The four orcas together in the performance pool looked an imposing sight, dark and circling. Kathy spoke precisely, and paced along the ramp like a drill sergeant.

At five foot eleven inches, Emma stood a good few inches taller than her chief trainer, and still retained the gangly awkwardness of youth. Jodie, though several inches shorter, still managed to top Kathy's diminutive height when she wasn't slouching. Kathy was well aware that a large part of her young charges potential success as dolphin trainers would be in developing their own sense of poise and self-confidence.

Despite the age difference, there was an easy connection between the three trainers. Kathy saw so much of herself in them, though she was acutely aware that growing up the daughter of a single mother had pushed her towards an early independence and rugged self-sufficiency. She had started smoking at fifteen, dragging on a last cigarette before cooking dinner for herself and her mom. More often than not her mother returned from work after dark, and Kathy had grown accustomed to the routine of eating alone before retiring upstairs to complete her homework half-heartedly. Usually she would find herself absorbed in her father's old National Geographic collection. She devoured any article on wild animals, and especially anything that involved marine life, be it sharks, turtles, whales or dolphins. It was the love of animals that filled that space in Kathy's heart, where humans failed her.

'Remember from your basic training the keys are confidence and timing, just like dancing.'

'We go to clubs these days boss, not dance halls!' laughed Emma.

'You damn kids! I'm talking partnered dancing, as in ballroom dancing. Did you never do that at your Prom? You take the lead firmly. A killer will sense any lack of confidence and you run the risk of confusing her.'

She shot them a wry smile. They were good kids, keen and enthusiastic to learn.

'Remember you are communicating with an animal that doesn't speak your language. So the language that you use – your hand signals, your key commands and your bridgework must be perfectly clear and concise, otherwise you'll just frustrate them.'
She let her words sink in.

'And believe me, you do not want nine thousand pounds of frustrated killer whale in a pool with you!'

The four orcas continued to circle the pool, quietly curious. Their staccato blows sounded like the whoosh of a nearby steam train; occasionally sending a fine wet mist over the trio with the sudden pistoning might of an exhalation.

'Woomfh-woomffh-shhh'
It was a sound that Quick had come to know and love. She found herself comforted by it; the hollow 'plastic pipe' tone of their breathing, often sounding just like a drain unclogging. The sudden thick wash of spray and stale breath. The drain hole, or blowhole as it is known, atop the ebony black heads deftly opening and closing rapidly following the intake of breath. Perfectly waterproof and sphincter-like.

'OK guys, so this is a general relationship session to break in our new arrivals Pandora and Leda. Tondo and Kyrie are old hands, so there may also be an element of observational learning here as the newbies pick up on their behavior. Watch out for this and make sure that you give the youngsters plenty of reinforcement as and when they do.'

With the gate to the large circular performance pool now closed, the four orcas weren't distracted by the privacy of their 'dormitory' lagoon, with its rocky walls and the wide barred sea inlet. Kathy handed Emma and Jodie a plastic bucket filled to the brim with fish, before picking up her own bucket and casting a scrutinising glace at the broad expanse of concrete ramp which ran into the dark waters of the pool.

'Emma, wave Pandora to one side of the ramp and Jodie, you take Leda on the other side. Let's start getting them used to target training, please.'

The girls, thought Kathy, were enthusiastic and engaging as she watched them slowly gain the young blackfishes' attention and trust with their hand gestures and deft movement. Spy-hopping and shaking their heads, open mouthed, the young orcas gratefully accepted each fish reward for their efforts.

Happy with the progress, Kathy made her way to the far side of the pool to engage with Tondo and Kyrie and allow her trainers the space to bond with the new arrivals. She loved days like this – the warmth of the sun and the sharp aroma of nearby ocean wafting through the palms lifted her spirits and reminded her that it was good to be alive. At a distance she could see the difference in behaviour and body language of the two young orcas. Pandora, the older of the two, had a deft grace and authority about her. Almost a maturity beyond her years as she followed Emma's commands with an easy fluidity. Leda, by comparison was reluctant and unsure. Tondo and Kyrie neatly surfaced simultaneously, vocalizing noisily to attract Kathy's attention.

'Well, well who do we have here? Fred Astaire and Ginger Rogers! Hello, you two!'

The big orcas shook their heads in acknowledgement, batting at the water with their broad fins. Casting a quick glance back to where the two trainers stood busily engaged, she decided that she would need to give the little youngster some extra attention and reassurance. As she cooed and scrubbed at the shining rostrums of the two larger orcas now vying for her attention, she couldn't help but feel the twinge of empathy for little Leda.

'Why can't they understand us?' asked Tristesse.

'They speak a different language,' replied Persia.

'Xai'ałax and Snx speak a different language, yet they can understand us perfectly.'

'Xai'ałax and Snx have the Harmony and these beings do not.'

'Persia, no being can live outside the Harmony. Who are they?'

'Tristesse, I only know that they cannot understand us, so we will simply listen to them.'

'I won't listen to someone who took us from our family. What right have they to talk and expect us to listen?'

'Little one, right here and now we have no choice but to listen.'

'I don't agree, Persia,' Tristesse thought for a while then added accusingly: 'Shadow would not agree.'

Persia was taken aback by the unusual defiance in her young pod-mate's reply, and patiently reminded her of the wisdom of the Harmony:

'Shadow *would* agree. Know what can be changed Tristesse, and simply flow with what cannot. You know the Way.'

'Persia, these are the hunters who did all those things to us. Who killed little Constant. Who killed Oberon and Ganymede.'

'No, these are not the same ones who did those things.'

'They are of the same clan. The blood is on their hands too.'

The young orca fin-slapped the surface angrily at the recollection.

Persia eased herself backwards from the wall, keeping her eyes riveted on the figure at the edge of the pool. She felt the steadily growing despair – her mother would know just the right thing to do and to say. Mother. She closed her eyes and took a measure of strength from the recollection. *Wooomfh-sshh.* Drawing a steadying breath she raised herself further out of the water and spoke firmly. Authoritatively.

'I'm asking you to follow what they ask and let us see where it leads us.'

'I fear it won't lead us home, Persia.'

'Follow what they ask of us Tristesse. Remember, water always flows back home eventually.'

Tristesse broke her gaze from the tall figure who offered her another fish and turned to face her friend.

'The water here is still, Persia.'

ઝ✿ﹾ

People are coming and going here all the time. New names, new faces. After a while the dreary procession slowly becomes a blur, and it seems that the greatest human constant here is the 'lifers', who become something of a fixed backdrop and a foil to the changing face of the unit. Some of these long-termers are loud, brash and openly threatening; confident in their knowledge of the 'lay of the land'. They bark louder than the other dogs. They posture and draw attention in brute display. Mostly it is just that – a display. Others are quietly resigned to their lot, the hard abrasive edges worn down like beach stones by the incessant ebb and flow of prison life. A great many are old men.

Dependent on their behaviour, the lifers are open contenders for the prized luxury of a single cell; a nod to their status born of longevity and long-standing within the prison community. This week I have a new neighbour in the single cell next door to mine – a pleasantly mild-mannered Hispanic by the name of Vasquez. So far he is polite and unobtrusive. He is probably older than he looks, a courtesy of the fortunate genetics of his race. Beneath a severe military style buzz-cut he possesses lively brown eyes and a ready smile.

Coming back from lunch he is scurrying toward his cell, nursing a large grapefruit in much the same way that a mother lovingly nurses her newborn, or a champion athlete proudly claps the shiny gold trophy to his chest as he mounts the winner's podium. His brown eyes are wider and shinier than usual, if that is humanly possible. Catching my eye excitedly, he declares triumphantly:

'I've got a grapefruit!'

'Yes, you do. Enjoy!'

The brown eyes are shining wetly, quite literally on the verge of tears.

'I haven't eaten a grapefruit for eighteen years, homme!'

The Federal Bureau of Prisons euphemistically refers to this grimy godforsaken place as a correctional institution. The sum of its pieces is a process which is destined to break the individual – ostensibly to disrupt the less desirable patterns and the old ways of the offender, and ultimately to foster 'correct' behavior. And so, each piece part in the process supposedly plays its role in contributing to this desired end result, by enforcing some form of denial, control or restriction upon the individual. All except for one, in my humble opinion. One incongruity of prison life has stood out starkly for me ever since Day One. Looking back now, I am still at something of a loss to explain it.

Never have I seen so much good food in plentiful supply. And yet, judging from the number of complaints and disputes around me with regard to the subject of food, it would seem that many here would strenuously object to my observations. One thing I have quickly learned about jail is that it is a festering wound that constantly oozes negativity. Its unwilling residents have a pent-up bitterness and resistance to absolutely everything from the general running of the penitentiary system right down to the brand of toothpaste that is freely distributed to them. With regards to food, I believe that what I have to say on the matter is both fair and reasoned.

You fly by the seat of your pants. This is perhaps the best way of explaining just how it is to walk in here as a newcomer. Everything in prison involves a procedure which you must very quickly fall in with. It might be better described as a series of routines and sub-routines, all hampered by the fact that most of them are not explained fully to you. Whether you are an agitator or a person bent on compliance, you are equally barked at or belittled should you fail to comply. So you either pick up the routine from those around you, in a *'monkey-see, monkey-do'* kind of a way, or you learn very painfully by trial and error.

Answering the 'dinner bell' proves to be one of the easier routines to master, although so far the greater majority of fights and altercations I have witnessed all seem to have revolved around food in some way. At twelve noon every day the public address system blares, and every day I struggle to hear what is just one of literally dozens of badly distorted announcements from the ancient speaker system. My mind casts back to my student days, when I took a backpacking holiday to the UK. A Londoner referred to the subway PA system as a Tannoy. Recalling this, I decide that the Tannoy is aptly named. It contains the word 'annoy' which was perhaps a clever measure on the part of the manufacturers to exonerate themselves from blame when user complaints arise.

Straining to understand the PA system becomes a draining ordeal in itself, however the noon call is a constant. It directs all prisoners to muster – to stand at attention by their cell doors for a head count by the small platoon of surly blue uniformed guards. This quasi-military parade marks the commencement of lunch each day. Satisfied with the muster count, we are dismissed with the shout *'Break off!'* whereupon the forty-odd prisoners on the wing scurry to collect their blue plastic plates to queue at the small stainless steel kitchen area for the 'dish-up' of lunch.

I often discreetly observe the cluster of guards who stand by and watch us impassively as we eat. If I let it get to me, meal times are a humiliating exercise in dominance and submission. More often than not there is a signature look of revulsion or contempt in the countenance of at least one or two of our jailers. It is the look one might get in passively observing cockroaches scurrying across a dinner table. Wishing you could despatch them with a few strategically aimed swats. I never make eye contact with them. It can really get to you if you let it.

The menu varies from day to day – chicken and vegetables, burritos, roasts with potatoes and pumpkin, lasagne, battered fish and fries and the aptly named 'brake pads' – thick circular meat rissoles.

Once all have been served, there comes the veritable call to battle:

'Seconds!'

This results in a mad frenzied rush and many with plates still full return for a second helping. The sagging plates are piled higher still, and yet despite this there is still invariably a mound of perfectly edible leftover food being thrown into a bin with little more than a casual glance. What stands out most stridently for me is not just the sheer amount of food that is available, but the sheer amount of good food that is senselessly wasted. In the midst of a punitive system which takes so much away from an offender, the jarring extravagance is a bitter pill for me to swallow. The pessimistic side of me suggests that this isn't an act of mercy or benevolence. Based on the aggressive voracity of appetites in the rag-tag hordes around me, I settle on the far more plausible explanation that a lack of food in a place like this will merely end in dissent and argument. Or perhaps in – perish the thought – a serious loss of order and control. Looking at the six and a half foot slab of angry tattooed muscle just a few tables away from me, I squirm inwardly and shake the thought off briskly like an unwelcome bug.

There are more than enough low level rumblings and latent angst around me without a food-fuelled riot breaking out.

'Just keep the food coming,' I muse to myself; my maximum-security issue plastic knife wobbling drunkenly as it struggles to cleave an almost comically thick slice of beef. Fortunately the brake pads are in plentiful supply. I can see the advertisement now:

Brake Pads – the rissoles that stop riots. Fast.'

A prison is no place to be plagued by addictions of any kind, and there are some tangibly real addictions centered around food. Despite its plentiful supply, this is not a place for extremes of gluttony or selectivity. Or a combination of the two. A very real addict in here is the 'junk food' junkie. For those so afflicted, the hit of fatty saturated food is a high as real as grass or smack. I have seen just as many terminal crazies on edgy rollercoaster rides from massive sugar hits as I have seen riding the blurring rush of amphetamines. MacDonald's smarmy red and yellow clown is as much a pusher as your friendly neighborhood drug dealer. And here, laid bare for all to see like twisted museum exhibits are the sad by-products of our society. The end-users of all the temptations offered legally or illegally on our streets. This is the suppurating ugliness that western society would prefer to sweep under the outwardly respectable mat of 'culture' and 'civilisation.'

I am blessed with a non-addictive personality. I am not a substance user, I drink very rarely and by and large I lead a healthy outdoor lifestyle. Perhaps that made me the most unlikely deckhand back on the old trawlers. Actually I know for a fact that it did, as I was so often the butt of the many jibes and blue jokes from my buddies out on the rancid after-deck as it heaved and rolled through the wash. With the sea air in my lungs and salt spray matting my hair, I am in that special heaven on earth. This is my hit and my high. I suppose that is something of an addiction in itself, isn't it? In many ways I am the prefect profile to survive this place as I am not a slave to many of the things that burden so many in here.

The dinner table fare on a working boat is a dish-up of heavy, fat laden food. Heavy on the carbs and heavy on the fats. It is deliberately copious and calorie loaded in order to fuel the massive energy demand of a working deck hand. The act of simply standing upright on a heaving deck demands strength and energy, even before the hard work of hauling and rigging begins. You first learn to overcome the debilitating paralysis of seasickness as a matter of pure self-survival. Initially, my reaction to the unfamiliarity of life on water both terrified and intrigued me. Humans do not take naturally to water.

It is said that all life on Earth was born from the waters, but the oceans are no longer our home. You fight against the overwhelming bodily desire to violently reject food, knowing full well that you need to do the complete opposite to survive in the hostile seafaring environment. You eventually force yourself to swallow and keep down the heavy glutinous grub, and you develop the mental resilience to overcome the stomach's sickly reaction to the sensory assault of smells in the steamy stale closeness of the crowded galley. The cloying stench of working men; sweat, flatulence and tobacco. The pungent aroma of roast meat. The greasy reek of sausages and mash.

All of this has positioned me well to weather the dark slurry of mental and emotional bilge that this depressing place constantly throws up. Not so with many others, and the 'junk food junkie' phenomenon surfaces very early in the piece.

Lunch call Sunday. The mid-day routine breaks the monotony of a painfully slow day. A ragged string of motley prison greens armed with blue plastic plates expectantly begins to form, commencing at the steel counter of the servery area and threading like a rogue's gallery around a wall lined at close intervals with gritty off-white cell doors. Weekends are always something of a mixed blessing here in the pen. Actually, the more that I think of it, the more I realize that they stand testament to one fundamental of the prison experience – even the smallest joy comes at a cost. Very often a weekend shortage of guards means that we are locked down in our cells far into the morning.

Imagine, if you will, being locked down for hours in a small shabby cell not much larger than a broom closet. You will be sharing this cell with another soul, and hopefully that 'other soul' is a congenial one. Or at the very least given to good personal hygiene; the choice is largely out of your hands. Body odor, bad breath and bad flatulence by themselves will make your communal broom closet an intolerable nightmare.

Now imagine that your broom closet contains one metal framed bunk bed. Drizzle it with rust and toss two emaciated single mattresses with similarly tired, thin pillows onto it. The barred window lets in a harsh afternoon sun that glares rudely over the razor wire outside. Using a cleverly shaped stub of plastic knife handle, simply wedge an old metal shower rail across your window opening and hang a rotting green curtain over it to blot out the mid-afternoon heat. Better. Now, against your grubby red brick wall, stand an old painted cupboard and alongside it bolt up an equally world-weary pin-up board. Use blind bolts, because screws can be removed by cunning lags and sharpened into stabbing implements called shanks. If you manage to scrounge some thumb tacks, pin some photos of your lady here. Place a tiny scarred wooden desk underneath it. Now, alongside the heavy cell door with the observation peephole cut into it, bolt a stainless steel toilet bowl against the wall with an aged, stained washbasin and scuffed polished metal mirror hanging by two screws.

The ancient, poorly maintained toilet will leak often, so be careful to return the flush button fully upright when using it. Two days ago an upper floor toilet leaked through the night, overflowing down through the ceiling into the cell below, making life on the downstairs wing a misery. Gazing at the rust stained mirror, you notice that the two bottom screws have been neatly removed, presumably by the cell's previous occupant. They probably now reside, sharpened and dangerous, on the end of a covertly fashioned shank – a stabbing blade with a handle made from a length of old toothbrush or a simple ballpoint pen. In prison necessity becomes the evil mother of invention, and sometimes in a very cruel twist on the popular saying the pen indeed proves mightier than the sword.

Sunday means that we are allowed access to the exercise yard for two hours – one of the small joys that I mentioned earlier. A depressing old gymnasium with heavy barred windows and ancient weight machines is available; the paint on its walls flaking and stained from years of rising damp and old sweat. It opens onto a timber floored basketball court, and a dark passageway leads outside to a small grassed oval ringed by stark concrete walls and tangles of razor wire. The downside of this relative freedom is the gauntlet of noise and aggravation that must be run before you physically reach the exercise yard. Scores of inmates are trooped through a series of locked doors and a maze of passageways, each as ancient, stale and grubby as the next. This is usually an angry battlefield of shouts and traded insults. Away from the stern view of the guards, threats and taunts are traded in the relative anonymity of the messy scrum jostling each other at close quarters. The shanks are often there too.

I always take the option of Sunday afternoon recreation largely because it is the only opportunity that we have to visit the small prison library; the only place in this mad house where I have any sense of peace and normality. The neat rows of books seem to have a quietly reassuring and comfortable aura about them; a safe familiarity which even a state penitentiary and its loon constituents cannot perfectly erase. So, when the whistle blows I join the crazy charge, pushing and shoving. Doing my best to weather the jostling bedlam of lock, gate and passageway until I reach the inviting sanctuary of those neat ranks of quiet books and bound manuscripts. Here for thirty short but welcome minutes I lose myself in the tranquil emotion of Wordsworth and the bold assertation of Whitman; noble men who are deserving of far worthier an audience, rather than to while out their days in this dank hole. Here at least I have one perfectly small island of quiet sanity and for the next precious half hour, I am a thankful scrubby green castaway.

And if that is the week's high, then the standard Sunday lunchtime fare is the low point of the week for me. Predictably it is always two hotdogs per person. That said, I'm amazed at the mad feeding frenzy that is stirred up by the dish-up of bland commercial hotdogs. As 'seconds' is called, it signals the usual jostling feeding frenzy. But today the sharks are circling. In the scrabble further down the queue, frenetic raised voices suggest this is something more than the usual ragged food scrum.

Adrenaline kicks in and I steel myself against the sense of rising danger, eyes darting. Behind me, one man is down and the kicks to his head repeat in slow motion as the first spray of blood spatters a grimy cell door. His well-aimed return kick evinces a sharp scream as the perpetrator folds, hands cradling his groin as he collapses against the wall, vomiting. The crumpled bleeding body becomes lifeless. Screaming bloody murder like portly blue banshees, four overweight guards send the bystanders caught in the crossfire flying like so many skittles; protectively hunched and still carefully nursing plates piled high with their booty of hot-dogs. Small skirmishes break out, and two broken bodies are quickly cuffed and roughly manhandled to the punishment cells. Barked orders and threats keep the others at bay. The spill kit is rapidly deployed and the offending blood stains carefully removed. The trampled remains of hotdogs are ground into the threadbare carpet like the lost spoils of war.

The sudden outburst of violence has cast a damp blanket over everything. I sit morosely, half-heartedly munching on my hotdog which is now liberally coated with a savory disguise of ketchup and mustard. Across the bench table from me, Dave sits in silence; his sombre mood matching mine. We avoid eye contact, lost in private thought.

We compare notes some time later that day over a coffee, both feeling a little more composed.

'What the hell happened there?' I ask Dave. 'And why all the angst over a few goddamn ordinary hotdogs?'

We decide that it must be either a generational or a socio-economic thing. Further evidence of the junk food generation.

'Never come between a greedy man and his hot-dog,' says Dave sagely, breaking the gravity of the situation.

Once again I thank several lucky stars that I remain addiction free and physically healthy. So far it has taken all my mental and emotional strength to cope with the trials of day to day life in the pen. Occasional phone calls to Maree back at home help to maintain my sanity; they are a small welcoming life raft that I can cling to albeit briefly – I find I can usually reach her at night, and feeling that familiar friendly energy reminds me there is a quiet normality waiting for me somewhere outside the wire.

On the subject of food, it seems that our newly acquired house cat Tin-Tin is also a finicky eater. Little is known of Tin-Tin's origins save for the fact that he was a sea-faring cat, having been found prowling the fishing boats on the docks of Friday Harbor. Proud and sure-footed, he carries himself with the stately demeanour of the old Spanish navigators who had boldly challenged the rolling main in their voyages of discovery to these far-flung shores. A lustrously thick jet-black coat endows him with the appearance of billowing pantaloons, which only serves to reinforce the impression. The day that he chose Maree, Tin-Tin's regal and measured approach was announced by the cry of a solitary red-tailed hawk wheeling overhead like some majestic winged envoy. Its presence seemed to speak of some higher purpose. And so it was in that measured communion that the cat thus chose for himself a companion human with whom to complete his journey.

Tin-Tin immediately took to life at our secluded forest home overlooking the river as if he had been born into it. Apparently more than content to end his nomadic sea-faring days, he chose the more homely comfort of snuggling up on an inviting cushion strewn meditation chair in a warm sunlit bay window, satisfying his wanderlust by lazily overseeing the incessant ebb and flow of the river outside. Even his diet proved a mystery. Despite the sacrificial offering and subsequent feline rejection of numerous variations of fresh fish and endless brands of cat food; thus far Tin-Tin's only known culinary constant remains his routine nightly forays to the cat bowl for a nocturnal feast of bland dry food. I smile to myself; the enigmatic black feline is most definitely not a prison cat.

But I digress. For the sake of anonymity, I will simply refer to the next character as 'Seagull'. The choice of nickname may give some early insight into the nature of the character I am about to describe. I'm sure most readers have encountered the seagull in real life. One of the most prolific and pedestrian coastal inhabitants, it is the gulls' scavenger tendencies that often put them off-side with so many.

Uninspired yet potentially versatile flyers, they unashamedly stalk the rusting garbage scows and rubbish barges that ply the slack inland waters, and festoon themselves over wharf and dock on the promise of morsels of rank smelling by-catch from the returning trawlers. In return they contribute little more than the thick white crustings of guano that coat everything indiscriminately from the timber planking of the jetty landings, rusting bulwarks and sea walls, ropes and railings. Many a fine Sunday picnic has been all but ruined by the unrelenting skulduggery of the ragged hordes of uninvited feathered invaders intent on the pillage of picnic basket and patience.

Seagull is a morbidly overweight young fellow sporting a mop of tousled greasy black hair and unkempt shaggy beard. He has so far lived up to the reputation of his namesake of the feathered variety. My sympathies initially fell squarely on the side of the corpulent crim who strikes me as something of a bumbling social outcast, of itself a blameless fault. In a theater of war, these guys are the first casualties. Large, easy targets wandering aimlessly back and forth like plastic ducks on a shooting range, studiously oblivious to the looming threat of bullet and shrapnel. They are targets here too. Sadly my sympathies are very quickly worn down by the cloying personality. It is in the dish-up line where Seagull really comes into his own. Catching my eye in the dinner queue, he enquires expectantly:

'Are you eating today?'

I am instantly affronted on two counts; one – my presence in the dish-up line should render that stupid question moot. And two – there is more than enough food for everyone. I cut him quickly short with a curt reply. Crest-fallen the shaggy scavenger scans the line for a more yielding candidate; his shoulders rounded and slumped as though a fragile spirit has been crushed. I immediately feel the accusing stab of pity and regret. That pity is very quickly snuffed out when the scene is repeated in its entirety the very next day. In pointed terms I explain to Seagull that it is best that he assumes that I eat every day, and that he saves his breath.

He waddles away again; a wretched cartoon-like study of abject defeat, and I am forced to remind myself that sometimes you must be cruel to be kind. This still does not deter him from urging me to return for seconds on his behalf when Sunday 'hot dog lunch' rolls around. Despite my dogged non-compliance, I still see him wobbling to a table like a gelatinous bulk, the rolling oscillations produced by his shuffling gait threatening to tip a plate of four hot dogs overboard. The very same Sunday evening sees my illustrious friend the Seagull tucking happily into three generous slabs of chocolate cake, piled high like a virtual chocolate replica of the Great Wall of China in his blue plastic bowl.

Recounting this story to you, I am more so struck by the desperate tragedy of the man; my annoyance all but dissolved in looking back at events. In point of fact I am somewhat ashamed and chastened that I have described all of this in such derisive manner.

I leave this on record though, because that is what this place does to you. It gets to you every day, and it eats away at you. How easily one can become worn down by the foibles and follies of others in here. Gluttony and food cravings simply drive home yet another nail of addiction. I can truly say that I have borne witness to all Seven Deadly Sins here. Pride, greed, lust, envy, gluttony, wrath and sloth. They are here displayed in all their ugly glory.

Did you know that the ancient Chinese believed that it was not the heart but the liver that was the repository of the soul? The ancient Etruscans were said to be able to read the future by looking at the livers of the animals that they sacrificed.

Every abusive substance we ingest, be it alcohol or drugs, sugar or fatty food causes damage to the liver.

It leads me to wonder just what exactly we're hitting out at.

CHAPTER FIVE

OF SKINS AND HEART

My mind's distracted and diffused
My thoughts are many miles away
They lie with you where you're asleep
Kiss you when you start your day.
–SIMON & GARFUNKEL - 'Kathy's Song'

THE LOW RUMBLE of distant traffic was the only man-made sound in the pre-dawn stillness. Tondo and Kyrie were logging side by side in their usual position at the ocean end of the lagoon, alongside the sea gate. Tondo's rising dorsal stood out in sharp relief as the morning sky slowly gave way to the onset of the new day, and the world of velvety-purple night retreated.

Gently widening wakes of swollen water marked Persia and Tristesse's deft movement through the semi-darkness.
Side by side they made their way to the corner of the pool and waited, spy-hopping expectantly. Minutes passed, and then the first questing rays of the sun spilt from around the empty pavilion at the eastern end of the pool; concentrating to a finger-like point which

stealthily crept up until it picked out a craggy rock just above the waterline.

Seeing this the youngsters raised themselves further out of the lagoon, flicking deftly with their powerful tails until the broad flattened pectoral fins were all but out of the water. The first ray of light was caught and reflected by their pale white bellies until it danced crazily on the water's surface around them. Pink mouths opened wide and ivory rows of serrated teeth flashed; ancient and dinosaur-like in the diffuse glow.

'*Pittt-uuuu,*' They sounded plaintively in unison: '*Pittt. Pittt-uuuu*' From her discreet vantage point at the performance pool, Kathy shivered at the sound. She sensed the yearning and the melancholy as it found a point of resonance somewhere in the vicinity of her navel.

'What the heck was all that about, do you think?' came the old man's voice.

Kathy hadn't even noticed old Casper sidle up alongside her, lost as she was in the moment. He stood intrigued, hands on hips. Confounded by the scene, as though it was yet another curiosity to be unravelled.

'You can't figure it out, boss?' Kathy replied. Casper's eyes remained on the dark pair of bobbing heads out at the sea wall, fascinated at the display. Without a glance at his chief trainer he finally ventured a considered response:

'Some sort of a game, perhaps?'

'They do this every morning. Just Pandora and Leda.' There was no response from the dry old manager, who casually folded his arms in thought. She shrugged and ventured the answer:

'They're greeting the sun, Casper. It's their ritual welcoming in of the new day.'

'Well I'll be. And they do this same thing every morning, you say?'

'Every morning. They seem to know exactly where and when the first light of the sun will appear, and they wait for it to arrive.'

'What goes through their minds, do you think?

Kathy smiled patiently. She had learned a long time ago that the easy connection that she shared with animals wasn't something that everybody naturally understood. To her it was as plain as the nose on her face.

'Can't you hear it in their voices? Or see it in the way they're moving?'

'I think that they're just curious, like a budgerigar is fascinated with a sudden flash in a mirror.'

'You're looking but not seeing, Casper. They're in touch with the sun, and the seasons. They feel it all around them. This is their way of praying and giving praise.'

'To the god of killer whales you think?' Casper seemed bemused;

'You have a wonderful imagination, young lady!'

She shook her head with a wry smile. The aging manager tapped thoughtfully on his temple, his mind forming the idea:

'You know what Kathy, we just might be able to work that into the show somehow. Talk it through with the team and see if you can choreograph something. Let's have a talk about it at the weekly meeting and see what we come up with, eh?'

Kathy stopped short of explaining it further to the old man. This was something special to them, a ritual to be held sacred. Their plaintive calls sounded again over the morning traffic. It would have to be enough that she felt their pain and understood it. She never mentioned it again, nor did she remind Casper of it.

The sun brought with it a quiet sense of hope. A promise for the future and a reminder of the past. It was night-time that Tristesse despised the most. By day Kyrie was sultry. Aloof. She stuck to her routine of shadowing Tondo everywhere; flanking him possessively as they swam aimless circles around the lagoon perimeter together.

The daily performances provided an almost welcome distraction of noise, activity and movement.

The two older orcas carried the more intricate choreographies and routines. Persia and Tristesse, for their part, would open the shows with synchronised leaps and playful fin waves. Circling the performance pool together waving at the crowd before the mighty Tondo appeared in an unexpected leap, rising up from the center of the pool, having entered stealthily underwater. A barrelling black-and-white rocket firing skyward in a perfect study of power and symmetry. His imposing entrance never failed to draw gasps of delight from the crowds watching on from the pavilion bleachers, and it was a masterful touch.

Tondo hung weightless for a split-second like some dark-finned scimitar, before a precise flick of his tail pitched him nose down and he descended cleanly out of sight. Cleaving the water with unexpected grace before re-appearing to repeat the performance. This was Persia and Tristesse's cue to exit the pool underwater and head through the open gate to the lagoon.

Tristesse liked those times and the distraction that they provided. It was the interminable hours of nothingness that wore her down. The cramped confines of the lagoon. Logging fitfully, or lazily circling with eyes half-closed, she felt cloistered and lost. Endless days of nothingness. Of course there was Persia, but when night fell there was also Kyrie.

At night the simmering tension often became open aggression, particularly on the days when one of the orcas had made mistakes during the performance, missing a cue or a bridge signal by one of the trainers. Often the food supply would start to dwindle long before the show finished, especially if one of the junior trainers misjudged the handing out of food rewards. The orcas could tell from the rattle of the ice at the bottom of the metal bucket that the food was getting low.

It spawned a deep brooding anxiety that added a further layer of psychological pain to their situation.

Tristesse hated the night-time. The nasty looking rake marks would slowly heal, only to be replaced with new welts on her flanks and belly. Red, suppurating and angry. She hated the night-time and she hated life. And hate in any being's language is never a good thing.

Just why Kyrie lashed out at her can be easily explained. Orcas are no different to humans in this respect. It was borne out of a sense of jealousy and rivalry on the one hand, and fuelled by a pent-up frustration at the hopelessness of their plight. Tristesse, being the youngest and the smallest female, became the target of all of this rage by default. And try as she might to come between the pair, Persia was all but powerless to deal with the situation.

Brad's eyes remained riveted to the report that he was scribing on the messy desk. His entire vet lab office was messy if the truth be told. A faded wetsuit hung over the back of an old wooden chair piled high with papers and surf magazines. A large dog-eared color poster occupied a goodly portion of the far wall, depicting all the different species of whales and dolphins.

Kathy leaned on the door frame, wondering whether the park vet was deliberately ignoring her, or just not given to multi-tasking. Deciding that it was likely a combination of the two, she shrugged in vague resignation and rapped three times on the open door.

'What's up?' he murmured. Offhand, distracted.

'You might want to do another check on Leda before you head off for lunch.'

'More problems?' he asked airily, looking up from his desk for the first time.

Kathy nodded, lighting up a cigarette and taking a first bracing drag before replying.

'Looks like Kyrie attacked her again overnight. She's got fresh wounds on her belly.'

Brad pinched the bridge of his nose, wincing before blinking a couple of times to clear his head.

'I'll give her a thorough check. We might need to consider isolating her in the performance pool overnight again, until things settle down.'

'I think that might be a good idea. She can't fend for herself in there, especially when Kyrie gets in these moods.'

'It's a bit of a territorial thing I think, Kath. I'm pretty sure the moods will settle down as they adjust to each other. There's plenty of space in the lagoon, so it's not like they're on top of each other full-time.'

'I think we need to talk seriously about a captive breeding program.'

Brad shifted his weight, giving her his full attention.

'We're a way off that yet I think. That might solve problems in the longer term, but you know as well as I do that it raises more problems of its own with the cost and ongoing management.'

'Brad, what I know is we have a juvenile killer whale getting distressed and helpless to do anything about it.'

'Kathy, they face these same issues in the wild. There is always a hierarchy and there is always competition for the top spot.'

'So, kill or be killed?' Kathy threw the vet a dumbfounded look.

'Law of the jungle, Kath.'

Manning leaned back in the chair, locking his hands behind his head.

'You're not comparing apples with apples, Brad. In the wild they have thousands of miles of ocean to escape into and they're not stuck in a glorified swimming pool.'

'Glorified swimming pool?' The retort caught Brad by surprise;

'You're not going all leftie-greenie on us are you Miss Quick?'

Kath snorted and ground the stub of cigarette out with her heel.

'I'm not a lefty or a righty. Brad. Or an innie or an outie. I just call it as I see it, so don't go using that puerile labelling crap on me. That might impress the young 'uns but it doesn't wash with me!'

'OK thanks, I'll make a note of it.'

He returned to fussing with the papers on his desk and called out without looking up: 'I'll check on Leda as soon as I'm done with this report.'

'I'll be out at the pool with Tondo so I'll see you there. Thank you. *Doctor.*'

She spat the title back with a sarcastic formality and turned on her heel. Pausing in the hallway for a moment before striding back into the doctor's cramped office, hands on hips:

'And just for the record, if you want to persist with your left wing, right wing trash, I might point out that our hearts are on the left side of our bodies, not the right.'

'What's that supposed to mean?'

'You figure it out Brad.'

౧⊛౨

Sun. Sea breeze riffling through her close cropped hair. The powerful yet reassuring surge beneath her was exciting and cathartic all at once. She needed to clear her head. Of Brad Manning and his obstinate attitude, and everything that was holding her back. She needed to clear her head and think straight and this was the perfect medicine. When Kathy was dorsal riding the orca it took her back to those halcyon days of riding in the front seat of her father's car.

Perhaps it was these warmly rekindled memories that seemed to endow her with a glow; a grace and a surety that made the sight of whale and human a thing of effortless beauty. Kathy had that natural sense of connection from the first time she had attempted the dorsal ride as a junior trainer in Orlando. Her chief trainer had recognized the incipient quality in her. Even now with her feet planted firmly on Tondo's broad back, she was still filled with the same sense of marvel and wonderment that these creatures inspired. His powerful dorsal fin rose, deftly angular behind her; a perfect foil to her dimunitive athleticism.

If Tondo despised the act he never did show it. Rather he pulsed his way steadily around the periphery of the pool like a fine thoroughbred with each precise flick of his muscled peduncle and splayed tailfin measured and perfectly controlled. Kathy could feel his skilled measurement up though the soles of her feet and knew that he was born to master the ocean. She felt him and he in turn felt her, carefully holding his breath so his exhalation wouldn't break her concentration as she made the fine countering adjustments of weight and balance.

Woooomph-shhh. Kyrie sounded from the other side of the pool gate as she surfaced to meet their pass.

'You've got a gorgeous girlfriend there, Tondo!' called Kathy.

Tondo lifted imperceptibly and the electricity as he passed the gate was palpable, at least to Kathy. Many were the times she had marvelled at just how perfectly oblivious people can be to these things. How the language of animals seemed to escape them so completely. Just like Casper at the pool this morning. Animals are talking all the time – for all our intelligence, we just haven't really cared to learn how to listen.

Cleaving water effortlessly, Tondo thought about stepping up his pace now in preparation for the finale and Kathy anticipated it nicely, leaning back slightly to compensate for the acceleration at the precise moment that he powered up. The wind shifted and cut across her face, sharp and bracing. Passing the ramp, where Jodie and Andrea stood, whooping with delight. *Wooomphh.* One short sharp readying breath from Tondo, eyes shut momentarily in the spray. Rooster tails of white water plumed back from Tondo's rostrum as he made for the center of the pool.

'Up, Tondo!'

The bulbous black head submerged slightly like a diving submarine, pectoral fins drawn in tight against his body like aerodynamic blades. Kathy tensed through her thighs and calves, bracing for the launch. Tondo tensed at the same time, their two minds locked. He drove on like a freight train; rising up like some dark banshee to flick Kathy skyward. Her body a taut graceful curve as fluid as a ballerina; the perfect beauty to Tondo's beast.

The first day that Kathy rode Tondo was also the first time she slept with Brad Manning. He had 'spotted' for her that day, keeping a wary eye out for her by the side of the pool. Although Tondo was a veteran, he was still an unknown quantity as far as the fledgling marine park was concerned. And Manning knew that a wild animal will always be just that – an animal not given to unnaturally enforced hierarchy. This was an oceanic top predator they were dealing with after all, not some domestic house pet. If Manning had any reservations about the capabilities of the new chief trainer, they were very quickly dispelled. She was quintessential control and grace, her body language and signalling clearly and perfectly executed.

Perhaps as a surfer, Brad saw in her a kindred spirit – that perfect sense of attunement with the natural marine world. It was heady and alluring all at once. Perhaps that was what had attracted him to her so compellingly.

As Tondo's dive went vertical, Kathy neatly flicked into her own diving arc to follow him. Watching him descend to the bottom of the pool before neatly reversing in one fluid motion and accelerating wildly to propel her like a catapult into the air. Looking on, her young protégés whooped and hollered from poolside. Kathy with an athletic grace, toned and whippet-like as she reached the zenith; a curvaceous streak of tan and blue neoprene. Tondo, a shiny streamlined powerhouse tracing her trajectory before completing the choreography with a bone shaking dive into the pool below.

Hair slicked back and streaming water from her wetsuit, she surfaced alongside the ramp. Tondo proudly appeared alongside, spy-hopping with his huge pink mouth agape, displaying the row of ivory teeth. He gratefully accepted the fish from the two young trainers who doted on him affectionately, scratching his rostrum and patting his slab-like flanks. The big orca shook his head playfully in response to the attention.

'That was awesome, chief!' gushed Amanda; still on a high from the spectacle.

Kathy hoisted herself out of the pool and paid her own respects to her mammoth counterpart; fussing over him and ensuring he was well fed for a job well done.

'So now you see what I mean when I say you don't want a frustrated nine thousand pound killer whale in the pool with you!'

The sun over the withered palm fronds had a bite to it now, and sheltered from the salt breeze the day smelled of concrete and stale heat. Kathy glanced at her dive watch.

'How about we get some suds at Broncos, girls? I could do with a beer after that.'

'Amen to that,' replied Jodie.

'Lock down the kids and meet me at the car in twenty, ladies.'

Kathy turned on her heel and headed for the change rooms, wondering to herself just how many beers it would take to wash Brad Manning out of her psyche.

The days passed and blurred. The routine was always the same. Sleep. Welcome the Sun. Eat. Morning show. Return to the holding pen. Afternoon show. Eat. Night. Even the Sun bore little significance or meaning these days, and eventually Persia lost interest, barely aware of its presence as it furrowed the sky in an incessantly familiar arc. Nothing mattered and nothing could hold her or captivate her anymore. She nursed her younger pod-mate and kept a close protective eye on her, sensing the growing mood of despair.

More often than not these days, Tristesse spent the nights locked into the performance pool alone. Persia would keep her company, logging alongside the narrow connecting gate while Tristesse slept on the other side. It brought back bitter memories of that first night, tired and hungry in the cramped sea pen. She was almost grateful for the cloying gray overcast which had insinuated itself across the west coast overnight; infusing the water with a sense of bleak weariness which hid own her misery from her captors.

When dawn finally broke across a clear sky, neither of the two young orcas felt the need or the desire to welcome in the Sun.

ᛦ

'How's it going, brother? Penny for your thoughts?'
Slingshot's cheerful voice snapped me out of my lazy reverie, causing me to spill my coffee on the old common room table as I jumped back in surprise.

'Slingshot! You surprised me!'

'Did I? I seem to remember hearing you saying last week that nothing surprises you anymore!'

'Correction, only crazy old hippies like you surprise me these days!'

'How many of those have you drunk today, buddy? That might explain why you're so damn edgy!'
He nodded toward my now half empty coffee mug.

'Never you mind! I've stopped counting, and this being my only vice, I think I'm entitled to a little comfort.'

'I can't argue with you there brother!'
His brow furrowed into what I had now learned was his look of concern. Slingshot was a likeable fellow who spent most of his days

working as the unit gardener; mowing, raking and trimming the lawn around the prison and visit center. With his long oily hair tied back permanently in a ponytail which ended just between his shoulder blades and a pair of 'John Lennon' style silver rimmed glasses, he could easily pass as a retired hippie, quietly whiling away his time in peaceful solitude. Working outside took him away from the often manic environment of the cells and common rooms, and precious little would be seen of him come the end of the working day.

I only ever knew him by the nickname Slingshot – apparently a throwback to his days of working for the US Air Force with rocket technology. When he wasn't busy with gardening he chose to squirrel himself away in his cell, reading books endlessly into the quiet hours of the morning. Despite his cloistered existence, he still seemed to possess a canny sense of all the goings-on in the unit.

'I've been worried about you, Adam. You've not been yourself of late.'

'I've had a lot on my mind, Slingshot. A lot I've been trying to make sense of.'

'And are you winning?'

'I'm not sure. I'm starting to question my mental state, if the truth be told.'

'Well you've certainly come to the right place then, my friend!' He gave an amiable hoot of laughter, clapping me on the shoulder warmly before pulling up a chair to sit down. I fussed over wiping up the puddle of coffee.

'I know what you're saying, buddy. About the mental state, I mean. This place can do that to a person. What bothers me is that you seem pretty low of late, and I worry that you're doing it tough. You hardly speak to anyone these days.'

'I guess I'm getting tired of constantly seeing the ugly side of humanity. I can see why some people devote their lives to animals.'

'Yep, I'm right there with you on that one, brother. I used to work with animals.'

'Really? I've been meaning to ask you. They tell me you worked with rockets?'

'That I did. Do you know much about the space program?'

'I read a lot about the Apollo program while I did my degree.'

'OK, well I was a technician on the Mercury program. I worked at Alamogordo on the Holloman Air Force Base.'

'That's out in New Mexico, near White Sands?'

'Yep, White Sands missile range is where the rocket test launches took place. I worked with the chimponauts on the rocket sleds at Holloman.'

'The chimponauts? So you mean there was more than one chimpanzee on the Mercury program?'

'There were dozens, but most people don't know the whole story, Adam. John Glenn made the first orbit in a Mercury craft in early 'sixty-two, but do you know the name of the first chimp that orbited the Earth?'

'Well I have to be honest and say I don't. I know a chimp flew the test flight before Glenn.'

'Actually, three chimps flew spacecraft on the Mercury program, and a whole bunch were killed in rocket tests before that happened. We launched four chimps in tests with V2 rockets out in the desert. Ended badly for all of them.

'How bad?'

'Like they all died, bad. Parachutes failed, rocket motors failed. A couple of chimps died on impact when the rockets crashed and a couple died of heat exhaustion after being lost out in the desert.'

'I never knew that.'

'Well, most folks don't know. History is always kinda fuzzy on those sorts of things. The US actually sent an expedition to Cameroon in Africa to capture chimpanzees to train for the space program. Bet you never heard that either. Stories went round the base about how they were trapped. Rumor was they killed the mothers to get to the chimps, then they were shipped back to Holloman for training.'

'I think I recall at the time Kennedy said the space program was *'the most hazardous, dangerous and greatest adventure on which man has ever embarked."*

'Yeah, well it was fucking hazardous and dangerous if you happened to be a chimpanzee. They had an AeroMedical unit on the base where they trained them, and it was pretty brutal.'

'How so?'

'The AeroMed guys said the chimps behaved pretty much like humans. They spent hours teaching them the controls and sequences for handling the capsule. They used food and pain to get the correct response. When the chimps did a sequence right they got a banana pellet.'

'And when they were wrong?'

'When they did it wrong they got an electric shock. The Mercury capsules they flew in were rigged up the same way. They weren't passengers – they were actually flying the ship.'

'So they reckon they behaved like humans? You wouldn't treat a human pilot that way.'

'Hypocrites aren't we? We never gave it a second thought back then. They were treated like slaves. I worked on the on-board systems so you kinda shut off to what happens behind the scenes so to speak.'

It wasn't hard to imagine the geekish Slingshot in a white lab coat, fussing with wiring looms behind open metal patch panels in the tiny space capsule. He sipped on a glass of water and continued:

'Anyways, the first chimp to fly the Mercury capsule sub-orbital was selected from a pool of chimps. They named him Ham – short for Holloman Aero Medical. AeroMed said he was picked because of his personality. He was easy to work with and they ever had to cuff him like some of the others. So Ham flew in 'sixty-one and he had a rough ride. The fuel burned way too quick you see, and he was subject to massive G-forces. Massive acceleration. The capsule overshot the landing site by a hundred-odd miles and made a hard splashdown. When they reached it, the ship was talking on water with Ham still strapped in.'

He paused and pondered the water in his glass, as if imagining what it must have been like for the helpless chimpanzee.

'When they got him back on the recovery ship the press were hungry for photos, so they tried to strap him back into his flight seat. He just went crazy and fought them, rather than get back in that damn chair.'

'So what happened to him?'

'Well Ham ended up on the cover of Life magazine, press made a bit of a fuss then he was forgotten. He was eventually shipped off to a zoo in Washington DC.'

'Great way to celebrate a hero.'

'Yep. The human gets the credit and the monkey gets the zoo. It gets worse, brother.'

'I worked one the ship in the full orbital tests in late 'sixty-one. After Ham there was Enos, and Enos wasn't as easygoing as Ham. He was quite a handful, though the electric shocks during training probably had a lot to do with that. When you look at the old photos he is usually cuffed. So Enos flew the Mercury on the first orbital flight which was supposed to last three full orbits. We had to bring him back early. The capsule's on-board systems failed and for every correct input he made he got an electric shock instead of a banana pellet. The poor little guy endured three hours of electric shocks and he still made all the correct moves.'

'Shit.'

'Yep, shit indeed. So three months later John Glenn makes the same flight as Enos and becomes an instant celebrity. Everyone knows Glenn, but I bet your bottom dollar they've never heard of Enos. All poor old Enos got was three hours of shock therapy for his trouble. When Caroline Kennedy met John Glenn her first question was 'Where's the monkey?''

'So where is the monkey? Enos I mean?'

'Well by the time John Glenn flew in February 'sixty-two, Enos was dead. He died of an infection two months after his flight. AeroMed guys claimed it had nothing to do with his space mission.'

'I seem to remember Buzz Aldrin said something about the chimps during the Apollo program?'

'Yep, that he did. Aldrin, with the celebrity status of being the second man to walk on the moon spoke out for the chimponauts. He said mankind couldn't have done what we did without them, and they should have the peaceful retirement they deserve.'

'So did the Air Force retire them?'

'There's no Hollywood ending if you're not human, Adam. The remaining chimps ended up in medical labs and testing facilities as 'lab rats.' There were over a hundred of them as far as I know.'

'I'm amazed, Slingshot. And disgusted. I just didn't realize all of this happened.'

'Well that's the thing. These things tend to be kept quiet. What do they say – if abattoirs had glass walls, no-one would eat meat?'

I felt the sting of shame and wondered if there was some sort of deal I could strike with the Devil to make it all go away.

'We're a hell of a species, Slingshot.'

'That we are, buddy. That we are.'

It's funny how it all works. Chimpanzees share 98.6 per-cent of the same DNA structure as man, so we justify using them because they're so much like us. Then with all of our arrogant superiority, we treat them as though they are little more than sub-human slaves.

For all our genetic similarities, it seems that tiny 1.4 per-cent difference is enough for us to behave as though we are the cousins of angels, not the cousins of apes.

CHAPTER SIX

REQUIEM

No place for the meek -
Their inheritance unrecognized
Within these walls
No place for the faint of heart -
Their light put out
As surely as the fall of night
No place for tears -
Best they be shed in private place
No place for privacy -
Except in thought, O blissful of dimensions
And night a softly preferred reality
To sink unfettered in a
Field of dreams
To hold fast to ones I love
No place for dreamers -
The brash Tannoy reminds me
No place, it repeats
No place for Me

CHAPTER SEVEN

THE TIES THAT BIND

With every goodbye we die a little more.
—ROBERT CHANDLER

I DON'T KNOW how long he had been there. Dave had mentioned him to me once before, pointing him out as the quiet guy who had kindly given him some woodworking glue when his own was stolen. I couldn't even begin to tell you his name.

All I remember is that he was fairly young, fresh faced and neatly shaven, and always politely unobtrusive. Most of the time he remained in his cell, keeping to himself and rarely mixing with the other prisoners. On the brief occasions when he did, you just knew he didn't belong here. He was undoubtedly college educated and comfortably middle class. Probably fresh out of studying for a career in something sensible like accountancy or law. Borrowing the car off dad on weekends to take his girl out on a date. Coming home on a Sunday to the smell of the roast dinner his mom always loved to prepare for the family sit-down meal.

Mainstream penitentiary life in the maximums is a nightmare existence in a world gone mad. At its worst it is a wild ride of payback and drug debts; of knifings and gangs, standover tactics and sexual abuse. At best it is rumors and gossip, simmering tensions and latent aggression. You quickly learn that the game is all about pushing. You push to get what you want, and you prove to others that you're not a pushover. This is basically a human trash dump where the rules of your quaint upper middle-class suburban world do not apply. There are a small handful of guys just like him, either buried by the penitentiary system, or voluntarily burying themselves in it. Flying underneath the radar for reasons mostly known only to them.

The justice system is a large sausage factory and the prison machine struggles under the sheer weight of numbers as the courts condemn a seemingly endless stream of offenders to life behind bars. Faces come and go with monotonous regularity. Every inmate so inducted is considered to be maximum security until such time as they are individually assessed, scrutinized and reallocated to another prison, dependent upon their threat level. Here in prison the sands are always shifting, the incoming tide from the courthouses leaves another dozen penitents in its wash, before receding and taking with it a further score of inmates to other permanent prisons, other shores.

After a while you think you know everyone on your unit; not necessarily by name, but mostly by face or appearance. And then one day you spy an unfamiliar face passing you by in the common room, or perhaps standing behind you in the dish-up queue for dinner. You do a double-take and wonder if it's yet another new arrival on the wing.

Then you realize that you've seen him once or twice before, coming out from the cell around the corner from yours. A chameleon perfectly camouflaged, living the cloistered existence of a hermit crab; scurrying from the relative safety of his burrow to snatch a scrap of food then beating a hasty retreat before being discovered.

Everyone has a coping mechanism here in confinement, and in a very broad sense those mechanisms can be neatly categorized as either 'fight or flight'. Some folks while away the time in endless card games, playing the much favored game of 'prison rummy'. Others languish semi-permanently in the common room around the pool table, shooting the breeze between rounds. This is usually the preferred domain of the gang members and the heavies. The talk here is usually of crime; who did what to who, and who is in jail where. There is an unabashed sense of pride here in the crimes committed, and those crimes are invariably harsh, graphic and extremely violent. I will not regale you of the specifics of their stories here. Suffice it to say that they boast of some of the worst acts that one human being can visit upon another, and they wear their inhumanity like a badge of honour. Drugs and addictions seem to form an intrinsic part of this dark underbelly.

Some men never rise above themselves.

But there is another breed here too. The handful who never give up their focus on their real life; their true selves. They live with a passion. Their love is for someone, or *something* beyond themselves. They cast tall shadows. In truth many should probably never have been put here in the first place, but sometimes we lose our way. Put simply there are bad people who have done bad things and good people who have done bad things, yet in the eyes of the law they are all damned and tarred equally with same stern brush. For these few, every single day becomes a battle to rise and return home, and a prison merely constrains them physically until they are once again free. Ultimately, they will transcend this place quickly because they never truly belonged here. They do not make any part of this their home.

But for other souls, life ends at those bars and the outside world may as well be a barren wasteland where nothing grows. They no longer live; they simply exist.

There are some fundamental reasons why a person chooses the path of solitude and isolation, but each of them has one common underlying motivation. *Escape*. The loners are generally seeking an escape from one of two things.

Firstly, there are those seeking release from a prison of their own making. This prison goes by the name of 'Self-Judgement', and its jailers are called Guilt, Shame and Regret. Haunted by the ghosts of their past, these souls exist as virtual sleepwalkers, condemned to their own personal hell and all but oblivious to the world around them. In many cases, the demon on their back has also brutally snatched away their lives and their livelihoods. The collateral damage for many so condemned is the collapse of a marriage, or estrangement from family, friends and loved ones. The loss of children, homes, finances and reputations. For some the damage bill is total, and so they simply live on in a state of Limbo. No longer a part of the world which they knew, but neither truly existing in their harsh new reality of razor wire and prison walls.

And the second group? Well, they seek an escape from the horrors of their immediate surroundings, finding themselves at odds with a harsh environment with which they struggle vainly to cope. This is well beyond the capacity of some, who up until now have only had to deal with nothing more confronting than the odd drunken lout at a baseball game.

How many lives here have been wiped away completely in a single fall of the gavel, I wonder?

To best describe the general prison environment, it is a little like swimming with sharks. The hard-core criminal elements are the top predators in this barred ocean. They can and will prey upon the weak, and suitably roused they will make short work of them. But just like their razor toothed counterparts, for the most part their probing advances are simply bluster; a pseudo-aggressive display of power mostly aimed at establishing boundaries and testing a potential victim's mettle. Facing down such a feint attack will usually send a signal back to the circling shark:

'Back off, I'm not a pushover'.

Usually. You see the trick is in knowing exactly where the line between bluster and blade is; learning how to ignore the bluster and avoid the blade. Sadly the meek do not have the heart for this game, and simply beating a retreat to the safe haven of a locked cell becomes the safest solution. Tragically for some of them, there are still voices lurking in the dark that can put an end to their lives as surely as the blade. And running is useless when the voices are inside your own head.

Like I said earlier, I don't know exactly how long he was there. I don't know what demons he faced or the name of the one that finally got to him. Whatever caused the final straw to break is now a moot point; the cold fact of the matter is that somewhere in the still of the morning, the demon won.

They cut his limp body down and carried it away, with the rest of the unit under careful lockdown. When the cell doors were finally unlocked several hours later, all that remained for us to see were the shards of bed sheet that had cradled him in his final moments, still tied to the top floor balustrade alongside the wooden staircase that led to the common room area. I didn't even know his name, and doubtless few others did either. His passing, like the final miserable days of his life was a lonely one.

In the weeks that followed, a working crew secured wire netting across the gaps along either side of the old wooden staircase where he had hanged himself. It was a hollow gesture that merely added insult to injury, as the polished top floor balustrade stretched away unprotected in both directions, affording plenty of space and opportunity for others to do the same. Precious few people gave it more than a passing glance as they scurried underneath it to push into the meal time dish-up queue at the nearby kitchen area. And so life went on, and he was very quickly forgotten. You see, many inmates here already have an intimate relationship with death, having made the dealing of it a handiwork and a lifestyle. From them there was precious little by way of acknowledgement, and certainly no grief for the suicide of one solitary mixed up loner. Hell, the sad asshole didn't even belong here.

For my part, I was given to fitful introspection. Where exactly did he belong, and what was his untold story? Was there a grieving mother somewhere out there beyond those stern walls? Or a heartbroken girlfriend? Who mourned his passing? Undoubtedly someone did, for I like to believe that there is always love. But then that's the thing about love: It is one thing to be loved, but it is another thing for someone to *feel* that love, or to feel that they are deserving of it.

What causes this disconnect from love? And what exactly must one lose; what circumstance could bring a person to this point – this place of lovelessness – that they would choose the loneliest of deaths over life?

The thought percolates quietly at the back of my mind for several days afterwards; usually as I go through the mind-numbing tedium of my labors in the prison laundry. I decide that I cannot simply apply my own life experiences to another's road. By comparison with many here, mine has been a fortunate and blessed life. I live with regret for what I have done, but what would I know of addiction; of under-privilege, destitution or true hardship? What do I know of true loss? Indeed, what right have I to issue this lofty challenge; raised from the materially comfortable higher ground of social privilege and education? I have always felt love, and felt more or less loved. Perhaps I should re-phrase my question a little more universally:

What is it exactly that makes us want to *live*?

There are so many sad stories, all around me. If it were humanly possible that these pained souls be given voice, the banshee din would be oppressive. The truth of it is that many have died in here, but the following day there is no evidence of the burn of rope, or the slash of blade to mark their passing. I see it in their eyes, however, as a back-light gone dim. A slow measured retreat of spirit. Sometimes the sense of loneliness and fragility that accompany its withdrawal tear at me to the point of raising silent inner tears. My soul cries for them.

Many times I have been told not to take on another's pain. But if one cannot or will not at least acknowledge the resonance of pain in others, what is the point of a heaven? When you can truly feel the pain of another's spirit you are a blessed man, I think. You have opened yourself to the truth of a larger world, and in doing so you touch upon something that is both intimate and sacred. So, why do some of us *want* to live? There must be some commonalities; some universals that are so worthwhile that we will grimly endure the storm in anticipation of the rise of the sun upon a brand new day.

So it dawns on me that I'm looking at this the wrong way. It seems to me that it isn't actually what one *loses* that causes someone to give up. Rather, it is what one *possesses* that keeps them living when all around them falls apart.

I have now weathered a fair few storms in my short seafaring life. The old salts are quick to tell you that foul weather and stormy seas is an accepted part of the profession and to deny that is folly. Perhaps a key to my resilience lies therein. I have had an enduring love affair with the ocean; a passion which has persisted through my youth. She is rather like a second home to me now, and over seasons past I have come to know her as both a generous lover and a scorned mistress. And many are the voyages where she has shown me both her faces. The trick in venturing out is always preparing yourself for both eventualities. To simply expect timeless balmy days of plain sailing is madness, and the ignorance of this fact has proven to be the undoing of many a would-be sailor. This same recipe must logically form the basis of a desirable mindset for weathering difficult times. But what then are the ties that secure us to this mortal coil; that anchor us as securely as rope or chain when our life's ocean whips into a hellish fury around us?

Life here mimics life on the outside. There are always divisions. There is a perceived hierarchy and pecking order. Racial groups form territorially and woe betide the person who dares cross those boundaries. By unspoken agreement the prison is divided into racial go- and no-go zones. Similarly there is the brotherhood of the street gangs, and then there are the heavies. These groups deem themselves to be hard-core criminals and they place themselves a cut above what they perceive as the lower life forms – the addicts and the petty criminals.

Yet there are some things powerful enough to cross divisions of race, creed, language and color. Let us put judgement aside for one moment, in the observation of this universal. It seems painfully simple, but here it is:

The singular thing that sets the living apart from the others is that the living possess a well-developed sense of purpose and meaning. It is as simple as that. Those who survive are the ones who live a meaningful life; those who have a purpose to their lives. We live for love, and for someone or something beyond ourselves. And one of the most powerful ties is the deep bond of family.

 C3❀80

The death of a star is a spectacular celestial event. In its dying gasp, what we perceive from our distant Earthly perspective to be little more than a faint twinkle in a velvety-black night sky is actually a sun which burns at its brightest just before it slowly implodes in upon itself. Who knows just where a star goes when it dies? Such is the power of its influence that even in its cosmic death throes a star still possesses a potency capable of drawing nearby objects into its vortex, in the same way that a sinking ship will drag her own floundering sailors down to their own watery deaths as she finally slips beneath the surface.

Similarly, as a star recedes it takes some of the fabric of this physical universe along with it in the self-same way, just like a virtual burial shroud as it were. A dark hole torn in the void of space and time becomes its parting legacy. And in some small way, we are no different to the stars.

With each passing day Tristesse was slipping away. Persia knew it and she sensed the deepening abyss as her friend slowly turned in on herself and increasingly rejected the outside world. Surfacing neatly alongside Tristesse, Persia nudged the smaller orca gently with her flank, trailing an outstretched pectoral delicately along her companion's side to attract her attention. They bobbed lazily together for a moment, not unlike two submarines at harbor – all power and might at rest. Locking eyes, Persia coaxed the smaller orca back from her dalliances in the Other world. Tristesse far preferred it that way, spending more and more of her time in 'logging', trance-like against the concrete wall. In the Other world she was free.

Like many other beings. an orca instinctively knows of the Other world and travels there regularly. For those of you who cannot conceive of it, the best way to begin to understand this whole concept is to picture an iceberg floating alone in a smooth clear ocean. Hold the image of an iceberg in your mind's eye for a moment and focus your thoughts. What is it that you see? Perhaps you picture a perfect glacier-white monolith; a solid small island quietly jutting from a cold deep emerald sea. Most likely that is exactly how your image will appear, especially as you are used to viewing your world through human eyes. What you are looking at is simply the tip of the iceberg. It is in actuality no more the iceberg than the summit of Everest is the mountain. In the same way, your physical body is not You.

Look deeper.

The greatest bulk of the iceberg exists beneath the quiet concealment of the waters. In fact, almost eighty per cent of it in fact lies quietly unseen by the human eye, leaving the remaining twenty per cent jutting up into view above the surface. For the whole to exist, the massive hull beneath the surface anchors the protruding top of the ice mountain. For its part, the peak simply becomes the interface for the whole as it probes into the world of air above.

As an interesting aside; human science observes that *Homo sapiens* possess something of an equivalency when we speak about the conscious mind. It led Austrian psychoanalyst Sigmund Freud to insightfully conclude:

'The mind is an iceberg; it floats with only 17 per cent of its bulk above water.'

The water which Freud was referring to was the realm of the unconscious mind. Co-incidence, you might say? I would beg you to ponder this revelation when you find yourself in a quiet moment. The Harmony observes that there is no such thing as co-incidence, and the keys to many universal secrets are there for us to find, if we so choose to seek them out. The mind, like the iceberg exists in two worlds. So too does the orca, in natural balance. This potential is accorded to you also, though your bloodline has all but supressed it. Of this truth, the Harmony simply observes:

'As Above, so Below; and Balance keeps it so.'

Persia eyed her smaller friend, noticing the new rake marks across her side, stretching forward of her dorsal. Angry red welts that cut cruelly into her flesh, deep enough to reveal the pale layer of blubber underneath. It was the damage to her blunt snout that was far more sinister, and Persia recoiled visibly in the instant she noticed it. Rough abrasions, weeping a pale gauze of blood into the water. Visibly rattled, Persia flicked into a fast lap of the pool's perimeter, scanning frantically as she went. The concrete wheeled around her; Tondo and Kyrie in the far corner of the pool. Tristesse bobbing dazed and subdued; the blood cloud now freely weeping from her snout and curling lazily into the salt water around her. Fuelled by frustration and fear Persia tail slapped violently, sending plumes of white-water across the ramp. Her eyes were drawn to the damning red mark. *There.* In the concrete wall directly alongside the ramp was a dark reddening stain marking the spot at which Tristesse had charged the wall.

When Kathy Quick arrived later that morning in the trainers' common room, she was already rattled. Muscling the yellow Stingray into the parking lot a full twenty minutes late, she muttered under her breath as she realized that the acrid carbon smell of this morning's hurried burnt toast still clung to her favourite UCLA windbreaker. At least it conveniently masked the suspiciously sweet aroma of surfboard wax, she told herself.

With her usual flurry of nervous energy, she slammed the door and caught a fleeting glimpse of herself in the chrome wing mirror. Even under the carefully teased mop of cropped blonde thatch and the obligatory Raybans she looked rattled. *Fuck.* At a loping jog she fumbled in the pocket of her track pants to confirm the presence of keys.

Nothing.

Returning to the Corvette she peered through the side window, cupped her face against the smoky mirror tint and confirmed the worst. The stub of metal key peered back blankly; the brown stitched leather Chevy key fob still swinging back and forth accusingly in a lazy arc on the steering column. *Double fuck.* She tried both doors, hoping for an easy out. No such luck. *Fuck squared. Fuck to the power of three.* Making a quick command decision, the lithely slender chief trainer decided that a late check-in followed by a welcoming cappuccino in the staff lounge to re-group was a good initial course of action. The 'Vette wasn't going to go anywhere in a hurry, and there were enough testosterone-fuelled drones who would willingly coax the car keys from their present lodgement, on the sugary suggested promise of her amorous attention. Quick smiled to herself at the thought. She hadn't risen to the position of chief behavioural trainer for nothing.

When the junior trainer threw the glass door open, breathlessly skidding on the fluted rubber matting, she was galvanized immediately; her training instantly telling her that there was trouble. Her bad day was about to get worse. A good dolphin trainer very quickly learns to understand and respond to the subtlest nuances in body language, and since her days as a driven young post-graduate Kathy had always been a natural. This one however was a no-brainer. Jodie's ungraceful stumble on the non-slip surface didn't exactly fall on the subtle end of the scale, but the look of sheer fright and concern on her wind burned face more than ably told the story. Hazel eyes wide. Still dressed in a polo shirt and running shorts, she stood dripping wet, hair bedraggled.

'At the main pool – it's Leda!' she screamed.

Kathy was already past the open door, taut athletic legs sprinting hard.

When the two trainers arrived, Persia was struggling to wedge Tristesse against the rough concrete edge of the ramp, desperately trying to keep her blowhole above water. As quickly as she applied the pressure with her broad flank, her friend's arterial blood simply pumped harder and further stained the water's surface a dark rosy crimson. She had found to her dismay that the younger orca kept rolling inverted, and already the heavy bulk of her young friend was draining her strength. Kathy reached the pair first, almost overbalancing into the pool in her haste. The blow from the young orca sounded panicked and wet; like a clogged drain. A heavy spray of water infused with thick blood clots dislodged itself and rudely spattered the chief trainer. It told of the gravity of the situation.

Vocalizing desperately, Persia struggled to support the pair with strokes of her broad tail; sending rivulets of stained water over the concrete hard standing. Her deep eye locked onto Kathy as she battled with the weight. Despite her measured distrust of the head trainer, Persia knew the situation was desperate. They needed to work together. Human and orca both knew the grim reality. Tristesse was dying.

The larger orcas, Tondo and Kyrie roamed the pool, passing close around the pair of young orcas in broad protective sweeps. Their usually measured fin movements were sharp and erratic; an adrenaline rush coursing through them. Kathy knew from the frenzied waves of panic that were telegraphing through the pool, there could be trouble. Though not of the same bloodline, the older orcas' protective instincts still remained dangerously strong and human intervention, however well-meaning, would be barely tolerated at best.

The risk assessment took her little more than seconds. Steadying herself against the flailing orca at the extremity of the ramp, she took to clearing the rapidly clogging blowhole. *Airways and breathing first.* Kathy glanced back at her younger charge, standing paralysed by fear and inexperience. Without taking her eyes off the agitated orcas circling in the background, she yelled a curt instruction back to her young protégé:

'Jodie, call Brad out here, now! Full trauma kit, stat! She's haemorrhaging!'

Having seen the commotion at the main pool from his office window, Casper rushed out into the bright morning sunshine and quickly covered the length of cobbled red brick walkway to the main display area. Squinting as his rheumy eyes slowly accustomed themselves to the stark glare of Californian sunlight, he moved at a slow jog to the concrete trainers' ramp which sloped down into the pool area where the limp body now lolled like a broken rag-doll. Rivers of clotted blood had already stained the young orcas ivory eye-patch the color of rust, and even to Casper's untrained eye it was painfully obvious that she was slowly drowning in it. The thought confounded him. Even in the noise and confusion, Casper was aware of how jarringly odd it seemed that a magnificent specimen of ocean predator like Leda could actually be capable of drowning.

He drew up alongside Kathy on the smooth wetness of the incline, puffing slightly from the exertion and looking oddly out of place; pristine in business slacks, shirt and tie against the scene of bloody carnage on the hard standing.

'You shouldn't be down here wearing those,' Kathy gasped distractedly; punctuating her comment with a hasty slant of her head towards Casper's feet.

She had sensed rather than seen the approach of the old man, focussing herself fully on the fevered task of constantly clearing Tristesse's blowhole, remaining in a steady crouch alongside the young female's blunt snout. More often than not, a whale or a dolphin in distress will begin to show signs of relaxing in the company of a human positioned in the sector forward of her pectoral fins; that is, in her range of vision.

'Keep clear and give me space,' she breathed heavily with the effort; 'And watch your damn footing. You know the rules, Casper!'

At thirty-eight years of age, Kathy was a good ten years the senior of most of the other trainers, and she had seen more than a dozen incidents of well-meaning bystanders being swatted accidentally by a sweep of broad tail fluke

'My rules, I'll break 'em,' came the dry retort.

'Is it bad?' Casper blurted, immediately cursing himself inwardly for questioning the obvious.

'It's fucking bad. She's bleeding out internally.'

'Brad?'

'He's on the way, but we need him *here*, not out on fucking Huntington Beach chasing tail. We're losing her.'

Casper recognized the barely disguised tone of accusation in his chief trainer's voice. As stressed as she was, he knew her feelings about his decision to keep the chief veterinarian on a loose on-call roster. She had made no bones about her disdain for his attitude of 'cutting Brad some slack'. And he in turn had made no bones about his stance. He willingly allowed Dr Bradley Manning the luxury of calling the shots with his own scheduling, knowing full well that the advantage of having the young man's qualifications and depth of knowledge with orcas and dolphins was too good an asset to lose by reining the pro-surfer in with too many rules and restrictions. And for such an asset, he was fully prepared to overlook the occasional leave of absence or transparently obvious 'sick day.'

Casper had recognized the breed immediately, the day the muscled, bleached blonde vet had applied for the job. The surfboard lashed to the racks of his open-top black Jeep Wrangler spoke clearly of his passion. The only ties that these young guys willingly endured were the rubber leg-ropes that bound them to their fiberglass boards as perfectly as any wedding band.

Privately bemused, it had conjured in his mind the imagined scene of every schoolboys private dream – the nubile young Californian goddess lying waxed, wet and ready; pert breasted and flat bellied. The perfect prize adorning his bed expectantly in all her diaphanous lace-pantied glory, only to be spurned and all but cast aside as her muscled champion fired up the Jeep to chase the 'perfect set' that had just rolled in off Huntington Beach. Adding insult to injury by leaving her with a hastily proffered feast of last night's Taco Bell leftovers and a cheap white spritzer as poorly considered compensation.

Yes, Brad Manning was a nomad at heart. One of the golden breed who lived for the oceans. For the next unspoiled set of tubes; the perfectly shaped curling walls of green water that called out a challenge – all salty might and white-capped fury – to young men like Brad Manning. That wanderlust had taken Manning across the oceans of the southern hemisphere. He would reel off the now-familiar names endlessly during sessions at the coffee machine in the common room. Waimea, Bondi and Bells Beach. J-Bay. The Banzai pipeline. Just how perfectly and completely he held the all-female contingent of trainers in thrall did not go unnoticed by the hawk-eyed old eccentric. Spellbound, they hung off his every word just as the legendary Brad Manning hung off the crested curls of green water.

Casper knew that the man's pull went well beyond hormonal superficiality. Beyond his audiences secretly imagined thoughts of gracing his bed; of capturing his tantalisingly free spirit and making it their own. There was no doubting that his head veterinarian was the perfect specimen of alpha male-hood, but Brad's natural magnetism went far deeper than that.

When he talked shop, it was spoken with an authority borne of years of skilled work as a marine mammal vet. Firstly, with the bottlenose dolphins of the Australian east coast, and then with captive orcas in Florida. The work of the husband and wife team of Brad and Andrea Manning in the Solomons with sea turtle rescue was now the stuff of legend. Their Ken and Barbie looks more than cementing their popularity with the fledgling *'Save the Whale'* movement, until the good doctor upset the eco-warrior apple cart with his subsequent move into more lucrative service with captive dolphins.

Now that Waterworld had acquired the complement of four orcas, with tentative plans for two more in the coming season, Casper knew that however much of a loose cannon Dr Manning may have appeared to his fiery chief trainer, he was a considered asset to the enterprise. He was well acquainted with Quick's disapproval of the man and his patchy work ethic. And he graciously afforded her that leeway, recognizing her own sense of professionalism and dedication was sorely tested by Manning's cavalier attitude toward the workplace.

The autism spectrum was still something of a mystery back then. Sharp as he was with logic and fine detail, what Casper Barrett couldn't glean was the deeper source of his chief trainer's present brooding frustration with the park's vet. It was by now common knowledge amongst the cadre of park trainers. A poorly kept secret furtively debated in hushed undertones in the common room. By general consensus, there was now no doubting the sordid fact of the matter. Just exactly how long Manning and Quick had been playing out their lusty agenda of furtive gropings and stolen liaisons was the current point of contention for all concerned.

In a year from now however, it would all be like proverbial water under the bridge. Stranger fates were to intervene, both mystic and statistic. And as is so often the case with affairs of the heart, it would soon become apparent to the two lovers that their respective depths of commitment to one another simply didn't match.

The painful implosion of their relationship would be like a dread spreading ripple, seen and felt by many. The illustrious doctor was destined to become another tragic statistic at the hand of a betrayed spouse with a handgun. The first bullet would enter his groin, completely missing the femoral artery. Though judging by the subsequent massive tissue damage in the region of his manhood, it was likely that Andrea Manning was not targeting the blood-rich vessel specifically. The second bullet that took out the left side of his cranium delivered the killing blow.

Kathy Quick narrowly escaped a similar fate, and though the angry furrowed crease across her right temple healed rapidly to a permanent line of ugly tissue scarring, the emotional scarring never did. As a struggling single mother, the fiery relationship with her son was marred by her own personal calvary of substance abuse and private nightmares. The much loved Corvette ended its days ignominiously in a small wrecker's yard after an alcohol fuelled accident in Santa Monica.

Exactly how Quick escaped so perfectly unscathed, to be found wandering on Venice beach miles from the crash site at the precise time her car reportedly hit the tree, confounded the team of crash examiners. They rejected her story out of hand and continued their search for the driver, despite the fact that five independent witnesses separately identified Quick as the sole occupant of the canary yellow 1968 Chevrolet Corvette bearing distinctive Nevada plates. Hospital staff and examining surgeons also chose to ignore the puzzling fact that the scar tissue from her prior episode of horror had not only perfectly healed, but vanished completely. The accident marked a turning point for Quick, who emerged from a hushed sabbatical and back into the public arena as a tireless and vocal campaigner for animal rights.

But that is yet another hidden fold in our story and is, as bewildering as it reads, largely irrelevant at this present moment in time. Indeed, on that September morning, Quick's current biological state and her ultimate destiny were known only to four individuals; none of whom were human.

The idea of precisely what constitutes the actual point of death is a topic of conjecture amongst the various human cultures and races. Humans, quite naturally have a vested self-interest in the subject, and predictably they turn to analytical and clinical scientific methodology to explain and understand the phenomenon. They fuss over their morgue tables and microscopes, tissue samples and electroencephalographs in order to dig Death out. To graph it, quantify it and isolate it. Their best thinking minds constantly return to the tip of the iceberg to trek over its smooth surface and chip away cold samples of its bulk in bold scientific expeditions largely designed to subjugate the lingering fear of death that haunts the quiet corners of each human mind. In more recent epochs, Western human science has proposed that death occurs when the vital body functions cease; specifically breathing and circulation.

The Harmony recognises the point of death as the time of the Separation. That is, the precise moment at which the super-conscious life force uncouples energetically to fold in on itself and transit the vortex to All That Is. The orca naturally understands this. Ironically it was ultimately this disparity between the two species fundamental understandings of death that led to the second fatality that day.

Casper Barrett's time of death was officially recorded as 10.19am Pacific Standard Time; a full eight minutes after Tristesse made the silent journey to All That Is.

The impassive coroner's report simply stated that: 'The largest of the four orcas, a male known as Tondo, had charged the ramp causing a surge of water to swamp the concrete incline as he launched himself onto it in an aggressive maneuver which marine mammal trainers refer to as a 'bodyslide'. It was the backflow resulting from the bull orca's subsequent slide back into the pool which caused both the victim Mr Casper Martin Barrett, Managing Director (aged 73) and Ms Katherine Quick, Chief Trainer (aged 38) to lose their footing in the backwash of the receding waters. From a health and safety aspect, neither party was suitably attired for entering the water; however it is most likely that Ms Quick's crouched position at the pool end of the ramp alongside the deceased juvenile orca named Leda, together with her non-slip training shoes, protected her from the powerful suction effect created by the retreating orca.'

The report went on to note that: 'Mr Barrett was not wearing suitable footwear and his resultant fall from a standing position at the centre of the ramp resulted in him being dragged into the centre of the performance pool. Contusions and trauma to the back of the scalp, together with abrasions to the shoulders and upper back region indicated that he had likely struck his head as he fell backwards, impacting the concrete ramp at its mid-point. These particular injuries were classified as non-fatal, and the cause of death was determined as massive heart attack.'

A full page of the report was given to describing the behaviour of the three surviving killer whales, and in particular that of 'the main aggressor Tondo, who was observed to deliberately drag Mr Barrett underwater and hold him under the surface on two separate occasions. Mr Barrett broke free from the first attack with the assistance of Ms Quick, who had dived into the pool and positioned herself between Tondo and Mr Barrett in order to allow him time to swim to the safety of the ramp. Ignoring her presence in the water, the male killer whale again lunged at Mr Barrett and dragged him underwater a second time, partially severing his left foot at the ankle in the process. After several minutes the victim managed to surface briefly, though it was observed from his demeanour that he was clearly distressed and weakened from the ordeal and the ferocity of the prior attacks.

At this point the vocalizing of the remaining female orcas Pandora and Kyrie, who had remained stationed alongside the deceased animal Leda throughout the ordeal appeared to distract Tondo, who in retreating to the pool's perimeter struck the victim unconscious with a resultant blow from his tail fluke. The retreat of the male killer whale to the western end of the performance pool allowed Ms Quick to remove Mr Barrett to the safety of the perimeter hard-standing where she and Miss Joanne Rose Michaelson, Behavioral Trainer (aged 25 years) subsequently administered cardio-pulmonary resuscitation until the arrival of the Los Angeles Paramedic team at 10.45am. Mr Barrett never regained consciousness and was pronounced dead at the scene.'

The only human to observe the actual passing of Tristesse to the Other World that morning was Kathy Quick. From her station alongside the stricken young orca, she instinctively felt the shift of light as Tristesse held her gaze long beyond her final breath. The dying orca had lost the physical strength to hold onto Persia as her body slowly shut down, but she nevertheless felt her loyal friend's comforting presence in those final moments; the sole representative of her bloodline and her family.

In the compression of seconds prior to the Separation, her breathing appeared to rally in rapid deep draughts, before giving way in one final longing sob before she found herself Home. The beauty of that one pure moment of intimate union was never lost to Kathy. Rather it remained as a perfect seed deep below her consciousness, which quietly and subtly wove the fine filigree alterations into her DNA in preparation for her calling. It was the final unselfish gift of a deeply sentient being.

Had Casper Barrett not been present on the ramp, approaching Tristesse at that particular point in time, Tondo would most likely not have reacted the way he did. But no human could possibly have known this, not for certain anyway. Many humans were quick to speculate; for the death of one of their own kind at the whim of a wild animal was a perverse curiosity that piqued their fascination for cheap sensationalism and tawdry controversy. Grim aerial footage of the lifeless orca lying alone on the ramp, and the sobering sight of what was undoubtedly a human body covered discreetly with white canvas, played and re-played endlessly across the evening news.

News anchors seized on the opportunity; likening old man Barrett to a modern-day Ahab gruesomely killed by his nemesis, the black whale. The post-apocalyptic setting of Waterworld provided a fitting visual backdrop for the telling. The story also carried a perfect 'Beauty and the Beast' angle; a photogenic Kathy Quick telling the flock of hungry spellbound journalists that it was only her deep connection with the park's killer whales that had spared her from the same grim fate as her aged employer. What she couldn't know at the time was that her reprieve had absolutely nothing to do with any sense of cetacean respect for her professional standing. Rather, the 'birth spark' which all three orcas had already instinctively recognized within her had become her saving grace.

No orca would willingly separate a human mother from her baby. Interestingly this same maternal connection was also recognized in the case of Casper Barrett. Quick, for all her innate skill and sensitivity with regards to the fleeting and often minute behavioural 'tells' of her oceanic charges was too traumatized to recognize it at the time.

It happened in that heart-rending moment when Casper surfaced exhausted for that final time and chillingly cried out for his mother in a fragile child-like voice. Kathy all but missed the fact that in that precise instant the two female orcas vocalized agitatedly in perfect unison and Tondo immediately broke off from his attack.

CHAPTER EIGHT

CALLING

'Five miles deep underwater you hear their voices sing
Surely that must be to every man a most fantastic thing'
–GARY ANDERSON/JOHN MEYERS - 'Calling'

AS A YOUNG man I was always drawn to the realm of the Sea. It was heady, mysterious and inviting, all at once. I was taken by her myriad moods; drawn siren-like to her all stretched out sensuous and opaline blue as far as the eye could see.

In summers past I rose triumphant, all salt and tan from a rolling surf, drying her from me before heading off to chase bikinis and beer as young men are wont to do. I stood in fear and awe of her powerful majesty; an insignificant solitary figure chilled to the bone and perched precariously on the rocks in the face of a wild winter gale. Yet the very next day I could be drenched in bright sunshine by her shore; the bay becalmed and peacefully silent, her ferocious rage now passed and all but forgotten. I think it was some vague promise of adventure in that duality that I feel in love with.

I remember my father shaking his head and telling me that I had saltwater in my veins, as I returned from summer vacation several shades of brown darker than my winter skin. Despite his quiet hopes that I might follow in his footsteps as a mechanical engineer, I already had a sense of where my destiny lay. Having reluctantly gone through the motions of completing a science degree to assuage the old man's urgings, I couldn't return to her quick enough.

My first introduction to dolphins came as a young rookie deckhand, getting my sea legs on the deck of a wildly pitching trawler out in Bristol Bay. Scores of wild dolphins would routinely accompany the fishing boats out of the harbor, breaching and charging our hull playfully, before riding our bow wave like joyful silver-gray bullets. It was here while still serving my time as a greenhorn on a salmon trawler that I experienced the first taste of my aquatic friends' keen intellect.

A male dolphin, who we had named Top Notch on account of a distinct triangular notch on his dorsal fin, had taken to watching me intently as I tied off the securing knots on the bottom of our trawl net. Once a trawl was completed, the catch would be winched aboard the boat and held suspended by the crane over the flat expanse of the aft deck. The knots would be untied and the catch disgorged over the deck for sorting. With the net now emptied, the knots could be quickly re-tied and the net made ready to go back over the stern for the next trawl. As the rookie crew member, the task fell to me to untie and re-secure the knots, whilst the senior deckhands busied themselves around me sorting the prized catch.

All had been going well and with the season now in full swing, I was pleased to note that the leather-faced old timers were slowly but begrudgingly welcoming me into their on-deck banter and conversations. It was a hard proving ground for an unseasoned newbie, and the drop-out rate from the first season was high. The skipper had even given me a smile for the first time; firm testament to the fact that their confidence in me was steadily rising. Perhaps there was some seafaring blood in me after all, as my surname had suggested! I must admit to suspecting that my Nordic surname had a lot to do with the captain accepting me over the score of other hopefuls. Sensing this, I went about subtly nurturing this perception of my proud Viking roots. Actually to be downright honest, I milked it for all it was worth; boldly surveying the vessel with my best professional eye, hands on hips (praying that I was correct in referring to the front end of the boat as the bow), and doing my level best to disguise a paralysing bout of seasickness that had struck me down on the second day out of port. In truth, the closest I had come to touching on the proud seafaring blood of the Vikings was owning a kayak. The Svenson clan can thus far only lay claim to a proud history as landlubbers – engineers, factory owners and the odd accountant. And I really do mean odd, though that is another story in itself.

Discovering that I had plans of further study for my doctorate, the rough-cut crew had enjoyed several laughs at my expense. The idea of someone with my credentials working the deck of an old salmon trawler was something of a crude novelty to them. I had been dubbed 'the Doctor', rather a letdown for me and not at all in keeping with the romantic pirate persona which I had eagerly hoped to cultivate.

Today however, feeling the growing sense of acceptance by the tight-knit crew, I felt much less the erudite university educated bookworm and more the salty old sea dog far befitting my Nordic heritage. Basking in my recent elevation in status, I proudly stood on the aft deck with the old salts, fighting the swell as best I could while desperately trying to affect their off-hand swagger as we casually whiled away the time, waiting for the first trawl to be hauled in. For the past couple of days I had taken to talking aimlessly to Top Notch, who seemed to have acquired a keen interest in proceedings as I scurried around the wildly pitching after-deck. Busying myself with steadying the swaying net and releasing the securing knots, whilst he spy-hopped alongside. Waiting by the winch as it steadily wound in the trawl cable, I scanned the choppy sea off the stern, looking for my newest buddy Top Notch. Today however he was nowhere to be seen. No doubt off with his pod, doing whatever it is that dolphins do to while away another perfect blue day.

Suddenly, the call to 'haul in' was issued from the bridge, and I snapped easily back to the task at hand. The deck crew hove into action making ready the crane as the trawl began to winch in easily. Far more easily than usual it seemed, drawing a little more than the standard off-hand glance from the wheelhouse window. The winch would up quickly and it purred rather than strained. I scanned the metallic trace of cable critically. Even the greenhorn knew something wasn't quite right. Several pairs of eyes were now trained on the trawl net as it surfaced, shedding plumes of salt water as it heaved clear of the surface and into the air. The net was empty, deflated and as sorry looking as an old discarded condom; raised condemningly high for all to see. I felt the blood rush to my cheeks in pained embarrassment.

The knots were untied. All ten of them.

Nervously I shot quick glances at the old deckhands now scrutinizing the limp offering, as if seeking their reassurance. Refusing to hold my eye contact, their faces told it all – the greenhorn had screwed up. Flustered and somewhat confused, I busied myself in securing the net, re-tying the accusing strings in double quick time as penance for my perceived blunder. I knew in my heart I couldn't have made a mistake. Not all ten knots. Sure, I had been guilty of miss-tying one or two knots in the past, in my haste to perform on the madly pitching boat. But never all ten. Never. My task completed, I swung around to signal Duke Delaney, the skipper in the wheelhouse up for'ard. His curt businesslike nod told me everything:

Don't screw it up again Doc, or you're toast.

As the net went down again, a flash of gray caught my eye off to starboard. It was Top Notch, surfacing with a sharp burst of expelled air like a sleek diver returning top-side. Immediately his eye caught mine, and in that instant I knew the truth of it.

'*You….bastard!*' I mouthed soundlessly.

A dolphin seems to wear a permanent smile, but this is simply the fixed physiology of its upturned mouth line. But today Top Notch really did smile at me. Not with his mouth but with his eyes which flashed a deep knowing glint, and spoke of his clever indiscretion. It was a smile that spoke right to my soul. And with that, as quickly as he had breached, he was gone in a powerful flick of tail fluke that playfully showered me in salt spray. I groaned to myself. I knew exactly where he was headed. Back downstairs for another fish buffet.

So, there it was. All that time he was closely scrutinizing my work, he was worked out not only how to untie the knots, but exactly where they were all located. I was left both impressed and betrayed in almost equal measure. I could only begin to wonder if Duke and the boys would buy my story.

'Ohhh,' they would all laugh as they slapped my back with gloved hands, bursting with gleeful merriment.

'Of course, it wasn't the rookie. Hell, it was the *goddamn dolphin!*'

And with that, walking down the wharf with arms around my shoulders like old buddies, they would shepherd me into the port tavern; roundly arguing over who would buy the first round of beers for the newest crew member of the *Liberty Belle*. Highly unlikely.

For the next two hours, I sat with my back pressed hard against the bulwark on the gently rolling after deck and waited. Mentally I had already packed my bags and phoned for the taxi to catch my flight home. My seafaring days cut embarrassingly short by a common dolphin. One thing still haunted me though; that singular knowing look in his eye. That recognition and the pure sense of deepest understanding stuck with me, and it does so to this day. Perhaps, looking back it was that simple yet powerful communion that set me unwittingly upon the misguided course that I ultimately took.

But I digress here and of course, you perhaps want less in the way of profundity and more in the way of entertainment. So what became of the bumbling rookie deckhand and his arch-nemesis the dolphin, you ask? I'm fairly certain that I know which of us you're now rooting for, good reader. For pious is the cloth, and knowledgeable the beard my friends, but deeply wise is the dolphin! As you may already guessed, the inevitable once again happened in a near perfect repeat of the earlier debacle.

For the second time in succession a pathetically limpid trawl net was drawn up behind the trailing cable, and my worst fears were realized. No catch and eight of the ten knots hanging open accusingly from the bottom of the empty net. This time however, there was no restrained silence from the deck crew – Dash, Jimmy and Curtis. With some very colourful expletives they made their sentiments loudly and patently clear. Speechless and flustered, my eyes ranged from the bedraggled net to the wheelhouse and back to the steel-gray ocean; half expecting the real culprit to surface alongside and reveal himself. But Top Notch was once again conspicuous by his absence. Even the large flocks of marauding seagulls had withdrawn from the vicinity, as if the word had got out to all and sundry. The greenhorn was turning the *Liberty Belle* into a ghost ship.

What followed was a curt dressing-down from the skipper, who then insisted on a rather humiliating public demonstration of knot tying, stopping just short of explaining the technique to me with sock puppets. And so it was left up to me to again prove my mastery of the skill under his stern glare.

In the days that followed I never missed a beat. By season's end that year I was an accepted crewmember of the *Belle*, even being entrusted to bring the old girl back into port on the final home run under the proud watchful eye of Duke, ever the old Master. Some weeks later, when Top Notch was caught red-handed untying a knot as the trawl was being recovered; the whole matter was finally put neatly to rest. Although I never felt truly exonerated, I could now lay claim to my very own 'tall story' just like the other salty old sea dogs.

The day came when I revisited the story of Top Notch and the trawl net with old Duke. I was at the point of steadily gaining a sense of surefootedness and direction; A feeling that I was moving beyond the wild flush of youth, and developing my seafaring skills nicely. And as ever, that ocean rolled before me, mysterious and wide. Yet I was still left with questions. Sheepishly I recounted to Duke the distinct sensation of deep knowingness I had felt in the dolphin's animated eyes. I was cautiously treading that unexplored ground of laying bare emotion and innermost feelings; a sensitivity so rarely displayed in public by these gruff men amongst men.

Carefully studying Duke's deeply lined face, I saw no sign of rebuke or disbelief, and it emboldened me to bare my soul a little further. Somewhat naively I spoke to him of the knowingness that I had felt at my very core, the distinct sense of spiritual connection. I asked him if we could be looking at some measured intellect far beyond that of other animals.

When Duke finally spoke, it was not the sharp, colorful language of an old nor-west trawler captain, but rather the thoughtful, measured lilt of a wise man.

'Son,' he said, focussing on some unseen point on the horizon, through the bay window of the cosy dockside coffee shop, 'I wanna share a story with you. Actually it's a tale that I like to tell in bar-rooms and pool parlours. Never fails to raise an eyebrow. Most think it's just a tall tale. Mostly I just leave it at that; a fisherman's story from a crazy old fella who's spent too many days at sea. I think you'll appreciate it though, because it involves dolphins. Actually it involves an orc-.'

He paused. An uncustomary shyness overtaking him as a tall waitress with a shock of long red hair placed two steaming cups of coffee on the table in front of us. Her blue eyes seemed to sparkle as she smiled, and I could imagine her swimming in the nearby ocean like a mermaid. Duke shifted uncomfortably, and his demeanour told me that this was something that he needed to share. Satisfied that we had the room to ourselves he continued, almost conspiratorially:

'Actually the story involves an orca.'

'You mean a killer whale?' I countered.

'Some call 'em that. Mostly those who don't really know 'em.'

'I wasn't much older than you at the time,' he continued without pause, 'Back in the day I had a love of yachting. I'd saved up and bought an old eighteen foot Endeavour. You know the boats I mean?'

I nodded. Actually, I had taken more of an interest in powerful ski boats, but I had often dodged the little Bermuda rigged yachts with the sharp white triangular sails which scudded across the Strait when the winds were favourable.

'I would often be out on weekends with a couple of buddies. The old girl had a cabin area with plenty of sleeping space, and a small rear cockpit area with tiller steering. Perfect weekender boat for camping and fishing trips. Mostly I'd be out with buddies, but with the winds being good, I'd often sail her single handed out in San Pedro Bay.'

He sipped distractedly on his coffee, and I sensed it was more to allow him to weigh his words, rather than to draw on the steaming brew. A sudden tell in his eye confirmed my estimation.

'I saw something out there one day, Doc. Out in the Bay. I don't know the hows and the whys. I only know that I saw what I saw.'

'Go on,' I urged softly, allowing room for Duke's story to unfold.

'Well, it was early morning. Beautiful spring weather with a light breeze coming out of the sou' west. I had the old girl on a long lazy tack, taking the wind off to starboard. Just sitting back nicely at the tiller in the sun, enjoying the day. Anyway, that's how it was when I sighted something off to leeward, coming towards me from the coast. Maybe a mile, mile and a half away. It's a pretty common sight to see big old gray whales breaching in the Gulf. You pick 'em up from a distance by the blow if the visibility's fair. So this particular day I'd sighted a blow in the distance and I was keeping an eye out. What was odd about this was that whales will normally blow and then dive again. You won't see 'em again for a good ten, fifteen minutes, so you get into a knack of scanning the water across a wide area, waiting for the next breach. The funny thing was this one was staying on the surface. As it closed in I could see it's dorsal; there was hardly a swell to speak of. So it's coming closer and closer, and then I could see there was something on its back, trailing right behind the fin. It blew several times more. Never dived once. I figured it must have been a whale that had picked up a ghost net; old abandoned fishing gear or suchlike. Probably got tangled up and couldn't dive with all the buoyancy floats wrapped round its dorsal.'

I had heard about this before. Migrating whales passing close to the coast would often find themselves entangled in discarded fishing gear. Many are the times that I have seen birds and even sea turtles strangled to death in floating plastic beer packaging. Further out the seas are being strangled by plastic and floating junk. Carelessly discarded old nets, rope and plastic floats; hundreds of miles of tangled fishing line float aimlessly with the currents.

Across the table, Duke toyed with his coffee cup nervously, perhaps sensing my mind wandering. This was clearly something more than an entangled whale story.

'Tell me Doc, have you ever seen an orca up close?'

I considered my response. Of course I had seen photos of them; that unmistakable blunt bulk and tall triangular dorsal made an imposing sight. Sheer brute power. Duke's years of experience often put me on the back foot, and I was a little chastened by my clear lack of real life experience.

'*Orcinus orca*,' I quoted: 'I think in the Latin it means barrel or cas-'

'Yep, it does….in the Latin as you so quaintly put it,' came the bluntly mocking retort.

'Comes from their distinct body shape. And why the hell do you always talk so damn fruity? It ain't befittin' a trawler man. Anyways, from a distance I could make out that distinct body and the high black dorsal fin. I could even see the white side patches back up behind its eye. It wasn't a gray whale, it was an orca'.

He clinked the porcelain cup against the polished wood of the table and focussed nervously.

'Now that by itself isn't that a big of a deal. Orcas cruise up and down the west coast all the time, though usually out in deeper water. That was when it hit me. That tangle on its back? It wasn't fishing gear. It was a man hanging onto its dorsal fin for dear life.'

The unexpected twist in the story caught me by surprise. I searched the skipper's eyes for the wicked glint that so often accompanied his mostly bawdy jokes. This time there was no such glint. Instead, he was patiently staring me in the eye, the wrinkle of crow's feet around his eyes deepening as he studied my face for a reaction to this revelation.

'A man? What do you mean a man? You mean it was a drowned body?'

'No Adam,' he grabbed my hand conspiratorially, as if sharing some dark, long kept secret, 'That's just the thing. He wasn't dead. This guy was alive and hanging on to the orca's fin like grim death as she headed out to sea.'

I pondered the weight of his story; the froth in my coffee cup looking for all the world like sea foam in a gathering storm.

'That isn't the half of it either,' he continued: 'The orca was heading for a nearby navigation buoy on a collision course, just a few hundred feet from my yacht. By this I was hollering at the top of my lungs, trying to attract the guy's attention, but he didn't even seem to notice me. He was wearing jeans and a sweatshirt; hard to tell much more than that with the massive wake streaming back from that dorsal. The orca was booking it, that's for sure.'

'Where is this going, Duke?' I enquired, sensing the weight.

'Can you keep a secret, Doc?'

'You know me, Duke.'

'Yep, I do son. And somehow I figure you'll understand the truth of it.'

He put down the heavy cup he was distractedly cradling and drew a long centering breath.

'As they neared the buoy, the guy simply vanished. Just like that.'

'He let go you mean?'

'No, Adam. He *vanished*. I mean, in the one moment I'm looking at him, large as life. In the next he just vanished. Disappeared, right before my eyes.'

'Well, he mostly likely tired and let…'

'Adam,' he grabbed at my sleeve again, an urgency rising in his voice, 'I know what I saw. There was kind of an odd ripple which mushroomed out around them – it's hard to explain. Looking out at them across the water, I could see him holding on with both hands. Kinda straddling the orca's back. Then there was this almighty ripple, like the air around them shimmered, and he was gone.'

There was an edge to his voice; almost as if he were telling the story for the very first time.

'And the orca?' I enquired.

'The orca slowed down. It had come up abeam the yacht by this, and it simply raised its head and stared at me. It saw me, I knew it. Looked me right in the eye, just like your buddy Top Notch. Just for a few seconds and then it dived and was gone. She never came back up.'

'And what about this guy? What happened to the body?'

'Well I searched the area down current of where he disappeared, using the shipping lane marker as a reference. I figured the body would drift slowly, if there even was a body.'

'So, I'm guessing they never found the guy?'

Old Duke paused for a beat, and then continued in a hushed conspiratorial tone.

'Spot on, Doctor. I contacted the authorities. Coast Guard did a search and never found a thing. No-one was listed as missing, so they just closed the case. End of story. At least they took my report seriously. I must have looked pretty shook up when I ran into the Harbormaster's offices.'

We sat in silence for a few moments, listening to the quiet metallic tinkle of a wind chime catching the first breath of sea air near the open window. The soft riffle of moist air was comforting and familiar.

'So what do you think it all means?' I asked, aware of the slightest break in my voice as my words filled the measured silence.

The red haired mermaid opened another window across the silent room, letting the familiar sounds of the harbor in. Out through the oiled timber framed windows I could just make out the white dome shaped Furuno radar atop the *Liberty Belle's* main mast as she bobbed lazily in her berth, three down from the wharf. Rigging tinkled prettily as the breeze lifted and fell in restless sighs.

'What it means? Nothing and everything.'

Duke shook himself out of his introspective fug.

'It's not like you to talk in riddles Duke. That ain't befitting a trawler man.'

'Ha ha, OK smartass! What I mean to say is every other time I told this story, it was always light-hearted you know? Didn't mean anything if folks didn't take it serious. Today when I tell you, it kinda means everything that you believe me.'

The sense of akwardness that carried in his voice drew me to study him carefully. Suddenly coy, he shrugged off my glance and turned away, fussing over the dregs of his coffee. A ruggedness not given to the vulnerability of baring one's innermost thoughts. The realization of what had just taken place flushed me with a sudden unexpected sense of pride. It seemed as though I had the confidence of the man. But there was something more to it than that. True, Duke's story was something straight out of the *Twilight Zone*. But I think we could both feel a common denominator to our questions. We were seemingly bound by some shared intimacy of connection with these enigmatic warm-bloods from the depths.

'For what it's worth Duke, I do believe you. I think you saw something that can't be explained. And I don't think it was just your imagination.'

Duke smiled his laconic half-grimace, the signalling of his thanks. A clumsy school-boy shyness betraying his gratitude for the timely intervention of the flame-haired mermaid, returning to unobtrusively slip the tab between us on the polished table with a warming smile. I picked it up with a flourish, as Duke took this as the cue to neatly close our intimate conversation. The rugged captain returned, all 'bullshit and business' as he always described it.

'Well, the *Belle* sure as hell ain't cleaning herself out there. Time we weighed anchor, buddy.' His voice now officially three tones louder.

'Best we do. I don't think I can top that story Duke, and I'm not sure I can even begin to give you an explanation for it!'

I grinned broadly at the 'buddy' reference.

'Yep, well I'm certainly older but no damn wiser,' he shrugged.

The air outside the café was that familiar heady mix of salt, seaweed, diesel and old rope. It was a comforting smell of adventure that now seemed tinged with mystery.

'Oh, and Doc? The answer to your original question was 'Yes.''

I thought for a while, confused.

'What question?'

'Your original question. About whether we're looking at some sorta high intelligence with dolphins.'

'Oh yeah, right. Well, I guess we've pretty much answered that already.'

'Adam, you throw a ball to a dog, and the dog will just bring that ball right on back. You throw a ball to a dolphin, and it will make up an entirely different game, just for the hell of it.'

'Do you think maybe they know something that we don't know? I asked in all seriousness.

Casting me a sidelong glance, Duke snorted at my sudden gravity.

'OK son, tell me – how many dolphins graduated from university with you? None I'll wager. Not so long ago I watched Neil Armstrong walk down that ladder and plant his big 'ole foot right on that damn moon. And there sure as hell weren't any flipper marks up there! What I'm saying is, let's not get carried away. They're smart all right, but there ain't nothing magical or mystical about them, son. They're just smartass flippered sons-of-bitches'

The crusty old skipper had returned, firing on all cylinders and drier than sandpaper.

'Who are you trying to convince, skipper?' I asked in quiet voice.

Catching his eye for the briefest of moments, I saw the retreating mask of the wise old man, casting a furtive weather eye out past the harbor mouth as if looking for an answer that lay buried deep in the growing swell. Waiting to be discovered like some coral encrusted treasure. Looking back, I suspect perhaps he had been chasing that answer for longer than he cared to admit. He fended off the question with a dismissive shrug.

The gangplank up to the *Liberty Belle's* deck creaked and groaned in protest as we planted our full weight on it, sending a gathering of gulls reluctantly back into the air, squawking their rude indignant disapproval as they went.

'Just you watch how you tie those knots in future, Adam. Don't let a goddamn dolphin bring you undone again!'
He laughed from the belly and slapped me on the back as he prised open the old wheelhouse door, which gave way with a jarring shudder.

I served out another two fishing seasons on *Liberty Belle*. Following a chance meeting shortly after that in the old harbor café, my seafaring life took a new and exciting path. Perhaps Duke's story came as a portent or omen. Come the following season I shipped out as a deckhand on a whale chaser – an imposing black ex-survey vessel. I still recall Duke's parting words the day I reluctantly told him of my new posting. Sensing his reticence, I pressed him for his thoughts and advice. He cocked his head thoughtfully and measured his words:

'Son, I've never known any black ship amount to anything good or holy.'

Little did I know back then just how badly the knot was going to come undone.

CHAPTER NINE

TIME & TIDE

*'An eye in a blue face saw an eye in a green face. That eye is to this eye,
but in low place, not in high place.' said Bilbo Baggins.
Just as Bilbo was beginning to hope that the wretch
would not be able to answer,
Gollum brought up memories of ages and ages before:
'Sun on the daisies it means, it does!' he said.*
—J.R.R TOLKEIN - 'The Hobbit'

I AM LYING in my bunk, having dozed off whilst engrossed in Tolkein's *'The Hobbit'*. Outside the tightly bolted porthole, the Pacific is trying its damnedest to hurl the aged book from my hands. Such is its relentless persistence that I am left with an all-pervading sense that it is using all of its elemental might to distract me from the reading of those words; perhaps for fear that I may touch on some ancient and fundamental truth.

The constant background howl of the squall rises to a chilling banshee wail each time the ship rolls drunkenly into another trough between the crazed whitecaps beyond my spume-starred window. Twice the old book is flung from my grasp as I scrabble at the fiddles of my bunk for a handhold, and the secrets of Middle Earth are temporarily lost in the wild turbidity. I reach for the water bottle wedged alongside me and draw a couple of deep drafts. Perhaps I am losing my mind. Perhaps these delusions are an ancient mariner's curse – this would sit nicely with my long-held romantic notion of a life at sea, plying the heart of a heaving swell. Sadly, the more likely explanation is that I am badly dehydrated from two days of uncontrolled vomiting and retching brought on by the foulest of offshore conditions.

We have been at sea for three days now in the miserable grip of squally weather; unable to sight our quarry through the fathoms of crazed white water, and I am questioning my reasons for being here. The skipper, Chris Mackie has taken on an almost Ahab-esque demeanor, keeping us offshore for the past forty-eight hours based on a hunch. The old hands assure me his hunches are more often than not spot on the money. Far from being consoled by this; in my nauseous misery I rather feel as though we are taking on more an aura of a ship of the damned.

The *Pacific Dark* is leaping and falling like a punch-drunk boxer and my nights have been fitful. I'm running a slight temperature and waking in a cold sweat with my ribs aching painfully from fits of non-stop vomiting, until there is nothing left to throw up. Each heaving retch then wrings a further knot of pain from my sides. The dreams are still there and the tablets don't seem to do anything to stop them though I can't keep them down long enough for them to work anyway. I imagine the ship foundering on jagged rocks and breaking its back, leaving me to float away on a polished timber coffin; the Ishmael to Mackie's Ahab. For a moment I am alone on a becalmed ocean save for the ragged flock of hopeful seagulls wheeling overhead and the words of Melville ringing in my ears:

'*Aye, it was Moby Dick that tore my soul and body until they bled into each other.*'

My soul and body are bleeding into each other.

The dream is always the same. The sudden blinding whirlpool that drags the broken ship down throws me against the whale and I am pinned to its side; powerless to move against the force of churning water. The whale's skin against my back is soft and yielding and has a rubbery 'give' just like soft neoprene; I am surprised by this revelation, having fully expected to come up against a roughness like coarse sandpaper as I first collided with the dark bulk. For long cloistered minutes the eddying maelstrom continues, paralysing my limbs as we sink downwards into it. Despite this I can breathe easily.

How am I breathing underwater?

The sound which envelops us is like the roaring of a hundred jet engines echoing and bleeding in concert. And all this time the whale remains steady, tucking protectively behind my body as we spin together. Protectively. Yes, the whale is actually protecting me! The realization jolts me, and I am suddenly aware that the dark form is deliberately spinning around its nose-to-tail axis, pirouetting like a ballerina in order to keep itself between my flailing body and the central core of the spiralling vortex which pulls us close.

The dream continues and one by one the boundaries that define our worldly plane seem to dissolve in our whirling Dervish dance. *From breath to breath, I am*. I am hanging suspended between the moments. There is no longer any definable orientation – no up or down. Time seems to hold no meaning or sway here, and the hourglass is a thousand crystal shards of empty irrelevance. There is no memory of times past and no thought of the future. There is simply a Here and Now in which every possible thing, everything which has or will happen occurs all at once. I can feel that potential all around me, everything that ever is, was or will be, whispering like a million small feathery voices that dodge and weave as I try to follow their thread. It is too much, and I find myself drunk, fuzzy and ungrounded as I start to lose myself in the rich weave of thought and idea constantly wheeling about me in the maelstrom.

In that moment I come to the realization that I can move my head, and craning backwards I see my guardian for the first time.

And she sees me, her deeply knowing eye gazes back at me like some all-knowing Mother of the Ocean. I am instantly both comforted and drawn to her.

'Am I dying?' I ask her, still struggling to still my mind.

'No,' comes the unexpectedly soft reply; 'You are Living.'

'Listen carefully. I am close and your time is at hand.'

And with that she dived into the eye of the whirlpool, drafting me along with her. Beyond that I cannot rightly find appropriate words to describe the remainder of the dream. I somehow feel compelled to use the word communion. On second thoughts I think perhaps *transformation* is the better word. Somewhere in the dreams I become one with the whale. I don't think I can describe the experience any better than that. So there it is. I never spoke of it to my lawyer and neither did make mention of the experience as I testified in that stately courtroom. No, it was circumstantial evidence best kept to myself.

Since that day the dreams have continued unabated and I can find no rhyme or reason to them. They come uncontrolled and unbidden, and they color my thinking and my judgement until they transform me. Change me. Perhaps our mental hospitals and institutions are brimful with crazies who saw fit to describe their lucid dreaming. Who blabbed and dithered about mystic whales and maelstroms; the screws at the back of their tongues worked loose in the cathartic purging of long-held psychosis. Perhaps the whale knows this. Perhaps that is its game. A measured payback for the years of decimation and horror visited upon its kind by the oil greedy Yankee whaling fleets; for cold flensing knives and bubbling iron blubber pots. For miserable demise by harpoon and bomb lance; calculated retribution for the collective memories of painful writhing exsanguination.

When I awoke, the storm outside had broken and the ship was bobbing on a becalmed ocean; sitting in the eye of an expectant silence. Though eight full hours have passed, *'The Hobbit'* remains neatly propped open in my hands, despite my earlier struggles to simply hold it against the force of the gale blowing desperately outside. Even the ornate woven bookmark that I always carried with me when I travelled remained neatly in place, crumpled but intact. Fascinated, I read the words that it pointed to.

Gollum had decided that the time had come to ask the hobbit Bilbo Baggins something hard and horrible. He asked his riddle in the darkness, certain that timid little Bilbo could not guess the answer:

'This thing all things devours. Birds, beasts, trees and flowers. Gnaws iron, bites steel. Grinds hard stones to meal. Slays kings, ruins towns; and brings high mountains down.'

Bilbo pondered this for mere seconds before proudly answering:

'Give me more time! Time! Time!'

Shivering I drew back and closed the book tightly, tucking it back under my pillow. *Time.* This was the first time I had read the passage and yet a sickly sense of déja-vu overtook me in a nauseous wave. *What did the whale say about Time?* The absence of sound was suddenly unsettling and I deliberately reached for my radio, desperate for something, anything to fill the space. The smooth familiarity of Steely Dan's *Reeling In The Years* reeled me back to present reality. A loud knocking on the cabin door finally snapped me out of the confused fug that had settled on me.

'Svenson!' yelled the brusque disembodied voice from outside the cabin, 'You're up for deck watch in ten. Skipper reckons we're close!'

I rubbed my tired eyes, my muscles protesting loudly as I rolled off my bunk and pulled on a heavy sweater and over it, my old oilskin jacket. Layers. The open deck would still be shrouded in the bone-numbing chill of pre-dawn.

Opening the heavy watertight outer door, I took a few unsteady steps over the bulkhead and made for the worn grab-rails of the steep staircase like Lazarus raised from the tomb.

It is often said that the eye is the window to the Soul, and I for one hold that to be true. But there is still one more window beyond that, because the Soul itself possesses an eye too, and to gaze into that is to be able to see into the realm of the infinite. The *'Everything That Possibly Could Be'*, if you will. And the Soul is intimately connected to this *'Everything'* by some kind of ethereal anchor line.

Perhaps this eye that exists at our very essence is the thing which mystics call the *'All Seeing Eye'* and perhaps it shows us the way Home. I believe that in all likelihood it does. These days I seem to be waking up with more questions than answers. I feel as though I am a hundred questions in search of an answer. Who or what am I?

I remember taking a meditation session once with a Buddhist monk. I can still recall how he looked, sitting cross-legged in the centre of that rough timber floor. Striking ochre and burgundy hues of his flowing robes complimenting his fine olive complexion. Those knowing eyes set behind a pair of unpretentious spectacles with fine silver frames had an almost hypnotic energy. I felt an immediate sense of calm, sitting there quietly at the warmest edge of that welcome aura. His energy was transformative and it seemed to reach easily into the corners of that sun-dappled room. The hippies and holiday-makers making up the gathering fell silent in a ragged huddle of bleached blonde locks, jewelled nose studs, board shorts and bronzed tans. The nymph next to me smelt alluringly of jasmine and tanning butter. We the sun-drenched. The rising hum of the brass singing bowl sent a sudden resonant shiver down my spine, and I fell into the easy tempo of my breathing as he instructed. The rhythmic rise and fall of my chest; the sandalwood incense warm and heady. Breathe. *And so from breath to breath I am.* It was exactly the same with the whale. I do remember that by the end of our dance what remained was a complete sense of oneness that made me think the Buddhist monk was on the right track. The whale is a state of 'knowing.' Knowing all that I needed to know, and knowing that *I* was all that I ever needed. Maybe *I am* the whale, I cannot say for sure.

What I do know for certain is that later on that day after the storm, I watched a whale cry. It actually shed tears. And that is an image which has haunted me ever since.

ര⊛ൟ

They say that the hardest acts to follow are children and animals. I would like to put it on record here that the hardest act to write for is a mystic whale who insists on me discussing time and space!

As I write these words, the black whale remains close by and she quietly urges me to speak this truth. So I hope you will accept the following with good grace, bearing in mind the difficulty I face in presenting it to you whilst remaining true to the original cetacean storyteller.

So here is that wisdom she would like me to share with you. It begins to explain *who* we truly are and just *what* the hell we are all doing here. After a great deal of thought on my part, the best way that I can translate the imagery that my friend the whale imparted is to give you this exercise that I would ask you to now try for yourself.

Find a blank sheet of paper and place it flat in front of you. Any size piece of paper will do. Mid-way down from the top of the left hand side, draw an '*x*' close to the edge of the page. Now, at the mid-point of the right hand side, draw another '*x*' once again as close to the edge of the page as possible. Finally from the first '*x*' that you marked, draw a straight line across the width of the paper from left to right, joining the '*x*' at the far left to the '*x*' at the far right. And before you ask, I am not going stir-crazy and neither have I touched any of the drugs that the heavies were peddling around the unit this morning.

Let us say that the first '*x*' that you drew represents 'You' in present time and space. In the human form that you presently find yourself in, time can be considered as a rigid dimension. The line that you have drawn represents the path that you must physically traverse across time in order to reach some point in your future. That future point is represented by the second '*x*' that you drew so neatly, way over there on the far right edge of the page. Thus in our human form we are at the mercy of the fourth dimension – Time. I say we are at its mercy in the sense that as physical beings we are condemned to travel it in a straight line, moving from the present toward some fixed point in the future. We shall call this method *'travelling in linear time.'*

If you could magnify the neat pencil line that you drew and examine it up close, we would see that it is not in fact a perfectly smooth line; rather it is a series of '*x*'s all joined up point to point along the line that you drew. The more that you magnify the line, the more '*x*'s reveal themselves. In other words we move forward constantly from moment to moment. Day to day, hour to hour, minute to minute and so on. Now, I'm quite sure I haven't told you anything thus far that you didn't already know, but please stay with me. Let's pull back out of fine focus and return to our original exercise of joining those two points – the present and the future.

The most important point that needs to be made at this stage is that in travelling in such a fashion, you are compelled to experience every single minute step along the journey. Your conscious mind is not registering every single microscopic instant along your path but mark my words at a deeper level of your being, in your virtual 'black box flight recorder', you are recording and processing every single event in each and every millisecond of your life's journey! *For some reason you are on a deliberate journey of experience.*

And that leads me to the next point. Look again at the flat piece of paper lying in front of you, neatly scribed across its middle with the straight line that you drew joining present and future. As you consider time flattened out before you, let me begin by asking you this question. Travelling this straight line laid out before us, do you think that we may rightly refer to ourselves as time travellers?

I am going to suggest to you that the answer to this question is 'No', at least not in our human form. If you were to throw a stick into a fast flowing river and watch it float away, carried by the current; would you call it a swimmer? No, the stick is at the mercy of the waters in which it is immersed and it is simply being carried along by the flow. And so it is with our beings in physical form. Time carries us along with it as surely as the tide carries driftwood along until it finally reaches a faraway shore. And so in our human form night follows day, winter follows fall and the years pass like the steady falling of leaves.

Don't throw your paper away just yet my friend, as the best is yet to come! In order to explain the next step I must firstly hark back to an observation that I made earlier on. You may have missed the significance of it, engrossed as you were in hand sketching that neat straight line across your paper. I mentioned that in the *human form* in which *we* find ourselves, time exists as a rigid dimension.

Let us make an important distinction here: the 'we' that I refer to here is not in fact our physical body, for that is little more than a neat costume to clothe us. Our essence, what *we* truly are is a conscious energy form – an essential stardust which permeates and animates the outer shell that we see as our human form. This is truly *what* we are. *Who* we are is a function of the collective sum of our experiences, shaped by the life lessons that we take on-board as our physical vehicle makes the steady measured crossing over the blank potential of time.

When we started this conversation, I told you that the whale explains that this might begin to explain who we are and what we are doing here. We have touched a little on the *'who'* we are, so how about a little more on the *'what'* we're doing?

Our life here on Earth is really just an experiential journey, and our human form merely serves as the interface through which we interact with the physical world. It is a convenient sensory vehicle via which we see, hear, smell, touch and taste. It slips neatly over us like some flesh-and-bone glove puppet, and through it we sensually reach out to others as we journey across the physical plane. So through this body we Live.

We fall and we skin our knees.

We cry.

We quietly share our lunch in the playground with the tearful shy girl who accidentally left hers at home.

We break hearts unthinkingly and uncaringly, only to then have our own heart painfully broken but the person we had trusted the most.

We mix beer, wine and spirits. At least once we try to mix them all in the same glass.

We lock our keys in the car and work out how to get them out again using only a simple wire coat hanger.

We buy waterproof mascara but still manage to end up with panda eyes.

We chase love in a series of hit-and-miss relationships, seeking that impossible perfection.

Then we fall quietly in love when we least expect it; when we're not looking for it.

We come to the realization that we didn't need someone who is perfect, but rather someone who is perfect for us.

We bring life into the world and realize it brings with it both responsibility and vulnerability.

We watch them take their first steps and ride their first bicycles.

When they no longer need us to pick them up when they fall, we grapple with the notion that our children came from us, but somehow do not belong to us.

We wonder about 'belonging'; some leaving partners and homes in an attempt to find it.

We begin to sense the passing of an age, and realize that we are aging. Some of us more comfortably than others.

We desperately try to fit into the old pair of stonewash jeans we used to own twenty years ago, for the high school reunion.

We try vainly to recapture our lost youth, and talk excitedly about revisiting the wild old days of mixing beer, wine and spirits.

We feel that old sense of youthful rebellion.

Then when it comes to the crunch we think the better of it, buy some takeaway and snuggle on the couch together and watch a movie; far more comfortable with painting the town a sensible beige rather than a gaudy red.

We finally reach a point where we can accept ourselves warts and all, and truly love what we have become.

We lose our life partner to Death, and a small part of us dies with them.

We age and wither, and on our death bed we cry out for the mother who brought us into the world and gave us life.

Life. Through the sensory world of physical dimension, that shard of essential stardust that You are transforms and ages on a bittersweet journey. It is our long slow trek through time that makes this so, for only in this way can we truly experience action and consequence, cause and effect. Aging and growth.

Look once again at your piece of paper, scribed with the trek of your human vehicle across the timescape. I would now like to give you an insight into just what You are truly capable of, when you are not in physical form.

Imagining yourself now as the essential You, free from the restrictions of your physical body, I would like you to pick up the piece of paper and fold it so that the two 'x's meet and overlap. Your flat piece of paper should now be a cylinder, and the straight time-line is now irrelevant, as the two 'x's representing your present and future now overlap one another. You have folded space and time to instantly transport yourself from the present moment to that future point. And so it is with your essential form. Freed of the constraints of the human vehicle, You are no longer limited by linear time! Time and space can in fact be folded, so that physical distance becomes an irrelevance.

If you have patiently followed my explanation so far, I would like to complete this exercise with one final step in order to show you the full potential of your essential form. Imagine now a multitude of 'x's dotted randomly over your blank page of time. Draw some on in random spots if it assists you to visualize this. Draw as many as you like.

OK? Now, crumple the paper up into a ball. Imagine if you will that all the 'x's that you drew now all precisely overlap each other inside the crumpled ball of time. A conscious decision by your essential self re-opens the ball of time and lays it out flat again. And in that instant, You can transfer to any one of those multitude of overlapped points you choose, instantly re-locating Yourself to that point in time and space. Time is a strange thing, you see; and outside of the physical world everything that ever happened or will happen in time is occurring all at once. At some point in the process You are potentially at all of those reference points in space and time at once, until such time as You make a conscious decision to re-locate to one specific point. For the geeks amongst you, we call this the ability to *travel in superposition*.

Or put another way, You have the inherent ability to be *everywhere* and *everytime*.

Perhaps at this point you are asking 'If we possess this truly amazing capacity to leap through time and space at will, why would we even contemplate incarnating in such a primitive human form?'

Perhaps that question may be best explained like this. A prison sentence is often referred to as 'doing time.' To punish a person for a misdeed, society removes that person's freedom. The prisoner forfeits the right to move about at liberty. Instead he is confined to a defined space where he must remain for a pre-determined period of time, in order to reflect on his actions and make amends for them.

In the same way, it can be said that in your present human form, you are also 'doing time' in order to work on your shortcomings – to learn and to grow. Your 'prison' is the confinement on an elemental plane of being, where time only travels in a straight line.

Our true essence knows that it has the ability to be everywhere and everytime, but the knowledge of this ability is all but lost to us when we are in physical body. There is good reason for this forgetting – it allows us to focus fully on the physical experience without distraction. It allows us to fully experience the 'wakefulness' of Here and Now. The experience the moment, and then the next moment after that. And so on. My aquatic friend urges me to stress the importance of this understanding. With further incarnations, a state of knowing begins to develop as we wake from our corporeal slumber. The closer that we come to journey's end, so the more we begin to touch upon our true essence and potential. We have truly been on the journey of a lifetime, or more correctly a journey comprised of *many* lifetimes.

To travel in linear time is also to grow and to resonate in accordance with the natural rhythm of things. To experience day and night and the progression of the seasons as our planet 'breathes'. There is a harmony which we become a part of, and in doing so we become one with a greater harmonious whole. The whale interrupts and corrects me; begging me to honor the latter by referring to it as 'the Harmony.' For it is the Harmony beyond all harmonies, she says; if that at all makes sense.

At this point you may decide to do one of two things, and I leave the last step to you without judgement. You can take all of this as a flight of fancy and simply toss the crumpled up paper into the black hole of your wastepaper basket. Or, if you feel so inclined you can carefully unfold the 'time ball', consciously choose to be in the Here and Now, smooth it out and finish the exercise by writing neatly somewhere along the bottom of the page *From breath to breath I am* to reinforce the message to yourself.

These are rather important understandings to grasp and if you feel so inclined, this might be a good time to pause, find yourself in a quiet place and time with your favorite herbal tea or brewed coffee and just *Be*. Perhaps fill your sacred space with a nice earthy incense and breathe.

The whale is always close and she waits for the day you reach a point in your journey Home when her message will resonate at the very core of your being. At that point in time and space you'll be truly ready to meet that essential Self and realize your place in the concordant whole. The Harmony, she says with a quiet respect, belongs to each of us. And we each belong to It.

 C3❂80

Chris Mackie glanced at his watch. It was an overly large one, even for his pudgy wrist; a heavy brushed-metal divers timepiece. The black cardinal points had almost completely worn off the chunky outer rotating bezel, and he could practically hear the sweep of the second hand with the boat's twin diesels now switched off and silent. With the squelch turned down on the VHF radios in the cramped wheelhouse, the sound of water lapping against the hull slapped a relaxed counterpoint to the muffled static white-noise grating from the chipped metal speaker box above his head. It sounded like sandpaper on ice he thought, privately impressed by his own sudden eloquence in describing it in such poetic terms. He really must write a poetry book someday. Now that would really impress the girls.

Raising the Zeiss binoculars to his eyes he ran a slow sweep of the calm waters out to the north, feeling rather like the proud master and commander of a frigate at the blockade of Trafalgar. The thrill of the chase always stirred these crassly bold sentiments in him. They were close and he could feel it in his bones.

Glancing up at the thick scuds of low cloud overhead, he sniffed at the air like a squat bloodhound. There is some vague intangible; the subtlest of feelings which many people report experiencing when whales are nearby. For those who make the chasing or the catching of whales a profession, this is often referred to as a 'whaley' sensation.

Just between you and me, the reason for this sensation is revealed by a closer inspection of the fundamentals of the Harmony – all matter is vibration, and whales are not only very well attuned to this fact, but they are also highly capable of manipulating this basic fabric of time and space. Those gifted with the Attunement will recognise the almost ethereal distortion of the space-time continuum which they are capable of effecting at will. To be in the company of dolphins as they perform this is to experience a distinct sensation of 'missing time' as you become enveloped in the localized warp that they deliberately create. But we shall hold their secret as sacrosanct; an insight shared discreetly between you and me as true lovers and protectors of the whales and dolphins. Chris Mackie was not such a person, and his interest in the enigmatic ocean dwellers was a motivation born merely out of greed and vain self-interest.

After three successful and lucrative seasons of trapping orcas, Mackie seemed to hold a franchise on tuning in to that whaley sensation, and his buyers knew it full well. As the respect grew and the money rolled in, Mackie's ego had grown as large as his waistline and his reputation. At forty years of age, and standing barely five foot six in loafers, he had taken on the stature of a squat cannonball; a far cry from his halcyon years as an ex-life guard turned commercial spear fisherman in the Gulf of Mexico.

The gas embolism that caused a nitrogen bubble to lodge dangerously in his spinal cord and threaten permanent paralysis put paid to 'a promising career and a lucrative business', to quote Mackie's own words. Just how lucrative his spearfishing enterprise had actually been was the subject of some conjecture.

In truth, the boasts of booming profit from the self-styled 'Mouth from the South' were largely bluster designed to increase his appeal with the 'bar bimbos' as he referred to them – the young nubile tourists who had been drawn to the sun and sand lifestyle of the Keys whom he plied with endless cocktails and in the fug of their giggly inebriation, sought to entice with stories of his wealth and fame. A large wallet and a faded lifeguard's shirt had been the tools of his insalubrious trade. Athletic as he was in those days, Mackie was no oil painting and his loud arrogant swagger did little to bolster his appeal. The leering, misogynistic barbs which he freely hurled at the affronted young women grew in direct proportion to the inevitable knockbacks which he increasingly received. After the dive accident, the wallet became progressively thinner and the lifeguard shirt ridiculously tighter around the bulging midriff. The fact that he couldn't see the sad incongruity between actuality and warped self-image further added to the pathetic absurdity of the situation.

The truth of it was that the hunt for red snapper in the Gulf was heavily labor intensive, with long hours of toil invariably laced with the inevitable fisherman's tales of 'the one that got away' variety. Unfortunately in the game of commercial spearfishing, a few days in this vein meant the loss of hundreds, if not thousands of dollars. It came as no surprise then that a man of Mackie's lower ideals, inflated sense of self and the desire for the adulation of pretty young women, led him to adopt some less than legitimate business strategies to make ends meet. Dirty pool was played, with some unscrupulous skippers taking to stealing the GPS co-ordinates of lucrative dive spots off of other operators. Mackie wasn't averse to paying off rival newbie crewmembers in return for some good inside information. Despite his best efforts, the business began sliding. In truth, to be a successful long term fisherman in the commercial spearfishing game, you had to be a canny businessman and an operator of good repute. Sadly Mackie was neither.

In a way, the gas embolism that had temporarily crippled him and threatened his future health had in some ways come as a blessing in disguise. Using this as a legitimate excuse for abandoning a haemorrhaging business came as a serendipitous face-saving move, and Mackie left the Sunshine state behind, chalking the whole encounter up to bitter experience. The ensuing years were marked by a lifestyle of beer and bad eating which transformed him physically to the point that bluster and old stories no longer coaxed a second glance from the painted ladies at the bar. So Mackie turned to bigger fish in order to up the ante.

His journey took him north to Alaska, on the promise of big money from one of his apparently endless stable of 'good buddies'; the portly ex-lifeguard traded the sun for the snow and the ice chill of Sitka Sound in Alaska's desolate south. A place where the vista of cold sea and sky often blur into starkly unbroken shades of gray. It perhaps came as no surprise that the majestic pods of shining black and white orcas that cleft long wakes of white across the drab seascape as they breached in formation caught the eye and the imagination of the man.

At the time, Mackie was 'riding shotgun' in a small spotter plane – a tiny two seat Piper Cub, more reminiscent of the old fabric and wire airplanes of the Great War than their modern day predecessors.

High winged, and equipped with oversize tyres to accommodate snow landings, it resembled a slow ungainly white albatross wearing a pair of clumsy over-sized black boots. The little single engine plane served its purpose well however, despite its ugly duckling appearance. From three hundred feet above the Sound, Mackie and the pilot had a grandstand view of the migrating schools of herring that they were pursuing. More correctly, their high vantage point allowed them to easily sight the brownish-gray herds of marauding seals and the ranging black orca pods that were attracted to the schooling herring. Where there is smoke there is fire, and the gatherings of these predators in the choppy gray waters below easily telegraphed the position of the running schools of prized fish.

Mackie kept up a running radio commentary to his mate's trawler below, vectoring the *Easy Lady* toward the run of plump herring. Using the little Cub was a stroke of genius – as the pilot rolled into a steep bank to port, Mackie could see the two dozen Ketchikan trawlers tightly clustered down below; wheeling around each other in confused circles and drawing long churning furrows of disturbed water in their wakes.

Fishing grounds the world over have been shockingly depleted by Man over the years, and a fisherman's lot is no longer an easy one. The catch has become smaller, the demand for fish greater, and the competition fiercer.

Each tiny boat was jockeying dangerously close to its competitors; all looking to gain the upper hand on their rivals in order to drop their circular seine nets right into the midst of the herring run and thus grab the lion's share. The Sitka Sound herring fishery was set and regulated by the Alaskan Department of Fish and Game and unlike many other fisheries it was not dictated by a set closing date. Rather it was based on catch numbers – once the season quota was reached, an official radio call to all boats, broadcast across the hailing frequency marked the end of proceedings.

As the days wore on the battle hardened old skippers knew that fortunes would be increasingly made or lost in the cast of a net, or the position of a boat. Last season a crewmember had died of exposure after falling overboard into the icy sea. Crewing here in the Sound was no place for the meek. Mackie, with his eyes riveted on their boat in the confused mêlée frantically called out the course changes to Leroy in the *Lady's* wheelhouse, aiming to plant the trawler square into the school which was changing directions wildly.

The court findings were fair but damaging nonetheless. Both captains had taken instinctive, narrow avoiding action, distracted by the breaching killer whale pod. Whilst neither the *Easy Lady* nor the *Shadow J* carried the legal culpability for the collision, the hull loss plus the subsequent downtime and lost income on the season were enough to put Leroy Blake out of business, and Chris Mackie found himself once again out of pocket and out of a job. The *Easy Lady* rusted quietly for a period in a Ketchikan dry-dock before the breakers hammers finally took to her and stripped her down for salvageable parts. Mackie however refused to rust away; back-broken like the shabby old Alaskan veteran.

They say the name Alaska is derived from an Aleut word meaning *'Great Land.'* She is a rugged and wild majesty – a land of impressive mountains and deep, high-walled fjords. But she is also surprisingly a land of contrast and extremity; a place of fire and ice. Slow-moving glaciers are countered by fierce volcanoes, and ice floes complemented by bubbling hot springs. She is also affectionately called the Last Frontier, not only by virtue of far-flung location, but also because of the wellspring of opportunities and fortunes which were born here in the past.

Here on the frontier, for Chris Mackie the seeds of a new idea had similarly been sown. The misfortunes of his past weighed heavily upon him. So by the time that he arrived in Washington State waters aboard his newly acquired ex-survey vessel, purposely painted to resemble an all-black man-o'war, Chris Mackie was a bitter, angry little man.

CHAPTER TEN

SHADOW BOXING

'You will never catch a shadow in a darkened room'
—LEN VARLEY

MERCURY VENUS EARTH Mars Jupiter Saturn Uranus Neptune Pluto.

O-B-A-F-G-K-M-R-N.

The Sun. Sol. G3 Classification; warm yellow.

Red-orange-yellow-green-blue-indigo-violet.

Black.

There is a man standing in the corner of my room. At least I think it is a man. He is bipedal, upright. He has no face; nothing by way of facial features or fine anatomical detail. Rather, he is a silhouette; a shade. And yet tangible somehow. Real. A shadow endowed with the intensity of perfect substance. He seems to be dressed entirely in some sort of shiny black wetsuit. It covers him completely from head to toe, giving him the appearance of a slick rubber mannequin. I don't like his energy. He runs towards me suddenly, and then is gone. Yet the fear and the sense of death that he evokes is terrifyingly real. Who is he? *What* is he?

A lesser mind might make slanted connection to fetish or distorted sexuality. The tightly glistening body-hug of black neoprene suggesting cloistered secrets of bondage and subjugation. I say a lesser mind, yet the thought did occur to me, now didn't it? Maybe that is the explanation for all this. Perhaps I am that lesser mind?

After it happened I talked to close friends about the dreams and the whale. About the sudden intrusion of the terrifying black figure. They listened to my tale with a polite detached interest; nothing more, nothing less. It strikes me as an odd reaction. I wonder if they listened to the survivors of Belsen or Auschwitz with the same courteous reservation. Nodding sagely and intently at the soul-wrenching recount of tales of the gas chamber and random death? It frustrates me, the lack of engagement. Frustrates and confounds me. Maybe they are in on the joke? After allowing them time to ponder the gravity of my words, and receiving the same muted response, I resign myself to the sad fact that I must deal with this largely alone.

It brings to my mind the story of the Spaniard Cortés and his conquistadors who plundered the lands of the Aztec and the Inca. It is said that the sight of his armoured men riding on horseback was a sight so alien, so foreign to the eyes of the Mezo-American natives that they simply could not distinguish between horse and rider, and decided that this was some strange creature outside the scope of their imagination. Beyond their primitive frame of comprehension. In the same way it seems my friends cannot begin to comprehend my dilemma. Nobody really can.

The prison psychologist seems friendly and matter of fact, in a perfunctory sort of way. Balding and middle aged, his spreading bulk seems to pour into his large high-back chair in an oddly surreal Dali-esque melding of fat and leather. His breathing has an annoying nasal wheeze, and every so often I catch the whiff of stale coffee breath. The signs of vainly deliberate pulling and teasing of sparse oily hair at his liver-spotted temples suggests that the good doctor is in the formative stages of a bad comb-over period. I become aware that my body language is hunched and instinctively closed, and as he fusses over reports and papers, I slowly and deliberately open my posture and try to visibly relax despite my wariness.

I decide not to tell him about the dreams. About the whale. The glistening black figure in the corner of my room. Perhaps if I did, he too might nod sagely, leaning forward off his high back leather chair with politely intense interest. Perhaps. Most likely he would take to the writing of reams of notes in the dog-eared folder perched on the corner of his cluttered desk; boldly underscoring some entries with an accusing red pen. Pausing momentarily to swivel around and select an imposing volume from the polished wooden bookshelf behind his right shoulder; to pore over the scholarly weight of scientific discourse by some lofty explorer of the human psyche. His reverence and respect rising in perfect proportion to the number of credential letters behind the author's name.

Perhaps, in a perfect moment of studious navel-gazing, he will arrive at some psychological epiphany, proudly announcing:

'Mr Svenson, it appears that you have (*insert some very large important scientific word here*)-osis.'

'Ooooh, that sounds terrible. Can it be treated Doctor?'

'I have absolutely no idea, but I'll prescribe you some nice chemicals that will make you feel better about yourself in the meantime. Here. Take some of these. And these.'

'Thank you so much Doctor! My goodness, I do feel as though a tremendous weight has been lifted!'

'Oh, come now. Don't thank me, thank our wonderful modern medicine!'

Beaming broadly, we sing a rousing chorus of *Kumbaya* together, then proceed to the warmly mutual shaking of hands. The healer and the healed. And with that we break camp and raise flags to mark the bold conquest of the summit. Our journey across the ice complete. I head to the nearest Starbuck's for a celebratory coffee, and greet a welcoming world with an unaccustomed lightness of step. The doctor retires to the solace of his quiet corner office, and busies himself with the sweaty hunched perusing of wigs and kinky fetish clothing from the sordid on-line specialty site which he increasingly frequents.

No, I don't tell him about the dreams, or the whale. Or the ominous black intruder. And I leave time travel strictly out of the discussion.

Tap-tap-tap. TAP-TAP.

The impatient tapping of a pen against the wooden corner of the desk becomes progressively louder, and the room pulls back into fine focus. The doctor glances over his thick glasses at me, his voice flat but measured:

'This is your general psychological assessment Mr Svenson, to check on how you are progressing here and to determine what intervention by way of treatment needs you may require.'

My prison report folder lies open on his desk. After a few brief jottings and businesslike rustling and reviewing of pages over glasses perched precariously on the bulbous stub end of nose, a series of seemingly unconnected questions ensue; apparently some sort of a psychological 'join-the-dots' game. I answer each question truthfully.

'Were you exposed to violence as a child?'

'No, sir.'

'Any history of domestic abuse? Did your parents argue or fight?'

'No sir, not at all. I had a good family life and we all got along fine.'

You nosy old bastard....

'Would you describe yourself as an angry child?'

'Only when my mom served Brussels sprouts, Doc.'

No reaction.

'Do you ever want to have sex when you are angry?'

'Well no, that would be the last thing on my mind.'

'Have you ever been at risk, or entertained thoughts of self-harm?'

'No, never.'

Though if these stupid questions continue I may be at risk of harming certain others….

'Do you like to watch violent movies?'

'No, nature documentaries are more my thing. But I do watch Fox News regularly, so I guess you could say fiction and comedies are also high on my list.'

I follow that with a wry smile. There is still no response from the humourless old doctor.

He glances up from his paperwork at long last, looks me in the eye for the first time since I walked into his office, and smiles. Not in a condescending way. Rather, he smiles along with me. Perhaps I have passed judgement a little too prematurely. Putting down the expensive looking gold clutch pen which he has fussed over since I first sat down in his cramped office, he draws back in his chair – a spreading belly protruding over the thin leather belt – and finds a comfortable seating position for his large frame. The overworked chair groans woefully in protest.

'How are you coping with prison Mr Svenson? What bothers you?'

The whale insinuates herself and responds; I spontaneously blurt out her words playing inside my head:

'We are a species of pretenders.'

There is a strangely keyed flatness to my voice.

'How do you mean?'

His professional curiosity is piqued by my left-field observation.

'We pretend that what we do doesn't hurt others.'

'Go on…'

I fumble for words. For context. The whale has gone and I am on the stage alone. The good doctor seems a little unseated by my outburst. He weighs it and decides upon another investigative tack, following a trail of psychosomatic crumbs like some loping festive bloodhound.

'Let's talk a little more about your offending behaviour. I see that when you were arrested, you had been trespassing on private property?'

'Yes, that's correct. I worked as a crewmember on the ship.'

'And you were removed from employment earlier that day?'

'I was sacked, yes.'

'Yes, that's right.' He turned away to the bulky file on his desk again, smacking his lips thoughtfully.

'For theft and property damage?'

'Well, that was the official explanation. I had a disagreement with my boss. Doc, this sounds like an interrogation. It wasn't the navy. Do you want my rank and serial number?'
I immediately regret the dryly sarcastic resistance. Fortunately the doctor seems unfazed and continues without distraction.

'It seems to be a little more than just a simple disagreement, Mr Svenson. The transcript says you also violently assaulted another employee. You had on your person a stolen camera belonging to your employer, and evidence also suggests that you had made attempts to open the, what is it, the water taps to the inside of the ship?'

'The sea cocks in the engine room, yes.'

I shut my eyes tight at the sudden recollection. I am dancing with the whale again. Then the dark shape reappears and rushes towards me. The memories flickering in amber fire around the insides of my darkened head like the eerie silhouettes thrown up from an old mechanical shadow-play projector. As always it ends in a blinding flash which feels like sharp needles in my temples.

The doctor takes my momentary distress and my tired welling tears to be symptomatic of my regret. A good sign. Progress is being made, he thinks to himself. His body language; his indifferent observational stance softens noticeably. The protruding fat belly relaxes, and I can all but hear the pained sigh of relief from the straining leather belt.

'Do you think I could have a glass of water please, Doctor?'

Grateful for the breathing space that it allows, I look at the proffered glass with the fascination of a person seeing something for the first time. I take quiet comfort in it somehow.

'Water is seldom still,' I muse to myself.

Turning the glass around carefully in the light like some quiet remembered dream. The water is hypnotic. Enticingly familiar.

'What exactly do the sea cocks do, Adam?' the calm voice continued, coaxing me out of my reverie. I realize he has been watching my reactions carefully all this time.

The night had closed in. The harbor all but asleep in the soft small hours of the morning. The darkness hid the white angularity of hulls and masts, but the wet lapping of water and strained creak of rope spoke of their restless restrained presence. Despite the heat of the previous day, the steel bulkheads in the bowels of the ship were cold to the touch and weeping moisture from the day's earlier humidity. The cramped engine room smelt of sweat and old diesel. Amidst the confused run of cooling pipes, the heavy sea cock took some shifting from its closed position. A thin coating of rust had built up despite the lubricating slick of oil against exposed metal thread. I applied steady force to the knurled red circular handle atop the gate valve, barking my knuckles painfully against an adjoining water shroud as my hands slipped suddenly from the damp metal. A low gurgle became a steady wet rush.

'The sea cocks will effectively scuttle the ship if they're left open.'

'Sink it, you mean?'

'Yes, sink it. Scuttle is the term.'

Shadows. The shiny smooth black figure in the corner reflected the veined scatterings of light in the darkened room, his work complete. I held the side of my head; cradled it like a fractured limb. Why did he do that? What gave him the right? I felt oddly small. Vulnerable and childlike. The frustrated confusion of tears welled up again, against the rising pain and the sense of violation. Questions. Many questions, but no answers.

'Was that wise, do you think?'

'Hmmm?'

'Opening the sea cock to cause damage and risk life. Was that wise?'

Frustration gives way to anger; rising like a heavy sodden gourd in my innards.

'*Wise?* What the hell would you know about wisdom?'

I grab the smug psychologist by the scruff of the neck, bashing him roughly against the oak bookshelf – his hallowed repository of perfect human knowledge.

'We are nothing! *You* are nothing!' I am screaming, blind with sudden rage;

'Fuck your books and your human science. *And fuck you!* Two-and-a-half million years of evolution to spawn you – a simpering half-simian full of your own fucking self-importance!'

The pasty-faced fat man cowers in terror, pathetically raising one pudgy hand in a half-hearted protective gesture against my railing fury. Undeterred, I hammer his scalp with a heavy book, catching sight of the gold-lettered spine as it bounces onto the floor. *The Ascent of Man.* I am aware of the hysterical edge to my laughter, pealing maniacally at the neat irony of the title.

'You fat overstuffed fuck-up!' I spit venomously, 'A whole planet and you've fucked it. Bled it dry. Raped it, like it was yours for the taking!'

I am rising and whirling like the avenging Fury, all writhing snakes of hair and blood dripping from my eyes. Wheeling and tearing papers and books from their quiet resting places in a whirlwind of righteous rage. The maelstrom opens; compliant and hungry like a gaping wound in time. The deafening roar of it rumbles and moans as the fat psychologist and his cluttered office slowly disappear into it like so much detritus. Eyes wide in confused terror, his gelatinous form becomes skewed, distended. Nothing in his quietly measured scientific journals could prepare him for this. Drawn elastically by the rolling curl of vortex, he is pulled along with it like so much fat lint. Sucked into the whirling vacuum until he becomes nothing more than a wet pin spot, deep down in its yawning epicentre.

Silence. Measured, total.

A clock ticks comfortably on the far wall, dutifully measuring time. Outside, the industrious chirp of small birds continues, oblivious to the human interplay going on in the old red brick building.

'Adam,' comes the patient voice.
'*Adam!*'
The punctuation of reedy nasal breathing is jarringly loud and obvious in the still silence of the small room.
'Hmmm?'
'Adam, you drifted off.'
Breaking his steady scowl of quiet concern, he takes to scrabbling a fat thumb and forefinger over the stapled reports in the folder. There. Finding a particular loose-leaf typed document, he scanned it briefly; sucking his tongue in small clucking noises before delivering the measured summation like a sentencing judge:
'Your medical report shows concentration difficulties, which the prison doctor attributes to severe mental and emotional distress.'
I do not grace the observation with a reply, allowing the good doctor to fill the void in space:

'He reports you have experienced recurring nightmares, or bad dreams as it were. That you are often withdrawn and reserved. You were prescribed medication by your family physician prior to entering prison, but this was discontinued at your request, is that so?'

'Yes, Doctor. The medication didn't seem to be doing much for the nightmares, so I stopped taking it.'

'And you've refused similar medication whilst in prison for the same reason, yes?

'Yes.'

'Have you ever taken any non-prescription drugs, Mr Svenson? Marijuana? Amphetamines or ice?'

'No doctor, I'm not a drug taker.'

'How often do you consume alcohol? I mean before you came to prison, obviously.'

Obviously….

'I don't really drink much at all, sir. The most I would have would be a beer or two on special occasions, or a dinner out.'

'So no history of substance abuse at all?'

'None whatsoever.'

'Are you telling me the truth?'

'As God is my witness, Doc.'

Sucking in his tongue once again, the good Doctor looked me in the eye once again.

'Adam, I'm approving your re-classification as minimum security. Your offences were extremely serious but appear to be very much out of character, given your background and prior clean record. I am however recommending that you serve out the remainder of your time in a low security rehabilitation facility. Your progress reports note a general lassitude and sometimes confused behaviour. You remain generally pro-social but with a tendency to withdraw on occasions. I would like to see you moved to a more positive environment which better caters to your needs. Do you understand?'

The sudden implication takes me by surprise, and hits me like a savage, wet slap.

'So you're saying I'm crazy?'
Even as I speak the words, I am aware of the twinge of sudden desperation in my voice.

'No, not at all Adam. Quite the opposite in fact. My reading of all this is that you are emotionally exhausted. At your mental wits end, so to speak. You've let all of this get to you. Your sacking. Your offending. Your time here in prison.'

His soothing tone does nothing to assuage me. I ignore his studied professional opinion; a diagnosis limited by my partial disclosure. He doesn't know about the whale. Or the missing time.

So, I'm crazy. There it is. I stare dolefully at the glass. Gazing through the elemental ether and feeling the pull of sorrowful yearning. The water is still. *Why is it still?*

'I see that you have already been undertaking some voluntary personal development courses here, with some very positive feedback from your facilitators.'

'The courses have been good. I've done my best with my time in here to better understand my situation. To make sense of things,' I counter; subdued, contrite.

That wasn't a lie. The whale shines a wry glint at me, my co-conspirator in spirit. My head is heavy and I feel thick and confused like someone in the fog of post-operative ether.

'Yes, I'm pleased to see you've made good progress towards your rehabilitation.'

'Thank you Doctor. It certainly has been an effort, coming to a point of understanding it all.'

A nod of approval from the whale. A synchronistic nod of approval from the shrink; his work done here. Another scrubby penitent on the road to moral recovery. He closes the large creased manila folder and beams at me with an almost beatific smile. Pompous ass. For one fleeting moment I actually consider belting him with his hard bound copy of *The Ascent of Man* just for good measure. After weighing up my options, I choose discretion as the better part of valor, and decide to leave well enough alone.

'I'll put the paperwork though this afternoon, so you can expect a move in about a week. Your unit officers will assist you with any further questions you might have in the meantime. Good luck to you, Mr Svenson.'

With an offhand wave he gestures toward the door, signifying the end of our official proceedings.

Case closed.

Svenson, Adam; Federal Bureau of Prisons ID #KAR403847. Reclassified *'Low Risk'*. Recommend transfer to minimum security rehabilitation facility. Re-evaluation required before release. Unit and medical reports noted; inmate's general behaviour and attitude satisfactory.

The world does not exist as we think it does. Green grass and solid rock. Our senses mislead us. Or put more correctly, they do not tell us the whole story. It's a little bit like the iceberg. Our physical senses only ever collect a narrow band of available information from our surroundings. So we only ever exist in a sliver of what is actually there. Grass only appears green because our brain is converting electromagnetic waves into color. That chunk of rock is really ninety-nine per-cent empty space, yet our brain insists that it is solid. How much of what is going on around you are you not seeing?

Here and there the knots of shabby green clad prisoners lounge and chat. The endless turn of days continues unabated, unchanged.

Punctuated by the constant backdrop of card games, the thugs and the heavies hovering around the pool table still recounting their glory days of dealing drugs and death. The coarse shouts and the blue language. Every second word is 'cunt'. Nobody ever seems to be able to talk quietly in this monkey cage. Heavy, low vibrations that give the air the literal consistency of treacle. It drags me down until I feel I can no longer rise above it.

Vibration. That is the one thing that I have distinctly noticed since the maelstrom – the vibrating and rippling of every single thing. Ripples that overlap and play against each other. How have I never seen it before? And color. Not just the color that we see with the human eye. Every vibration creates its own color. Every thought and every passing emotion colors us. And what they say is true – you really *are* green with envy. Red with rage. Or feeling blue. And that 'color' can remain with us if we let it. Until we take it on like a chameleon. Leaching down into our physical bodies and taking root, and making its presence known to us in the distortions of cancer, disease and malignancy.

Black. The shape shifter in the corner of my room intrudes again. It is the absence of all color. A nothing, as it were. And yet, it is a nothing with a very real and tangible presence. Does it represent good or bad, and what is its intention? There's the thing – only in opening the box can I possibly know if Schrödinger's cat is alive or dead. Right or wrong. Good or bad. The time is fast approaching to open the box.

Unlock the box. Where have I heard those words before? I constantly feel as though I am searching for jigsaw pieces in a junkyard. The pieces are there, hidden carefully. Placed deliberately. Scattered in small corners of my mind which I never knew existed. I can *see* them, but only at those times when I don't actually *look* for them. Does any of what I'm saying even make sense?

Coffee. Give me coffee. That will fix everything. My head hurts and I distractedly pour myself a cup of very average prison brew and sit in the quietest corner of the common room. *Unlock the box.* The sharp *unlock* crack of cue ball against *the* wood slaps angrily against my consciousness *box* like wet leather. My head hurts. No, actually hurt is not quite the word. It feels different. Unbalanced somehow. As if some vitally small segment has been carefully removed with a scoop. Re-sculpted and re-assembled differently. I see careful strands; molecule chains re-forming. Performing a slightly different curved dance. One-two-*four*-three. One-two-*four*-three. Same rhythm but a slightly different sequence. What does it all mean?

UNLOCK. The distress rises in a sudden nauseous wave, beating to a sudden crescendo. *THE BOX.* Rehabilitation facility is such a neatly sanitized antiseptic term. Politically correct and far more palatable than lunatic asylum. And I swallowed the bait so easily. Maybe the good doctor was far more cunning and calculating than I gave him credit for. I was played! Gazing vacantly I gulp at my coffee, a bitter aftertaste rising. Maybe I should have belted him with that book after all. A lunatic asylum. Yes, that would explain everything. *UNLOCK.* The dreams, the episodes of anxiety. The paranoid wash of imagery. The black whale. The wetsuit. *THE BOX.*

The whale first appeared to me just two days out of Friday Harbor. And she has been with me ever since. I feel the sudden urge to contact Maree. To hear her sweet voice. To anchor me to reality; to some quiet remembrance of my life before all of this. To *normality*. Before I am snatched away like so much flotsam. Yes, that term is so very apt. Flotsam.

I am little more than floating wreckage.

They came for me just after breakfast, and I gathered together my meagre belongings from my shabby shared cell in B-wing. This in actuality took little more than fifteen minutes, for my possessions are woefully few. And now they sit on my stripped down bunk, zip tied into small plastic bags. A rising wave of sadness washes over me and becomes a deluge. An outpouring. I lift one tiny plastic bag and examine it timidly, childlike. I have a writing pad, a few envelopes. A bundle of letters bound together with an elastic band. Three pens. A few toiletries in an old plastic container. Photos. Of Maree and Tin-Tin. A nice old shot of me aboard the *Belle*, hair dishevelled and grinning like an idiot; my buddy Top Notch surfaced and chirping, mouth open like a comedic gray photo bomber off my right shoulder.

And then the tears come. Heavy sobbing tears which I cannot stop. I am surprised by the sudden unexpected reaction. Surprised and confused as to the meaning and the cause. I allow the waves of sorrow and despair to wash over me without further examination or judgement. The sobs wrack my body, and a simple glance at my meagre belongings merely evokes a further rising of tears. I close my cell door so no-one will see me. I feel vulnerable and alone.

The sorry looking bundle lying on my bunk is all that is left of me. All that I have become. *All that I am*. And that, I decide, must be the source of my pitiful sorrow. Or maybe it is because I no longer know just *what* I am any more.

CHAPTER ELEVEN

TICKING

For man's Karma travels with him, like his shadow.
Indeed it is his shadow, for it has been said,
'Man stands in his own shadow and wonders why it is dark.'
—ALAN WATTS -'The Spirit Of Zen'

THE TRACK THAT Mackie had carefully plotted out for the two vessels had neatly bisected the course that Shadow's pod traced as they passed tangential to the nearby protuberance of coastline. They had been making their way toward the meeting ground of the Three Pods. Mackie's canny sense of reckoning had in fact placed the *Pacific Dark* right into the centre of her pod, effectively splitting the pack into two as he came in from their seaward side.

His seasoned eye had picked up the dynamic in the instant that the nursing mother breached immediately alongside the *Dark's* port side. Sweeping the waters around the ship, it wasn't long before he found what he was looking for; a ragged vee of four towering triangular fins surfacing on the starboard quarter, about a quarter of a mile further out to sea. Those were the 'men-folk' of the pod, flanking the mothers and young protectively and ranged around the perimeter of the pod as scouts.

Mackie's pudgy right hand danced quickly on the chrome throttles, cribbing back on the power in order to lose a little forward speed. His head craning feverishly left and right to scan the restricted view from the broad rectangular side windows. A clutch of stubby black fins breached close on the port side, the tinier accompanying fins marking the juveniles amongst them. Mackie called to his quartermaster alongside him at the chart table:

'Get on the blower, Buzz. Tell the *Jonathan Lee* to go out wide of us and cut those bulls off.'

The interception had been near perfect. He matched speed as best he could with the fins now paralleling his course, pleased that he had so neatly divided the pod. A dull throaty roar issued from just behind the small starboard bridge-wing. With both bridge doors swung wide open for better visibility, the outside noise reverberated through the bridge. The *Jonathan Lee* barrelled past the open door, heeled over in a curving arc which would effectively cut the bull orcas off from the rest of the pod, and scare them further out to sea.

With the *Lee* now making way off his forward quarter, Mackie could now make out the sister ship's ungainly profile. Smaller and more nimble than the *Pacific Dark*, the *Jonathan Lee* was equipped with a towering structure atop the fly-bridge roof – a tuna spotting tower – giving the ship a top heavy look like a grubby white mobile crane. They were close enough for him to make out the two crew with binoculars high above the waterline in the enclosed crow's nest atop the tower.

The squelch on Mackie's VHF radio array was broken by a sudden broadcast; the voice loud and clear through the overhead speaker by virtue of the other ship's proximity.

'Chris, you've got all of 'em on your port side. Swing out a little wider for a few secs then close them down back toward the inlet. We have six bulls cut off out here.'

Mackie nodded his acknowledgement of the call to his bridge mate, and swung the wheel out to starboard. A sudden astringent burst of fresh salt air blew through the open bridge as the big ship answered the helm and swung its black nose through the wind. The little cannonball of a man could imagine the thrill of an old Yankee whaler heeling on a broad reach with the wind filling the big sails with a sudden crack of billowing canvas. He felt his blood surge with the thrill of the chase.

'Tell the *Lee* to give me regular updates, and get Svenson to call me up regular reports from the foredeck. And ready the RHIB for launch.'

On the after-deck of each vessel, a small inflatable boat, or RHIB was slung high over the stern railing in a pair of davits, ready for the close-in chase. Mackie knew the mother ships would need to stop to launch the small boats, and visually selected a point inside the looming mouth of the inlet to anchor the *Dark*. Running his sightline from that point, he swung the black hull back into the pod, shepherding them hard left toward the inlet.

The bleak overcast made the sighting of the whales that little bit harder. It turned the choppy waters a complimentary shade of gray which effectively disguised the ebony orcas until they rose to the surface for breath.

'Svenson counts about seven young 'uns in the pod, boss.'
The unshaven quartermaster leaned in from the platform of the port bridge-wing.

'OK let's nail these motherfuckers. Its payday, buddy!'
Mackie was living his dream, and now the money was all but in the bank:

'Radio the *Lee* and tell them to drop their RHIB now. The inlets coming up and we don't wanna over-run it.'

Abeam the towering steel slab of hull, Persia and Tristesse were running alongside Grace and Aura. The two mothers had swung instinctively between the dark intruding monster and their youngsters, trying desperately to fend off the danger. Persia struggled to pick up the frantic calls across the pod from amongst the deeper pitched mechanical noise of propellers and diesels. They had changed their calls up to higher frequencies to make themselves heard over the lower baritone blatting of the hunters' ship.

The pod was loosely trailing behind Shadow, and in her slipstream Persia sensed the old matriarch's confusion with a growing sense of dismay. Always the cool deft navigator despite her advancing years, Shadow's course changes were now hesitant and uncertain. To her left, her sonar had registered the shoaling bottom and the shoreline coming up dangerously close. She knew she needed to move the pod to the right, toward the safety of open water. But each time, her feint move to cut across the bow of the interfering hull was easily defeated. With over two dozen orcas straggling behind her, she knew there was little chance of them all making the dash. Her nervous energy telegraphed through the shallow waters, and the pod began to break ranks in fear.

Persia overtook young Constant; tiring rapidly and struggling to find her mother in the confused melee. The pod was now running for its life. Up ahead Shadow was commanding a dive, but with the seabed rapidly rising up to meet them, this was becoming a vain impossibility. Sweeping the area with her sonar, Persia had already picked up the welcome gap in the shoreline up ahead and swung deftly toward it, taking the pod obediently with her.

Up in the cramped wheelhouse, Mackie could now clearly see the gaggle of orcas wheeling frantically towards the wide inlet, and he continued pressing home the attack. He jockeyed the big ship around the sleek shapes with deft pulses of power. The engine note of the powerful twin diesels rose and fell in concert with his nimble adjustments at the throttle quadrant. Dark oily clouds of diesel drifted around the superstructure and mingled with the fresh tang of sea air.

With the pod under control, Mackie took stock. The *Jonathan Lee's* inflatable boat with its crew of six was now in the water and rapidly weaving about the periphery of the pod like a sheep dog; nudging the stragglers back into the loose stream which was funnelling into the inlet. Beyond that lay the blind bay, which the crew would quickly net off behind them. Mackie counted the fins on the breach, making out the youngsters amongst their mothers. Only one or two males remained, but one was yet to be seen. Mackie pondered the thought. Where was the alpha male?

Almost on cue, the frantic yells and gesticulations from his crew amidships answered his question. A sudden resounding thud made the hull shiver and for a moment Mackie wondered whether they had hit an obstacle in the shallow water. Mars had charged the black hull as it came to a stop, hitting it squarely amidships with the force of a blunt torpedo the size of a dump truck. It was enough to rock the boat wildly as the hull steadily lost way through the water. The impact had dazed the massive orca and he surfaced like a punch-drunk boxer beside the *Dark's* solid black flank.

Catching the ship as it swung back through the vertical like a pendulum, Mackie's hand punched the chrome throttle levers once again. Whooping with delight, he swung the ship on differential power, fish-tailing the aft end toward the dazed orca. Deliberately gaging the proximity of the propeller shafts to the orca's drifting bulk; he pushed the paired throttles through the gate and felt the blades shudder as the big ship swung to.

The twin brass screws tore huge gouges of flesh out of Mars' flank and threw them skyward in a bloody flume of churning water. As the mighty orca rolled reflexively in pain, the sharp scimitar-like curve of accelerating blade tore through his broad trailing pectoral fin, all but ripping it away from his body at the root.

Mackie eased off the throttles, the severity of the jarring vibration through the prop shafts bad enough for him to fear that the heavy watertight seals may come adrift and flood the ship. In the sudden silence, Mackie could hear the distant chorus of surprised yells from the crew on the after-deck. Pushing past the dumbfounded quartermaster, he grabbed the digital camera from the drawer under the chart table; pushing it into his offsider's hand.

'Get aft and get some photos of that dumb son-of-a-bitch. Asshole needs to learn some fucking manners, trying to ram my ship like that.'

☙❧

The stench of blood and newly exposed viscera was overwhelming, even for a couple of the more experienced members of Mackie's crew. It didn't seem to upset the blocky little man though. These days very little did. He kicked at the closest body, more to roll it into a position to look into its small dead eye rather than out of any sense of spite or malice. Though still a juvenile, the lifeless blackfish still presented a solid, imposing sight. The corpse was easily as large as a small pony; its pink tongue lolled to one side, endowing the whole with a rictus of painful death. Already starting to bloat, the once streamlined body now appeared grotesquely accusing to the fat man, and he knew that they had little time.

Unlike the younger men who stood by awkwardly, Mackie appeared determined. Businesslike. He cast a quick glance towards the distant curve of roadway, hidden from view behind the stands of dry salt bushes high above the beach. There were no onlookers, but he would need to move fast nevertheless. The noise and commotion often drew a crowd, fascinated with the mechanics of the capture. Today they had managed to sling and load the live catch without an audience, but now that the dead whales had been retrieved from the nets the plump black and white bodies lay accusingly in the shallow water. Mackie had quickly formulated a plan to avoid further complication.

'Slit 'em open, guys. Right down the belly. And grab some of those big rocks.'

He motioned towards the nearby groyne with one stubby finger. Two of the rookies gladly complied and took to collecting a pyre of loose granite, grateful to be upwind of the rapidly decaying carcasses. The taut black skin was already bubbling and expanding along the dead animal's upper surfaces after the heat of the noon day sun. Up to his knees in water, Mackie busied himself with making fast a thick length of rope to a cleat on the nearest RHIB. He threw the other end roughly towards the closest deckhand.

'Lash that around the tail,' he commanded, 'we're gonna stuff these suckers full of rocks, drag them out and sink them in the bay. The rocks will weigh 'em down.'

Secretly he hoped the powerful outboard would take the weight. The last thing they needed was a field day for the local press. Two of the younger crew staggered under the weight of a gray slab of rock, before dropping it into the gaping maw in the dead whale's belly.

'Don't weight 'em down now, jackass! We'll never drag them out off the beach with the RHIBs that way.'

He loaded a couple of rocks into the closest inflatable boat himself, demonstrating the method for the dog-tired crew.

'Load the rocks into the boats, boys. We'll weight the bodies down after we've towed 'em out into position.'

He softened – heartened by his lads' quick compliance.

'And someone make ready to shift that net enough to let us out.'

Since the deliberate ramming of the bull orca, Mackie had sensed the shift in mood. The elation of the chase had rapidly been replaced by something approximating a simmering solemnity. Still, the day had been long and spirits were flagging following the exertion of the capture. Now that the prize catch was on its way to the floating pens, the boys were quietly hankering to wind down.

Mackie, ever the master of subterfuge and coercion, pressed them to stay focussed on the business of the clean-up. He kept them busy; making as light of the debacle as possible, whilst casting a roving eye secretively on each crewmember's demeanour and responses. Remove the rotten apples before they poison the rest of the barrel, he thought to himself.

Beyond the taut line of yellow floats, strung like gaudy beads across the mouth of the bay, the surviving members of Shadow's pod gathered. Restrained by the vile criss-cross of netting, they huddled together protectively as the light faded on them sympathetically. With the harsh daylight gone, the bay took on an almost serene countenance, painted in more sombre tones of deep aqua and purple. The late afternoon breeze which had blustered its way up the inlet had fallen steadily away as the orcas spy-hopped together hopefully; bobbing up and down like so many shiny black bulbous corks. A noisy flock of gulls dotted the beach, screeching and arguing amongst themselves over the piled entrails lying in the surf.

After the cacophony of sound that had accompanied the capture – the rasp-toothed sawing of outboards, the blunt yells of the crew and the high-pitched calls of the pod; the ring of darkening hills above the beach had fallen into a breathless eerie silence. Pushing up against the rough net barricade, Aura and Grace surfaced together disconsolately, pectorals fins brushing gently; their daughters now the latest victims of a stolen generation. Their breathing, when it finally came was subdued. Dejected. In the gathering stillness, their cries carried over the netting as low, mournful notes punctuated by the gentler sighs and questioning squeaks from the remainder of the pod.

Shadow bobbed fitfully, readying herself to say final goodbyes before shepherding the survivors back to the relative safety of open water. And Mars. What state would she find her mighty Mars in when she re-joined him? Anticipating Shadow's imminent move, the younger males had ceased their spy-hopping and taken to circling the gathered pod, preparing to escort them through the restricted neck of the inlet.

On the shore, the hunters were making ready for their final unexpected task. With two of the dead orcas now roped securely against the sides of the RHIBs, the precious silence was once again torn by the raucous note of powerful outboards. The sound ran like wildfire through the pod. Fearing a renewed attack, Shadow placed the muster call urgently and tail-slapped the becalmed waters. A dozen bobbing black corks slid backwards into the bay; flick-turning the length of their long axis whilst submerged to take advantage of the shallow draft of darkening water to make good their escape.

With the threatening bulk of the *Pacific Dark's* hull rocking slowly at anchor off to one side of the inlet, the young bulls drew in tighter around the pod, urging Shadow to speed her selection of the exit track. The metal hull loomed large as they passed, continuing its lazy side to side motion in mute reply. The tight rank of the pod slipped past with a sullen wariness.

By the time the pod had transited the inlet and felt the reassuring surge of ocean once again, the hunters had already manoeuvred the limp eviscerated bodies of Constant and Oberon into position at the deepest point of the bay.

∛❅√

Persia traced her usual path around the periphery of the lagoon. Sensed without seeing the jutting bulk of submerged sea wall. The rocking slap of backwash pushed at her persistently as she scudded through the warm water with long easy strokes. She welcomed the scant exercise it provided and tightened against its opposition. The water was a deep green murk and it felt nicely welcoming as she immersed herself languidly in it. Her dorsal fin cleft a fine swirling ripple through the salt water, tracing out her slow endless circles in a faithful symphony. Beneath the surface, diffused swathes of mottled light broke the solid darkness of weed encrusted rock; marking the rusting bars of the old gate. She could close her eyes and feel the proximity of the gateway on each lap. The ingress of water through it came as a fresh surge of brine, pulsating and alive. Small schools of fish, shining like silver dollars followed it through the grill. Occasionally the mottled brown tendrilled squirt of a curious squid or octopus rode in with the pulse. Hanging motionless; suspended like some odd tentacled spacewalker before contracting and diving in a pencil-like blur for the protective cover of nearby rock.

Persia coasted past the entrance each time, allowing the in-rushing sea to carry her temporarily in its familiar drift, like the old times, before she left it behind with a deft flick of peduncle and broad tail-fin. She loved the feeling, and she expectantly looked for it each day. It gave her hope. It meant that life still existed beyond the bars. The familiar beckoning of tide and current insinuated itself into the lagoon; bringing with it all the wild promise and imagination of open sea before succumbing to the private soliloquy of the rocky sea pen. It reminded her of home.

The young orca could make the transit around the entire lagoon easily with her eyes closed. In fact she was beginning to prefer it that way. Until it occurred to her that this was the steady path of recession and withdrawal that Tristesse had taken not so long ago. Poor little one. She was painfully missed, but still alive in Persia's memory.

Her paced quickened, causing the backslap of water in her wake to increase until the water's surface was alive with ripples. She would not give up hope. She would hold out and keep herself strong.

He would come back for her one day, she knew.

Wooomph-shhhh. The staccato punch of her breath scattered the small flock of gulls that had congregated in the shadow of a stand of palm trees. They quickly resettled, ignoring the coating of fine wet mist on their flight feathers which would quickly dry in the heat of the day.

CHAPTER TWELVE

SCAR TISSUE

*'The birds possess an honour and courage that man does not possess.
Man lives in the shadow of laws and customs which he made and fashioned
for himself, but the birds live according to the same free External Law which
causes the Earth to pursue its mighty path around the Sun'*
–KAHLIL GIBRAN

I AM TIRED. Right now all I want to do is go home. I am ready. I'm sure that everyone in my situation voices that same threadbare yearning. For me though, I have the creeping sensation of a destiny calling. The distinct feeling that my time is fast approaching.

The dreams continue. Some days I can recall them, and other times the information remains tantalisingly hidden from sight. Days have slowly become months, spent mentally tilting at windmills. And sometimes I feel that I am no closer to either solution or reconciliation. But then maybe that is just how madness insinuates itself.

I have conjured up several possible words for myself and it seems many of them are 'D's if indeed that fact bears any relevance or key to my condition.

Delusional. Disturbed. Demented. And one underlying it all – Denial.

Ockham's razor offers a bold suggestion. I am currently in a rehabilitation facility, surrounded by mentally challenged individuals. Go figure. Maree remains a perfect constant and despite the pain of our separation she playfully reminds me that if I continue with this random line of soul-searching the only 'D' I will end up as is Divorced. Or Dead. She has been my rock through all of this. And I am Devoted. There – a new label. That one sounds so much better.

I have been cautiously aware of my state of mind ever since arriving at the rehabilitation center. Being moved here has been an immense shock to my system; a damning indictment of my mental state. And now finding myself surrounded by the criminally insane, it is slowly becoming harder to hang onto that promise that I made myself all those months ago – to remember who I was, no matter what.

There is something to all of this which studiously defies human logic; which perhaps I am not yet ready to acknowledge as bold reality. An intangible. Darkly enigmatic, and my straining Aztec eyes simply cannot comprehend the astounding sight of it raising billowing canvas sails on the curve of my imagination. I swallow hard and deliberately open my eyes wide. I make the conscious decision to see the truth of it, and if this means the acceptance of madness or worse, then so be it.

It is a clear crisp morning and the trees surrounding the rehabilitation center are perfectly still. The change of environment and the relative freedom of being outdoors seem to be doing my mental state a world of good. My world has suddenly expanded itself from cramped clamouring enclosure to a broader serene vista of open space and fresh forest air. Though the bars still remain, I feel a difference in vibration. As I write, a scattering of green parrots busy themselves with picking amongst the broad swath of newly mown grass alongside the old dormitory block, unaffected by my close proximity. Their distracted chatter is the only noise that hangs in the stillness of morning air around me.

The scent of fresh cut grass is wildly pungent and heady. It reminds me of lazy Sunday mornings. Nature is slowly claiming sway here, and the wire of fences and restrictions seems quietly subjugated by its rule. Eclipsing this entire scene is a sky washed in a watery pastel blue, and from it the autumn sun insistently warms my back and shoulders. It sends a warm contented tingle up the length of my spine to the nape of my neck. I ponder that sensation. *Contented.*

The feeling catches me unaware, and it strikes me as something of a jarring contradiction, given my present circumstances. I smirk to myself. At least it is not another 'D' word. Perhaps I am making my way slowly and progressively up the alphabet of the deeper mind. And surely contentment follows acceptance? A-ha! I seems I have arrived at the penultimate 'A' word. *Acceptance.* Aren't we making amazing progress today then, Adam?

And if that follows, then what is it exactly that I have accepted? I look carefully, and count seven different shades of green in the surrounding landscape. Could it be that I have accepted my place here?

Drawn by the quiet stillness of the day, I decide to find myself a secluded spot to sit amongst a peaceful grove of sycamore trees at the extremity of the lawn area and investigate this feeling a little more. An inmate in a wheelchair paddles his way up the slope of concrete walkway across the broad lawn, breathing heavily with the effort. Apart from him I am alone with my thoughts. Seated comfortably, my thoughts return to the question of contentment and acceptance.

I'm now being referred to by both the medical and prison staff as a 'short timer.' A heartening sign. Having been poked, prodded and generally observed over the weeks since I arrived, it seems the powers that be are more or less satisfied with my state of mental health, and I hope that in a few short months they will return me to the world. To me this all feels like it has been no less than an eternity. Times works that way, you see.

So, could it possibly be that my quiet sense of contentment means that on some level I have accepted this place as my home? It can certainly be said that there is a greater measure of freedom accorded to inmates here in the low security rehabilitation complex. There is the relative luxury of being able to wander the grounds outside into the late evening. The hard-core heavies of maximum security are left behind. The threats of bashing, gang violence and the drug culture ever-present but now distinctly diminished. Mellowed and replaced by the more real and pressing concerns of mental state. Thankfully, once again there is the welcoming solitude of a large library. Larger and better equipped than the narrow old bookshelves in the pen. And as ever, it is the hallowed sanctuary from the hurly-burly which renders me a welcome breathing space in which to collect my thoughts. My first day of arrival was spent here, simply touching the books and inhaling the reassuringly familiar scent of ink and binding. *Remembering*. Like an old friend; a sensory reconnection with a far more comforting reality.

So – back to the question of acceptance and contentment. Consciously returning to the scene that triggered this moment of introspection, I decide to take it in, as one might meditate upon the steady intake and exhalation of breath, or upon a solitary thought. Perhaps my answer lies here, and I simply allow the moment to take me where it will.

I can once again feel the whale, dark yet reassuring against my back.

Minutes pass, and the more that I allow it, the more an innate sense of connection and deeper understanding pervade my sense of being. In that quiet introspective moment, the warm fingers of sunlight which have never once broken their reassuring embrace on my shoulders whisper something to me. That I am recognised and loved as a part of something bigger than myself and my present predicament. A green bomb-burst of parrots take flight, passing closely around me to left and right, close enough for me to see the streamlined beauty of their clean lines, and aerodynamic splayed feather array. The small eyes simply acknowledge my presence momentarily before they are gone, in perfect aerial balance. This is new. Has something changed, or was I simply not aware of this before now? Within those eyes – albeit for no more than a fraction of a second – I can now recognise the quiet passive acknowledgement of life force.

We are so many, yet we are One.

In that sublime acceptance we are recognised by the One, with all our faults and our failings and we are lovingly welcomed. We are enough. *I am enough.* A feeling of infused amber fire deep in my solar plexus returns once again, and in the shiver of that perfect moment my question has been all but answered. In this unexpected awakening, rushes of golden moments re-introduce themselves in a perfect frisson; rising in flood like a spring tide.

Standing on a flat rocky outcrop with the cloak of evening chill around me, watching the steady twinkle of stars in the upturned bowl of night sky.

A shooting star perfect and alone over open water.

The splendid display of crimson and gold picking out clouds and painting the western sky to mark the going down of the sun.

Each moment brought me to hushed reverent silence, as surely as any temple or shrine. Each moment endowed me with the same perfect contentment, and quiet reassurance. Anchored me to the Here and Now, yet promised me far more beyond it. *We belong somewhere.* In a larger sense, we have an essential place of belonging, and wherever and however we find ourselves is simply just another step on that long journey Home.

Some find a sense of peace in the base level of contentment that this place offers, but by and large it is precious little more than simply a yearning of the flesh. An imprinted memory. Base desire;

food, clothing and shelter. But we have a choice. To accept where we are, or to transcend it.

This place – this prison – is not my home. It exists as a realm which lies tantalisingly close to the physical world that we all share a quiet longing for. The pull of that world draws us; each of us for reasons of our own like a siren call, and yet it remains inaccessible. Out beyond a stern partition of metal and wire. Something in the acknowledgement of this sends a dread chill down my spine and the now familiar 'body jolt' grips me once again.

Where am I? Where is this place? *When* am I?

The people around me here, save for a few exceptions, are little more than shells. Sleepwalkers. Still given to living out a cycle of old familiar patterns – hatred, anger and violence. Lust and perversion. They seem to see nothing more beyond that. Seem to desire nothing more beyond that. Maybe as my old cellmate Dave said to me, this is a prison of their own making; either haunted or enthralled by the sins of their past.

For me though, the heart and spirit quietly pine for more. I feel different, *look* different. I realize something that I have known deep down from the very start – I am not one of the sleepwalkers. Somehow, I do not belong here. I am living a life of meaning and purpose.

Lived a life, rather.

In the days that followed, I found myself on something of a personal quest to further understand a little more about the notion of 'equality'. You see, there is an inequality that a prisoner senses every single day that he languishes within these confines. It is very hard to feel any sense that you are the equal of anyone outside these four walls. In here there are constant reminders of position and standing. My identity card simply describes me as *'Prisoner'*. I received an official notification slip the other day, titled in bold as a *'Notice to Offender'*. Stung by this address, and painfully aware of the accusatory labelling, I coursed through all of the explanatory jargon on that official slip, to find that the word *'offender'* appeared no less than ten times.

It seems that the system is hell-bent on reminding me of my status. It matters not that I have performed a great many good deeds throughout my life, or that I have given so much of myself for the benefit of others. I am now simply defined by a solitary criminal act, and no deeds or evidence to the contrary can seem to balance the scales. It becomes extremely hard for me to now see myself as a good man, despite the fact that I should know better. Dear reader, I no longer feel myself to be your equal because I have been judged so by a jury of my peers.

But, here's the thing I have realised since then – they say that nobody can make you feel inferior without you giving them your acceptance. If I were to search my soul, I would have to say that in truth, it is not simply the judgement placed upon me by society that has led to my recent bouts of mental self-flagellation. More tellingly, it is a judgement which I have imposed on myself. An acceptance of my own wrongdoing. Not the wrongdoing that I was found guilty of in a human court of law, but rather, a wrongdoing that I have enacted against my own moral compass. I have passed a judgement on myself, and I am owning a greater guilt.

It is interesting to observe that even here amongst the judged, the condemned themselves decide upon who amongst them may be viewed as equals. Who is to be welcomed and accepted, and who is to be shunned. And so the judged sit in judgement of themselves. Perhaps this is a fundamental part of the human condition. Is it not true that as a race we live in almost constant judgement of one another?

We enact a set of discriminations based upon color, creed and religion. On gender and sexual preference; on body size, shape and appearance. Upon social and financial standing. Wars are fought in the wake of judgement. Slavery in a myriad of sanctioned and unsanctioned shapes and forms underscore our nations, our communities, even our marital homes. From slavery and oppression many a 'fine civilization' grew. Governments, corporations and individuals grow wealthy from it, whilst scores of others are all but crushed in its wake. O we, the inhuman race. Is there any other species on the planet capable of wreaking such multi-faceted judgement upon its own kind? Indeed our propensity for judgement extends beyond our own species.

A light-bulb moment. Going back to that 'A' word – Acceptance. It now occurs to me that it isn't a case of what I have accepted in this place. It is more a case of understanding what I have accepted in myself, and more importantly, what has accepted *me*. Because what I am experiencing is a yearning of spirit. And that yearning is increasingly being met with the reassurance that I am a part of something all-pervading; a harmony that transcends my present circumstances. I realize that I have my place. Indeed, we each have our place in it, if we choose. And we will be warmly welcomed into that greater 'something' as equals.

ೞ ❧ ೞ

It was in the late-sixties, during the 'space race' period of the Cold War era and NASA's Apollo moon landing program was in full flight. Departing Earth's atmosphere on a mission to field-test the lunar landing equipment in the relative safety of Earth orbit, it was the crew of the *Apollo 9* spacecraft who bore witness to a uniquely breathtaking sight. Forty miles high, above the steady wheeling turn of Earth, they gazed back at our planet through the ship's tiny window. As they did, they were presented with a view of our home only seen by a mere handful of privileged individuals. Breathless and in awe, they took a photograph to capture that perfect moment. What that photograph revealed for the first time, was the face of the Earth bathed entirely in sunlight. A perfect disk without shadow.

The public release of that photograph sparked a major sensation. For the first time in the history of Man, we saw our home world with fresh perspective. The cold naked eye of the astronaut's camera revealed us in all our glory. A perfect blue orb spinning silent and alone, pinned against a vast velvet backdrop of space, as perfectly as a butterfly in a cosmic display case.

In that one halting image, wars and territorial disputes seemed to fall away, lost with the benefit of vast distance. Hatred, violence and crime became matters of relative insignificance. Divisions of color and religion dissolved into one monochromatic universal. We were Humankind, adrift on a small fragile home planet that we called Earth. And we were alone.

Dubbed *The Blue Marble*, that iconic photograph remains the most widely circulated image in recorded history. That striking imagery heralded a major shift in our collective consciousness. It triggered an almost primal urge to reach out, to connect; to seek out other intellects and to reassure ourselves that we were not alone in the vastness of space. That one perfect photograph sowed the seed for programs such as SETI – the Search for Extra-Terrestrial Intelligence. I am making these observations to highlight to you one implicit, underlying fact. Whenever we are given to speculate on the existence of intelligent life forms, have you noticed where we all collectively turn?

SETI's telescopes, radar dishes and listening arrays uniformly turn themselves upward and outward; expectantly looking and listening deep into the vast wellspring of the cosmos for a kindred intellect. *Away* from planet Earth. And in this one orchestrated act we have effectively passed one definitive judgement. We have settled on this fact – Humankind has searched the world over, and we are satisfied that no other intelligent life-form exists here worthy of, or indeed capable of engaging in intelligent communication with us.

So there it is. As far as intelligent life on planet Earth is concerned, we are it. So say we all. But how exactly are we gauging this thing we call 'intellect'?

The answer to that question was framed rather neatly for me in a scene from a 1950's B-grade sci-fi movie. Picture this scene if you will – a classic looking flying saucer has just landed on the grounds in front of the White House. Seamless, polished silver. Doorless and windowless and emitting an ominously low resonant hum. A large crowd has gathered expectantly to witness the extraordinary sight, held back at a respectable distance by a knot of soldiers and military police. Suddenly, without warning, a hatchway opens in the smooth metallic exterior, and a ramp extends itself with a buzzing electric whine. The gathered crowd draw a collective breath and, after a pregnant silence, a humanoid form emerges from the shadowy interior. The unearthly visitor cuts a dashing figure in his close fitting one-piece silver suit. With smouldering movie star looks and a slicked down James Dean hairstyle, he brandishes a rather clunky and obtrusive ray-gun in one hand. He casts an assessing glance at the stunned ranks of soldiers, and then proceeds to address the gathered throng in a perfect clipped Atlantic accent.

So how exactly do we gage intelligence? Well, clearly our underlying yardsticks appear to include culture, language (preferably English, spoken with an American accent) and a clear mastery of technology. Being a good-looking bipedal humanoid specimen who nicely fills out a body-hugging spacesuit is clearly a much coveted bonus. And so by these criteria we have effectively ruled out all other co-habitants of planet Earth. Another sweeping judgement is passed. How supremely arrogant are we?

Jacob Bronowski, in his work *The Ascent of Man* observes:

'The human being is the mosaic of animal and angel'.

In so doing, Bronowski accords humankind with a capacity suggesting our greater spiritual standing over animals, or perhaps some sort of custodianship over the natural world. And if that were the truth of it, wouldn't that embodiment of angelic sensibility manifest itself in Man in the form of a benevolent, harmonious being?

Nothing in fact could be further from the truth, and I submit our woefully poor environmental track record as living proof of my contention. In just over two million years of foolhardy existence we have stumbled across the environmental landscape of planet Earth like the proverbial bull in a china shop; mortally upsetting the balance of biosphere and ecosystem as we go. We are nothing more than the master's apprentices. How blindly arrogant are we then, to accord ourselves the pedigree of angels? And what precisely leads us to believe that animals themselves do not naturally possess any form of greater connection with the world of Spirit?

Could it possibly be that we have some important lessons to learn from our fellow voyagers on this planetary ark in space? I for one believe that we do. Yet, full of our own self-importance we fail to realize this. We are not the only species on the planet who possess a defined culture and language. Indeed, on the subject of language, it is acknowledged fact that every animal has an ability to communicate with its own kind. And nature neatly utilizes every means and media available to make this communication possible, be it visual, auditory or olfactory signals. Some signals are beyond human perception in VHF and HF soundwaves; infra-red and UV light, vibration and electrical fields. All of this communication and cross-talk going on right under our noses while, dumbly oblivious, we the master species order our burgers at the drive-thru and race each other home through the peak hour crush to watch endless re-runs of old television shows!

After my brush with Top Notch, I found myself wanting to know more about this enigmatic creature, the dolphin. I read many books and I spoke to many people. I watched them up close, and saw them at their best and their worst. Working on the *Pacific Dark* with people who made a profession out of capturing them put a further dimension on my study. Here is what one of the old deckhands on our sister ship the *Jonathon Lee* told me about a bottlenose dolphin called Kelly. (If you've ever watched the TV show 'Flipper' you will know just what a bottlenose dolphin is.)

Kelly was one of the resident dolphins of a marine park, and when not performing she lived with the other dolphins in a natural sea pen. Due to the local sea breezes, the trainers were forever having to skim the surface to remove debris and leaf litter which had blown into the pool. So one day they hit upon an idea. Given the boisterous gray dolphins' natural playfulness and thirst for mental stimulation, the trainers decided to invent a game for them and solve the problem of pool litter at the same time. So they taught the dolphins to collect any trash – leaves, paper and Styrofoam cups – that blew into the pool, and to present it to a trainer for collection.

The dolphins quickly learned that by presenting an item of trash to a passing trainer, they would be rewarded with a fish for their troubles. The idea rapidly caught on and the dolphins all embraced the game enthusiastically; Kelly moreso than the others. The deep thinking Kelly had very quickly figured out something rather important. Regardless of whether she presented the trainers with one leaf, or a clump of leaves, she was always rewarded with one fish in return. So she changed her strategy, collecting leaves from the water's surface and hiding them under a rock at the bottom of the pool. Whenever a trainer passed, she would quickly dive to the bottom and remove one leaf from the hidden stash; rising to the surface to present it to the trainer and collect her fish reward. Kelly had learned the important business concept of 'profit maximisation'!

But it didn't end there.

One day Kelly discovered a dead seagull floating in the pool. She grabbed the lifeless bird and casually threw it at the feet of a trainer, and was rewarded with not one, but five fish for her troubles. Watching the enterprising dolphin, the trainer noticed that she ate four of the five fish, before diving to the bottom, to hide the remaining fish under the rock. Why? This new twist had the park crew intrigued. It seems they didn't have to wait too long before they got their answer. Later that day, as the local flock of seagulls came home to roost at the pool's edge; Kelly was seen casually trawling the fish along the surface in full view of the flock, hoping to entice an unsuspecting feathered victim. The enterprising young dolphin had taken things to the next level!

After my experiences as a rookie deckhand, with my enigmatic buddy Top Notch the story of Kelly, entrepreneur of the bottlenose dolphin world, only served to deepen my sense of admiration and intrigue for their kind. Because this, my friends is an example of the *highest level* of learning and application of a concept that any individual – human or dolphin – can possibly attain!

Charles Darwin, the noted English naturist best known for his theory of Evolution challenged the popular view that animals acted purely on instinct. His peers at the time claimed that intelligence was based upon an individual's ability to reason, and this therefore excluded animals. Darwin begged to differ. Many animals, like Top Notch and Kelly demonstrate the higher reasoning ability which comes with high intelligence. And yet, apart from a few small-scale projects and experimentations they are still all but ignored by mainstream science as a kindred intellect. We seem to be far too busy pursuing the superior notion that we have something to teach them.

You may be surprised to learn that dolphin trainers rely on hand signals to communicate with their charges. What makes this particularly relevant is that dolphins do not have hands and therefore are not able to use the 'language' to communicate back to their trainers. Of course, our human arrogance implicitly recognises this. If we genuinely sought a two-way communication, we would have used a 'common' language which could be used equally by human and dolphin alike.

And so we busy ourselves with training dolphins to leap through a hoop. Or domiciling noble tigers in petting zoos, safely doped and compliant for human interaction. Neat rationalizations are concocted to permit this abuse. The arrogant display of our dominance over other species is dressed up neatly and passed off as education. The education of our young. The opportunity for people to see a wild animal they wouldn't ordinarily see in their daily lives. The opportunity to learn about their 'habits'. Because of course dolphins leap through suspended hoops all the time in the wild, now don't they?

What exactly are we teaching our children? What messages are these displays sending? That it is acceptable for a human to dominate and subvert an animal or a 'lesser' being? And where does that dominance stop? Does it perhaps reinforce other innate social and cultural prejudices? Does it by extension cultivate a sense of superiority over others?

As long as willing patrons push their way through the turnstiles and fill the cash registers with blood money, this cunning ruse will continue. And as the unwilling performers invariably succumb to illness and premature death in custody, there are plenty of specimens either purpose-bred or captured specifically to replace the fallen ranks. Pressed into service to perform for us until they day that they too die. There is no retirement program for captive dolphins and whales.

Faced with these accusations, the dolphin trainer with the benefit of his vast experience and self-proclaimed intimate connection with his or her charges, will invariably voice a bitter rebuke:

'What do you know about dolphins? The fact is that they love to perform. They love the company of humans and they compete with one another for our attention, just like small children'.

How very superior of you, Mister Trainer. What the wide-eyed public never get to see are the cruel training methods which slowly break the spirits of these noble wild animals. The food restraint system which denies them nourishment should they fail to comply with their captors' requests. Or how a creature that will naturally range up to hundreds of miles a day with its family fares when faced with a painful solitary existence in a synthetic tank no larger or deeper than a hotel swimming pool.

Given no option but to perform amusing tricks, you will conveniently pass this off as normal behavior. The marine park veterinarian, in his turn will tell argue:

'Dolphins live fuller lives in captivity. They are kept safe in our protective care. Here they are free from their natural predators and safe from the slew of natural ailments and diseases that beset them in the wild, thanks to modern human technology and medicine. When it comes to birthing, we are on-hand to help deliver their young and attend to any complications, which could otherwise have resulted in the death of mother or baby in the wild.'

What the marine mammal vet stops conveniently short of telling you is that the natural life span of the dolphin is cut sharply and prematurely short in captivity – a dolphin that rightly expects to live for half a century in its natural environment is lucky to live a life of half that duration in the charge of humans. How exactly then are they *'living fuller lives in captivity?'*

And just where exactly do you get off playing God, Mister Veterinarian? Whales and dolphins have happily procreated, given birth and raised young, endured disease and predation and populated the world's oceans and seas successfully for the past *fifty million years* without the intervention of the 'wise man' and his medicines.

Humans. On the evolutionarily scale you are still in short pants and wet behind the ears. And yet, in your relatively short *two-and-a-half million year* tenure you are solely responsible for the extinction of thousands of plant and animal species. No other living species on the planet can boast this capacity for wholesale destruction. Not a single one. Where other creatures blend and harmonize, you destroy and bulldoze. Where a plant or an animal finds their place within the balance of life, you view the Earth through greedy eyes, and turn it into your house, your table and your dumping ground.

If all insect life on the planet were to be removed, *all life* on earth would cease to exist in less than a decade. On the other hand, if all human life were to be removed by some cataclysmic event, life on earth would continue. Who exactly are the primitives here?

Of whales and dolphins, I can say that my journey has been something of a quest to understand more about these enigmatic beings. Personally I suspect that they know far more about us than we do about them. Make of that what you will.

I feel especially qualified to make these observations and to speak these words on their behalf. I am ashamed to say that I am equally qualified to speak on the subject of their subjugation at the hands of man. Of the mistreatment of a fellow intellect which possesses a clearly refined culture, social order and language.

Long before I wrote these words, some people recognised this fact and urged others to speak out as a *'Voice for the Voiceless.'* With due respect to those good men and women I would make this further qualification. The time has come to teach others that these noble creatures do indeed have a voice. It is time for us not simply to *be* their voice, but to finally *hear* their voice. To make every effort to further understand their language and their culture. To put aside our singular superior attitude and to carefully consider our relationship with them.

Bold though the concept may be, we have arrived at an age where we need to seriously consider the forging of a unique set of non-human rights for these special intellects; as empowering and as protective as our own human Bill of Rights. Freedom is not solely the birth right of humankind, and it is time we stepped into a far wider world.

In my short career, I have already borne witness to clear acts of understanding, reasoning and compassion from our fellow warm-bloods of the deep blue. They should not have to prove themselves to us. On the contrary, with our disgracefully shambolic environmental track record, I believe it is we who have everything to prove to them.

My writing here is as much a celebration of these amazing creatures as it is an act of recompense for the harm that I myself have done them. A desire to set the balance to rights. And maybe this is why I have brought you to this point – as a act of contrition for something that weighs heavily upon my heart and soul.

CHAPTER THIRTEEN

RISING DAMP

'Meet our Orcas. They're dying to entertain you'
—ACTIVIST BANNER - 'Waterworld Protest'

SOMEHOW THE PEACEABLE old wood panelled boardroom seemed more like a bunker to Kathy Quick these days. She took in the room thoughtfully. The long polished wood conference table, the Spanish stucco wall above the dado rail lined with neatly framed photos which captured the heady excitement of the orca shows. The late director's favorite picture took the pride of place, almost twice as large as the others. The photo of Casper proudly kneeling alongside Tondo; pink mouth yawning wide in almost childlike glee formed the centrepiece of the room. Ironically the scene was captured on the very ramp where the two had clashed so tragically and finally just a few weeks ago. The blonde trainer shivered at the memory. She made a mental note to request that the picture be removed at the earliest opportunity.

Strange that the thoughtful accoutrements and trappings which just a few short weeks ago had given the nook a comfortable air of respectability and consummate professionalism – of bold direction

– now endowed it with the desperate military aura of an embattled Pentagon war-room. Kathy hunkered down into the boardroom chair, balled and catlike. A vague chill caught the air and harried it, in spite of the playfully beckoning glow of sunlight which was insistently filtering and slanting its way through the small rectangular window to pick out minute sparkling flecks of floating dust.

A noisy clattering and the astringent waft of after-shave announced the presence of Brad Manning. Kathy rolled her eyes. How the hell did the man always manage to make an entrance with the bare minimum of props, yet sound for all the world like he was toting a collection of pots and pans with him? The quaintly suburban imagery that it conjured raised a wry grin. She would be a psychologist's joy, she imagined. How interesting that his processional clatter should provoke such imagery of shackled domesticity. Was that the secret of Brad's animal magnetism, or perhaps a darker imagining pointing to her own deeper yearnings? The inevitable biological call to nest, perhaps? She shuddered at the thought and pushed it deftly aside.

'Morning, Miss Quick.'

The clatter drew up a seat alongside her and shoehorned into it, scattering keys, phone and miscellany onto the table in front of him. The random chaos of it was just like a small replica of his apartment, she thought. The musky headiness of body spray was a perfect complement to his brute outdoorsy frame. She felt the quiver of loins and the corresponding rise of wetness.

'Nice of you to join us, Doctor Manning. And so early too! Wet your bed this morning then?'

She threw the offhand quip with a clumsy crossing of legs, feeling just a little betrayed and undermined by her body's traitorous arousal.

'I guess so. Quite novel that it was me for a change,' he countered, as playfully slick as a sea otter. Eyebrow raised like an exclamation mark.

'Touché' she muttered, disguising her off-balance state as best she could with a theatrical fussing over a pile of park reports.

Since the accident, the pair found themselves carrying a lot more of the administrative hack work. It created a surface tension between them. Despite the superficial role-play of dramatics and barbs, Quick was quietly encouraged with just how perfectly Brad had stepped up to the mark as the de-facto spokesperson for the embattled marine park. He embraced the role, uncharacteristically responsible; perhaps reprising his glory days in the Solomons. She measured it against their own romantic situation hopefully; fighting down the niggling feeling that they were merely painting over the cracks.

'How are you feeling?'
The genuine tone of concern in his voice was at once comforting and reassuring; instantly de-fusing the barbed brevity of their exchange.

'I'm feeling OK. Much better. Thanks.'
Kathy felt herself softening; the dropping of wary guard. Damn it. How the hell does he manage to do that? Despite the passing of weeks, this was the first time the pair had discussed their feelings at any depth. *Discussed!* She laughed inwardly at just how pitiful she was becoming these days. He asked how you were feeling, Kath. *Once.* One brief exchange. The shellacked superficiality of it totally at odds with the gravity of the situation. A superficiality that stood as testament to the true depth of their secretive, unconvincing connection. She recognized it, all at once, and hated the truth of it.

There had been the convenient backdrop of distraction. Press interviews and coroner's reports. Media and money problems. Ongoing inquiries and public scrutiny. There was a stark nakedness to it all, and Kathy felt it pressing down on her. Microscopic, observed. Waterworld, forced onto the back foot by the tragedy, had been in a wary state of damage control. And now, the icing on the cake for Quick was the unexpected queasy bouts of morning sickness. An unshared secret, she would deal with that later.

'There was nothing more you could have done Kathy.'

She shook herself out of her reverie and measured his words. Deciding that he was referring to the recent tragedy.

'I keep telling myself that Brad but I still can't truly feel it, you know?'

'What you did on the day was textbook perfect, Kath. Believe me. I've watched people fall to pieces in far lesser situations. You couldn't be faulted.'

The knot in her gut loosened and warmed. Funny, how the body carries stress unrealized for long periods. It's not until the unravelling of it that you begin to realize just how tight its grip on you has been. Brad was only echoing the same words that everyone had piped, ever since that horrible day. Yet those same words, delivered with the benefit of qualified experience gave a firm credibility to what she already privately knew to be true. She gripped his hand and squeezed; her heartfelt thanks for his quiet belief in her.

Closing her eyes deliberately, she tried to re-invent the room. The way that it used to be. Casper busying himself with reports. Holding council at the head of the table, engaged and involved. Passionate. You couldn't help but become caught up in his energy and vibrancy. His vision. His drive became your drive somehow; a warm synergy of activity and ideas. The way that it used to be before all this. If she had that pair of fabled ruby shoes she would have gladly clicked them three times to turn back time. Red shoes. Those leather shoes didn't help Casper now did they? Put it away Kathy, she told herself. The ghosts of the past are just that. Shadows. Shades. Put them away.

A ring tone reverberating outside in the long hallway heralded Morrie's arrival. Kathy cursed silently. The abrupt pull back from her snuggled proximity to Brad was just a little too obvious, her body language smacking of guilt and seminal conspiracy. Christ, she was getting paranoid these days. Neurotic perhaps. Or hormonal. She needn't have worried though, as the hunched little businessman had neither seen nor heard, focussed as he was on fielding yet another telephone enquiry. These days the phone seemed to be fused more or less permanently to Morrie Lambert's ear.

Since the tragic loss of his old friend, the blustery New Yorker was spending more and more time on-site; tending to the myriad commercial wheelings and dealings that seemed to crop up each day. As the Finance Manager, Lambert ran a tight ship but when pushed, would openly confess to the unsettling feeling that he was out of his depth when it came to the general running of the park. Oh the irony, he mused. *Out of my depth in Waterworld.* That might make a great title for a biography someday. He lit another cigarette and inhaled hard, before entering the boardroom.

'Good morning, troops' Morrie exhaled a cloud of smoke at the ceiling; his half-hearted nod to the dangers of side smoke. 'The jury's in.'

'What's the verdict, boss?'

Brad's voice had more than a hint of expectancy, and Morrie capitalized on the moment to pause, comedically deadpan, for dramatic effect.

'Well folks, it seems I have some good news and some good news.'

'So, tell us the good news first.' Brad lightened.

'So, the good news is the preliminary report paints us in a good light. We've got a couple of minor health and safety points to address, but they're just that – minor.'

Brad exhaled an audible sigh of relief, leaning the chrome framed chair backward until it made the first creak of protest. Kathy took in the news with a vacant gaze. Leaning forward onto the glossy table with hands clasped, looking for all the world like Joan of Arc in deep prayer.

The aftermath of the tragedy had wreaked a separate toll on each of them. The elfin chief trainer did not speak for the longest time – preferring to savor the almost tranquil wave that overtook her, before finally breaking the reverie of the room:

'What did they say about Casper's death?'

'Well, they said it was an accident which could have been avoided, but Casper had breached his own regulations by being on the ramp that day. And the report acknowledged your directive to him to stay the hell clear.'

'It doesn't bring him back, Morrie. Actually it feels like we're just desperately trying to make ourselves feel better by blaming him.'

'Well I don't see it that way. Not at all. His death was a tragedy whichever way you look at it, and we need to learn what we can from it to ensure it never happens again. Hell, I want every single one of us to go home safe to our families each night.'

'Leda didn't, Morrie.'

Kathy's words touched a raw nerve with Brad. The body language was telling.

'Leda was depressed, Kath. It happens to humans, and it happens occasionally to killer whales. It's something that's out of our control.'

'Is it?'

Manning sensed the shift but couldn't quite define it. Anyone who spends time around the ocean develops an intimate 'sixth sense' for shifting energy. A sailor worth his salt can sniff a subtle swing in the breeze just before it occurs. So too do the tides telegraph their impending changes to the canny; in the same way a musician feels the spaces between the notes.

The sharpness of tongue still remained, yet Kathy was softer somehow. Glowing.

'So go ahead, somebody ask me what the other good news is!'

Morrie broke the hiatus; determined to keep the mood in the boardroom light.

'OK, so what's the other good news, Morrie?'

'Thank you very much. I'm glad you asked. The other good news folks, is we have a very healthy bottom line. And I'm not talking about your ass this time Bradley!'

He pushed copies of balance sheets across the polished table with a dramatic flourish; one for each of his deputies. Brad scanned the figures; tapping a pen noisily as if to punctuate each line of the ledger.

'Figures look good. Sales are holding steady, though we're still in early days yet.'

'True enough, though my gut tells me we're coming through this well. And the new rehab initiatives are going to build on it.'

'Well, I trust your gut when it comes to business. So how are our preps for the open day coming along?'

'We're still on track for next month guys, and thanks to you both for your individual inputs. I like to say offence is the best form of defence so the public open day is a go, and this positive report seals the deal.'

'In other business, what do we propose to do about replacing Leda?' Kathy led into the concern that had played on her mind since the loss; 'Have you guys given some thought to a breeding program?'

Brad pushed pen and paper aside, giving Kathy's question his full attention.

'From past experience, captive breeding is a complex undertaking. We would need to bring in expertise from other parks, possibly from the east coast. And it's a pretty labor intensive exercise.'

Morrie nodded thoughtfully at the marine vet's observation. Although a canny businessman, he sensibly deferred to the input of experts before making any call.

'The problem with wild captures is that we run the same risk as we did with Pandora and Leda,' replied Kathy. 'We run the risk of aggression because they're forced into an unnatural situation which leaves them nowhere to go to avoid a conflict. In the wild they have thousands of miles of ocean to escape into but it's a different ballgame here.'

'OK, well let's look into this, guys. At the end of the day I want happy families out there in the pool, and happy families here in the staffroom.'

'OK, Morrie. Happy families.' Kathy nodded unconvincingly. Happy families.

It rained the day Kathy's father walked out of her life. She remembered that only because she could still picture the way her socks and sandals had felt. Sodden and heavy around her ankles as she stood by the old letterbox with its coat of peeling red paint. Expectantly waiting for his car to round the corner beyond the old ash tree one more time. Sometimes she thought she loved that car as much as she had loved him. The plush red leather upholstery had a heady scent which made her dizzy as she rode proudly in the front passenger seat of the Thunderbird, imagining herself as a movie starlet making her way to some big gala event. Those were the days when she felt ten feet tall, with the sun washing everything with a glow that matched her father's adoring smile as he edged the big convertible easily through the loose weave of Sunday morning traffic.

She remembered that day that he left for the rain, and also for little Gypsy. That very same day her mother had quietly left the little jet black feline in her bedroom; a ball of sleepy fur, tucked carefully into an old cardboard box full of shredded newspaper.

Over the following months the pair became inseparable, the little girl and her cat.

The cat, who patiently took all of Kathy's tears. All of her grief. And in return showed Kathy an unconditional love that told her nature held a promise for her. That everything would be all right. That she would always, *always* be loved, no matter what.

Her father was the director of a large aluminium siding company, and he had talked the exact same language as Morrie – a language of bottom lines and balance sheets. When he talked business on the phone, he gave her little more than a second glance. As if nothing in the world mattered more than those balance sheets and that bottom line.

His work took him away from the family home for increasingly longer periods, and he grew to become more the stranger who popped in and out in some strange cameo, as Kathy's life rolled on. As the money grew so too did the arguments, and the Sunday drives which she had so loved in the big car became fewer. By that time however, there were other things in Kathy's life. She was growing up, and there were more pressing distractions. Boys and parties. Though of course, underneath it all she never quite forgot. None of us ever do. The hard shell of an exterior neatly covered all the hurt that she tucked up inside, just like that little defenceless ball of fur in her cardboard box. The day that Gypsy disappeared was the day her own fragility re-surfaced, leaving Kathy with the sting of a loneliness and betrayal which she had carried ever since.

Hugging her stomach protectively in the vague chill of the boardroom, Kathy could not fight the strange feeling that she had seen the fleeting glimmer of Gypsy in Leda's eye as she drew her last sobbing breath, out there on the ramp.

ʚ●ɞ

'HONK 4 THE ORCAS' the hand painted sign read. Morrie Lambert instinctively hunched lower into the driver's seat but kept his speed to the moderate pace he had adopted since turning into the long tree lined boulevard. Casual, but not too casual. A knot of ragged protesters held the signs high and jiggled them, whooping and hollering as he approached. He didn't honk. Though it didn't escape his attention that the three family sedans surrounding him did. He felt the growing flush of redness infusing his cheeks and rising to the tips of his ears.

Damn you Casper. You really left me holding the baby this time. The boulevard seemed to have transformed magically into a raucous street festival with people lining the road and spilling over the broad median strip. Colors alternately muting and flaring in the shadowy wave of the overhanging palms. At least the palms seemed to be enjoying the mêlée, swaying fronds casually in time, like the excitedly compliant pom-poms of so many leafy green cheerleaders. Music was blaring from small PA's, competing for air space with the metallic crackle of megaphones leading the onlookers in ragged rebellious chant.

Closer to the marine park entrance, the signs and banner wavers increased in number, until the streetscape became a virtual sea of signage – canvas and cor-flute artfully punctuating the milling crowd. Ragged boldface slogans teasing and tempting the eye:

'Thanks but NO TANKS.'

'Meet our orcas. They're dying to entertain you.'

'You wouldn't stick your nanna in a bathtub.'

That last one was Morrie's favourite. His creased leathery face broke into a broad grin, and he snickered nasally despite himself; feeling nonetheless just a little stung by his own betrayal.

Interlacing the rag-tag assembly were the dark uniforms, caps and badges of the LAPD. Their officious demeanour seemed somehow conspicuously formal and draconian amidst the passionate outpouring. It was not without its moments though. He trolled past one flustered old motorcycle cop shepherding three young girls dressed in black and white orca jumpsuits across the busy traffic lane, to the relative safety of the shady median strip. The youngest of the excited pod of juveniles, a beaming freckled girl with horn-rimmed glasses, innocently handed the besieged officer a bunch of yellow California poppies. Looking more than a little sheepish with a floral arrangement in one meaty hand, he waved Morrie's sedan through with a look approximating something between wonder and bewilderment. The trio of orca jumpsuits re-joined their family group to cheer and wave from under the protective sway of palms.

Alongside Waterworld, the amusement park was in full swing, the multi-colored lights topping the dim covered entranceway flashing and cascading. Heavily bolstered by the influx of protesters, the huge Ferris wheel with its multi-hued canvas covered gondolas worked its age old magic with a material vigor; turning confidently and faithfully amidst the sparkle and pop of carnival noise and the echo of gay bagatelles. The sickly sweet smell of hot buttered popcorn and candy-floss laced the air and mingled in wafts with the salt tang of the nearby Pacific.

The rising crags of twisted gun-metal architecture and industrial decay of the marine park next door appeared for all the world to be a time-worn throwback to a much older and darker world era. Morrie imagined the victory scenes that had repeated themselves across the beleaguered towns and cities of the Third Reich; color and celebration returning like so many inevitable spring buds amidst the backdrop of war – all charcoal and austere grays. The ruins of astute former glory and quiet civility razed and blackened. The imaginative post-apocalyptic dreamscape that Casper Barrett had created now appeared as a grimy portent of its own destiny. Inevitable, he thought. Was all of this inevitable?

The happy squeals of delight from the young children as the towering Ferris wheel described its constant circle overhead provided neat peaceable counterpoint to the metallic urging of protester's megaphones. They somehow seemed perfectly complementary to one another, setting Morrie to wondering as to whether his plan for the day was really sound enough to hold water.

Water. Right now it felt like he was treading water.

The airy common room had been transformed into a lecture theater; the staff lounges moved to one side to be replaced with rows of white plastic chairs, set out neatly to face the small podium. Already three or four local reporters were occupying seats in the front row, casually sipping coffees and trading small talk. Through the full length glass panel windows, Quick could see outside toward the main display pool, where the afternoon show was in progress. The sound of rock music was punctuated by gasps and applause from the appreciative crowds.

A sudden deep thud which shook the tall glass windows marked Tondo's closing power-dive through the center of the pool. Pressing through the chaos of the unusually large crowd outside, Morrie Lambert seemed buoyant and unfazed. Quietly confident, even. Shaking off his earlier misgivings as he approached the park, he was now comforted by the ragged knots of spectators. The activists who had found their way into the park were swallowed and diluted by the milling family groups and excited children, just as Morrie had anticipated.

The park had taken on a vibrancy and life, and the presence of the activists merely underscored it with an electric expectancy. Rather like the build-up to a stadium concert, a wave was rising. And Doctor Manning, in presenting the exciting news of Waterworld's new rescue and rehabilitation program was the perfect man to put the stamp of credibility to it. Already, threads of curious spectators were drifting in and studying the impressive static displays set around the periphery of the room. A large drift net hung suspended across the row of floor to ceiling windows. The web of rough sisal ropes and weathered white floats softened the ambient light and cast the softest of shadows across the sea of plastic chairs, making the room cool and inviting. Set in front of it was an imposing full-scale model of a sea turtle, the net falling from the ceiling tangling and lacing itself around two of the model's broad flat swimming flippers.

Wide-eyed youngsters gazed fascinated at the huge glass aquarium. In it, a spawn of leathery flippered baby sea turtles dotted the bubbling waters. Newly born and still assimilating; their movements were ungracefully jerky and random, rather like a score of dimpled brown helmets beetling their way through the water.

'Who let the fucking greenie in here?'

Brad Manning's voice had a hysterical edge to it. Enough of an edge to draw Morrie away from the small talk he was making as he circulated the room, getting a feel for the prevailing vibe. The little New Yorker drew him into a corner of the room nearest the glass paned doors, out of the earshot of the clutch of reporters who were gravitating toward the row of seats nearest the small podium.

'What's the problem, Brad?'

'That's Shannon Jasper.'

Morrie followed the accusing finger to the far corner of the room, where a tall bleached blonde with an athleticism rivalling his chief trainers was dropping a rucksack and a bulky file on a vacant table.

'So?'

'So, what the hell is she doing here?'

'She's doing a presentation on killer whales, why?'

'She's presenting? What exactly? Why the hell did you choose her of all people?'

'Well Brad, the fucking Queen of Sheba was unavailable at the last minute so I took second best. She's a goddamn marine expert. What's your problem?'

'My problem is Jasper has made her views on captivity pretty crystal clear in the past. She's poison, Morrie. Poison. Damn it, why in the hell would you call her of all people?'

'I called her in Brad. Me. Not Morrie.'

Kathy insinuated herself into the conversation, sliding around Morrie's squat bulk to face off with the fuming marine vet.

'*You* called her? What, so you're adding crazy to your resumé now too? Did you even consider asking me, or are you calling all the shots now?'

Brad's words were spat with an unnatural venom. Kathy recognised it and knew it had become personal.

'You, as I recall,' she countered hotly, 'didn't even bother to show for the meeting. Don't you read the damn minutes?'

'Listen, you don't go making decisions like this when I'm not in. You know as well as I do we need to be very careful about how we come off.'

'First off, Brad, I'm sure you were 'in' someone. Just not in the fucking meeting that you should have been.'

'That's not very funny, Kath.'

'And I'm not laughing, Brad. Second, if we're operating above board – which from my side of the fence I can assure you we are – we should have nothing to worry about. We'll 'come off', as you crudely put it, just fine.'

'OK you two. *Enough.* Shut the hell up and listen to me for a sec. Whatever your private beef with each other, just deal with it. *Privately.* See a counsellor, spank your inner monkeys; I don't care, just get it done. While you're on duty I expect you to both behave like the senior staff that you are. We're on display here.'

Morrie paused for a beat to allow the sentiment to sink in. Deftly continuing before either of the pair could interject:

'Kathy made the call and quite frankly as senior behavioral trainer it's in her ballpark. Brad, if you weren't at the meeting – you snooze, you lose. Hell, I know you two are under a great deal of strain, we all are OK? I need you guys working with me on this. Now excuse me, I've got work to do.'

Clapping the pair roundly on their shoulders as if to signal the end of the matter, Morrie wandered off to settle into a round of rousing handshakes with two local news anchors, all smiles and banter.

'If this turns to shit, it's on your head, Kath.'

Manning was not about to letting the matter go.

'If this turns to shit, I'll shoulder responsibility and wear it, like always. Brad.'

Turning abruptly on her heel, she threaded her way through the throng of milling onlookers, feeling both stung and galvanised by her lover's acid attack.

At the table, Shannon Jasper had pulled her hair back into a ponytail. It seemed to somehow complement the black multi-pocketed cargo pants and sky blue top, in a sort of a para-military kind of way. Eco-warriors, thought Kath, dismissing the idea almost as quickly as it came.

'Hi Shannon, I'm Kathy Quick, the chief trainer. We spoke before on the phone.'

Kathy wondered to herself why she felt she had needed to assert her position. Perhaps Brad's tirade had put her on edge unnecessarily.

'Oh hey, Kathy. Yeah, I've been very much looking forward to finally meeting you.'

The hint of Canadian twang in her lilt was succinct.

'Have you got everything you need for your talk?'

'Yeah, Morrie's shown me the projector set-up. Just my slides and I'm good to go. You've got a great turn out today.'

'Yes, it's kind of beyond our expectations. Did you manage to get down to the main pool?'

'I did. I've spent almost an hour and a half down there with the orcas.'

Shannon picked up the slight shift in Kathy's expression; a fleeting glimmer of awkwardness. A sadness almost.

'Andrea and Doug were just great showing me around.' Jasper shifted awkwardly; 'Look, I know we come from different sides of the fence as far as captivity goes, but I kinda want to clear the air from the get-go. I know that you care for the orcas and I want to say that I truly appreciate that.'

'Thanks. The thing is we do genuinely love and care for these guys. More than most people could know.'

'I guess by 'most people' you probably mean us lot from the '*If you love birds put them in trees not cages*' camp!'

Kathy relaxed her guard somewhat and conceded a thoughtful smile.

'Our marine vet refers to you as a fucking greenie, by the way.'

'Really? Oh well, I've been called far worse.'

'I'm sure.'

'Hey listen, I know you were at the pool during the incident. And I wanted to say I'm really sorry. I know that you did all you could.'

Kathy pondered the striking blonde's turn of phrase, deciding that the term 'incident' rather whitewashed the whole frightful affair. Her breath caught in an involuntary sigh as she re-lived the curious light-shift as life passed for orca and human.

'I did my best for Trist… for Leda. And I did my best for Casper. And I lost them both.'

Shannon sensed the sudden pained ripple and immediately rued her social awkwardness.

'Look, Kathy I do apologise. I lecture worldwide and I never miss a beat. But when I'm faced with a situation like this I never seem to find the right words. What you went through would have been hell for anybody. I read the coroner's report. What you did was flawless, and they were lucky to have you there.'

The activist's words passed, barely registered. Kathy instead pondered the deeper truth that had risen unexpectedly from deeper waters.

The water had surged up the ramp so quickly that it caught Kathy unawares; crouched a she was with her eyes locked on Tristesse.

That deep sorrowful eye. Kathy felt that telling condemnation far more than any harsh word or backhander from her ex-husband. And yet it wasn't anger or resentment she saw reflected back. It was the deepest sense of sorrow in that eye that overcame her far more perfectly than the surge of rising water that carried Casper away.

'Kathy, you OK?'

Shannon's words hung in space, long enough for Kathy to realise that she was staring vacantly at a point beyond the conservationists tanned shoulder. Out to where the main pool lay, behind the cloistering stand of palm trees. Tristesse, that was her name.

'Yeah,' she replied, lost in the sudden recollection; 'Yes, thanks Shannon. I still kinda struggle with it on a daily basis. It's all still so raw.'

'Yeah, I can see that in your eyes. But you know what? Time is a healer. And in time you'll begin to see things as they truly are.'

'I really do hope so. Maybe we need to continue this conversation over a coffee, some other day.'

'You know what, I would really like that' nodded Shannon.
A subtle shift in the background chatter of the room drew the pair's attention just as Morrie took to the podium in typical brusque and businesslike manner to formally open proceedings. Giving Kathy a discreet sideways glance, Shannon wondered if the chief trainer might still feel that same way about that social coffee tomorrow.

'Ladies and gentlemen, I am Morrie Lambert the General Manager of Waterworld. I would officially like to bid you welcome and I sincerely hope that you have all been enjoying the day's program. Since the opening of our facility, we have gone collectively gone from strength to strength. And whilst we have suffered unfortunate setbacks recently, we have remained true to the memory and vision of the recently departed founder of Waterworld, Mr Casper Barrett.'

The mention of Casper Barrett's passing drew an expectant murmur from the compliment of media types, their presence at the proceedings for the most part driven by the controversy of the park owner's grim death. Morrie, true to his nature, had chosen to take the bull by the horns and play from the front foot.

'I am particularly proud to be able to outline to you today our exciting new initiatives in marine rehabilitation and rescue, plus a new round of school education programs. This was Casper's plan for the facility, and to be able to bring his dream to life is very exciting for all of us. It's also very exciting for the stars of our show, the killer whales, who I can today announce are expecting the arrival of two newcomers to complement the family.'

The final statement caught Kathy off-guard. *Newcomers?* Glancing across to where Brad Manning stood, off to the side of the podium; she searched his eyes for confirmation of his knowledge of the unexpected revelation. Her questioning look was met with a smugly knowing raising of eyebrows that told her all she needed to know.

'Now who's keeping secrets, you prick,' she muttered through clenched teeth, as Manning prepared to take the podium.

'Without any further ado, I would like to present to you our senior park veterinarian to explain our new wildlife rehabilitation program. His international accomplishments in marine wildlife rescue are legend. Folks, I give you our very own Doctor Bradley Manning.'

The welter of applause seemed as much for Morrie as it was for Brad. Visibly buoyed by the vibrancy and acceptance of the room, Morrie yielded the floor to the charismatic marine vet, slapping him playfully on the shoulder as they passed to exchange places. Fired by the unexpected revelation, Kathy descended Lambert like a dark cloud.

'*Two newcomers?* When the hell were you planning on telling me this, Morrie? I am the chief trainer here, dammit.'

'Would you relax for a moment? I just got the call from Chris Mackie's outfit this morning. He has a new catch in the pens. We haven't signed up, or gone through any of the fine detail as yet.'

'The fine detail? Morrie, we haven't even agreed on the major detail of whether we go down the track of more wild captures, remember? Or is this just some secret boy's club decision I don't know about?'

'Kath, now you're just overreacting. There ain't no secret squirrels here. Like I said, nothing's been set in stone. But we need to capitalize on opportunities like today to market ourselves. Stay ahead of the game and show 'em our progress.'
He flicked a casual nod of his head towards the audience.

'Progress?' she chortled, 'Is that what you call it?'

'Take a look around you. This is what Casper would have wanted.'

'Don't bring Casper into this, Morrie. Don't ever.'
A ripple of laughter and broken applause washed across the room like a wave. Brad had the measure of the room; his voice and body language confident and compelling as he delivered his slick presentation.

'We'll talk about this later, kiddo.'

'Yes, Morrie. *We'll* talk about this later.'

Morrie's introduction of Shannon Jasper as a 'fellow conservationist and staunch supporter of the facility' did not go unnoticed by the score of journalists occupying the front rows attentively. From the back of the room, Brad Manning looked on expressionless. Kathy knew him well enough to know that he was tense. Suspicious. Her own stomach knotted with a growing apprehension; feeling that old sense of ugly, angry energy which she had now come to expect from her men.

If she had come planning to cause trouble that afternoon, nothing in Shannon's easy demeanour and keen warmth betrayed it. Kathy glanced at the crowded room and relaxed slightly, allowing their easier familial vibe to wash over her. Brad did seem to be overthinking the situation just a little.

'Good afternoon folks. My interest in dolphins began some years ago. It led me to study their patterns in the wild, and I work as part of a network of groups tracking migrating orca. Oh, in case you guys didn't know, orcas are in fact large dolphins. They form part of a sub-group known as 'blackfish'. So, I would like to tell you something of that we know about our friends the orcas. As you probably have already figured by now, they are highly intelligent and engaging animals. But hey, pigs and cows are intelligent too, right? So what is all the fuss with orcas?'
Kathy allowed a taut smile. Yeah, what was the fuss?

'One big thing about orcas is they have a highly defined culture and social order. Orcas are the one creature that will live their entire lives with their family group, or matriline. Can you imagine living your entire life with your family, guys? Geez, I was glad to get away from my folks at age nineteen!'
The crowd took in the observation with good humor, and Kathy relaxed visibly.

'The thing is, orcas have social ties and loyalties which far surpass that of us humans. Pandora and Leda out in the pool there belong to Alpha One's down-line. Alpha One, or A1 as we refer to him is the dominant male, and we know his pod forms part of a 'clan' of three extended family pods who meet and socialize annually off the coast of Washington state. They are basically nomads – they're what are referred to as a 'transient clan' and they can travel as many as a thousand miles in a day.'
Impressed murmurs issued from the gathering as Shannon continued:

'Alpha One has not been sighted for some time, and anecdotal reports from local fishermen indicate that he may have been involved in a shipping strike from something like a large container vessel. With increased boat traffic, collisions with whales are sadly becoming far more frequent. Anyway, reports showed that a big orca matching A1's description has been sighted swimming with difficulty and with massive fin damage.'

Morrie and Brad cast a furtive glance at one another. Brad loosened his tight cross-armed stance. It seemed it wasn't Shannon's intent to preach the typical 'anti-captivity' talk of the environmental activists.

'We have managed to get some photographs of A1, and before I show the next set of images I warn that some are a little graphic.'
A ripple of murmured confusion ran through the room. Shannon continued without pause. Brad cast Morrie a warning look, taking the opportunity to move closer to the stage.

'This series of shots was taken during the capture of Pandora and Leda earlier this year. The first few shots are from the deck of the chaser vessel *Pacific Dark*, showing A1 in the water behind the ship after he was deliberately rammed and mutilated by the ship's own propellers.'

Lying in a stained pool of rich dark arterial blood in the water directly below the bulbous stern deck, the massive tissue damage Mars had suffered was painfully obvious. Torn chunks of flesh and blubber floated accusingly, as Shannon moved impassively; deliberately from shot to shot. Confused exclamations of horror ran like terse electricity around the room. The succession of images slapped quickly onto the overhead projector were raw. Naked. The photographer had captured the bloodbath carefully; categorically. Shannon continued without pause, knowing her time was now short:

'We know that two orcas, Pandora and Leda were captured that day. What the hunters wanted to keep quiet was the fact that three juveniles and a nursing mother were also killed; having tangled themselves in the nets and drowned in a blind panic.'

It was the photograph of poor little Constant; eyes bulging and tongue lolling, strangled by the tight tangle of netting , that now drew angry questioning cries from the stunned audience. Morrie recognised the sudden flashpoint and charged the podium, colliding awkwardly with the burly park vet.

'This is lies and bullshit. Shut her down Morrie! Shut her down or I will!'
Brad was yelling like a madman, pushing toward the stage with arms flailing.

'Let her finish!' yelled a voice from the throng of confused spectators.

'To cover up the deaths, the bodies were sunk in the bay!' Shannon was yelling now to be heard over the commotion; 'You'll probably find the remains still there.'

At the back of the room, the ensuing chaos wheeled in slow motion for Kathy. The dread rush of images from the ramp – Leda lying panicked in the pool of her own blood, Casper losing his footing – now superimposed and inter-played with the sight of Brad and Morrie jostling to drag Shannon Jasper away from the offending images. She yelped painfully as Manning charged her, continuing to yell at the confused crowd:

'They have plans for another capture early in the new year. A1's pod has now lost five juveniles, plus one female of breeding age. A1 himself may not survive his injuries. This means their lineage is at risk and questions must be asked about the legitimacy of live captures.'
Manning now in a red-faced fury placed his body between the projector and the screen. The accusing footage playing over the back of his white polo shirt as he yanked out cables, scattering the accusing slides across the floor.

'You can say goodbye to any credibility you had. We'll sue you, you fucking evil bitch!'

'Feel free, Doctor Manning. Ladies and gentlemen of the media, I have taken the liberty of sending you all copies of the photographs with supporting information. So, I guess this is the end of my talk here.'

Kathy pressed her way toward the big double doors, as Manning roughly shoved the tall conservationist toward the waiting security guards, her eyes wide and questioning:

'Shannon, what the hell?'

'Kathy, think about this carefully then decide for yourself what the truth is. I think you already know it.'

Shannon's words were shaky; spoken as she was roughly jostled and shoved by the angry guards. It was her final words that hit Kathy like a wet telling slap:

'Take care of the little one.'

Struggling to regain order, Morrie took to the podium once more, dusting himself down and issuing one last call before realizing that precious few left in the room were still listening   :

'Sorry folks. You probably saw the small group of protesters outside. It seems these militant greenies will do anything to destroy a legitimately run operation that they disagree with.'

Still in shock from the surprise turn of events, Kathy grabbed the beleaguered businessman as he left the stage.

'Is this all true, Morrie? Did you know about this?'

'Right now I know as much as you Kathy. Diddley-squat. But I want some goddamn answers. And quickly.'

Morrie hadn't failed to notice that the media cronies who he had presumed had been on-board with the park had all but followed Shannon Jasper as she was hustled out of the door in a confused gaggle of security guards and cameras.

'All we need now is another goddamn media circus.'

'I think that's the whole problem, Morrie,' came the reply. 'We're running a circus.'

Kathy's words stung the little New Yorker.

'Jesus Christ, Kath. Don't you start on me. Not here and not now.'

A picture they say is worth a thousand words, and the most telling photograph from the afternoon was that of Bradley Manning; his face frozen in rage, as he twisted Jasper's arm cruelly behind her back. The pain on her face neatly underscored the bloody death scene which was so neatly captured as it played across his broad back as neatly as any movie screen. By the time the stolen photographs hit the newspaper stands, Waterworld was already reeling from yet another body-blow.

SUN HERALD NEWS
Los Angeles CA.
Controversy has once again hit the stricken beachfront marine park Waterworld, mere weeks out from the tragic death of park owner Casper Barrett, aged 73.

Ever since the shock unprovoked attack by bull orca Tondo, which saw the elderly Barrett dragged to his death, Waterworld have faced intense scrutiny and a barrage of criticism from both the public sector and governing bodies.

A further blow to Waterworld's ailing credibility was struck yesterday at the marine park's public open day event, when guest speaker and leading Canadian marine conservationist Shannon Jasper revealed leaked photographs from an unnamed source, depicting alleged acts of animal cruelty and mishandling during the acquisition of the orcas from Washington state waters. Early claims suggest that four animals, including three juveniles were drowned in a mass panic as hunters botched the netting of a wild orca pod. Even more damning are the gory photographs of a badly mutilated male orca, which appears to have been rammed deliberately by the hunt vessel.

Waterworld had acquired their four orcas which included Tondo, the killer whale involved in the earlier fatality, from Pacific Marine LLC; the Friday Harbor based operator at the center of the controversy. The Washington based operator was engaged in the live capture of dolphins and small whale species for supply to domestic and international marine amusement parks.

It is understood the NOAA is now investigating the allegations. A spokesman for the authority declined further comment pending the completion of their investigation.

Christopher James Mackie, registered owner of Pacific Marine stated that his operation was fully compliant with NOAA requirements and all transfers were made in strict accordance with approvals granted by the regulator. Yesterday evening he confirmed that he was assisting NOAA officials with their enquiries. Mackie claimed that his operation had been the target of 'unscrupulous left wing eco-militants' and the photographs no more than 'clever forgeries designed by bitter people with a grudge' in order to discredit him.

Waterworld, who were found to be in minor breach of health and safety regulations, were exonerated from direct blame for the incident which claimed the life of their owner. Director of Waterworld, Morris Lambert yesterday released the following statement:

'Casper's death was a tragedy felt deeply by all of us here at Waterworld. We have pro-actively put into place a set of new measures which include a 'no contact' rule precluding our trainers from displays such as dorsal riding with the orcas at any time.

Our commitment always remains to the safety and wellbeing of our patrons, our staff and our animals. With regards to the recent allegations, I would point out that at this point they are just that –

allegations. We have a vested interest in the findings and we await the outcome of the NOAA's investigation.'

In the meantime, Waterworld continue with their schedule of daily park displays and an intensive sea turtle conservation program. Yesterday's open day event drew large crowds, surprising police and city authorities. Anti-captivity protesters turned out in force for the event, and large numbers of banner waving groups which included parents with young families suggests that the question of the legitimacy of keeping wild animals such as orcas and whales in captivity is very much on the table.

The shock leakage of damning photographs further fuels activists claims that the hunting and capture of a highly intelligent and social creature such as the orca is a primitive and cruel practice which has little place in today's civilised society. If proven legitimate, the claims may well herald the end of the live capture industry and muddy the waters further for marine amusement park operators.

Ms Jasper was unavailable for comment last night, following unconfirmed reports that death threats had been made against her following yesterday's shock exposé.

CHAPTER FOURTEEN

THERE ARE NO CAMELS IN HEAVEN

*'Earth's crammed with heaven
But only he who sees, takes off his shoes'*
—ELIZABETH BARRETT BROWNING

THOSE WHO DO not learn from history are doomed to repeat it. Never a truer word was spoken. Let that sink in for a moment, because these words apply to us on many levels. We can take away a vital lesson from this; personally and collectively. Here in my present reality I bear witness to this blind repetition.

Very few things truly anger me. What I'm mostly annoyed by are selfish people – those far too absorbed by self-interest to truly consider others. They bring me undone, and they seem to be everywhere. Here behind bars you are routinely treated to the very worst of it.

I watch them every single day. The same people jumping the queue at the dish-up line. The same people loading up plates of surplus food, only to then throw half of it away after gorging themselves until they can eat no more. Hoarding scores of clean clothes in their rooms, causing others to go without. Stealing from others. Leaving a mess for *someone else* to clean up. *Someone else* will do it. *Someone else* will fix it. And it is always *someone else's* fault, or *someone else's* problem. Ironically, these are the only times that they think of *someone else* and therein lies the problem.

The underlying nature of these individuals is always the same – a studied ignorance of the feelings and rights of others. Theirs is a narcissistic world view in which everything exists simply for their own benefit. One might argue that this is no different to the outside world, and I would agree save for one subtle difference. I see a kind of hardness here. A hardness born out of lifetimes of repetition; all gathered into this one place so that it seems nurtured and magnified. What becomes of these souls once they're released back into the real world? What will they have done with their time here? What lessons will they have learned about themselves, and of life? I know that many of them will return to re-live their former patterns of self-indulgent behaviour.

Time is a funny thing. From the glimpses that I have seen, I can say that the theme seems to remains the same; just played out on a different stage with different props.

Drug use and abuse is a common theme. By drugs here I don't just mean chemical substances. We 'drug' ourselves in order to escape reality. With chemicals. Or alcohol. Sexual excess. Food. Even with things like overwork or filling our quiet spaces with noise and distraction. You see a drug is *anything* which we use in order to escape our reality.

Here's the problem with this – by constantly drugging ourselves, we don't *transcend* our reality, we merely *escape* it temporarily. The irony is that the low vibration that results actually prevents us from permanently transcending our present state. There is no such thing as a 'social' drug. Let that sink in.

So we drug ourselves to escape reality, and we drug ourselves to numb all of the bad things that we feel. The thing is, we cannot actually selectively numb emotions. In drugging ourselves we numb everything – we numb our capacity to feel – and we lower our resonant energy. Our vibrations then prevent us from doing what we set out to do in the first place – to transcend our present state.

So how do I know all this? Like I said before, time is a funny thing. I have seen a great deal; more than I can comprehend. Some of it is ugly. Of the far distant future, I can only give you this brief spoiler:

'Darkness cannot exist where there is Light. And there is always Light.'
To tell you any more than that would mean the writing of another book.

What we seem to be doing is disconnecting ourselves from a greater truth. I am reminded of the words of French philosopher Jean-Jacques Rousseau:

'Let us set down as an incontestable maxim that the first movements of nature are always right. There is no original perversity in the human heart'.
If that is true, then where did we go so terribly wrong? And more importantly, how do we go about making it right again? Have we somehow managed to slip out of sync with nature? It seems to me that the further we drive ourselves from nature, so the greater is the divide between us and that underlying fundamental truth.

As children, we almost instinctively assume the natural cadence of nature, don't we? So the connection must be there in our fundamental state of being. As kids we were always in tune with nature. It was always there all around us - in the playful drag of a stick; running along the Sunday sidewalks lined with trim tall hedges ad newly mown grass. In the idle toss and catch of a baseball in the grassy diamond of park. In the quiet solitude of sky-gazing – lazily picking out the imagined shapes and distortions in slow passing clouds. Sun-baked and tingly warm under a mile of summer sky, with the ticking background chorus of a thousand sunning cicadas. We lived according to the sun and the seasons.

Then as we grow into mortgages and overdrafts, rosters and overtime, buses and trains, mowers and washing machines; we slowly but surely begin the regimented march to the beat of a different drum. The manufactured backbeat of industry and mechanization. We forsake sun for fluorescent light. Sea breeze for scrubbed, recirculated air. Temperature control allows us to neatly ignore the seasons. We can now eat virtually any type of food, anytime we choose. We defy Circadian rhythm and slip out of any natural sense of synchronicity at will. Night can now be transformed electrically into day.

We effectively remove ourselves from the Present. We are stuck in the Past – slaves to guilt and regret. We are stuck in the Future – slaves to fear and anxiety. So, we numb reality and live anyplace but Here. Anywhere but Now. I told you time was a funny thing! So how then can we possibly live in harmony with a world going on around us in the Here and Now if we are not truly present?

Imagine what a symphony might sound like if the lead violinist of a string orchestra was constantly looking ahead on his music sheets as the orchestra played on around him. Imagine if he played on robotically, his mind on the pages yet to come, rather than immersing himself in the sounds and subtleties evoked by his fellow musicians. Or imagine if he stayed focussed on the two bum notes he played two pages ago. They are already long gone and forgotten, yet his mind cannot get past them. How pedestrian and lacklustre would his performance become?

This is how most of us are currently living our lives, and the symphony of the world is suffering as a result. We weren't designed to be this way. We most definitely weren't meant to be this way.

I don't recall exactly what time I nodded off, and nor do I recall just how long I was gone for. These episodes are all characterized by this weird sense of 'missing time.' I seem to be getting used to this, and my body clock now re-adjusts and patches up the time anomaly rather quickly. So now I only feel 'out of sorts' for a few hours, before I'm back in sync and feeling grounded once again. I realize I've been negative and in a rather massive blue funk for the past few weeks; the mental and emotional strain of living in a human zoo starting to get under my skin.

The whale relaxed her now familiar dance, and our wild rotation slowed. She gazed at me thoughtfully, sensing my mood.

'I have never seen you quite like this. What troubles you, Adam?'

'Apart from the obvious, you mean? Because I always have these strange conversations with a large whale in some weird kind of time vortex.'
The tiniest glint in her eye suggested that whales too had a capacity for sarcasm and dry humor.

'Go on' she urged, ever-patient.

'Days go by endlessly and I just feel so lost. As though I've died, yet somewhere life still goes on without me. I'm so tired these days. I'm tired of the noise and the angst and the hatred. It wears me down, I guess.'

'I understand,' she replied. 'Hatred is a quicksand that drags you down and sucks your strength. And it is always the absence of love that allows hatred to take root.'

'I wonder about that, too. Love, I mean. Sometimes we seem like such a loveless race of beings. I've met people here who have done the most evil things to others, yet see no wrong.'

'Adam, the greatest force in the world is the power of love, and the greatest threat is the love of power. This power emboldens people to wreak evil upon other beings they perceive to be lesser than them. Where there is love there is Light, and the absence of Light is the Darkness which brings this evil into being.'

'There is darkness and low energy around me all the time here. I try not to let it get to me or defeat me. So, I just pick myself up day after day, and I keep going. But when I look in the mirror, I don't see happiness anymore. My eyes have gone dull, and it bothers me what this place is doing to my soul. I miss my sweetheart. I miss my life. Not that I'm the greatest of believers, but sometimes it kinda feels like we are alone, you know? Like God just isn't listening anymore.'

'When the sun leaves the sky at night, and there is darkness all around you; do you stop believing in the Sun?' she asked.

'Well no, of course not.'

'And so it should be with God.'

'OK so tell me – on the subject of God - do all whales believe in some divine Creator? Or do you have different religions?'

'We have different clans and tribes. All speak different languages.'

'That's communication. I was talking about religion. Beliefs.'

The whale held my gaze patiently, as if waiting for some answering glimmer of understanding on my part. I felt just a little chastened; like an awkward schoolboy.

'Does it matter whether I choose to call you Adam or Doctor?'

'Well no, I don't mind what name you prefer to use. I'll still answer you, whatever you call me, if that's what you mean.'

'And will it change *who* you are, if I call you by the name Adam or by the name Doctor?'

'No, of course not. I am who I am no matter what name you decide to call me.'

'And so it is with God. Let me explain it in a different way. Blindfold three men and ask each of them to touch a camel. One man feels its long fetlocks. The second feels its hump. The third it's long curved neck. Then ask each man to remove his blindfold and describe his experience to the others. The first describes a spindly creature; smooth and fine haired. An ancient being, gnarled and knobbled. A fragility belying its quiet inner strength. The second decides that this was not his experience. He insists he had felt a mountain; solid and rising up toward the heavens. Unmoveable in its vastness. The third has a different story again. He describes the trunk of a fine palm tree, draped with fronds. A rough curving arc giving shade over the hot desert sand.

I took in the whale's story and allowed her the space to continue, anticipating the conclusion.

'Without being able to see the whole, which of the three men do you think was correct?' she urged.

'Well all of them felt a small part of the whole camel, so all of them were technically correct.'

'Precisely. You seem to connect religion with God, as if they are inter-related. As if the one leads to the other. Religion is simply the worldly act of choosing which man you thought better described the camel. But just like the blindfolded men, that is only a limited view and All That Is cannot be truly understood and fully experienced that way.'

'Well I guess that answers my question as to whether whales have religion.'

'We have no specific word for what you understand as religion. Perhaps our closest word is 'ritual.' There is only All That Is and we each simply acknowledge it, sense it and communicate it differently.'

'I guess that's really not that different to us humans. I've always thought that different religious faiths are simply interpreting one and the same thing.'

'Quite so. It is actually the same camel.'

'So how then can we fully understand this thing that you call All That Is?'

'Remember the three blindfolded men?'

'Yes.'

'Remove the blindfold and step back!'

'So, that's all there is to it? Take off the blindfold?'

'And step back! The blindfold goes by many names, Adam – intolerance and superiority, racism and species-ism, bigotry and sexism – just to name a few.'

'I understand what you're saying, whale. I must say though, I find this all vaguely amusing. I'm either floating in a time pocket listening to a giant mystic whale talking about a camel, or I'm bat-shit crazy. Which one is it?'

'Which explanation would you prefer?' the whale enquired, 'And why does the experience of something outside of your normal reality automatically imply insanity? I might point out that you yourself began this conversation with a discussion about God – an entity that you have never ever seen or heard. And yet the word 'insanity' seemed far from your thoughts as you did so.'

'OK, point taken. So, can I assume from our conversation that there is a God?'

'There is simply All That Is', the whale patiently repeated, 'It is a part of us, and we are a part of It. To acknowledge this and to live by it is to be at one with the Harmony.'

'But I've seen you whales and dolphins out there at sea. I watch you all the time. Don't get me wrong, I love you guys; but I see you argue and bicker amongst yourselves sometimes, which to me seems anything but harmonious. Surely our kinds are not so very different?'

'Where there is reason and free will, there is always the capacity to choose. Good or bad. Yes or no. Love or hate. Yes, sometimes we argue and compete; that is true. And sometimes we are jealous. Or selfish. Or angry. Yet always underneath is the greater cosmic pull of the Harmony, and its dance is the dance of perfection.'

'I get that feeling of harmony when I'm with you.'

'That is only natural. Our bodies resonate with it, and that is what you feel and respond to. And when every single one of the atoms of our being resonate with it completely, we will find true perfection.'

'If it is that simple, why don't we all achieve perfection then?'

'Reason and free will' she replied, the celestial twinkle returning to her eye.

'Reason and free will. OK then. What about Heaven and Hell?'

'What do you wish to know about them?'

'Sorry, I should have been more specific. Do Heaven and Hell exist?'

'I thought you would have already learned something of this, Adam!'

'So are you're saying they actually exist? What are they like?'

'Hell is another camel.'

'And Heaven?'

'There are no camels in Heaven. There is no need for them.'

I leaned back onto the reassuring bulk of the whale, my mind beginning to spin.

'OK, what about angels? Are angels real?'

'Ahhh, angels,' said the whale, the playful glint returning to her eye. 'Wonderful beings. Not the greatest of conversationalists, as they tend to pick the topic and speak cryptically. They're not really that big on small talk either, so it's best you don't invite them to dinner parties. Still, you would have a field day talking with an angel, Adam.'

'Really?'

'Really. And great lovers of music. Oh my, such beautiful voices. When they sing their voices are rich like the finest imported silk.'

'Wow.'

'Wow, indeed.'

'Demons?'

'Black.'

'Black. That's it?'

'Black, as in the absence of all Light. They come at you through your weaknesses.'

'I see. So, this thing that you call All That Is…what does it want from us? I mean, should I be doing something great like inventing a cure for cancer, or writing a symphony?'

'A very deep question and a very good one, Adam! She allowed the thought to hang in space for a good while before she continued:

'Have you seen a jigsaw puzzle?'

'Yes whale, of course I have.'

'If every piece was shaped exactly the same way, the puzzle would not work.'

'OK, so we are all a unique piece of the entire picture? That makes sense to me.'

'When you are called upon, All That Is will simply ask you if you have been true to Yourself. It is not for all of us to invent cures for cancer or write symphonies, but there *is* a plan for each of us, and only by truly becoming Yourself can this greater Harmony be achieved. Only then does the Great Puzzle reach a solution.'

I closed my eyes and relaxed for a moment. My head ached from the effort of understanding, and I welcomed the feeling of simply floating, weightless and lucid without expectation or judgement.

'So, do we have anything in common, whales and humans?'

'Yes.'

'Does all life have something in common?'

'Yes.'

'What is it?'

'That which unites all life, you mean?'

'Yes.'

The dark bulk drew back; poised and graceful as a ballerina. When her words came, they were measured and reassuring:

'We each of us carry a spark of the original Light. All bearers of the spark are held sacred; to be recognised by the One. We see it and acknowledge it; all beings do. *The Light in me sees the Light in you.*'

'And humans understand this too?' I queried; realising I was speaking in a hushed tone.

'For your kind, reason and free will led to your rejection of the Harmony. You chose to walk your own path to perfection, in your own way. You bloodlines carry this forward from generation to generation.'

I let the mighty whale's words hang for a while, measuring them and feeling their weight.

'Are we a lost tribe do you think?'

'Nothing is truly lost, Adam. The Harmony is always there. Infinitely patient. It is always within and without. The secret to finding it is to reach in, rather than reach out.'

'You speak in riddles, you know that?'

'And what is the purpose of a riddle, if not to force you to think?'

'Touché,' I countered with a wry grin. 'So, explain to me what you mean by reaching in rather than reaching out.'

The shadowy cetacean took measure, and the momentary pause gave me time to notice that her broad spade-like pectoral fin had been dancing, curved and weightless around me all this time. Encircling me. It's slow motion serpentine dance giving her the aura of an astronaut walking in space. Her closeness was comforting, intimate, and I realized in that one perfect moment that I felt truly loved and accepted.

'By nature, we are travellers,' she continued. 'But we are also voyagers in more ways than one. Our ocean journey takes us many miles, ranging from one coast to another. And yet we know that the longest journey is achieved by the shortest path.'

'More riddles?' I mused.

'The secret is to reach in, rather than reach out.' she repeated, ever patient.

'I have the strangest feeling of deja-vu, like I've heard all his before. The feeling keeps hitting me lately.'

'Time and space work like this, my friend. Time and space are folded, and you simply reached in. Now rational mind, which lives in a more familiar linear realm is desperately assimilating, in an attempt to keep up with cosmic super-consciousness. It is rather like trying to paste a three dimensional shape onto a flat scrapbook page.'

'This is an awful lot to take in, whale. Heaven and Hell. All That Is.'

'Cosmic knowledge is like a rich diet. It is not enough to simply swallow each morsel. It must be digested and absorbed before you eat again.'

Perhaps it was the proximity of the great whale, or the measure of her words. With each weightless, suspended moment I felt more balanced; more at one with this newfound wellspring of awareness. She could sense the shift.

'What you are feeling now is the Harmony, Adam. And the Harmony welcomes you!'

'Why did you come to me, whale? My God, I've just realised I don't even know your name! Please, please don't think me rude.'

'Not at all. My name is not of consequence.'

'So why have you come to me?'

'My blood is in trouble, as is yours. Just as the fates of our two great tribes are intimately intertwined, so now are yours and mine.'

'Wait, are you saying that you're using me to solve our problems?'

'Nothing at this level is done without the agreement of the other. I came because you were ready. Be thankful, for you are one of the chosen few and the Light chooses who It works through carefully.'

'How will I know what I'm supposed to do?'

'Reach in. It will be how it is supposed to be.'

'That's it? Just reach in?

'Be patient. For now, take back what you have learned and assimilate it. *Time and space!* See, we are having this conversation in the Here and Now, but when you return you will discover that this conversation has in fact already happened a long time ago. Take back what you have learned and heed it well, for your time is close! Until next we meet, Adam.'

'Wait, please! Can't you at least offer me some advice?'

I felt the gentlest brush of neoprene rubber from the encircling flipper as she withdrew.

'Don't grow larger than your Ocean, human!'

'That's it?'

'It is a good start.'

'Not philosophy, I meant specific…'

The now familiar sound of jet engines roared in a perfect three-part harmony which sent shivers down my spinal cord. And with that I simply 'fell out' of the maelstrom. Rather unceremoniously, I felt, given the pure and reverent nature of our communion. The mundanity of flesh was like a rough, poorly cut suit after the serenity of the Harmony.

Rolling off the hard unforgiving single bed mattress, I pulled on the least worn pair of tracksuit pants and staggered out like a sleepwalker to the coffee urn. My nasty little world seemed like a harsh conglomerate of jagged edges and intersecting lines, and the light was painfully over-exposed. The prison soundscape crackled in my ears, rather like a cheap tinny AM radio.

Reader, looking back I am aware of my earlier negativity. In my defence, I have chosen to faithfully record these feelings in order to give you a taste of exactly what this life of captivity does to your mind. I have always thought of myself and well-balanced. Resilient, even. And yet, living with a constant cloud of negativity and noise around you day and night slowly gets to you. It comes at you from all sides. Rises around you like a winter damp, and progressively numbs you despite your conscious efforts to fight it off. Rises up until you are eventually colored by it; until your energy, if you do not pay close attention, begins to resonate with it.

After my time with the whale, I see this all the more clearly.

The light caught on the chipped glass tumbler in front of me and burst across the table in a neat spectrum of color. I liked this little sunlit corner of the room. Here with the big windows swung open I could catch the nice waft of afternoon breeze, which today carried with it the now familiar heady aroma of freshly cut grass. Out on the lawn by the nearby flowerbeds sat Baba; one of a handful of Muslims in the center. Baba is a refugee from Pakistan who keeps largely to himself and rarely speaks to the others. Wild tousled dark hair and a longish unkempt beard, he has taken to wearing an old green bed sheet around his waist like a caftan. An equally weatherworn blue pillowslip has been fashioned into a turban, giving him the wild look and demeanor of the prophet.

Baba has taken to sleeping alone outside in a corner of the long verandah, protected from the elements by the wide metal roof. The guards have all but given up on coaxing him back into the dormitory and have begrudgingly settled for ensuring his belongings are kept tidy, making sure any valuables are kept from opportunistic inmates. By day he is a solitary figure, sitting or kneeling in constant prayer out on the rising grass mound. His chants form a constant backdrop when I wander about the grounds; foreign and echoing like the call from a minaret. This has drawn much derision and abuse from the resident population, and the verbal threats and racist taunts are now a daily occurrence. If it upsets the solitary figure, he does not show it.

For my part, I have to say that I quietly enjoy the wild prophets presence; occasionally stopping to listen to his prayers on the rare occasions when he breaks into English. They are wise words; the blessings of Allah. His steady voice has a nice ringing energy to it. Comforting almost. Recently Baba has made himself more unpopular on account of the fact that he has taken to leaving food out for the birds and animals. Just why these small acts of kindness so agitate and enrage these people is beyond my comprehension. And yet there is something about the man that draws their derision and abuse. Perhaps they take umbrage to the words of a Muslim. Perhaps it is something in the way that he deflects their angry vitriol without reaction; like their taunts are so much water off a duck's back. Perhaps it is what is reflected back that they fear.

Once again the guards find themselves flabbergasted by Baba's behaviour, and threaten him with punishment if he continues feeding the animals. To make matters worse, a feral cat has brought its two newborn kittens into the compound and every evening they have taken to waiting cautiously under the protective cover of the bushes for Baba, who carefully lays out their food then retreats to sit quietly cross-legged whilst they feed. Twice now, I have watched Baba being led away to the punishment wing for his sins. And twice now he has returned and quietly continued to go about the evening chore of laying out some of his food for the cats. He is simply concerned for their wellbeing, he explains to the hovering guards with an offhand shrug. Imagine my elation when I learned the other day that the Superintendent himself has been forced to intervene and has provided no less than a formal letter approving Baba to continue feeding the cats, providing the area is left clean afterwards! This has not gone down well with either the guards or the inmates. Personally I can't help but think this world would be a far better place if the only crime these people were guilty of was caring about animals.

Today I spoke to Baba for the first time; simply thanking him for his care and concern for the animals. I felt he needed to know that at least one person appreciated him. He acknowledged with a simple smile, which left me wondering as to whether my words had registered.

Later on Baba returned and made his way over to the table where I sat. He spoke to me for the first time:

'I know that you are also a carer of animals.'

I smiled and nodded; caught somewhat off-guard by the unexpected approach.

'I enjoy listening to your preaching Baba, though I don't always know what you're saying.'

'I pray for everyone here, my friend. Mostly I pray all people may see themselves as equal. Guards and inmates equal. Doctors and patients equal. Humans and animals equal.'

'You speak wisely,' I replied; quietly impressed with the man's thoughtfulness despite all the hatred and barbed threats; 'I hope that we'll see equality one day. Though I sometimes wonder if some of these people will ever understand that in their lifetime.'

The wild prophet smiled amiably and looked out of the window expectantly toward the neatly cultivated row of flower gardens where the cats sat in wait for him each evening. His thoughtful brown eyes matched his dark skin.

'The skull is solid, my friend. Very thick. And yet one single word is capable of breaking through it.'

Three days later the smallest of the kittens fell from the roof, its hind leg obviously damaged. The commotion had drawn a small knot of curious inmates, whilst up above the mother cat yowled protectively from the guttering. Seeing Baba rising from his prayers one of his main antagonizers, a gap-toothed redneck of a man quickly scooped up the writhing kitten from where it had fallen and held it aloft. Catching sight of Baba, the kitten cried plaintively as it swung helplessly in the man's grasp; one small hind leg dangling uselessly. Staring fixedly at the robed figure approached the scene with arms outstretched pleadingly, Gap-tooth roughly snapped the kitten's neck with one sudden savage twist of his slab-like hand, before tossing the lifeless little bundle at the horrified Muslim's feet, with a wet thud. Baba's pitiful howl of anguish wringing a sadistic smile of joy out of his spotty creased face.

The others seemed entertained, murmuring their approval at the brutal act. Finally crazy Baba had gotten what he deserved. Satisfied with the outcome, they dispersed; returning to their card games and endless argumentative chatter. In the fading light, Baba scooped up the little tortoiseshell kitten and cradled it carefully, taking it out towards the flowerbeds. I followed him across the lawn sullenly.

'I'm really sorry about what just happened, Baba.'

'Don't be sorry. It is not your fault.'

The brown eyes gazed darkly, rimmed red with the salt sting of rising tears.

'I know, but I just don't understand these people. Maybe they're crazy, but this is just evil and heartless. That guy is supposed to be leaving in a couple of weeks.'

Baba lay the broken little body down gently amongst a spray of red flowering shrubs. He stepped back, allowing mother cat her space to reach her youngster and mourn. He looked at me thoughtfully:

'The little cat is free, my friend. But when that man leaves here he will still be in a cage.'

Sometimes from amongst all of this ugliness there comes an unexpected glimmer. Something that suggests that maybe, just maybe we might have a chance of making it after all. Perhaps, as the whale said, nothing is truly lost. Maybe it's simply waiting to be found.

CHAPTER FIFTEEN

SHADES

'But O shipmates!
On the starboard hand of every woe, there is a sure delight.
Delight is to him whose strong arms yet support him,
when the ship of this base treacherous world has gone down beneath him.
Delight is to him who gives no quarter in the truth and kills,
burns and destroys all sin; though he pluck it out from under
the robes of senators and judges.'
—HERMAN MELVILLE - 'Moby Dick'

THE CHROME PIPES caught the sun and concentrated the warm questing rays to a sharply wicked glint, widening to become a broad lens flare on the aging photograph. The jet black Harley sported a sharply raked springer front end. Long spidery-thin tubular chrome forks connecting the wire-spoked wheel with its skinny rubber tire to the rider clinging splayed-arm to the ape-hanger handlebars. A black lack tear-drop shaped gas tank, and a deeply shaped seat in tuck-buttoned black leather. The chopper was all rebel device. An evilly wrought masterpiece. Between the threadbare denim of the rider's legs, the heavy engine was deceptively pretty with perfectly shaped chrome head covers in the shape of plump upturned pie dishes topping the big vaned cylinders. A 'pan-head' engine, arguably the prettiest big block motorcycle engine that Harley-Davidson ever built.

Clifton 'Bozz' Bozwell was quietly impressed by my observation.

'You know your motorbikes,' he said grudgingly.

I realized that I had verbalized that last thought. I glanced from the tattooed strong man sitting in front of me back to the youthful jacketed rider in the photo, proud and focussed. It was clearly Bozz, riding at the head of the vee of three bikes; younger and more idealistic, perhaps. And definitely far fiercer, in spite of the warm mellowing effect of the old snapshot. The only nod to highlight amidst the boldly intimidating slurry of black and chrome was the curling flash of color adorning the back of his jacket; marking his defiant allegiance.

The club colors.

Maybe he caught the quick tightening flash of my distaste in that moment of recognition. Most probably he did. I sense that precious little escapes the man's steely gaze. He is what is called an outlaw biker - a harrier whose kind live outside the law and openly flaunt the fact. His twelve hundred cube Springer Softail is an open taunt to authority; a raised middle finger to law and society. And the bold gang colors emblazoned across his broad back fly as proud and fearless as any pirate flag.

The image rankled me. To say that I have never liked his kind is a bold understatement.

'I was with the association for twenty years,' he said unbidden, reading my face. I smiled inwardly at the reference. 'Association' seemed a vain rationalization. Paradoxically jagged. A neatly sanitized justification to allow a gang of thugs free reign.

'Altamont, 1969,' he continued with a brief nod toward the yellowing photograph. 'We ran security for the Rolling Stones gig at the Speedway. Outta control, brother. Three hundred thousand people. I drank Bourbon with Mick Jagger that night. Had to help carry him out to his limo afterwards.'

'Sympathy for the Devil?' I suggested wryly.

'Right on. But I guess that was a little bit before your time. They were crazy days back then my friend. Crazy days.'

I knew the story of Altamont and the gangs of the swinging sixties well. My older brother rode a Low Rider and I loved the throaty blatting roar of it, hammering its way out through the Pass; all shining, squat and chrome mantis-like. Crazy days indeed. The odd pairing of outlaw motorcycle gang and peace loving hippies was a jarring contradiction that challenged both harmony and good sense. Bikers and hippies – their movements seemed strangely interwoven throughout those Californian 'flower power' years of free love and expansion of the mind.

The nineteen-sixties was an exciting time to be alive. Martin Luther King had shared a dream and the colors of it were inexorably bleeding though our collective psyches. We reached for the moon and we saw the stars beckoning to us beyond it. On the one hand, the world stood on the brink of a new age of burgeoning cosmic consciousness. Our collective journey had inexorably drawn us here, in an almost incessant yearning of spirit. The sating of some winsome cosmic longing that seemed almost hard-wired into our DNA. To discover our rightful place in the universe, and to find a meaning to our lives. To arrive at some point of enlightenment. Crawling out of the flames of a world war, we shed skins – some gladly and perfectly, some gradually. Some reluctantly. We took fledgling first steps.

The hippie generation represented our spiritual 'growing pains' made flesh. They represented a challenging of the *status quo*. Of traditional ways of thinking and traditional conventions. Marriage, sex and union. A challenging of sexual and cultural inequality. Of personal liberty and the embedded bias of creed and complexion. On that one hand the hippie generation was calling for us to seek connection via the universals of peace and love. *To make Love and not War.*

Its call was insistent and compelling, and to be caught up in that seminal flow was to give oneself to the letting in of the Light. It came as no surprise then that the movement was characterized by all the colors of the rainbow, evidenced in the wild bohemian clothing and the token adornments of a spiritual and sexual liberation. It touched on connection with wild nature; the flowers in untamed long-flowing hair. The soul-scape of the sixties was psychedelic and expectantly ablaze; the burning of draft cards matching the lithium burning of spirit.

The polar opposite of the hippie movement was a far more brutish and dark masculinity – the nascent primal urge to physically express a darker claim. A throwback to exactly what the flower people were seeking to outgrow. The primitive stone and wood days of rape, pillage and plunder. Days of blackly elemental darkness, long before the golden dawn of Aquarius. The bikers – the lineage of a band of men who had originally faced fiery death together in the war-torn skies above Nazi occupied Europe. A brotherhood united by the common aim of wresting freedom by more violent means. Motorcycles ultimately replaced the aluminium overcast of multi-engine bombers, but the brotherhood, the bond still remained.

Hippies and bikers. Everything that has come to pass will come to pass again. Until we finally learn. I suppose in some strange way each faction were seekers of Freedom; the one borne out of the incipient welling of universal love and the other out of the fires of war. Different origins and different psychic wellsprings, yet each essentially acknowledging that the fabric of modern human society clothed a fundamentally broken machine. And so each faction arrived at some notional freedom via their own uniquely skewed route.

Ultimately it was the clash of those two freedom seeking countercultures that resulted in tragedy that night in Altamont.

While the Stones sang 'Sympathy for the Devil', the devil's reprise was the stabbing death of a peaceable concert-goer when the pack of Hell's Angels turned the scene of a minor skirmish into a frenzied bloodbath.

'I was the sergeant-at-arms for one of the local chapters for five years,' Bozz continued.

Another laughable reference, like they were still fighting a war. Most likely the military term was a throw-back to the seminal death or glory days of the *'Fighting Eighth'* – the US Army Air Force group which originally spawned them.

I stopped myself and deliberately took in the man's countenance; tried to see who he truly was. There is a quiet patience to Bozz's face. A strength mellowed with age, and I could easily see him as a leader of men.

'So what can I help you with Bozz?'

The wall mounted fan is sputtering and clicking; the large chipped blades wobbling drunkenly out of balance. It ignites a cluster of papers on the tiny scarred corner desk into a sporadic motion before leaving them dishevelled in its vigilant passing sweep of the small living space. The humidity makes the small room close and cloying. Bozz's room, like mine is cramped; the ancient badly applied paintwork tacky and flaking. I count four different colors, each as dirty and weatherworn as the other. The original decorator was either woefully color-blind, or well beyond caring. Quite possibly both.

Bozz handed me a folded wad of official paperwork with the state Parole Board's official logo emblazoned across the top.

'The Board have some reservations about my release, given my past history.'

A quick glance at the top sheet is all I need to confirm the picture that I have already suspected. *Multiple breaches of court orders. Driving whilst under suspension.* I sigh inwardly as the rap sheet rolls on accusingly. *Violent assault. Assault occasioning bodily harm.*

'Yes, well you've certainly been around,' I observe in the bold understatement of the year.

'I know it doesn't look good,' he replies, poker-faced.
Runner-up for the bold understatement of the year. I saw the veiled softness behind the aloof façade, and I felt an easy warmth which I liked. An authenticity, as it were.

'Look brother, I know you're good with words. I was really hoping that you might see fit to help me with writing my request for parole.'

My reputation was preceding me of late, and I was fast becoming something of a rare and prized commodity – a jailbird that could read and write. What had started as a favour to a cellmate had developed into a virtual occupation of writing letters to loved ones on behalf of semi-literate inmates, and finally writing their submissions for parole. I became privy to intimate slices of life; oft-times pained and tortured. Other times uniquely and fleetingly beautiful. Every single one seemed to have a deeper story; each drawing out some deeper facet of life. Each telling me that sometimes we have to look deeper to see the truth of a person.

'It sounds like a lame excuse, but I did it for her.'

He pulled the photograph from the top drawer of the desk. Unlike the other photos on display, tagged to the old pin-up board, this particular shot was pristine; un-punctured by the burred pinholes like the others. The colors still glossy and new. This was no gaudy pin-up, no casually pinned public display. Even the careful way with which the grizzled old biker reverently held it spoke of its importance and his obvious loyalty to the subject, framed in head-and-shoulders portrait.

'Your daughter?'

'Rosanna,' he nodded. 'She was twenty when that was taken.'

The young girl in the photograph could easily have passed for a woman in her late forties, had I not known. Sunken eyes in dark sockets. Gaunt cheekbones achingly prominent, like the sharp remnant outcrops of what had obviously once been a far softer and more welcoming landscape. Before the life-force had been meticulously siphoned from the once pretty face. It had been a windy day when that photo was taken, and there was a vibrant blue wildness to the backdrop of sky laced with the thin driven swatches of passing cloud.

The contrast between subject and background made the telling of it all the more gut-wrenching. Despite the wind and the sun endowing the scene with the benefit of natural compass, Rosanna appeared small and lost. Her oily hair blowing in limp straggles and conveniently veiling those eyes from the impartial gaze of the camera. There was a sad resignation in the wistful expression, the tired droop of eyelids suggesting that these were young eyes that had seen far too much. Hazel eyes which, despite everything, still retained the vaguest memory of innocence. Behind them I could see the ripples in the frozen gathering of light.

The blade like some frightful wasted mattock, vainly used in the scoring and the loosening. In the scraping of her pain, the desperate scrabbling to expose its root. There was pain, and intelligent measurement. Each time, only just enough to perfectly match the emotional pain with the applied physicality of razor's edge. The innocence lost in a blur of so many wasted days; perfectly wasted. The expiring of resigned half-breath at the weary submission to something which had become beyond control. Those acts of self-harm were the mind's desperate attempt to regain some vestige of control; struggling to regain conscious control over runaway emotion. I feel the astringent sharpness of first incision, and recoil abruptly at the unexpected spurt of blood and the sickly sweet smell of its essence. The sudden blinding tear of flesh. Saltwater tears.

Shaken abruptly back to the present, my involuntary shrug causes a sudden crick in the nape of my neck. No, I do not need to see. I do not *want* to see. The chill glimpses de-rail me like some runaway train. Fuck it, why do you keep doing this shit to me? How does the whale live with all of this knowing, I wonder? Can there be too much knowing? And does she perhaps refer to this particular affliction as *'the Knowing'* - the capital 'K' suggesting it is a knowing beyond those things which one rightly needs to know?

The whale does not grace my sarcasm with a response. What, I wonder will my own portrait look like when I leave here, cast hopefully against the blue yonder beckoning of sea breeze and sky?

Suddenly she is there. Surfacing, invoked. Her eye calls to me. That beautiful eye, patient yet insistent.

'Look carefully, Adam. Listen and do not judge.'

I soften, and deliberately put aside my thoughts of judgement; chastened by my companion's appearance. The grizzled biker continued;

'I was a wild man in my time, brother. Really wild. Outta control wild, I mean.'

'Go on.'

'Well a lot of things changed when Rosanna was born. Not straight away, mainly on account of me being too fuck dumb crazy to see it. I started arguing more and more with the old lady. She had her bags packed ready to leave me a coupla times, but she stuck by me. By the time our little girl was ten I began to realise that my lifestyle was not only going to kill me and the missus, but it would end up killing Rosanna too. Watching her grow up so priceless and new, it was like I was seeing the world through a new set of eyes. Her eyes.'

He drew a confessional breath, staring at some distant point in space as if re-playing some familiar old motion film.

'I didn't want her view of the world muddied like her old man's ya know?'

He picked up the rap sheet.

'Violent assault. I belted a dealer senseless one time. Got done for it, straight up and down. Wasn't hard on account of my colors and my past history. What the judge didn't bother to see was the dealer's gang who held Rosanna down and deliberately injected her. Laughed at her as she went into a fit. She was a drinker brother, but she was never a user. Not before then anyways.'

I watched his eyes glaze over wetly as he stared fixedly into the distance, his voice measured and flat. The film had played out many times in the past. And always the needle, like a blind shooting of sorrow.

'I didn't bother with his lackeys – they were just dumbass lap-dogs. Went straight to the top man and beat him to hell with a tire iron. They never went near Roseanna again. None of 'em, but by that time it was too late anyways….the damage was already done.'

The tears came, steady now. He held the rap sheet stubbornly at arm's length, straining to read.

'You don't have to do this Bozz,' I said quietly.

'Driving under suspension', he continued doggedly. His gruff voice caught plaintively in the back of his throat in the exorcising of personal demons:

'When I got the call, there was nothing else for it. If you were a father you would understand what it means – flesh and blood. Their flesh and blood is your flesh and blood, and it's a lifetime bond. Carly, that's Roseanna's flatmate, had come home to find her unconscious in a pool of blood. Rang me screaming. So I drove there like the proverbial bat out of hell. Who was I gonna call, the authorities? I was a fucking Hells Angel, goddammit. A one per-center. Cops tried to flag me down, but I wasn't having it. All they could do was tail me 'til I arrived at Roseanna's flat'.
His hands trembled, a latent cocktail of frustration and injustice.

'When the highway patrol tackled me off my bike in the parking lot and barred my way to the flat, I just took a swing. I dropped Cop

One flat on his ass. Cop Two thought about trying it on with me, but he was older and way smarter. Wasn't as gung-ho as his buddy. The sad bastard would have been far happier with his doughnuts and hot coffee. When Carly ran out screaming, covered in Roseanna's blood he finally got the message. It didn't stop them from charging me though.'

'So that accounts for the *Assault occasioning bodily harm*?'

'That's it brother. The thing is I fucked up and I let my little girl down. Truth is up until then I had loved my way of life too much, and I wasn't there for her. But I gave it all up after that night at Roseanna's flat. I gave it away because my love for her was stronger, and you just can't fight love. I handed my colors in and quit the association. Turned 'em in, took the consequences and walked away.'

Fixing me with gray eyes, he pointed a finger casually at the ugly thin scar over his right eye.

'The consequences', I thought. Seems you just don't simply 'walk away' from an outlaw band of brothers.

'I needed to show my daughter how much she meant to me.'
He shifted his frame uncomfortably, a weight seemingly lifted and he looked reverently at the photo one last time.

'Bozz, it's tough sometimes. Being a guy, I mean. We're supposed to be providers. Leaders. Protectors. Crying or calling out for help is seen as a weakness. I would go as far as saying you were most probably a born leader. You were a man of pride weren't you?'

'You can see it can't you? It took a lot of guts for me to ask for your help. A lot of guts. See, we're all in here for a reason, brother. We're all paying the price for something we done. Something that we can't let go of'

'You're a good man, Boz.'

'It's a hefty fucking price, man. I've been in here for ten years.'

His eyes were shining now; wet with his tears. His lip trembles and I see both strength and compassion. It makes me realize that we are all human, and we all have a story to tell. How we got here, and where we are going.

'Can you help me get back to my daughter?' he pleaded in a quavering voice; 'She's all I got. And she needs me.'

I realized that the whale was looking at me intently, and I think I understood what she meant.

cs❧so

Life behind bars is a sad futility and a death in captivity is nothing short of vain tragedy. And not only death by one's own hand. There is a sense of wan futility even in the unpredictability of natural death when it occurs in custody. A weary, senseless emptiness to it all.

For the second time since my imprisonment I am again faced with the spectre of death. It was a natural passing this time and once again I didn't even know his name, let alone anything of his life story. We would have said nothing more than the occasional hello or exchanged the offhand nodding of heads as we passed each other in the hallway. And yet, I was one of the few who bore witness to his passing.

There was no family to farewell him across the void; no loved ones to comfort him in his final breath. Only the impersonality of a ragged green rank of timeworn passengers, who by some seemingly random default had been destined to occupy that particular space and time with him. And you see, it is precisely that one lonely fact which so perfectly highlights the abject futility of the event.

It took me back to my father's passing. For the old man, it was an event that was softened for us by a life so well lived. Life for my Pop was an ongoing experience; an investigation of sorts. He threw himself willingly into everything; fuelled by a seemingly unquenchable desire to learn and to understand. If it was structural or mechanical, he would repair it, improve it, modify it, enhance it, paint and decorate it. If it was electrical he would connect it, solder it, tune it or tinker with it. Every single damn electrical item in our house seemed to end up with an extra switch on it for some arcane reason known only to him.

He was great with people though. He inspired them, provided for them, captivated them. Understood them. Sometimes frustrated the living heck out of them. On an electric buggy. He fought the Nazis in occupied France and won medals for bravery under fire. He shot and got shot at. And then he travelled as though he was struggling to escape something. Filled every moment of his ensuing life with enquiry and adventure. He trapped a wildcat in a wooden crate in India. Hunted game in the rainforests of Malaya with dayak natives armed with blowpipes. He questioned many things, and answered many others.

And so death itself, when it finally came, was something of a fitting summation to that perfect life of enquiry, and by that time the old man was more than ready to go. The mind had outlived the body and Pop, feeling the dead weight of its aging liability, had prepared himself for one last adventure. On his deathbed that day, he confided in me that he had memorized a long list of sharp probing questions to grill the Maker with. In illness he had lost nothing of his impishly stubborn charm. I smiled inwardly, imagining the impending chaos at the Pearly Gates that day! I guess even in death, there is still so much life!

Just before Pop slipped into a final morphine induced slumber, I was able to tell him to feel free to go and not worry about looking back. And so with the family quietly gathered around his bed in a vigil that persisted into the musky still of the evening, we sat and kept watch; each in our own taut private reverie, until the noble old man finally passed. His last frozen breath somehow endowing his aged features with a look which bridged both welcome relief and peaceable conclusion. The kind of look that I imagine a weary traveller enacts when the long overdue homebound train finally steams into the station, where he has sat numbed and fidgety awaiting its arrival.

You know, in looking back, I think I can begin to understand the meaning and relevance of the spiritual lotus – out of the dark hindering murk of our grief and worldly heaviness, the passing of his spirit, when it finally gave itself up, came as something of lightly delicate beauty. A subtle blooming of pastel light; an opening and a breathing like the flowering of lotus petals. And we were there with him, his earthly kith and kin, in that one perfect moment.

This is precisely what got to me when Arthur James Munroe passed that day. The futility of his passing (I was driven to find out his name afterwards, fuelled by some desperate urge to offset the pointlessness of it all) was that, unlike Pop he had to cross over all alone, save for the meagre few of us who bore witness that day. Eddie and 'Mad-Dog' Murray were heading to the kitchen with a trolley stacked with boxes of tinned fruit. Struggling over the thick wedge of grassy re-growth out the front of the self-care block, Eddie stubbed his toe and upended the topmost box onto the lawn. It had bounced and split, sending cans of apricot halves rolling down the concrete gutter like a tinny gaggle of clunky escaping cons. Much to Murray's squealed delight.

The three Latino 'brothers' (I call them the 'Three Stooges') Pablo, Miguel and What's-his-name (I know it but can't spell or pronounce it) were wandering up the pathway with a movie they had just borrowed from the library, jibbering loudly and animatedly amongst themselves in their native tongue. Maybe it was pure imagination but I'm pretty sure they said something about nachos. But then there is something about the language which makes every conversation seem to be about nachos. Or tacos.

And then there was me.

I had just stepped out of the small rammed earth chapel, snugged cosily into a grove of sycamore trees directly across the narrow bitumen roadway from the self-care living quarters. I had gotten into the habit of making a daily visit to the tiny rustic chapel, which was more often than not empty, save for my own humble presence. I much preferred it this way. The warm amber light, yellowed and softened by the natural timber pitched ceiling gave it an ambience of welcoming reverence. Of exclusively offered solitude. In it I always felt protected; a warming sense of some greater presence in the hushed airiness of timber and slate.

In truth, I waited there expectantly every day for the whale, but she never showed. She hadn't showed for the longest time and just as one moves on from unrequited love, I had begun to resign myself to the sterner possibilities of madness and delusional state of mind.

As I walked out through the infused slants of tempered sunlight that marked the heavy entrance portico, I squinted momentarily as my eyes adjusted to the noonday sun. And in an exact same instant, I bore witness to that pitiful choreography played out in split second freeze-frame. I watched the clanking runaway cans chase each other down the roadway. Heard the pitched boyish squeal of Murray's delight. Wondered about nachos. And saw Arthur James Munro crumple and fall as perfectly and helplessly as a casually discarded rag doll. One second he was there, and in the next heartbeat he wasn't; as if some master-switch had been thrown for the last time. The veiled membrane between this world and the next is as mystically thin as that.

I suspect the sense of futility is the inheritance of only those who are left behind. What I do know for sure is that the fact that he died without the comforting proximity of friends and family both upset and angered me. It grew to bitter seething rage when we were ordered by the guards to remain exactly where we were, bearing the uncomfortable intimacy of the next thirty minutes of CPR, liked shamed voyeurs. Our shuffling shoe-gazing presence was totally unnecessary, inappropriate and somehow irreverent. The guards' blue comments over the lifeless body a crudely undeserved violation which merely added mocking insult to injury.

So when the privacy screens and yellow crime scene tape appeared half an hour later, I made no apologies for yelling back at the imperious senior officer who barked at me angrily for walking away without official clearance. I had had enough of the disrespectful officious farce. A man had just died. No, not just a man. A *person* with everyday hopes and dreams. He was a husband and a father. And as it turned out, a war hero.

Arthur James Munro had been a member of an international peace-keeping force which helicoptered into war-torn Bosnia. Within twenty-four hours of their insertion into the dusty rural chaos one of their number lay dead, cut in half by a sniper's rifle. It was Munro, as the squad's sharpshooter who pursued the fleeing sniper; pumping rounds at him on the fly. It took six bullets to finally take the man down. Welcome to Bosnia. Arthur James Munro returned home from active duty some months later without fanfare, but that time he had witnessed too much. In that ethnic cleansing of Serbian and Croat, something of Arthur James Munro had been left behind on a dusty Bosnian road spattered with the blood of his comrades; leached perfectly from his weary frame.

He finally handed back the blue helmet of the peace-keeping force and put on the old familiar clothes of civilian life again, but the fit was never quite the same after that. *He* was never the same. By the time he finally arrived at the rehab facility, after a shambling nomadic existence which he routinely numbed and medicated with speed and painkillers, he was already damaged goods. It turns out the last of his team who returned home had hanged himself in a woodshed six months ago, leaving Arthur as the sole surviving member of the squad that choppered into the windswept Bosnian LZ that fateful day. Not that anybody really cared by then. Officially nobody gave a damn until the day Arthur broke the law by pulling a gun on a panicked shopkeeper he hoped to rob. Only then did the United States of America suddenly and righteously take interest in Arthur James Munro – violent criminal and recovering drug addict. A hopeless down-and-outer, deemed a risk to the very society which created him.

I watched on sullenly as they covered him with a white sheet. The body would need to remain in place until the coroner arrived, and being a weekend that was likely a few hours away at least. Due to be released in just two weeks' time, he had served six years behind bars. His family had already prepared a surprise homecoming for him, excited by the prospect of his return home, His long suffering mother, despite the frailty of advancing years had insisted on being there, having carefully prepared the score of yellow ribbons which already festooned the London plane trees lining the quiet suburban street. She never told the family that the arthritic pain racking those fragile liver-spotted hands had kept her awake crying for long nights afterwards. It didn't matter because Arthur was coming home where he belonged. Arthur, her beautiful son. Arthur, the carefree little boy who had always loved animals. The man who would do anything for anybody in need.

Little Arthur was coming Home.

Dying at home unexpectedly is one thing, but dying in some grimy prison so far from home, surrounded by people who couldn't care less for you, that's another thing altogether. And that was the point at which I decided to walk away. In every sense of the word, I walked away. I no longer belonged there, bearing forced witness to the remains of Arthur James Munro. I no longer belonged *here* anymore.

That one decision brought about a sudden immediate shift. I felt it, and then I saw it as a mysterious ripple which swept like a pulse across my field of vision. *What in hell was that?* A second pulse, stronger than the first burst soundless, like the shockwave of some unseen explosion. I stopped in my tracks and squinted, looking out beyond the fence. Had I just seen that? The scenery decayed in a spilt-second of static and white noise, before the image quickly re-adjusted itself. What the hell?

A darkly threatening voice from behind suggested in no uncertain terms that I should stand the fuck still. *Now.* Callous simple-minded piece of shit. I had endured enough, seen enough. And now I knew. In equally brash voice, and without pausing to look back, I loudly proposed that Deputy Superintendent Wallis, whoever or whatever he was, should go and fuck himself. Now.

'Now!' I screamed, feeling the word tear coarsely at the back of my throat.

And with that the maelstrom opened; dragging me upwards and away just like a rag-doll until the next moment I was floating face to face with the whale, feeling for all the world like Dorothy's little dog Toto.

'Hello, Dorothy,' I quipped despite the fury of my displacement, 'We really must stop meeting like this.'

'Hello, Adam. I see you can now make the jump for yourself. Well done.'

'Whale, I couldn't quite put my finger on what was wrong here, but I've just figured something out. They're not real are they?'

'Who?'

'The people that I've met since I've been in jail. Dave. Slingshot. Baba and Bozz. Arthur Munro. None of them are real. And neither is this place, I'll wager. And don't tell me it's the medication, because I haven't been taking any. This has all been a sham. *Nothing here is real.*'

'That depends on what you are calling reality.'

'I mean they're not actual people. None of them. There's something just a little too odd about them all. Something oddly familiar to their stories, and something common to them all which doesn't seem to be coincidence.'

'You are correct in saying there is no such thing as coincidence. Go on, Adam,' she urged, matching her graceful movement neatly to mine, so as to remain in the now familiar eye-to-eye position.

'All these people and their stories, they all seem to be reflections. Of me. Like they're all elements of my mind somehow.'
The whale paused momentarily before answering:

'They are called Shades, Adam.'

'Shades?'

'Reflection was an apt description. Perhaps you might also refer to them as echoes.'

'Echoes originate from somewhere, or more correctly *someone*. So who are they from, whale? Me?'

'Everything that we do, every action has a consequence. They create ripples through the time-stream. And sometimes those ripples are from actions severe enough to come back to confront us. To haunt us until such a time that we can move beyond them.'

The blood pounded in my temples as I struggled to comprehend.

'Shit, this is too much,'
A dark thought slowly dawned.

'This is Hell isn't it?'

'Only if you decide for yourself that it is.'

'It has that Hellish camel feel to it.'

'If you believe it to be so, Adam.'

'If *I* believe it to be so? Why does it seem like a lot of this whole clusterfuck is coming down to me? Tell me straight please whale, with no riddles this time. Where am I?'

'You are on what is known as the Plane of Forces,' came the cool measured response.

'And where exactly is that?'

'It is not the physical world that you are familiar with. Everything is dependent on vibration, Adam, as you already know. The Plane of Forces vibrates differently to the Physical Plane, but it is the closest and most easily accessible dimension to it.'
The whale allowed her words to sink in before continuing.

'There is a reason you feel the way you do. The earthly longings, the yearning that you feel is due to the fact that you are very close to the physical world, yet not close enough that you can touch it, or continue to be a part of it.'

'I'm in a prison, whale. That's why I can't be a part of it, as you put it.'

'Your mind rationalizes your situation as a prison, Adam. This is what conscious mind does. It has taken the elements of your present state of being and logically presented them to you in the best way that it can.'

'Whale, I'm sorry but this is bullshit. How can it not be the real world? I was talking to Maree on the phone the other day.'

'You spoke to her and she spoke back. *Energetically.* You feel her presence and she feels yours. In dreams, Adam. In earthly longings. Your mind simply painted the familiar image of the telephone into the picture for you.'
The weight of the whale's words was crushing, and my inners felt like molten liquid.

'Look deeper, Adam,' she urged, 'Look past the mind's construct. Remember the story I told you about green grass and solid rock?'

Green grass and solid rock. *The world we exist in is not as it seems, but simply as our limited senses portray it.* I remembered our previous conversation, in that same moment wondering just how many conversations with the whale I had forgotten about.

'But I swear the phone calls were real, whale.'

'Tell me Adam; Maree, does she visit you?'

'Well no. But then our home isn't just around the corner from here. It's miles away.'

'Yes Adam, it is,' she persisted softly, sensing my tears rising at the memory, 'And have you not wondered why neither of you ever discussed the possibility of her visiting you? How your talk is only ever about times past?'

'This is a lot to process, whale.'

'The world you are experiencing is very real, Adam. But it is not your familiar old world. Your conscious mind merely presents it as if you were still in corporeal form.'

The whale's gently persistent words washed over me, half-registered.

'So that explains my prison, I suppose. But where are we now, you and I?'

'Vibration, Adam. There are higher dimensions of Being beyond your present reality. Dimensions overlapping dimensions. What you are experiencing is your higher form. Have you noticed how much lighter you feel here? How much Light you feel?'

'I would love to stay here, whale. It is perfect peace after that madhouse of hate. So how come I can never remember our meetings when I return?'

'On some level, you do. But for the most part the fine details are hidden from your conscious mind for good reason. The fuller memory would prevent you from living in the Here and Now and distract you from learning the lessons that you need to learn.'

Once again I paused to allow the whale's message to sink in. I mulled over her last thought.

'OK, so maybe I should be asking myself what the lesson is that I need to learn in this place. This…this prison.'

'Yes. I think you put it nicely as Dave when you said: *All we really have is today. Yesterday has been written and cannot be undone. We can beat ourselves up continually over it, but that just keeps us rooted in the past.*

It paralyses us. Yesterday is done. But the choice is ours with what we do today, if we decide that we want a better tomorrow.'

'Well it seems to me there is something holding me back, whale. Something that I need to resolve so I can move on.'

'You are correct.'

'And these Shades are the echoes of that something reflecting back at me?'

'I couldn't have put it better myself, Adam.'

'So really I have created this prison for myself in a sort of *'As ye sow, so shall ye reap'* kind of way?'

'Some might call it Karma.'

'So am I stuck here?'

'No. Some move beyond it quickly. Others take an eternity of repetition before they figure it all out. Besides your Shades, most of the people you meet on the Plane of Forces fall into the latter category. They are sleepwalkers. Shells, who for whatever reason haven't been able to transcend their situation. Or have no desire to. The lures and temptations of the physical world are too much for some.'

'I'm pretty sure I can pick those people. And maybe that explains also the feeling that I don't belong here.'

'Your time is limited here, my friend. Your sentence is almost complete. And the Light has a plan for you.

'Yes, you mentioned this before. That whole *'reach in'* thing.'

'Let me share something with you Adam. There is a great battle being fought. A battle between the forces of Light and the armies of the Dark. Remember the iceberg? The battle is being waged below the surface, unseen except to those with the Sight. It is being played out on the battlefield of the Physical Plane.'

'Whale, how have I come to be involved in this?'

'My friend, we have hardly begun to scratch the surface of cosmic knowledge here. You have enough for now to begin your new journey.'

'It seems as though I've already been on one. Like I've been dragged through a wringer backwards.'

'Adam, you told me that you were worried about what this place was doing to your soul. Perhaps you need to see it as what it has done *for* your soul. It will only be a prison until you choose to widen your circle of compassion beyond it.'

'I really hope I can do that, whale.'

'I believe you have, Adam,' replied the whale with what could almost pass for a proud expression, 'I believe that you already have.'

A glint of blue caught at the corner of my eye. Strident and bottle-like amidst the softer green-yellow patchwork of sycamore and grass. I turned to seek out the source. Light danced and caught on the striking red and blue lead-light glass over the chapel entrance door. Scroll-like, the decorative words emblazoned across it read: *'Reach For Life'*.

So there it was, in all of its seemingly complex simplicity. *Life.* Have we really become so callous; so impersonal and hard-shelled that we can visit such wrongs and injustices on another? That we can claim any sense of superiority over another life form?

The greatest force in the world is the power of Love, and the greatest threat to that is the love of power. That was the moment in which a lot of things became clear, and I knew exactly what it was that I had to do.

CHAPTER SIXTEEN

HOME

'It is an interesting biological fact that all of us have in our veins the exact
same percentage of salt in our blood that exists in the ocean.
We are tied to the ocean.
And when we go back to the sea, whether it is to sail or to watch it –
we are going back from whence we came.'
–JOHN F KENNEDY (1917-1963)

HAVE YOU EVER seen a deck of Tarot cards? I would like to take a moment to describe one of the images to you. The first card of the deck is called 'The Fool', and it depicts a young man looking toward the horizon and striding purposefully forward, a small knapsack of belongings slung over one shoulder. On closer inspection, you will notice that he is walking dangerously close to the edge of a cliff. Had he been more observant of his immediate surroundings, he would have noticed the danger.

A small white dog is seen grasping the cuff of his shirt, warning him of the impending danger. Still, the youth is naively oblivious to the warning signs around him, and the peril he is in. He is the embodiment of youth and idealism and the woefully small sack of belongings he carries speaks of his scant worldly experience. Like so many of us his mind is in the future, not in the present.

When I look back on the chain of events that led me to this point, I realise that I have been a fool too. That was me - idealistic and naive. Rightly speaking, I suppose we all are 'The Fool' at some point in our lives. Every journey has a beginning, whether it be in cutting the apron strings and stepping out into the world as a young adult, or that first hormonal rush that marks the start of an exciting new relationship. Each journey begins stridently with high hopes for the future. My old university lecturer used to say a successful person has failed seventy per-cent of the time. We inevitably fall a great many times before we walk, and I think that is what life is all about. It's what we choose to do after we fall that defines us.

Pausing to gaze around the cramped confines of my shabby little cell, I realize that I have still acquired precious little by way of material trappings over the past months. Letters and photographs from home, each neatly dated and bundled together in a cardboard shoebox. A set of well-worn, dog-eared exercise books that contain all of my scribbled writings. This time however I'm able to assess my meagre inventory without tears, and something has definitely changed. These few belongings do not represent All That I Am and nor am I defined by them.

When I think back to when I started this journey I realize I carried precious little spiritually, just like the Fool with his meagre knapsack trussed jauntily over his shoulder. I realise now that the time when I sobbed fitfully over my scrappy bag of possessions, I was really crying for the Fool that I was. I realize that I am no longer that naïve young man, and time and tide have witnessed the changes.

My mind returns to the day when I first walked into this prison, wide-eyed and fearful of what I may lose. Today I am preparing myself to walk away, grateful for what I have found.

When first we met, I was entering a foreboding world. A world of prison cells and steel bars, of violence and vice. One of the harshest of existences a person can endure, where ordinary things are beyond your control and you are forever at the whim of others. The denial of freedom and liberty must be one of the harshest punishments that a sentient being can endure, short of the finality of death. I remember telling you back when we began that I longed for the comfort of home. My quiet home – safe with the ones that I loved. This is of course no surprise. Because home, as they say, is where the heart is. It is where the heart naturally yearns to return to in times of dire distress.

What I want to tell you now is that I have learned something deeper about this thing we call 'home'. Our flesh and blood yearns naturally for home and for family. But there is a far greater journey to be had.

When the time came to leave, it was not quite as I had expected it. Heaven knows I had stood at the shady rotunda near the tall wire gates to the rehabilitation center so many times before. Imagining what it might feel like the day that I donned my civilian clothes again and walked through the tiny processing area and out to the other side. No longer defined by an outfit of shabby prison greens, or limited by barbed wire and bars. I had often daydreamt about that moment of release, and how it would feel to return to the world once again. When my time came, it was all of those things and more.

My belongings had been packed into a bag and dropped at the reception area the evening before, so all I needed to do was eat a light breakfast and brush my teeth before saying my goodbyes to my roommates. I took my bundle of civvies from the desk clerk and shut myself into the tiny change area she pointed me to. It was the first time that I had seen my old clothes from what seemed like a lifetime ago. I held them up and examined each article with a childlike fascination. The lush palette of colors and the different textures of each of the fabrics, all quite foreign to sight and touch. An unfamiliar weight and weave to them. My favourite old grey coat. And shoelaces! My boots had shoelaces, and I drew a quiet pleasure from tensioning and tying them; feeling a growing sense of empowerment after endless months of shoes with velcro straps and a careful absence of anything which I might use to end my misery.

I was coming back to life, rising from the tomb like some wildly grinning Lazarus. I caught sight of my reflection in the small polished safety glass mirror. The long hair was gone, replaced by a far more sensible looking cut of dark thatch. I could see my old essential self in the unfamiliar eyes staring back at me. I was still there, distant and knowing like some weary traveller, jetlagged yet somehow defined and shaped by those bittersweet memories of passage.

A foreboding chill went through me. That odd feeling that old wives will tell you means that somebody has just walked over your grave. *My grave!* I squinted feverishly and stared into my reflection, misty and grained in the scratched mirror. Tried to find that slip of fleeting movement that hid itself in the shadows when it caught sight of me looking in. Grabbing at the mirror surrounds reflexively with both hands, as though I was making to tear it from the wall.

'Who are you? Where are you?' I called at the retreating shape.

The now familiar sense of paranoia crept up and tapped me on the back once again, making me spin around suddenly in fright. The world does not exist as we think it does.

'*Where* are you?'

Feeling a knot of panic tightening in my gut, I feverishly examined the walls of the small featureless room, like some crazed blind man scrabbling for an exit. *Solid.* Not a construct. The surge of pain in my fingertips was reassuring. Not a construct. That mirror was real, at least solid enough to resist my desperate grab at it. That's a good sign, isn't it?

'Everything OK in there, Svenson?'

The reception officer's enquiring voice from outside the room seemed muffled and distant through the thick slab of the door. I pulled myself together, vaguely aware of not wanting to sound rattled or unhinged. Don't blow this, Adam. Not at this late stage of the game.

'I'm OK. Almost done here.'

Hopefully she would mistake my manic edge to be simply the excitement of impending release. Drawing a centering breath, I opened the door.

'Are you ready, Svenson?'

'Yes, ma'am. I'm ready.'

'Hurry up then. They're expecting you.'

'Who's expecting me?' I enquired of the blue uniform.

'You'll see,' the desk clerk replied with a wry half-smile, 'Tabula rasa, Mr Svenson. Tabula rasa.'

Time from that moment on became little more than a vacant blur. Three signatures later, I walked through the double paned entrance door without fuss or fanfare, feeling rather than hearing it close firmly behind me. As it did, so too a set of conscious memories similarly closed shut. They remain there, in a deep pool of knowing, should I need to reach in to find them. *Tabula rasa.* The blank slate.

Beyond the small car park a bitumen road wound through a clutch of fir trees. I stood for a moment, sniffing the air. It hung suspended and still, a thinly dry electricity of vague expectation. The sky looked different somehow. The small forest was dark yet inviting and scatterings of light broke through as I followed the road, my first reluctant steps slowly becoming more confident. A self-assured fluidity slowly returning to my gait. There was no sign of a barbed wire fence, and small birds chattered distractedly in the tops of the trees, perfectly oblivious to my passing. Almost without warning, the quiet cloistering tunnel of trees and the low overhang of branches gave way to a blinding mid-morning sun, forcing me to clutch instinctively at my unaccustomed eyes in fright. It took me precious seconds before I realized that the racking cry of wet sobs was actually my own.

The bus trip down the west coast took several hours, though I have little recollection of the passage. For me the scenery through the window, every sight and nuance of color seemed somehow vibrant and new. The air-conditioned bus was barely half-full, and the other passengers seemed content to chatter amiably in their own small groups, as though the only bond we shared was the mere fact that we had all boarded the same southbound coach.

Personally I was happy with that arrangement, lost as I was in my own quietly percolating sense of detachment. I felt microscopic and raw. Naked and still forming. Every sight, sound and smell seemed to very rapidly overwhelm my senses. And so, I contented myself with jamming the small purple travel cushion between my temple and the plastic window surround, simply allowing the vista to scroll past my window like a green and brown patchwork quilt of hills and tall stands of trees. The rolling verdant panorama punctuated every so often by a staccato punch of compressed air which rocked the bus as cars sped by in the opposite direction, fired like so many bullets from a gun.

By the time that the granite grays, glass, steel and red brick of urbanity had replaced the softer rural scenery, the curious sense of detachment had been all but overtaken by a cold hard lump of anxiety that wedged itself against my solar plexus. I cast a furtive glance around the bus, concerned that my increasingly fidgety behaviour might telegraph my intent to my fellow travellers. I needn't have worried – no-one seemed to have given me so much as a sideways glance since we embarked all those hours before. Mackie would most likely be looking for me now, after yesterday's episode at the ship. Despite that, I reminded myself that it was unlikely he could have second-guessed my plan. He wouldn't think to be looking for me down here and if nothing else, the photographs were now safe. The knot of traffic grew steadily larger, and the stop-start drive through downtown Los Angeles now seemed to take forever.

Arriving at the depot, I muttered my thanks to the driver, descending the stairs to be met by a sudden ripple of heat. The bitumen felt hot and angry underfoot, and I was grateful for the shade offered by the sultry line of palms which lined the coast road.

It was late afternoon by the time I reached the old sea wall near the park, feeling dry and parched. Now that I had stopped walking, the balls of my feet were hotly raw and protested terribly; as if woefully unaccustomed to the sudden demand. Relieved of the load, muscles ached, and I cursed as my calves involuntarily contracted and throbbed. I had reached a point where I could spend hours on a rolling deck without so much as breaking a sweat, yet the hours walk under the yellow haze of the LA afternoon sun had all but exhausted me.

The last of my money was spent at a small hardware store, and now the solid handles of a pristine gloss red pair of heavy-duty bolt-cutters stuck obtrusively out of my old army green backpack. My offhand manner, borne of the bone weary tiredness of the journey raised nothing by way of suspicion from the pimply young clerk who had served me dismissively. The tall gangly youth seemed far more interested in returning to chat aimlessly with an equally disinterested youth with one lazy eye.

Pausing to catch my breath in the dying swelter of the afternoon, a picture came to my mind of one of the old tarot card images that Maree had described to me. The thought made me smile, for what seemed the first time in an eternity. The Fool had returned, the instrument of redemption slung like a heavy red crossbow over his back. Standing at the point where the sandy beach gave way to the long rocky bastion of sea wall I took stock of the situation, idly kicking at shaggy clumps of dry grass which peered from crevices in the charcoal-gray rock. The top of the wall was broad and flat, and rather reminded me of the rampart of a castle. It was an easy walk along the flat grassy expanse atop the wall. More importantly, there was no-one in sight, and the traffic sounds were distant and muffled. Even if I happened to be seen, I looked little more than a solitary walker, taking in the musky Californian sea air. That said, I nonetheless shoved the bolt-cutter as deep as it would go into the bulky backpack, before setting off stridently in the direction of the park.

Cutting my way into the amusement park was a simple affair. The chain mesh fence barely took the protective oil sheen off the shiny metal business end of the bolt-cutters, and the wire strands gave way like butter. Without the dizzying kaleidoscope of lights and sound the sideshow alley had a vaguely morbid atmosphere, a weird sense of foreboding which made me think of chimpanzees and popcorn. I brushed past the gaudily painted amusement rides with names like *'The Octopus'* and *'Python Loop'*, their cupolas and carriages all carefully tarped up against the weather; eying the path ahead cautiously before making for the common wall which hid the marine park from view. Nearer to the stucco wall, I could make out the metallic rise of an old water tank and the tops of palms peering over from the spot where I knew the dolphin enclosure lay. The sea breeze was little more than a solitary whisper which barely moved the fronds of the trees. When I finally heard the familiar sound of their breathing I knew that I was close.

The sea pen gates proved to be a nightmare after the ease with which the security fence had given way. Having carefully and sure-footedly crabbed my way across the rocky face of the sea wall I muttered softly under my breath, wondering what exactly I had expected. Up close, the barred gate rose up out of the water, thick and heavy like some old castle portcullis. A solid barred fence extended across the top of it, preventing anyone, or anything from leaping over the top of it. The sea gate was not one but two heavy barred gates which swung from big hinges on either side. Suddenly aware that the burnished glow of setting sun offered me little by way of protective cover, I cast a guilty look around me and furtively scanned the area, before popping my head up discreetly to peer into the park enclosure. Three shiny fins stood together by the rim of the lagoon nearest to me, looking like battleship row at Pearl Harbor. The familiar sight of those three dark fins brought back memories which rose and caught in my throat.

In a crouch, I thought hard. Once out along the sea gate I would be exposed, should anyone happen be looking back across the wide expanse of lagoon. Cautiously I inspected the hinges closest to me, deciding from the ancient ferrules of fused rust that the gate hadn't been opened in a decade. Think fast, Adam.

I decided on abandoning the backpack and swimming my way across the protruding top of the gate to tackle the centre padlocks. Cramming the handles of the bolt-cutter into my jeans, I let go of the rocks. The water felt cold and unfamiliar. The gentle swell pushed me neatly against the rough metal bars as I clung to the rusting barrier and carefully edged my way across. Clear of the sea wall, the vista of the lagoon lay before me. In the dying light I could clearly make out the three orcas, lying together like massive tree logs floating in a dam.

'*Wooomfh-shhh.*' The lazy sound of their slow steady breathing told me that they were sleeping. I reached the centre of the gate easily, despite the growing weight of my sodden clothes. The centre padlock was predictably solid and hung bright and shiny above the waterline on an equally weighty welded steel chain. Cursing to myself as I clung to the heavy bars, I decided there had to be at least another padlock below the surface. I checked the bolt-cutter was snugly secure, took a steadying breath and dropped into the water. My descent was easy with the cloying weight of saturated jeans and sweater, and my body felt awkward and unnaturally heavy.

Dark water. Even just a few feet down, what little light there was faded impotently to a murky dimness. I shivered soundlessly and pulled myself down the centre bars, feeling my way. Another heavy chain – that must be the mid-point of gate. I kept going, still descending easily. The old sea gates were easily two-thirds underwater, with just the top third projecting above the waterline. They had been secured together by heavy stainless padlocks at three points. Two underwater and one above.

I kicked my way back to the top, sodden and cumbersome. Surfacing I gasped instinctively, clumsily swallowing salt water with the reflexive intake of breath. I hunched low in the water for a moment, painfully aware of the noise I was making in the evening stillness. There was still no movement beyond the gate. When I finally managed to wedge myself into a position where I could lever the bolt-cutters against the heavy padlock, I found to my frustration that the heavy tool would leave little more than a score mark on the thick metal before slipping off impotently. Wedging my feet harder against the bars and raising myself out of the water for leverage I switched to attacking the heavy links of chain, with similar result.

Tiring rapidly, I crammed the handles of the cutter back into my jeans and crabbed my way back along the gate to the protective cover of the sea wall to rest and re-consider. Dragging myself clear of the water I lay with my back against the rock embankment, my breath coming in sharp shallow gasps which pulled at my stomach muscles painfully. I wrung what seemed like buckets of water from my sodden windbreaker and considered stripping off to lighten the burden of waterlogged clothing. Lying back, I turned my head to look at my new nemesis, the gate. *The hinges.* My mind kicked in – I hadn't thought about cutting away the corroding hinges. Galvanised I reached out and groped at the nearby top hinge, feeling the rough protruding pin. Swinging the bolt-cutters into position I made an exploratory cut into the old attachment from my position alongside, hearing the promising brittle crack of old rust and decaying metal.

The two uppermost hinge pins had sheared away easily causing the gate to sag, its weight now suspended on the hinge near the sea bed. Down here at the very bottom of the gate the ocean was a cold blanket which weighted me down and sapped my strength. Through the gloom the bottom hinge shone shiny and new, unlike its rusty counterparts. It refused to budge under the leverage of the heavy cutters, and my arms were heavy with repeated frustrated effort. With the blood starting to sing painfully in my ears as I fought the instinctive bodily urge to gulp oxygen, I kicked my way to the surface once again; pulling myself up onto the rock wall in the growing darkness to muster my strength for another dive.

I don't know how long he had been there waiting for me. His dark shadow separated from the top of the wall and lunged at me angrily.

A well-aimed kicked split my lip and threw the bolt-cutters from my hand. I tasted salt and the warm liquidity of fresh blood as the blow threw me backwards. I heard my instinctive groan as I fell awkwardly against wet, slimy rock.

'Get the hell back up here you little shithead!'
The guard screamed blue murder from the top of the wall, stumbling awkwardly as he clambered down the sharp angle of bastion wall.

The heavy cutter had disappeared into the steady surge of water and without a second thought I dived to follow it, pulling myself down the heavy gate desperately. Missing its top hinges, this time the heavy assembly 'gave' and shifted precious inches as I heaved against it. Not enough to open it though. Reaching the bottom, I stared blindly into dark water.

Moments later a freight train hit the gate.

A sudden shockwave of water threw me backwards and the rough bars flung themselves against my face, and the still dark water became a blur of unexpected color and movement. Pink and flashing white, the ocean thrashed and took form; dark and uncoiling, bluntly black. My face was inches away from the bulbous rounded snout which now filled my entire field of vision. As he pulled back from breach slightly, I caught sight of that eye, inquisitive and alive, and I immediately knew his intention. I felt an adrenaline surge of fear and incredulity at the bull orcas size and sheer sense of presence. Locking his gaze on me as he reversed; I steadied myself against the foot of the rock wall. The gate came away from the wall as the final hinge gave way under the orcas second charge, folding impotently and tearing great lumps of concrete away with it.

The ferocity with which the massive orca had rammed the gate was terrifying. My blood sang and it felt like victory. Then, here he was passing alongside me as though I had come up against the fast moving hull of a ship in the night. Solid, cold yet softly yielding to the touch. His broad flat pectoral fin shoved me aside as it displaced water and I gyrated awkwardly in its wake like some punch-drunk cage fighter. Sudden crazy water and foaming contrails like white water rapids streaming back at me and catching me up in its wake. High pitched creaks and rapid streams of clicks ringing in my ears.

Then more movement from the looming hole where the gate had once been; veering towards me. Close against the huge swath of departing tail, another black and white shape pulsed past me. Smaller, but still blocky and powerful, the second orca gazed at me as she slid past effortlessly. The dark inquisitive eye giving me once quick glance of recognition as she followed her mate to sea.

I recall the split second delay as I anticipated the shockwave behind her streamlined tailfin. *Bbboomphhh.* I was thrown like a loose sock in a washing machine, watching the plump lines of two dark torpedoes departing into the shadow-fall that marked the way to open ocean.

Dear Maree,

I'm hoping this message gets to you, so that you know just what an amazing strength you have been throughout these long months. *You* have been the unfailing constant through all of this, and for that I want to thank you from the bottom of my heart. Many have been the times that I have wondered how you could possibly love such a fool.

Do you remember that day when we finally met? Of that day, I particularly remember this one thing. We were standing close together in that cobbled square and we noticed our shadows, cast in the backlight of the setting sun. And looking down at those tall, tall silhouettes in that sun-dappled square, I remember thinking to myself that those were the shadows of bold people. That the shadows we cast were big. So perhaps it is fitting that the mark that we will ultimately leave on the Earth should be rightfully bigger than the both of us.

In truth, we are a part of something which is far bigger than us and when it speaks to us by name it is not a call that is always easy to answer. It requires us, in our turn, to be something larger than ourselves. To recognize just who and what we truly are. Many of us live our lives as virtual sleepwalkers, and some of us never wake up. But once your eyes are finally opened those days of slumber are over. That time has now come.

The world that we know, and take for granted; our comfortable façade of humanity and peaceable civility is wallpaper thin. It is a carefully crafted illusion and there is a dark brooding ugliness festering behind it. But beyond that darkness there is a Light, and we are answerable to it. Beyond the robe and the gavel, beyond the reach of self-serving politicians and overstuffed statesmen. We should speak that Truth, even if our voice shakes.

Maree, this is the one last thing I must do, and then I will be home. I promise. The truth is I am always nearby anyway, no matter what physical distance separates us. The secret is to reach in to find me. Remember this, and I will be seeing you very soon.

I am coming home!

Love to you and to Tin-Tin. Adam.

How much water I swallowed before I could elbow the muscly security guard in the ribs and break his cloying grip was anybody's guess. With the water still eddying and foaming from the departure of the two massive black dam busters, he had seized the moment to grapple me from behind. He hung on like grim death to my heavy sweatshirt, which stretched crazily as I struggled to break free from his grasp. Through the gloom I could make out his face, reddening and contorted. Realising a punch would not throw through the heavy water, I settled for digging fingers deep into his eye sockets. It worked. He recoiled slightly and released his death grip, angry bubbles of expelled air rising from him like some crazed skindiver.

The flash of approaching white belly grew suddenly and shoved him aside like a discarded rag doll, before revolving neatly to collect me up. Instinctively I made a grab as the stout fin descended to meet my outstretched arms. It was deceptively strong. Unyielding. And with that we were rising to the surface like a steam train, trailing bubbles and flume. As though I was strapped to a rocket. And then I was carried away, dragging air into parched lungs. Exhausted.

The evening breeze felt good against my face as I drew in deep lungfuls of it thankfully. As the adrenaline drained from my body I was overwhelmed with the painful need to sleep. The orcas body had a familiarity about it; softly yielding yet strong and purposeful. Behind us the sea wall had become little more than a gray distant line with just the thin white foam of breakers to mark its presence. The deep sonorous ring of a nearby shipping lane marker punctuated the hiss of our wake. And then there was only ocean.

'Adam'

'Oh, hello Persia.'

'Hello, Adam. I've been waiting for you.'

The rush of water came to a sudden crescendo, before falling away to a perfect hushed silence. And with that my body simply unburdened, as though all the anxieties and concerns that I had carried as a cross were lifted from my shoulders.

I turned to face the whale. Weightless and composed.

'Am I dying?'

'No, you are Living.'

'How did I get here?'

'You do not remember?'

'No, Persia. I'm sorry, I do not.'

I felt the pounding rush of blood in my temples, and my head hurt despite the welcome tranquillity of the moment.

'Think back, Adam and reach in.'

ଓଞ୍ଚ

The night closed in with a whispering of eerie familiarity. The harbor sleeping into the soft small hours of the morning. A familiar darkness hid the white angularity of hulls and masts, but the wet lapping of water and strained creak of rope spoke of their restless restrained presence. Peering in cautiously through the rectangular window from the shadows of the starboard bridge wing, I could see the bridge was silent and still; the comfortable leather chair at the helm vacant. Testing the chrome handle carefully, I found it moved easily; cold as ice to the touch. The door gave way with a ratcheting clunk and I squeezed past the captain's chair, making my way to the small chart table along the port side of the cramped cockpit.

On this side of the ship, the naked glare of the harbor lights illuminated the black steel flank of the vessel and lit up the radio array on the bulkhead behind the table; bright enough for me to make out the fascias of tuning knobs and dials. I moved in a steady crouch to avoid detection and a quick sweep from the port bridge windows to the dock below confirmed my entry to the ship had passed unseen.

The aft companionway leading down into the bowels of the ship was dark and silent. I would need to reach the diesel room and then double back to drop the Nikon back into Mackie's quarters before finally checking that the coast was clear for my exit across the exposed companionway.

Below decks, the steel bulkheads and fittings were weeping moisture profusely from the day's earlier humidity. The cramped engine room smelt of sweat and old diesel. Amidst the confused run of cooling pipes, the heavy sea cock took some shifting from its closed position. A thin coating of rust had built up despite the lubricating slick of oil against exposed metal thread. I grabbed the knurled red circular handle atop the gate valve with both hands, barking my knuckles painfully against an adjoining water shroud as they slipped suddenly from the damp metal. A low gurgle gave way to become a steady wet rush. The sea water which poured in through the open sea cock caught me by surprise and I jumped back instinctively, feeling my heavy socks and track shoes soaking up the cold water thirstily.

Moving to the opposing valve I went through the same procedure, finding the second one moved easily; sitting as it did under the warmer exhaust shrouding. The ingress of water became louder now, and it filled the silence of the metallic tomb accusingly. Suddenly galvanised by the deliberation of my act, I moved swiftly. The polished linoleum floor of the narrow corridor picked up the wet slapping squelch of my feet, and I winced at the noise which seemed to reverberate off the smooth walls in the silence. Worse still, I could now hear the dull in-rush of water from behind me. With the heavy engine room door wide open, there was now precious little in the way of soundproofing to mask it, and it reminded me of a battery of runaway washing machines in a Laundromat.

It was when I came back out of Mackie's room that I realized I wasn't the only soul on the ship. Perhaps I sensed it just moments before the blow – a ripple of darker energy that belonged to neither me nor the vessel.

The first blow sent me buckling to my knees; the shock delaying the white spur of pain for a millisecond so that everything moved in slow motion. Reflexively, I lunged at the black figure; smelling cheap alcohol and feeling a sub-layer of tensed muscle and sinew under the thick neoprene.

The second blow glanced off the side of my ribcage and I felt the sudden dry snap of bone.

'Persia....'

'I am here, Adam.'

The final delivered blow wasn't flesh but metal. I can still see the glint of the heavy spanner, all silver against black. I felt the finality of its weight as it collided with my temple and fatally splintered bone.

And then there was nothing except the endless summer.

Sand clinging to my sun-tanned feet.

Ice cold lemonade and the singing of a thousand cicadas.

The soft fall of leaves from the old sycamore tree in the front yard, and the rope swing that hung from it, where I fell and broke my wrist as a kid.

I heard my mother's voice in the orchard, softly pointing out the spider web in the old apple tree to me as she cradled me in her arms. And in that quiet moment I knew that I was Home.

The wave of comprehension swept over me and I felt the faintly distant longing for summers past, and the love of the most beautiful woman in the world. My tears mingled with the salt and I felt lonely and small.

'She'll be waiting for you Adam,' said the whale in quiet voice.

'Yes Persia, she will.'

And with that, the memories faded and neatly reacquired their rightful places in the stream, locking together as neatly as a jigsaw puzzle at its proud conclusion.

'Persia?'

'Yes, my friend?'

'How can you forgive me after all the pain I caused you?'

'Judgement is not mine to make, Adam. You have atoned and that is enough.'

We continued wordlessly, drafted easily in the current before the sleek dark whale finally broke the silence:

'Unarm, dearest friend. The long day's task is done, and for now we must sleep.'

The flesh beside me was cool to the touch, yet pliant and reassuring. We left long fingers of dappled sunlight behind us, yet their suffused glow remained reassuringly draped about us like the finest winter cloak.

The deeper water that we dived into was anything but still.

Love is a risk – take it. Take many risks.
The heart is blind, yet in that blindness there is truth.
Be in love with life, and live with meaning.
Be true to yourself, for in truth you are all that you have.
You are all that you need.
You are enough.
Never be afraid to let yourself be seen
For you are loved without condition or judgement.
You exist within a greater Harmony and the Harmony exists
within You.
Widen your circle of compassion.

At the end of the day, we are all just walking one another Home.

ADAM SVENSON
PERSIA - *Clan of Three Pods*

DECODING 'HOME'

SeaWorld to End Orca Breeding Program
By ABC NEWS
Mar 17, 2016, 11:41 AM ET

SeaWorld is ending its controversial killer whale breeding programs, the theme park operator said in a statement today.

Its treatment of the orcas has come under fierce criticism since the release of the 2013 documentary 'Blackfish.'

'SeaWorld has been listening and we're changing,' the statement said. 'Society is changing and we're changing with it. SeaWorld is finding new ways to continue to deliver on our purpose to inspire all our guests to take action to protect wild animals and wild places.'

It's changing the breeding policy, as of today, but none of the 29 orcas in SeaWorld's care will be released, according to the statement.

'The best place for them is at SeaWorld. No whale born under human care has been released successfully,' company CEO Joel Manby said.

'These majestic orcas will not be released into the ocean, nor confined to sea cages. They could not survive in oceans to compete for food, be exposed to unfamiliar diseases or to have to deal with environmental concerns – including pollution and other man-made threats. Instead, they will live long and healthy lives under love and care of our dedicated veterinary and other trained specialists where they can inspire this and future generations to be conservationists around the world through natural presentations that are fun, exciting and will educate guests about the plight of orcas in the wild.'

SeaWorld has operations in Florida, Texas and California.

And so, on March 17 2016 SeaWorld USA announced that it would end their in-house captive breeding programs for orcas, following several years of pressure from environmental groups and damning publicity exposing cruel and unacceptable practices. You might notice that they are still sticking to the same propaganda-like spin about *'long healthy lives in captivity'* and the *'fun, exciting presentations that educate guests about the plight of orcas in the wild.'*

I'm still to this day left wondering exactly how putting a creature which swims hundreds of miles a day with its family into confinement in a swimming pool is 'fun and exciting' for the orca, and how it could in any way educate people as to their 'plight in the wild.' By extension, perhaps one day we will be able to give a race of visiting alien beings an insight into how we humans actually live by showing them around a prison or a concentration camp.

To me, it says rather more about the orcas plight in captivity and the mentality of the humans who keep them there. Company CEO Joel Manby also conveniently omitted to tell you that the life expectancy of an orca in captivity has been proven to be about half the natural lifespan that an orca enjoys in the wild. I wish Joel the same 'long and healthy life' too.

Ironically when SeaWorld made this announcement, I found myself in an immigration detention centre which was the equivalent of a maximum security prison. After many years of advocating for the protection of marine mammals; just as a major blow was struck for their freedom, I found my own freedom cruelly snatched away.

This became my original inspiration for writing *'Home'* – to draw a parallel between the plight of the orcas in captivity and the trials of a human being in prison. Somewhere in the telling of this, the whale intervened and re-wrote both the plot and the ending; deciding that there was a far deeper message that needed to be relayed to you.

ఇ ENTER THE WHALE ఎ

Time, as the whale said to Adam is a funny thing. But what does the concept of time and space have to do with our cetacean friends? I believe they inherently know a little bit more about the subject than what we do. I also believe they know more about us than we do about them.

I have seen some strange things that led me to this conclusion; experienced some very unusual oddities around them. And one day if perchance we happen to meet down by Constitution dock and you would truly like to know, I will gladly sit down at the cosy table by the old stone fireplace and tell you over hot buttered rums exactly what I saw; just like old Duke Delaney did.

And so what of the whale? Who or what was she? I will simply grace this with the suggestion that perhaps she is my own interpretation of the camel.

"I can once again feel the whale, dark yet reassuring against my back." said Adam.

Who amongst us hasn't felt this reassuring presence at some time in their lives, and referred to it as a guardian angel, or a spirit guide, or a deceased loved one?

Or perhaps when you're busy feeling the camel and you finally remove the blindfold, the whale appears?

With regards to the era in which *'Home'* is set, there are numerous allusions to the 1960s. However, since the concept of time played such a pivotal role in this story, I did my best to remove as many references as possible that may allow you to pin down the precise year that this story was set in. For that reason Adam has a radio, not a cassette or a Walkman or an MP3 player. The 'three stooges' borrow a movie, not a video or a DVD.

And hence the specific objects mentioned are those with timeless qualities: Kathy's canary yellow 1968 Corvette Stingray, her father's Ford Thunderbird, Bozz's Harley-Davidson Springer Softail with a 1200 cube pan-head engine. OK, those are timeless 'boy things', granted. The nod to JRR Tolkein's timeless work *'The Hobbit'* draws on Gollum's cryptic reference to time. And Steely Dan's *'Reeling In The Years'* is not just a timeless classic but also a convenient tongue-in-cheek reference to time's passing.

And what about the characters? Well, the majority of them are based on real people. Shades, as the whale might say. The names have all been changed, except in one case. I will leave it up to you to decide who he is.

The tale of Kelly the dolphin is true, and so too is the story of the incredible knot-untying Top Notch. And orcas have been observed in captivity in at least one marine park ritually worshipping the arrival of the sun each day.

Reference to the Sun and to Light is one of the running themes of *'Home.'* In the physical world, the Sun is a natural reference which life synchronizes itself against – the diurnal variation of day and night, and the change of the seasons. In that sense the Sun represents life and a reminder of the Harmony.

In a spiritual sense, the Light manages to get in everywhere, and holds each character up to its enquiry. It filtered into Casper's office quietly and insistently, showed up the dirt as Kathy and Brad talked in the conference room, and caused Mackie to squint against its might. It remained around Adam and Persia in their final dive into deeper water.

In another veiled reference to the importance of the Sun, the names of all of Tani'm's pod of resident orcas - Skalus and Kosum,

Spukani, Lúkwał, Sumshasat and Luqał are words from the different native Salishan dialects each meaning 'Sun.' Tondo and Kyrie's pod names Xai'ałax and Snx similarly mean 'Sun' in local dialects. And what of Persia's pod? Well, being nomads and wanderers many of them are known by the names of distant stars, which of course are also suns.

Fellow geeks might also recognize Adam spouting things like O-B-A-F-G-K-M-R-N which are the official classifications of stars according to their temperature. Our own sun Sol is a warm and friendly yellow G-classification sun which sits nicely in the temperature mid-range as far as suns go. Just like a perfect bath it is not too hot and not too cold, and I think we could all stand to be a little more appreciative of its life-giving presence instead of taking it for granted.

I couldn't help but give a nod to cats, and to one special feline in particular. Jackie's cat Tiddles was sent by the Universe at precisely the time that he was most needed. And so Tin-Tin and Gypsy are both aspects of him. I'm sure that he won't mind me telling you this!

Green grass and solid rock.

Cats have an innate ability to see the Other side, and they seem to revel in the private knowledge of this, and also the fact that we mere humans cannot access their mystical cat dimension.

It probably comes as no surprise that both Adam and Kathy had a connection with the mystic whale and both also had cats who either came to them or were 'given' to them. Cats, I believe, choose their guardians and not vice-versa.

The cats also chose Baba, and it is also no surprise that the 'souls' who hated Baba and his cats with such passion happened to be those 'sleepwalkers' who were so drawn to the lower ideals of the flesh.

Being a person who likes to bury meanings within meanings, I felt it appropriate to work another iconic cat into the mix. For those of you who are unfamiliar with the concept, 'Schrödinger's cat' is a thought experiment devised by an Austrian physicist named Erwin Schrödinger in 1935. He ventured the theory of a cat locked in a steel box with a flask of deadly acid wired to discharge after an unknown period of time. Without knowing when the lethal gas is discharged, he proposes that we cannot truly know what state the cat is in - either alive or dead - until the box is physically opened and the cat is actually viewed by an observer. Until that time the cat may be said to be simultaneously both alive *and* dead, in a state known as a *quantum superposition.*

Yes, call me a geek but there is a relevance to our story on two different levels!

Firstly, it begins to explain the concept of time travel which Adam postulated. Adam actually makes the reference to the physicist's feline when he is haunted by the compelling urge to *'Unlock the Box.'* At that point he observes: *'Only in opening the box can I possibly know if Schrödinger's cat is alive or dead.'*

My intention was to draw the reader to the conclusion that Adam was being called to 'unlock the box' – a reference to unlocking Persia's cage. Schrödinger's cat also refers to Adam's present state of being, and the urge to 'unlock the box' points to his own subconscious desire to know whether he himself is in fact alive or dead.

The Plane of Forces is the closest dimension to the physical world, and as such, it vibrates in a similar way. This is why it can be mistaken for the physical world. It appears to be solid but it simply takes on a form by virtue of the conscious mind. Perhaps the best way to explain what I mean by this is to use the example of speaking to someone you have never met on a telephone. Although you have no idea of what the person looks like, your mind creates an image of the person for you, based on your own life experiences.

Conscious thought has energy, and therefore it has a vibration. The 'shades' that Adam encountered were the manifestations of those thoughts. They are the mind's ruminations over the actions of the past and they hold a soul back from higher vibration and hence from reaching higher dimensions of Being.

And angels? Angels are in fact terrible conversationalists and not given to idle chit-chat. If and when they do speak to you, I would strongly suggest you listen carefully and pay particular attention to the exact words that they use. They are economical with language, but each word has incredible weight and meaning.

○ THE CHIMPONAUTS ❀

The story of the 'chimponauts' is sadly also real. I wonder how many people have even heard of Ham and Enos and what they had to endure in order to send mankind on their 'greatest adventure' as JFK so boldly described it. So what became of the space chimps?

It wasn't until 1997 when the United States Air Force finally announced their retirement. 'Retirement' in the governmental sense meant handing them to a medical facility to be used in further experiments. They were required to go through a standard process of declaring the chimpanzees as 'surplus' and accepting bids from prospective buyers. They were awarded to a biomedical testing facility called the Coulston Foundation.

The bid process was questionable to say the least, and controversy followed when Coulston's animal abuse track record was exposed. Over the years, they had racked up numerous breaches and at one point 300 of their chimps had been confiscated due to improper care. Their bid for the space chimps was thus voided and the Air Force looked for a second bidder. Many former astronauts demanded the chimps go to a sanctuary.

Dr Carole Noon, with the backing of Dr Jane Goodall and Dr Roger Fouts, made a bid to get the chimpanzees to sanctuary. The

Air Force denied her bid on the basis that she didn't have a facility ready, and instead surprisingly awarded the bulk of the chimps to the Coulston Foundation once again. In what appeared to be a backhanded attempt at good faith, the Air Force sent 30 of the remaining chimps to a sanctuary in Texas.

The story didn't end there, certainly not as far as Dr Noon was concerned. Believing that the chimpanzees deserved far better treatment than what was being meted out to them, she promptly sued the Air Force for custody and raised funds to build a sanctuary. After a year-long court battle she was awarded custody of 21 of the space chimps. In 2001, the chimps arrived at *Save the Chimps Sanctuary*, Florida.

In the following year The Coulston Foundation went bankrupt, and Dr Noon purchased the lab in Alamogordo, New Mexico rescuing 266 chimpanzees and 61 monkeys, becoming the world's largest chimpanzee sanctuary in the process. Until her death in 2009, Dr Carole Noon worked tirelessly to improve their conditions, raised funds for their care, and trained staff to care for the chimps with compassion.

❧ ORCA CAPTURES – THE TRUTH ☙

There is of course no Waterworld, however SeaWorld is still more or less alive and well. The times are changing though and as our cultural sensibilities change, so too do operations such as SeaWorld. Slowly and begrudgingly. This however does not exonerate them and other marine parks from the sins of the past.

When it comes to the story of the orcas, *'Home'* is based on many truths.

Yes, orcas were cruelly and opportunistically captured in Washington state waters for sale to places such as SeaWorld. And yes, young orcas were drowned in a botched capture in 1970 which resulted in a lawsuit after three of the bodies were discovered by locals. SeaWorld, who were implicated in the captures, agreed on a court settlement which saw them promise never to capture wild orcas from national waters ever again. It didn't stop them from immediately sourcing orcas from further afield though. There was no deliberate ramming of an orca by the hunters, though inadvertent strikes by commercial shipping represents one of the greatest threats to orcas and larger whale species today.

The hunters did however drop explosive charges around the terrified pod to scare them into the blind bay where they were netted.

For those who would like to know the true story, here it is:

Orca captures in Washington state waters began in the mid-1960s. Although Persia and Tristesse were described as nomadic members of a transient pod, the actual hunters preyed on a clan of resident orcas. In early 1966 the hunters harpooned a nursing mother in Puget Sound in order to steal her youngster away from her, as a proposed companion for Namu – a teenage male orca who had been captured the year before in Canadian waters and displayed in a sea-pen on the Seattle waterfront.

Dying from her wounds, the mother deliberately dived and drowned herself, and her young daughter was taken away and named Shamu. Traumatised by the cruelty of the capture and her mother's death, Shamu fared badly in captivity and clearly despised her owner Ted Griffin, the entrepreneur who had captured her. She died just six years later, but this was never revealed to the public. Many orcas do not survive the shock of life in captivity and six other orcas were subsequently captured and secretively substituted; each of them named Shamu. The public never cottoned on to the deliberate ruse, and neither were they made aware of the 'revolving door' of Shamu deaths. The whole Shamu thing was just that – a sham.

The Shamu phenomenon marked the birth of the captive orca craze in the United States and the following years saw the captures increase in number to meet the burgeoning demand. Heading up a capture organization known as Namu Inc., Ted Griffin and Don Goldsberry routinely returned to Puget Sound to prey on a clan of resident orcas known as the Southern Residents, who met there each year. The capture operation was taking on an almost military dimension, and now included speedboats and light aircraft to spot and track the orcas. The orcas very often succeeded in escaping the capture teams. They had learned to recognize the engine sounds of the capture boats from miles away, causing the captors to continually change boats and engines to outsmart them.

It was the events of August 8, 1970 in Penn Cove, Washington that ultimately spelled the end for the capture operation. The hunters badly botched a mass round-up of over 80 orcas which they corralled into the blind cove by throwing explosives into the water to terrify the fleeing pod. Five whales, including four babies entangled themselves in the nets in a blind panic and drowned. To hide the atrocity from the public the hunters slit the bellies of the dead whales, filled them with rocks and weighted them with chains and anchors; secretively dumping the bodies after dark.

Seven young whales were taken that day, and sold to marine parks around the world. Notable amongst them was a 3-year old who was initially named Tokitae. Her name was taken from the greeting in the local native dialect which literally translates as *'nice day, pretty colors.'* It was far from being a 'nice day' for the plucky young orca, and she would never see her family again. She survives to this day in Miami Seaquarium Florida, having first arrived there September 24, 1970. The young female was swiftly re-named Lolita, in an attempt to hide the fact that she was captured in Washington state. She remains the oldest surviving orca in captivity and she has been a poignant and enduring inspiration, not only for the writing of this book, but indeed all that I do for captive whales and dolphins.

For me she is the living embodiment of all that is cruel and wrong with this world.

Lolita was intended to be a playmate for a young male orca named Hugo who had also been captured in Puget Sound two years earlier. Hugo was in fact from Lolita's clan, the Southern Resident community, but nobody knew that at the time. He struggled with life in captivity and over the next ten years he rammed the walls of his tank on many occasions, once slicing the tip of his rostrum (or nose) off when he broke the thick glass of the viewing window. The park veterinarian Jesse White sewed Hugo's severed rostrum back on. Becoming more and more depressed, Hugo took his own life in 1980 after ramming the tank wall for a final time.

Lolita lives on in a woefully small tank, which is roughly the size of two hotel swimming pool. She has never seen another of her own kind since Hugo passed in 1980. Her aging owner, Arthur Hertz has been approached on numerous occasions by conservation groups hoping to buy her and allow her to spend her remaining time in the relative comfort of a large sea pen in Washington state; close to where her pod pass by. Her mother is still alive and continues life with the greatly depleted Southern Resident clan. Hertz has turned down every offer point blank, stating her will never release her. She is doomed to continue performances at Miami Seaquarium until the day she dies. As Adam mentions in 'Home', there is no retirement plan for captive orcas.

Of the six other young family members who were captured with her, two were shipped to marine parks in Japan, and one each went to parks in Texas, the United Kingdom, France and Australia. They were all very young calves, and except for Lolita, they all died within five years of their capture.

So much for the 'long and healthy lives' which SeaWorld CEO Joel Manby described so enthusiastically.

Three of the dumped carcasses washed up on the shore of Whidbey Island on November 18, 1970. Six years later, SeaWorld settled in court, agreeing to never again capture orcas in Washington State to avoid publicly taking the blame.

The conclusion of their in-house breeding programs in 2016 now means that the days of orca captivity in the United States are numbered. This is of course cold comfort for the current captive orcas, whose deaths will effectively bring down the final curtain on a cruel era so cleverly disguised as entertainment and education.

Other species of dolphin closely related to the blackfish continue to be wild caught and sold into captivity. Participating countries include: United Arab Emirates, China, Taiwan, Russia and Japan.

ଓ TIME AND SPACE ARE FUNNY THINGS ଚ

Indeed, they are. And there is an observation to be made about our mindset here:

'We are Masters of Looking Out'

Let that thought sink in for a moment. When the whale talked about connection she suggested that we *'reach in.'* Consider this for a moment – when we talk about space, it is generally 'outer' space, not inner space. For those of religious persuasion (whatever camel you prefer), God is always 'out' there. The grass is always greener on the other side – 'outside' the fence. We are always on the 'lookout' for a better job. For a better life. For a partner. A lover.

It is always easier to look out and see the faults with others than to look in and see our own faults and blemishes. Some of you may go through an entire lifetime without getting to truly know yourself. Or truly loving yourself. And yet *you* are the only person you will spend your entire life with. *We are Masters of Looking Out.*

Have you ever had to carry a map? Some of them are quite large affairs, and can be very unwieldy. So you don't carry them around flat and opened out; you fold them. You will find that time and space, being inter-related, work in precisely the same way – massively big and ungainly when laid out flat. Neat, tidy, pocket-sized and easily carried when folded. Humans, the masters of reaching out, still think that the way to traverse space is while the map is laid out flat. Try folding it first. Until we truly come to grips with this fundamental, deep space travel will continue to elude us.

So too, the way to deeper connection is not whilst our lives are laid out flat, but in those moments when we turn ourselves inward like a quiet observer. Try it sometime. Those with insight (there's another in- word!) will realise that this is also a map, and everything that we actually need to know is plotted on it.

❧ DON'T GROW LARGER THAN YOUR OCEAN ❧

So, what exactly did the whale mean when Adam pressed her for advice and she replied: *'Don't grow larger than your ocean, human'?*

My last home had a most beautiful water garden occupying almost all of the front yard, and this was home to a school or thirty or forty koi. An incredibly hardy and peaceful fish, koi will live to a ripe old age of about eighty years. Watching their bright colors gliding peacefully amidst the pond plants, the thought often occurred to me that most of them would outlive me!

Just how a koi interacts and responds to its environment highlights one of the keys to environmental resilience and natural balance. You see, a koi like many plant and animal species will only grow as large as its environment permits. My tribe, as I liked to call them, were each a whopping two to three feet long. Contained in a small aquarium, they would only have grown to perhaps a quarter of that size.

The whale gave Adam arguably the most powerful key to the survival of our species. We need to adapt our behaviour and our activities to our natural environment. To blend with it, to harmonise and to find a balance. Or as the whale might put it – to live in accordance with the Harmony. *'Don't grow larger than your ocean, human.'*

Personally, I think the whale was famously understating the power of this seemingly simple observation when she said *'It's a good start.'*

In sharing this book with you, I truly hope that in some small way we have shared a part of our journey Home together, you and I.

Whoever, or whatever, your Whale is – whatever form she appears to you in – honor it, embrace it and be true to it. x

ABOUT THE AUTHOR

Len Varley is a passionate advocate for the protection of human and non-human rights. His love of the oceans saw him take up the cause of raising awareness for marine conservation issues and the protection of fragile ecosystems and endangered marine species.

Len has authored scientific reports on the decline of localized dolphin populations in Japanese waters and contributed research to Australian state bodies, challenging their controversial shark cull program. He has spoken publicly at conservation events and given radio interviews in the UK and Australia.

A former commercial pilot; his aviation background led to research into bird strike mitigation measures for the aviation sector and wind turbine farms.

www.ingramcontent.com/pod-product-compliance
Lightning Source LLC
Chambersburg PA
CBHW061654190726
48289CB00006B/1864